*Other macabre collections of Lovecraftian horror available from Titan Books*

*Available now:*
ACOLYTES OF CTHULHU
BLACK WINGS OF CTHULHU, VOLUME ONE
BLACK WINGS OF CTHULHU, VOLUME TWO
SHADOWS OVER INNSMOUTH
WEIRD SHADOWS OVER INNSMOUTH

*Coming soon:*
BLACK WINGS OF CTHULHU, VOLUME THREE
THE MADNESS OF CTHULHU

# WEIRDER SHADOWS OVER INNSMOUTH

# WEIRDER SHADOWS OVER
# INNSMOUTH

## Edited by STEPHEN JONES

*Illustrated by*
RANDY BROECKER

**TITAN** BOOKS

WEIRDER SHADOWS OVER INNSMOUTH
Print edition ISBN: 9781783291311
E-book edition ISBN: 9781783291328

Published by Titan Books
A division of Titan Publishing Group Ltd
144 Southwark Street, London SE1 0UP

First Titan Books edition: January 2015

2 4 6 8 10 9 7 5 3 1

Stephen Jones asserts the moral right to be identified as the author of this work.

'Introduction: Weirder Shadows ...' copyright © Stephen Jones 2013, 2015.
'The Port' by H.P. Lovecraft. Originally published in *Driftwind* Vol. 5, No. 3, November 1930.
'Innsmouth Bane' copyright © John Glasby 2005. Originally published in *H.P. Lovecraft's Magazine of Horror.* Vol. 1, No. 2, Spring 2005. Reprinted by permission of the author's estate.
'Richard Riddle, Boy Detective in "The Case of the French Spy"' copyright © Kim Newman 2005. Originally published in *Adventure* Vol. 1. Reprinted by permission of the author.
'Innsmouth Clay' copyright © August Derleth 1971. Originally published in *Dark Things.* Reprinted by permission of Arkham House Publishers Inc.
'The Archbishop's Well' copyright © Reggie Oliver 2013.
'You Don't Want to Know' copyright © Adrian Cole 2013.
'Fish Bride' copyright © Caitlín R. Kiernan 2009. Originally published in *Sirenia Digest* No. 42, May 2009. Reprinted by permission of the author.
'The Hag Stone' copyright © Conrad Williams 2013.
'On the Reef' copyright © Caitlín R. Kiernan 2010. Originally published in *Sirenia Digest* No. 59, October 2010. Reprinted by permission of the author.
'The Song of Sighs' copyright © Angela Slatter 2013.
'The Same Deep Waters as You' copyright © Brian Hodge 2013.
'The Winner' copyright © Ramsey Campbell 2005. Originally published in *Taverns of the Dead.* Reprinted by permission of the author.
'The Transition of Elizabeth Haskings' copyright © Caitlín R. Kiernan 2012. Originally published in *Sirenia Digest* No. 74, January 2012. Reprinted by permission of the author.
'The Chain' copyright © Michael Marshall Smith 2013.
'Into the Water' copyright © Simon Kurt Unsworth 2013.
'Rising, Not Dreaming' copyright © Angela Slatter 2011. Originally published in *Innsmouth Free Press* No. 3, February 2011. Reprinted by permission of the author.
'The Long Last Night' copyright © Brian Lumley 2012, 2013. Originally published in different form in *Weird Tales* No. 360, Fall 2012. Reprinted by permission of the author and his agent.
'Afterword: Contributors' Notes' copyright © Stephen Jones 2013, 2015.

A CIP catalogue record for this title is available from the British Library.

Printed and bound in the United States.

*In memory of*
PHILIP J. RAHMAN
( 1 9 5 2 – 2 0 1 1 )
*who cared too deeply.*

# TABLE OF CONTENTS

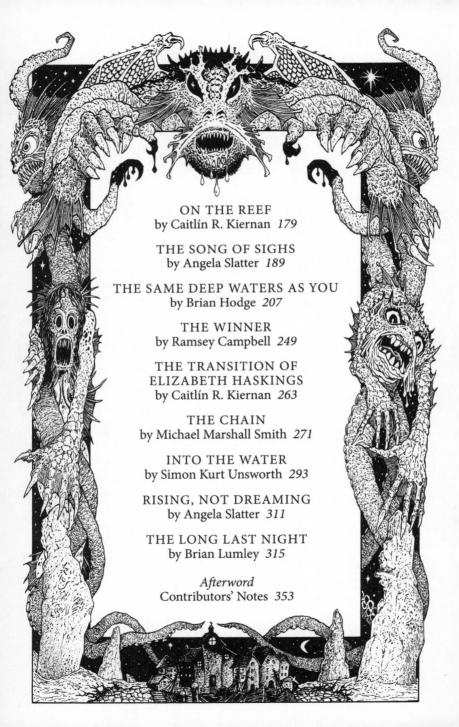

# INTRODUCTION

## WEIRDER SHADOWS...

F OLLOWING ON FROM the World Fantasy Award-nominated *Shadows Over Innsmouth* (1994) and *Weird Shadows Over Innsmouth* (2005), this third volume was intended to conclude a loosely connected trilogy of anthologies inspired by H. P. Lovecraft's 1931 novella.

As readers of the previous volumes will be aware, it has been far from plain sailing. After the trials and tribulations involved in getting the first book published, I had hoped that the follow-up volume would have found a ready and enthusiastic audience. Unfortunately, due to a number of reasons beyond my control, that did not happen.

After having turned out a number of worthwhile and beautiful books from the late 1980s onwards, by the beginning of the new century publisher Fedogan & Bremer was starting to struggle. Despite producing a number of new titles by Hugh B. Cave, Donald Wandrei and Howard Wandrei in the early 2000s, along with a new "Cthulhu" anthology edited by Robert M. Price, the money was no longer coming in as regularly as it had once been. The economics of book-selling were already beginning to change, and for a small operation such as Fedogan & Bremer, this meant that it had wait longer and longer for payment for bookstores and dealers, with the inevitable result that there was not always enough money to invest in new projects.

It perhaps didn't help that the publisher's accounting system was also not as good as it should have been, and orders went unfulfilled for long periods. Although they set up a distribution deal with Arkham House—somewhat ironic, considering that F&B was initially created to fill a gap in the market left by that imprint—even that venerable small press publisher was going through some tough times itself.

On top of all that, publisher/editor Philip Rahman had his own personal demons to contend with.

I therefore suggested to Philip that we do another "Innsmouth" anthology. The first book had been a success, going into a rare second printing for F&B and selling to a number of paperback markets around the world. If the follow-up volume did as well as its predecessor, then it should generate enough revenue to kick-start the imprint's publishing programme again.

Philip readily agreed, and in November 2005 he launched *Weird Shadows Over Innsmouth* with a terrific party at the World Fantasy Convention in Madison, Wisconsin.

And that was when it all started to go wrong.

Fedogan & Bremer's management problems worsened. Accounts were not being kept and royalties were no longer being paid regularly. Although Philip managed to get contractual copies of the book to the various contributors, for reasons not fully explained he was unable to send me my own personal copies. Perhaps even more traumatically, first Philip's old friend Peder Wagtskjold died, and then his second wife and long-time soul mate, Diane Landon, passed away only a few days after the couple were married. It was a double blow from which he would never really recover.

Not long afterwards the imprint all but ceased operations, and the hardcover print-run of *Weird Shadows Over Innsmouth* simply disappeared from distribution. Without any spare copies of my own to circulate amongst other publishers, there were no other editions produced.

Despite attempts by friends and family to help, Philip's health deteriorated as his situation worsened, and he was found dead on

July 23, 2011. For a while it looked as if his untimely passing would also mark the end of the publishing imprint that he co-founded.

But then something remarkable happened—with the aid of Dwayne H. Olson (who had helped rescue *Shadows Over Innsmouth* from being a "widowed" book back in the early 1990s), Philip's business partner and F&B's co-founder Dennis E. Weiler stepped in to sort things out.

Within a year he had recovered all the remaining stock—including all those unsold copies of *Weird Shadows Over Innsmouth*—from several warehouses scattered across the United States; he organised the royalty system, paying out long-overdue sums to those who were still owed money, and he even managed to finally get me my contractual copies of the second "Innsmouth" anthology.

Even better, Dennis reorganised the company—issuing a new catalogue to promote the existing stock and creating an online retail presence for the first time—while also looking around for new projects to publish.

During the course of our correspondence, I happened to mention that Philip and I had envisioned the "Innsmouth" books as forming a loose trilogy, and Dennis immediately asked if I would be willing to put together a third volume under the Fedogan & Bremer imprint.

Two years later, this present compilation was the result. Thankfully, this time nothing went wrong. Even better, Titan Books started reprinting the trilogy in handsome paperback editions, and the publication of this title from them marks the first time that all three volumes will have been in print in uniform editions at the same time.

Overseas reprintings of the earlier books continue to appear, and although this series was always envisioned as comprising only three volumes, it has subsequently been suggested that I should consider adding a fourth instalment entitled *Weirdest Shadows Over Innsmouth...*

But for now, once again taking Lovecraft's original story as inspiration, prepare to be introduced to the Massachusetts seaport and its ichthyoid denizens years before that fateful FBI raid in February 1928. From there, Dagon's blasphemous spawn spread out across the globe as the offspring of that decaying fishing town undergo their own, often bizarre, metamorphoses.

While the world changes, so through eldritch rituals and human sacrifices the Deep Ones' masters—the terrifying Great Old Ones themselves—make ready to escape their prisons throughout space and time when the stars are right, so that they may once again reclaim the Earth as their own.

As the final shadows gather and the waters continue to rise, mankind begins its ultimate struggle for survival against a pantheon of dark gods and their batrachian foot-soldiers...

*Iä-R'lyeh! Cthulhu fhtagn! Iä! Iä!*

Stephen Jones
London, England

# THE PORT

*by* H. P. LOVECRAFT

Ten miles from Arkham I had struck the trail
That rides the cliff-edge over Boynton Beach,
And hoped that just at sunset I could reach
The crest that looks on Innsmouth in the vale.
Far out at sea was a retreating sail,
White as hard years of ancient winds could bleach,
But evil with some portent beyond speech,
So that I did not wave my hand or hail.

Sails out of Innsmouth! Echoing old renown
Of long-dead times. But now a too-swift night
Is closing in, and I have reached the height
Whence I so often scan the distant town.
The spires and roofs are there—but look! The gloom
Sinks on dark lanes, as lightless as the tomb!

# INNSMOUTH BANE

*by* J O H N  G L A S B Y

I AM WRITING this narrative in the sincere belief that something terrible has come to Innsmouth—something about which it is not wise to speak openly. Many of my neighbours, if they should ever read this account, will undoubtedly assume that any accusations I make against Obed Marsh are based upon jealousy since there is little doubt that he, alone, is prospering while those of us who lost much during the years of depression are still finding it difficult to profit from this strange upturn in fortune which is his alone.

My name is Jedediah Allen. My family left Boston and settled in Innsmouth in 1676, twenty-one years after the town was founded, my grandfather and father being engaged in trade with the Orient, prospering well following the success of the Revolution. The war of 1812, however, brought misfortune to many Innsmouth families. The loss of men and ships was heavy, the Gilman shipping business suffering particularly badly.

Only Obed Marsh seemed to have come out of the depression successfully. His three vessels, the *Sumatra Queen*, *Hetty* and *Columbia* still made regular sailings to the islands of the South Seas. Yet there was, from the very beginning, something odd about these voyages. From the first, he returned with large quantities of gold trinkets, more treasure than anyone in Innsmouth had ever seen.

One rumour had it that this hoard of gold had been discovered by him concealed in some secret cave on Devil Reef, left there by buccaneers more than two centuries earlier—that he covertly ferried it ashore on nights when there was no moon. Yet having seen some of these artefacts for myself, for Obed displayed many of them quite openly, I was more inclined towards the former explanation as to their origin.

Certainly, the objects were beautiful in their intricate workmanship and design but this was marred by an alienness in their imagery. All of the objects appeared to have an aquatic motif. To my eye, they had disturbing suggestions of fish or frog symbols, totally unlike any of the Spanish trinkets from the West Indies.

There was also something strange about the metal from which they were fashioned, which indicated a non-European source.

My attempts to get Obed to divulge any information about them all met with evasiveness. He would neither confirm nor deny any of the rumours.

There was one man, however, who might talk.


Matt Eliot, first mate on the *Sumatra Queen*, was known to frequent the inn on Water Street whenever he was in port and it was from him that I hoped to learn something.

It was two weeks before an opportunity presented itself. Entering the inn just after dark, I spotted Eliot in the far corner, among the shadows, and for once he appeared to be without his usual drinking companions. After purchasing two drinks, I walked over and sat in the chair opposite him. He clearly had had a lot to drink although the hour was still early.

I knew him to be a man of violent temper, readily aroused, one who had to be approached with caution and diplomacy.

Setting the drink down in front of him, I sat back and studied him closely for several moments. I wanted him to be sufficiently drunk to talk, but not too drunk to fall into a stupor. For a time, he gave no indication that he had noticed my presence. Then his hand went out for the glass and he took several swallows, wiping the back of his hand across his mouth.

Leaning forward, he peered closely at me. Then he grinned. "Jedediah Allen, ain't it?"

I nodded. "I'd like to talk with you, Matt," I said. "About these voyages you go on with Captain Marsh. Where'd he get all that gold? I'd like to buy some of it for myself."

His eyes opened and closed several times before he replied, "Reckon you'll have to speak to Obed about the gold. He keeps all of that for himself."

"But you do know where he gets it."

"O' course I do. Every man on those ships knows where that gold comes from." He leaned forward a little further, pushing his face up to mine, and dropping his voice to a hoarse whisper. "Every trip he makes, Obed sails for Othaheite. Couple o' years ago, we came across an island to the east not shown on any of our charts. The natives there, the Kanakys, worship some kind o' fish-god and they get all the fish and gold they want in exchange for sacrifices to this heathen god. Obed gives 'em beads and baubles for it."

He took another swallow of his drink. "There's somethin' else, somethin'—"

He broke off abruptly, as if suddenly aware he was on the point of saying something he shouldn't.

"Go on," I urged. "This is just between you and me, Matt."

"There's another island close to that where the Kanakys live. That's where they offer their sacrifices. Obed got me and two others to row him out there one night. God, it was horrible. Not just the ruins that looked as if they'd lain on the bottom of the sea for millions of years, but what we heard and saw while we were there, on the other side of the island. Things comin' up out o' the sea like fish and frogs, only they walked on two legs like men, croakin' and whistlin' like demons."

I saw him shudder at the memory. "Obed never went back to that accursed island again. I reckon even he was scared by what we saw."

Finishing my drink, I thanked him for his information and left. As a staunch member of the Baptist Church, I knew that it was my duty to warn others of Marsh's activities. But without proof, it was doubtful if I would be even listened to. Obed was a prominent figure in town and after all, it had long been an established practice for sea captains to exchange goods with the natives of these far-flung islands. Before I could tell anyone, I needed to know a lot more about what Obed was bringing into Innsmouth apart from gold.

It was then I decided to wait for his return from his latest voyage. I already knew that both the *Hetty* and the *Columbia* had sailed some seven months previously, leaving the *Sumatra Queen* tied up at the harbour for repairs.


Over the next few weeks, I made discreet enquiries concerning these ships and finally ascertained they were due off Innsmouth some five weeks later. I had already decided upon the best vantage-point to maintain a close watch on any activity without exposing myself to view. Accordingly, on the night in question, I made my way along Water Street to the harbour. The night was dark and starlit with no moon, and I let myself into one of the large warehouses lining the waterfront.

Going up to one of the upper storeys, I crouched down by the window from where I had a clear and unrestricted view of the entire harbour. Although dark, there was sufficient starlight for me to readily make out the irregular black outline of Devil Reef perhaps a mile and a half away.

It was almost midnight when I spotted the two ships rounding Kingsport Head. The *Columbia* was in the lead with the *Hetty* about half a mile astern. Twenty minutes later, after following the movements of the two vessels closely, it became apparent that Marsh meant to bring them both into the harbour rather than anchor offshore.

By the time the vessels had docked, a further hour had passed. There was much activity on both ships and the tall figure of Captain Marsh was clearly visible. By shifting my position slightly, I was able to watch closely as the cargoes were unloaded onto the quayside. Much of it consisted of large bales, which were carried into the warehouse adjacent to that in which I had concealed myself. There was little talk among the men, much of the work being carried out in complete silence. After a while, the crews vanished along Water Street and only Marsh and one crewman were left on board the *Columbia*.

When they eventually disembarked they were carrying a large chest between them and it was this, I guessed, that contained more of the gold which Marsh was bringing back from that unnamed island in the South Seas.

I now had ample confirmation as to the source of this gold and, had Marsh continued merely with smuggling such trinkets, there was little that could be said against him. Prior to the war, during the privateering days, such activities were commonplace in Innsmouth and were certainly not frowned upon by the townsfolk.


By now, Marsh seemed to have fully accepted this pagan religion of those natives with whom he traded on a regular basis. He began to speak out vociferously against all of the religious communities, urging anyone who would listen to abandon their Christian faith and worship this pagan god, promising them wealth beyond their wildest dreams if they did so.

Had we all listened to the Reverend Joseph Wallingham, who entreated his congregation to have nothing to do with those who worshipped pagan gods and worldly goods, and had I known then what I was to discover the next time the *Sumatra Queen* returned from that accursed island, all of the ensuing madness might have been averted.

But few heeded the Reverend Wallingham, and it was a further year before that fateful night when the *Sumatra Queen* docked. Is it hard to say what gave me the notion that Obed Marsh was smuggling something more than gold into Innsmouth, or what brought to my mind the recollection of the old tunnels beneath the town, leading from the sea into the very centre of Innsmouth.

But remember them I did. For two nights I concealed myself on top of the cliff overlooking the shore, but without any untoward happenings. On the third night, however, a little before midnight, I observed a party of men moving along the beach from the direction of the harbour. It was clear the men believed themselves to be safe from prying eyes, for they carried lanterns and, as they drew near the entrance to one of the tunnels almost immediately below my hiding place, I recognised Obed Marsh in the lead, with Matt Eliot and five of the crew close behind.

But it was the sight of the others accompanying them that sent a shiver of nameless dread through me, so that I almost cried out. Without doubt they were natives brought back from that terrible island and, even in the dim light cast by the bobbing lanterns, I could see there was something distinctly inhuman about them.

Their heads were curiously distorted with long, sloping foreheads, out-thrust jaws and bulging eyes like those of a frog or fish. Their gait, too, was peculiar as if they were hopping rather than walking.

Trembling and shaking, I lay there and watched as the party entered the tunnel mouth and disappeared. Not until a full half-hour had passed was I able to push myself to my feet and stagger back into town.

God alone knew how many of those creatures Marsh had smuggled into Innsmouth under the unsuspecting noses of the population, concealing them somewhere in his mansion on Washington Street.

At the time, I could tell no one. Marsh had too tight a hold on all who sailed with him for any of them to talk. What dire purpose lay behind this wholesale importation of these natives, I couldn't begin to guess. I knew full well there had to be a reason, but Marsh kept it to himself and none of the creatures were ever seen on the town streets, even after dark.


Over the next two years, whenever he was in town, March continued his tirade against the established churches and, when several of the leading churchmen unaccountably disappeared, it became abundantly clear that he intended to become the only force in Innsmouth. Those who did not join him also had a tendency to vanish in peculiar circumstances or were driven out of the town.

Then, suddenly and without warning, disaster struck Innsmouth.

A terrible epidemic swept through the town, a disease for which there seemed no remedy. Hundreds, including my own wife, died during the outbreak. The few doctors could do nothing to stem the spread of the disease, merely declaring that it was one of foreign origin they had never encountered before. Almost certainly, they maintained, it had been brought into Innsmouth by one of the vessels trading with the Orient.

The dead and dying were everywhere. There was no escape since the Federal authorities, on hearing of it, quarantined the entire town and surrounding region. By the time the contagion had burnt itself out, almost half of the population had succumbed.

Now, for the first time, I spoke out of what I had witnessed that night on the cliffs. Other townsfolk then came forward to tell of curious foreigners glimpsed in the fog, particularly along the waterfront at dead of night, some swimming strongly out to sea in the direction of Devil Reef, and many more coming in the other direction.

We knew that something had to be done, and a meeting was hurriedly convened to discuss the rapidly deteriorating situation. There, it was agreed that no other course of action was open to us but to raid the Marsh mansion. Further action would depend upon what we found there. It was essential, of course, that no intimation of this plan should reach Obed, for there were now several of the townsfolk who appeared to have thrown in their lot with him.

Two Federal investigators, agents Jensen and Corder, were present at the meeting, and although at first reluctant to support this taking of the law into our own hands, they eventually agreed to lead the raid. One group, led by Jensen, would go in at the front, while agent Corder would command the second, which would enter by the rear.

Arming myself with a pistol, I accompanied the second group. In all, we numbered twenty-two men. None of us knew what to expect as we made our way silently along Lafayette Street towards the rear of the huge building. Once we were in place, we waited for the two blasts on a whistle, which would signal that the other band was ready to move in.

Lights were visible in three of the rear windows, and occasionally a shadow would pass across the curtains. Clearly the house was occupied, but whether the shadows we saw belonged to members of the Marsh family or to servants, it was impossible to tell.

The signal to attack came five minutes later. Running forward, three of the men smashed in the heavy door and moments later, we were inside the house. A long, gloomy corridor led through the house towards the front of the building. Several rooms opened off from it on either side, but a quick search revealed only two terrified servants and little out of the ordinary.

Meeting up with the first group, we found Obed Marsh seated in a chair before the fire. He had obviously attempted to reach for a weapon when the men had burst in, for a pistol lay on the table. Now he sat covered by the revolver in Jensen's hand.

"Did you find anything?" Jensen spoke directly to Corder.

"Nothing in any of the back rooms," Corder replied. "But if there is any contraband here, it's likely to be well hidden."

"You'll find nothing!" Marsh snarled. He half-rose to his feet, then sat down again at a gesture from Jensen. "And you'll all pay for this unwarranted intrusion. I'll make damned sure of that."

There was something in his threat that sent a shiver through me. I had long known him to be a man who never made idle threats.

While the rest of the men made a thorough search of the house, with five of them climbing the stairs to the upper storeys, I made a slow circuit of the room. A number of portraits of Marsh family members, going back for several generations, hung on the walls, but it was not these that made me feel uneasy. There were also other things, lining the mantelpiece above the wide hearth and on top of several long shelves around the walls.

There could be only one place where Marsh could have obtained them. Grotesque statues depicting hideous monstrosities, the likes of which I had never seen before. In particular, I came across a trio of statuettes, each about ten inches in height, which were frightful in the extreme. Apart from the nightmarish contours, which appeared to be hybrids of various sea creatures, the anatomical quintessence of these idols, the grotesque tentacular nature of the limbs and malformed torsos, suggested to me things from some distant pre-human era. The nature of the material from which they were fashioned was also highly peculiar. A pale, nauseous green, striated with minute black lines, it was extremely heavy and none of us could even hazard a guess as to what it was.

A sudden shout from one of the adjoining rooms jerked my attention from them. In a loose bunch, we made our way towards the sound, leaving Jensen to keep an eye on Marsh.

In one of the rooms, the men had come across a locked door which, on being broken down, revealed a flight of stone steps, clearly leading to cellars beneath the house. Lighting three of the lanterns we had brought with us, we descended the steps, almost retching on the stench which came up to meet us. It was a sharp, fishy odour, which caught at the backs of our throats, almost suffocating us.

At the bottom, in the pale light from our lanterns, we saw the shocking confirmation of what I had said earlier concerning my nocturnal vigils on the cliffs. There were more than a score of natives crowded into the cellar, and one or two of the men cried out as we tried to assimilate what we saw.

Several of us had sailed to many foreign ports during the prosperous trading and privateering days and were fully conversant with the many native races found on different islands of the Pacific. But what we saw in the wavering lantern light was something none of us had ever witnessed!

These were the most repulsive creatures I had ever set eyes on. Apart from some curious deformity of their bodies, their bulging eyes and oddly shaped heads held something of the aquatic physiognomy of fishes, and I could swear that some of them had hands and feet which seemed to be webbed!

Sickened by the sight and smell, I turned away, and it was then that I noticed the hastily boarded-up doorway in the far wall where the shadows were thickest. Drawing Corder's attention to it, we soon ripped away the boards and shone the light of one of the lanterns into the gaping aperture that lay behind them. There was no doubting what it was—the opening into one of the old smugglers' tunnels leading down towards the sea.

"So that's how he brought them here," Corder muttered grimly. "God alone knows how many more of these creatures are in the town, probably concealed in cellars like this."

Charged the next day with illegally importing unidentified aliens, Obed Marsh and several of his crew were thrown into jail to await trial, and for two days thereafter an uneasy quiet reigned in Innsmouth.

It was not to last, however. For then came the day which was to change Innsmouth forever.

As far as I was concerned, my suspicions were aroused when I noticed several groups of men in the streets adjoining the jail. All of them were either men who had sailed with Marsh in the past or those who had joined him later, when he had spoken out against the various religious denominations.

It was clear their intention was to secure Obed's release by force, and this seemed confirmed when they began moving in the direction of Main Street. Hurriedly alerting several of my neighbours and telling them to spread the word, we succeeded in gathering more than fifty men armed with muskets, pikes, knives and any other weapons they could lay their hands on.

By the time we reached the jail, we found it had already come under attack. Some of the raiders had forced their way inside, and the unmistakable sound of shots came from somewhere within the building. Moments later, we were set upon by the yelling mob, and I was fighting for my life against men I had known for years who now acted like crazed madmen.

For a time, since we outnumbered them by almost two to one, we succeeded in driving them back from their objective. But as they retreated along Main Street, a great horde of natives burst out of Waite Street, forcing us back towards the bridge over the Manuxet.

In the distance, I could clearly pick out more gunfire coming from all directions, but concentrated mainly near the centre of the town and along the waterfront, and I guessed that fighting had broken out in several places. Already we had suffered a number of casualties— seven men had been killed, and almost twice that number wounded.

Luckily, the majority of the natives were unarmed, relying on sheer weight of numbers to overwhelm us. Several were killed within the first few minutes, but the rest came on, heedless of their casualties.

It was the bridge that temporarily saved us. On either side, the riverbank as far as the falls was far too steep and treacherous to be readily scaled, and the Manuxet was in full flood after the recent rains, thereby preventing the creatures from crossing the river and assaulting us from the rear.

For almost an hour we managed to hold off the attackers, inflicting terrible carnage among their ranks. When they began to pull back, we believed we had beaten them off, and although firing could still be heard around the town centre, it was sporadic, and it appeared the situation was slowly being brought under control.

After what several of us had witnessed in the cellar below the Marsh mansion, I think we believed we were prepared for anything. But nothing could have prepared us for what came next.

It was Silas Benson who suddenly called our attention to the river below us. As I have said, the Manuxet was in full flood, but now it teemed with black shapes, swimming upstream against the racing current. That they had come from the sea was immediately obvious. Literally hundreds of them came swarming onto the bank, and one horrified glance was enough to show that these creatures were even less human than those we had stumbled upon earlier.

Hopping in a manner hideously suggestive of frogs, they clambered up the steep sides with ease. There was no chance of defeating such a multitude, and our only hope of survival was to flee across the bridge and along Main Street. Another bank of natives, surging out of Dock Street, attempted to halt us, and our ammunition was almost spent by the time we broke through them. Four more of our number were killed before we reached the relative safety of my house, where we barricaded ourselves in.

By now it was abundantly clear that those monsters from the sea had taken over the whole of the town. Sporadic firing could still be heard in the distance, but we all knew that further resistance was futile.

By the morning of the next day, after spending the night confined to the house, we finally pieced together the full story of what had happened. Obed Marsh and those imprisoned with him had been released. Both of the Federal investigators who had accompanied us to the Marsh mansion had been slaughtered. John Lawrence, editor of the *Innsmouth Courier* on Dock Street, who had often spoken out against Marsh, had been dragged into the street and murdered. The presses and printing equipment had been smashed and the offices set on fire.

Thus it was that Obed Marsh now controlled the whole of Innsmouth. His word was law. Within weeks, the old Masonic Temple on Federal Street had been taken over and replaced by the Esoteric Order of Dagon.

Only a handful of the townsfolk were allowed to leave Innsmouth. These were mostly Lithuanians and Poles. Whether Marsh considered that no one outside Innsmouth would believe anything of what they said about the town or whether, not being descendants of the original settlers, he adjudged them to be of no importance, no one knew. After they had gone, those who remained were allowed to join the Esoteric Order of Dagon. There were few who declined.

It was not only the gold which made people join this new religion Marsh had brought back with him, nor the fact that, by now, most folk were mortally afraid of him. What persuaded the majority to join was Marsh promised that, if they took his five oaths and obeyed him implicitly, they would never die.

When I was asked to join, I refused, as did my son. I had read sufficient concerning the rites that had been practised in nearby Arkham during the witch trials to know that similar inducements had been made then—that all who worshipped Satan would be granted eternal life. At the time, I knew it to be nothing more than myth and superstition, merely an enticement to get people to join in their unholy rites.

Now, however, I know differently. It soon became apparent that Marsh was involved with those deep ones much more deeply than was first thought. In return for their continued aid, he declared that the townspeople must mate with these creatures. He, himself, was forced to take a wife from among them, although she was never seen abroad and no one was able to tell who—or what—she was.

* * *

All of that happened almost twenty years ago. More and more of the folk, particularly the younger ones, acquired the same look as many of those natives we had found in Marsh's cellar and some, as the years passed, were even worse—being little different from those creatures which had come from the sea to take over the town. Almost all of the Marsh, Gilman, Hogg and Brewster families were affected by this 'Innsmouth look'. Curiously, Ephraim Waite's family remained untainted, even though he was one of Marsh's closest acquaintances.

Rumour had it, however, that Waite had once resided in Arkham and had a reputation as a wizard, some even suggesting that he was the same warlock as was present before and during the witch trials there, two centuries earlier. That this was nothing more than idle gossip, spread by those who were more afraid of him than of Obed Marsh, seemed undeniable.

It was now becoming more difficult and dangerous for me to keep watch on Marsh's activities. Even though the deep ones had returned to the sea shortly after Marsh's release from jail a score of years before, those who bore the 'Innsmouth look' were in the majority, and any of the population untouched by it were kept under close scrutiny.

Only those who belonged to the Order were allowed in the vicinity of the Esoteric Order of Dagon hall. Nevertheless, on a number of occasions I managed to approach within fifty yards of it under cover of darkness. Even on those nights when there was no service taking place, the building was never silent. Strange echoes seemed to come from somewhere deep beneath the foundations—weird sounds like nothing I had heard before.

But things were worse whenever a service was being held. Just to see some of those who attended made me want to turn and run. Scaled things that wore voluminous clothing to conceal the true shapes of what lay beneath, walking upright like men but with a horrible hopping gait that set my teeth on edge. And the chanting which came from within was something born out of nightmare. Harsh gutturals such as could never have been uttered by normal human throats—croaks and piping whistles, more reminiscent of the frogs and whippoorwills in the hills around Arkham than anything remotely approaching human speech.

Dear Lord—that such blasphemies as those could exist in this sane, everyday world! I found myself on the point of believing some of the tales spread abroad in Innsmouth concerning some deep undersea city, millions of years old, lying on the ocean floor just beyond Devil Reef. When I had first heard them from Elijah Winton, I had immediately dismissed them as the ravings of a madman. But hearing those hideous sounds emanating from the Temple of Dagon made me think again.

Something unutterably evil and terrible lay out there where the seabed reputedly fell sheer for more than two thousand feet into the abyssal depths. Whatever it was, from whatever internal regions it had come, it now held Obed Marsh and his followers in its unbreakable grip.

Then, two days ago, I found myself wandering along Water Street alongside the harbour. What insane compulsion led me in that direction I could not guess. I knew I was being kept under close surveillance all of the way—that eyes were marking my every move.

Where the sense of imminent danger came from it was impossible to tell, nor was it any actual sound. Rather it was a disturbing impression of movement in the vicinity of Marsh Street and Fish Street. I could see nothing to substantiate this, but the sensation grew more pronounced as I halted at a spot where it was possible to look out over the breakwater to where Devil Reef thrust its sinister outline above the water.

It was several minutes before I realised there was something different about the contours of that black reef. I had seen it hundreds of times in the past—I knew its outlines like the back of my hand. But now it seemed far higher than normal, almost as if the sea level around it had fallen substantially.

And then I recognised the full, soul-destroying horror of what I was seeing. That great mass of rock was unchanged. What distorted it was something huge and equally black, which was rising from the sea behind it.

Shuddering convulsively, unable to move a single muscle, I could only stand there, my gaze fixed immutably upon that—*thing*—which rose out of the water until it loomed high above Devil Reef. Mercifully, much of its tremendous bulk lay concealed by the rock and the ocean. Had it all been visible, I am certain I would have lost what remained of my sanity in that horror-crazed instant.

There was the impression of a mass of writhing tentacles surrounding a vast, bulbous head, of what looked like great wings outspread behind the shoulders, and a mountainous bulk hidden by the reef. It dripped with great strands of obnoxious seaweed. I knew that, even from that distance, it was aware of me with a malevolent intensity. And there was something more—an aura of utter malignancy which vibrated in the air, filling my mind with images of nightmarish horror.

This, then, was the quintessence of all the evil which had come to Innsmouth—the embodiment of the abomination which Captain Obed Marsh had wittingly, or inadvertently, brought to the town in exchange for gold.

I remember little of my nightmare flight along Marsh Street and South Street. My earliest coherent memory is of slamming and bolting my door and standing, shivering violently, in the hallway. I had thought those creatures which now shambled along the streets of Innsmouth were the final symbolism of evil in this town, but that monstrosity I had witnessed out in the bay was infinitely worse.

What mad perversity of nature had produced it, where it had originated, and what its terrible purpose might be, I dreaded to think. I knew it could be none other than Dagon, that pagan god these people now worshipped. I also recognised that I now knew too much, that neither Obed Marsh, nor the deep ones which infested the waters around Innsmouth, could ever allow me to leave and tell of what I had witnessed.

There is only one course open to me. I have set down everything in this narrative and I intend to conceal it where only my son, now serving with the North in the war which has torn our country apart, can find it.

Through my window I can see the dark, misshapen figures now massing outside and it is not difficult to guess at their intentions.

Very soon, they will come to break down the door.

I have to be silenced, and possibly sacrificed, so that the Esoteric Order of Dagon may continue to flourish and the worship of Dagon may go on unhindered.

*But I shall thwart whatever plans they have for me. My revolver lies in front of me on the table and there is a single bullet still remaining in the chamber!*

# RICHARD RIDDLE, BOY DETECTIVE IN "THE CASE OF THE FRENCH SPY"

*by* KIM NEWMAN

## I

### WMJHU-OJBHU DAJJQ JH QRS PRBHUFS

"GOSH, DICK," SAID Violet, "an ammonite!"

A chunk of rock, bigger than any of them could have lifted, had broken from the soft cliff and fallen on the shingle. Violet, on her knees, brushed grit and grime from the stone.

They were on the beach below Ware Cleeve, looking for clues.

This was not strictly a fossil-hunting expedition, but Dick knew Violet was mad about terrible lizards—which was what "dinosaur" meant in Greek, she had explained. On a recent visit to London, Violet had been taken to the prehistoric monster exhibit in Crystal Palace Park. She could not have been more excited if the life-size statues turned out to be live specimens. Paleontology was like being a detective, she enthused: working back from clues to the truth, examining a pile of bones and guessing what kind of body once wrapped around them.

Dick conceded her point. But the dinosaurs died a long, long time ago. No culprit's collar would be felt. A pity. It would be a good mystery to solve. The Case of the Vanishing Lizards. No, The Mystery of the Disappearing Dinosaurs. No, The Adventure of the Absent Ammonites.

"Coo," said Ernest. "Was this a *monster*?"

Ernest liked monsters. Anything with big teeth counted.

"Not really," Violet admitted. "It was a cephalopod. That means "head-foot."

"It was a head with only a foot?" Ernest liked the idea. "Did it hop up behind enemies, and sink its fangs into their bleeding necks?"

"It was more like a big shrimp. Or a squid with a shell."

"Squid are fairly monstrous, Ernest," said Dick. "Some grow giant and crush ships with their tentacles."

Ernest made experimental crushing motions with his hands, providing squelching noises with his mouth.

Violet ran her fingers over the ammonite's segments.

"Ammon was the ram-headed god of Ancient Egypt."

Dick saw Ernest imagining that—an evil god butting unbelievers to death.

"These are called 'ammonites' because the many-chambered spiral looks like the horn of a ram. You know, like the big one in Mr. Crossan's field."

Ernest went quiet. He liked fanged monsters, giant squids and evil gods, but had a problem with *animals*. Once, the children were forced to go a long way round to avoid Mr. Crossan's field. Ernest had come up with many tactical reasons for the detour, and Dick and Violet pretended to be persuaded by his argument that they needed to throw pursuers off their track.

The three children were about together all the time this summer. Dick was down from London, staying with Uncle Davey and Aunt Maeve. Both were a bit dotty. Uncle Davey used to paint fairyland scenes for children's books, but was retired from that and drawing only to please himself. Last year, Violet showed up at Seaview Chase unannounced, having learned it was David Harvill's house. She liked his illustrations, but genuinely liked the pictures in his studio even more.

Violet had taken an interest in Dick's detective work. She had showed him around Lyme Regis, and the surrounding beaches and countryside. She wasn't like a proper girl, so it was all right being friends with her. Normally, Dick couldn't admit to having a girl as a friend. In summer, it was different. Ernest was Violet's cousin, two years younger than her and Dick. Ernest's father was in Africa fighting Boers, so he was with Violet's parents for the school holidays.

They were the Richard Riddle Detective Agency. Their goal: to find mysteries, then solve them. Thus far, they had handled the Matter of the Mysterious Maidservant (meeting the Butcher's Boy, though she was supposed to have a sweetheart at sea), the Curious Affair of the Derelict Dinghy (Alderman Hooke was lying asleep in it, empty beer bottles rolling around his feet) and the Puzzle of the Purloined Pasties (still an open case, though suspicion inevitably fell upon Tarquin "Tiger" Bristow).

Ernest had reasoned out his place in the firm. When Dick pointed the finger of guilt at the villain, Ernest would thump the miscreant about the head until the official police arrived. Violet, Ernest said, could make tea and listen to Dick explain his chain of deduction. Ernest, Violet commented acidly, was a dependable strong-arm man... unless the criminal owned a sheep, or threatened to make him eat parsnips, or (as was depressingly likely) turned out to be "Tiger" Bristow (the Bismarck of Bullies) and returned Ernest's head-thumping with interest. Then, Dick had to negotiate a peace, like between Americans and Red Indians, to avoid bloodshed. When Violet broke off the Reservation, people got scalped.

It was a sunny August afternoon, but strong salt wind blew off the sea. Violet had tied back her hair to keep it out of her face. Dick looked up at Ware Cleeve: it was thickly wooded, roots poking out of the cliff-face like the fingers of buried men. The tower of Orris Priory rose above the treetops like a periscope.

Clues led to Orris Priory. Dick suspected smugglers. Or spies.

Granny Ball, who kept the pasty-stall near the Cobb, had warned the detectives to stay away from the shingle under the Cleeve. It was a haunt of "sea-ghosts". The angry souls of shipwrecked sailors, half-fish folk from sunken cities and other monsters of the deep (Ernest liked this bit) were given to creeping onto the beach, clawing away at the stone, crumbling it piece by piece. One day, the Cleeve would collapse.

Violet wanted to know why the sea-ghosts would do such a thing. The landslide would only make another cliff, further inland. Granny winked and said, "Never you mind, lass" in a highly unsatisfactory manner.

Before her craze for terrible lizards, Violet had been passionate about myths and legends (it was why she liked Uncle Davey's pictures). She said myths were expressions of common truth, dressed up to make a point. The shingle beach was dangerous, because rocks fell on it. People in the long ago must have been hit on the head and killed, so the sea-ghost story was invented to keep children away from danger. It was like a BEWARE THE DOG sign (Ernest didn't like this bit), but out of date—as if you had an old, non-fierce hound but put up a BEWARE OF DANGEROUS DOG sign.

Being on the shingle wasn't really dangerous. The cliffs wouldn't fall and the sea-ghosts wouldn't come.

Dick liked Violet's reasoning, but saw better.

"No, Vile, it's been *kept up*, this story. Granny and other folk round here tell the tale to keep us away because *someone* doesn't want us seeing what they're about."

"Smugglers," said Ernest.

Dick nodded. "Or spies. Not enough clues to be certain. But, mark my word, there's wrong-doing afoot on the shingle. And it's our job to root it out."

It was too blowy to go out in Violet's little boat, the SS *Pterodactyl*, so they had come on foot.

And found the ammonite.

Since the fossil wasn't about to hop to life and attack, Ernest lost interest and wandered off, down by the water. He was looking for monster tracks, the tentacle-trails of a giant squid most likely.

"This might be the largest ammonite ever found here," said Violet. "If it's a new species, I get to name it."

Dick wondered how to get the fossil to Violet's house. It would be a tricky endeavour.

"You, children, what are you about?"

Men had appeared on the beach without Dick noticing. If they had come from either direction along the shore, he should have seen them.

"You shouldn't be here. Come away from that evil thing, at once, *now*."

The speaker was an old man with white hair, pince-nez on a black ribbon, an expression like someone who's just bit into a cooking apple by mistake, and a white collar like a clergyman's. He wore an old-fashioned coat with a thick, raised collar, cut away from tight britches and heavy boots.

Dick recognized the Reverend Mr. Sellwood, of Orris Priory.

With him were two bare-armed fellows in leather jerkins and corduroy trousers. Whereas Sellwood carried a stick, they toted sledge-hammers, like the ones convicts use on Dartmoor.

"Foul excrescence of the Devil," said Sellwood, pointing his stick at Violet's ammonite. "Brother Fose, Brother Fessel, do the Lord's work."

Fose and Fessel raised their hammers.

Violet leaned over, as if protecting a pet lamb from slaughter-men.

"Out of the way, foolish girl."

"It's *mine*," she said.

"It's nobody's, and no good to anybody. It must be smashed. God would wish it…"

"But this find is important. To *science*."

Sellwood looked as if that bite of cooker was in his throat, making his eyes water.

"Science! Bah, stuff and nonsense! Devil's charm, my girl, that's what this is!"

"It was alive, millions of millions of years ago."

"The Earth is less than six thousand years old, child, as you would know if you read your scriptures."

Violet, angry, stood up to argue. "But that's not true. There's *proof*. This is…"

Fose and Fessel took their opportunity, and brought the hammers down. The fossil split. Sharp chips flew. Violet—appalled, hands in tiny fists, mouth open—didn't notice her shin bleeding.

"You *can't*…"

"These so-called proofs, stone bones and long-dead dragons," said Sellwood, "are the Devil's trickeries."

The Brethren smashed the ammonite to shards and powder.

"This was put here to fool weak minds," lectured the Reverend. "It is the Church Militant's sacred work to destroy such obscenities, lest more be tempted to blasphemy. This is not science, this is sacrilege."

"It was mine," Violet said quietly.

"I have saved you from error. You should thank me."

Ernest came over to see what the noise was about. Sellwood bestowed a smile on the lad that afforded a glimpse of terrifying teeth.

Teeth on monsters were fine with Ernest; teeth like Sellwood's would give him nightmares.

"A job well done," said the Reverend. "Let us look further. More infernal things may have sprung up."

Brother Fose leered at Violet and patted her on the head, which made her flinch. Brother Fessel looked stern disapproval at this familiarity. They followed Sellwood, swinging hammers, scouting for something to break to bits. Dick had an idea they'd rather be pounding on something that squealed and bled than something so long dead it had turned to stone.

Violet wasn't crying. But she was hating.

More than before, Dick was convinced Sellwood was behind some vile endeavor. He had the look of a smuggler, or a spy.

Richard Riddle, Boy Detective, would bring the villain to book.

## II

### QRS NDPS JA QRS DGGJHBQS DHHBRBFDQJM

Uncle Davey had let Dick set up the office of the Richard Riddle Detective Agency in a small room under the eaves. A gable window led to a small balcony that looked like a ship's crow's-nest. Seaview Chase was a large, complicated house on Black Ven, a jagged rise above Lyme Bay, an ideal vantage point for surveying the town and the sea.

Dick had installed his equipment—a microscope, boxes and folders, reference books, his collection of clues and trophies. Violet had donated some small fossils and her hammers and trowels. Ernest wanted space on the wall for the head of their first murderer: he had an idea that when a murderer was hanged, the police gave the head as a souvenir to the detective who caught him.

The evening after the fossil-smashing incident, Dick sat in the office and opened a new file and wrote *Qrs Ndps ja qrs Dggjhbqs Dhhbrbfdqjm* on a fresh sheet of paper. It was the RRDA. Special Cipher for *The Case of the Ammonite Annihilator*.

After breakfast the next day, the follow-up investigation began. Dick went into the airy studio on the first floor and asked Uncle Davey what he knew about Sellwood.

"Grim-visage?" said Uncle Davey, pulling a face. "Dresses as if it were fifty years ago? Of him, I know, to be frank, not much. He once called with a presentation copy of some verminous volume, printed at his own expense. I think he wanted me to find a proper publisher. Put on a scary smile to ingratiate. Maeve didn't like him. He hasn't been back. Book's around somewhere, probably. Must chuck it one day. It'll be in one of those piles."

He stabbed a paintbrush towards the stacks which grew against one wall and went back to painting—a ship at sea, only there were eyes in the sea if you looked close enough, and faces in the clouds and the folds of sail-cloth. Uncle Davey liked hiding things.

When Violet and Ernest arrived, they set to searching book-piles.

It took a long time. Violet kept getting interested in irrelevant findings. Mostly titles about pixies and fairies and curses.

Sellwood's book had migrated to near the bottom of an especially towering pile. Extracting it brought about a bad tumble that alerted Aunt Maeve, who rushed in assuming the whole of Black Ven was giving way and the house would soon be crashing into Lyme Bay. Uncle Davey cheerfully kicked the spill of volumes into a corner and said he'd sort them out one day, then noticed a wave suitable for hiding an eye in and forgot about the children. Aunt Maeve went off to get warm milk with drops of something from Cook.

In the office, the detectives pored over their find for clues.

"*Omphalos Diabolicus, or: The Hoax of 'Pre-History'*," intoned Dick, "by the Reverend Daniel Sturdevant Sellwood, published 1897, Orris Press, Dorset." Uncle Davey said he paid for the printing, so I deduce that he is the sole proprietor of this phantom publisher. Ah-hah, the pages have not been cut after the first chapter, so I further deduce that it must be deadly dull stuff."

He tossed the book to Violet, who got to work with a long knife, slitting the leaves as if they were the author's throat. Then she flicked through pages, pausing only to report relevant facts. One of her talents was gutting books, discovering the few useful pages like a prospector panning gold dust out of river-dirt.

Daniel Sellwood wasn't a proper clergyman any more. He had been booted out of the Church of England after shouting that the Bishop should burn Mr. Darwin along with his published works. Now, Sellwood had his own sect, the Church Militant—but most of his congregation were paid servants. Sellwood came from a wealthy Dorset family, rich from trade and shipping, and had been packed off to parson school because an older brother, George, was supposed to inherit the fortune—only the brother was lost at sea, along with his wife Rebecca and little daughter Ruth, and Daniel's expectations increased. The sinking of the *Sophy Briggs* was a famous maritime mystery like the *Mary Celeste* and Captain Nemo: thirty years ago, the pride of the Orris-Sellwood Line went down in calm seas, with all hands lost. Sellwood skipped over the loss in a sentence, then spent pages talking up the "divine revelation" which convinced him to found a church rather than keep up the business.

According to Violet, a lot of folk around Lyme resented being thrown out of work when Sellwood dismantled his shipping concern and dedicated the family fortune to preaching anti-Darwinism.

"What's an omphalo-thing?" asked Ernest.

"The title means 'the Devil's Belly-Button,'" said Violet, which made Ernest giggle. "He's put Greek and Latin words together, which is poor Classics. Apart from his stupid ideas, he's a *terrible* writer. Listen… 'all the multitudinarious flora and fauna of divine creation constitute veritable evidence of the proof of the pellucid and undiluted accuracy of the Word of God Almighty Unchallenged as set down in the shining, burning, shimmering sentences, chapters and, indeed, books of the Old and New Testaments, hereinafter known to all righteous and right-thinking men as the Holy Bible of Glorious God.' It's as if he's saying 'this is the true truthiest truest truth of truthdom ever told truly by truth-trusters.'"

"How do the belly-buttons come into it?" asked Dick.

"Adam and Eve were supposed to have been created with navels, though—since they weren't born like other people—they oughtn't to have them."

This was over Ernest's head, but Dick knew how babies came and that his navel was a knot, where a cord had been cut and tied.

"To Sellwood's way of thinking, just as Adam and Eve were created to *seem* as if they had normal parents, the Earth was created as if it had a pre-history, with geological and fossil evidence in place to make the planet appear much older than it says in the Bible."

"That's silly," said Ernest.

"Don't tell me, tell Sellwood," said Violet. "He's a silly, stupid man. He doesn't want to know the truth, or anyone else to either, so he breaks fossils and shouts down lecturers. His theory isn't even original. A man named Gosse wrote a book with the same idea, though Gosse claimed *God* buried fossils to fool people while Sellwood says it was the Devil."

Violet was quite annoyed.

"I think it's an excuse to go round bullying people," said Dick. "A cover for his real, sinister purpose."

"If you ask me, what he does is sinister enough by itself."

"Nobody did ask you," said Ernest, which he always said when someone was unwise enough to preface a statement with "if you ask me". Violet stuck her tongue out at him.

Dick was thinking.

"It's likely that the Sellwood family were smugglers," he said.

Violet agreed. "Smugglers had to have ships, and pretend to be respectable merchants. In the old days, they were all at it. You know the poem…"

Violet stood up, put a hand on her chest, and recited, dramatically.

"If you wake at midnight, and hear a horse's feet,
Don't go drawing back the blind, or looking in the street.
Them that ask no questions isn't told a lie,
Watch the wall, my darling, while the gentlemen go by.
Five and twenty ponies, trotting through the dark,
Brandy for the parson, 'baccy for the clerk;
Laces for a lady, letters for a spy,
And watch the wall, my darling, while the gentlemen go by."

She waited for applause, which didn't come. But her recitation was useful. Dick had been thinking in terms of spies *or* smugglers, but the poem reminded him that the breeds were interdependent. It struck him that Sellwood might be a smuggler of spies, or a spy for smugglers.

"I'll wager 'Tiger' Bristow is in this, too," he said, snapping his fingers.

Ernest shivered, audibly.

"Is it spying or smuggling?" he asked.

"It's both," Dick replied.

Violet sat down again, and chewed on a long, stray strand of her hair.

"Tell Dick about the French Spy," suggested Ernest.

Dick was intrigued.

"That was a long time ago, a hundred years," she said. "It's a local legend, not evidence."

"You yourself say legends always shroud some truth," declared Dick. "We must consider *all* the facts, even rumors of facts, before forming a conclusion."

Violet shrugged. "It is about Sellwood's *house*, I suppose…"

Dick was astonished. "And you didn't think it was relevant! Sometimes, I'm astonished by your lack of perspicacity!"

Violet looked incipiently upset at his tone, and Dick wondered if he wasn't going too far. He needed her in the Agency, but she could be maddening at times. Like a real girl.

"Out with it, Vile," he barked.

Violet crossed her arms and kept quiet.

"I apologize for my tactlessness," said Dick. "But this is vitally important. We might be able to put that ammonite-abuser out of business, with immeasurable benefit to *science*."

Violet melted. "Very well. I heard this from Alderman Hooke's father…"

Before her paleontology craze, Violet fancied herself a collector of folklore. She had gone around asking old people to tell stories or sing songs or remember why things were called what they were called. She was going to write them all up in a book of local legends and had wanted Uncle Davey to draw the pictures. She was still working on her book, but it was about Dinosaurs in Dorset now.

"I didn't make much of it, because it wasn't much of a legend. Just a scrap of history."

"With a spy," prompted Ernest. "A spy who came out of the sea!"

Violet nodded. "That's more or less it. When England was at war with France, everyone thought Napoleon…"

"Boney!" put in Ernest, making fang-fingers at the corners of his mouth.

"Yes, Boney… everyone thought he was going to invade, like William the Conqueror. Along the coast people watched the seas. Signal-fires were prepared, like with the Spanish Armada. Most thought it likely the French would strike at Dover, but round here they tapped the sides of their noses…"

Violet imitated an old person tapping her long nose.

"…and said the last army to invade Britain had landed at Lyme, and the next would too. The last army was Monmouth's, during his rebellion. He landed at the Cobb and marched up to Sedgmoor, where he was defeated. There are *lots* of legends about the Duke of Monmouth…"

Dick made a get-to-the-point gesture.

"Any rate, near the end of the eighteenth century, a man named Jacob Orris formed a vigilance patrol to keep watch on the beaches. Orris's daughter married a sea-captain called Lud Sellwood; they begat drowned George and old Devil's Belly-Button. Come to think, Orris's patrol was like Sellwood's Church Militant—an excuse to shout at folk and break things. Orris started a campaign to get "French beans" renamed "Free-from-Tyranny beans", and had his men attack grocer's stalls when no one agreed with him. Orris was expecting a fleet to heave to in Lyme Bay and land an army, but knew spies would be put ashore first to scout the around. One night, during a terrible storm, Orris caught a spy flung up on the shingle."

"And…?"

"That's it, really. I expect they hit him with hammers and killed him, but if anyone really knows, they aren't saying."

Dick was disappointed.

"Tell him how it was a *special* spy," said Ernest.

Dick was intrigued again. Especially since Violet obviously didn't want to say more.

"He was a sea-ghost," announced Ernest.

"Old Hooke said the spy had *walked* across the channel," admitted Violet. "On the bottom of the sea, in a special diving suit. He was a Frenchman, but—and you have to remember stories get twisted over the years—he had gills *sewn* into his neck so he could breathe underwater. As far as anyone knew round here, all Corsicans were like that. They said it was probably Boney's cousin."

"And they killed him?"

Violet shrugged. "I expect so."

"And kept him *pickled*," said Ernest.

"Now that *isn't* true. One version of this story is that Orris had the dead spy stuffed, then hidden away. But the family would have found the thing and thrown it out by now. And we'd know whether it was a man or, as Granny Ball says, a trained seal. Stories are like limpets on rocks. They stick on and get thicker until you can't see what was there in the first place."

Dick whistled.

"I don't see how this can have anything to do with what Sellwood is about now," said Violet. "This may not have happened, and if it did, it was a hundred years ago. Sellwood wasn't even born then. His parents were still children."

"My dear Vile, a century-old mystery is still a mystery. And crime can seep into a family like water in the foundations, passed down from father to son…"

"Father to *daughter* to son, in this case."

"I haven't forgotten that. This mystery goes deep. It's all about the past. And haven't you said that a century is just a heartbeat in the long life of the planet?"

She was coming round, he saw.

"We have to get into Orris Priory," said Dick.

\* \* \*

## III

## BA BQ WDP SDPY QJ ABHO, BQ WJTFOH'Q IS *RBOOSH*

"Why are we on the shingle?" asked Ernest. "The Priory is up there, on top of the Cleeve."

Dick had been waiting for the question. Deductions impressed more if he didn't just come out with cleverness, but waited for a prompt.

"Remember yesterday? Sellwood seemed to turn up suddenly, with Fose and Fessel. If they'd been walking on the beach, we'd have seen them ages before they arrived. But we didn't. Therefore, there must be a secret way. A smugglers' tunnel."

Violet found some pieces of the fossil. She looked towards the cliff.

"We were facing out to sea, and they came from behind," she said. She tossed her ammonite-shard, which rebounded off the soft rock-face.

The cliff was too crumbly for caves that might conceal a tunnel. The children began looking closely, hoping for a hidden door.

After a half-hour, Ernest complained that he was hungry.

After an hour, Violet complained that she was fed up with rocks.

Dick stuck to it. "If it was easy to find, it wouldn't be *hidden*," he kept saying.

Ernest began to make helpful suggestions that didn't help but needed to be argued with.

"*Maybee* they came up under the sea and swam ashore?"

"They weren't wet and we would have seen them," countered Dick.

"*Maybee* they've got invisible diving suits that don't show wetness?"

"Those haven't been invented yet."

"*Maybee* they've invented them but kept it quiet?"

"It's not likely…"

"But not *impossible*, and you always say that 'when you've eliminated the impossible…'"

"Actually, Ernest, it *is* impossible!"

"Prove it."

"The only way to prove something impossible is to devote your entire life to trying to achieve it, and the lives of everyone to infinity throughout eternity, then *not* succeed…"

"Well, get started…"

"…and that's *impractical!*"

Dick knew he was shouting, but when Ernest got into one of these *maybee* moods—which he called his "clever spells"—everyone got a headache, and usually wound up giving in and agreeing with something they knew to be absurd just to make Ernest shut up. After that, he would be hard to live with for the rest of the day, puffed up like a toad with a smugness that Violet labeled "very unattractive," which prompted him to snipe that he didn't want to attract anyone like her, and her to counter that he would change his mind in a few years, and him to… well, it was a cycle Dick had lived through too often.

Then Violet found a hinge. Two, in fact.

Dick got out his magnifying glass and examined the hinges. Recently oiled, he noted. Where there were hinges, there must be a door. Hidden.

"Where's the handle?" asked Ernest.

"Inside," said Violet.

"What's the use of a door it only opens from one side?"

"It'd keep out detectives, like us," suggested Violet.

"There was no open door when Sellwood was here," observed Dick. "It closed behind him. He'd want to open it again, rather than go home the long way."

"He had two big strong men with hammers," said Violet, "and we've got you and Ernest."

Dick tried to be patient.

He stuck his fingers into a crack in the rock, and worked down, hoping to get purchase enough to pull the probable door open.

"Careful," said Violet.

"*Maybee…*"

"Shut up, Ernest," said Dick.

He found his hand stuck, but pulled free, scraping his knuckles.

There was an outcrop by the sticking point, at about the height where you'd put a door-handle.

"Ah-hah," said Dick, seizing and turning the rock.

A click, and a section of the cliff pulled open. It was surprisingly light, a thin layer of stone fixed to a wooden frame.

A section of rock fell off the door.

"You've broken it now," said Ernest.

It was dark inside. From his coat-of-many-hidden-pockets, Dick produced three candle-stubs with metal holders and a box of matches. For his next birthday, he hoped to get one of the new battery-powered electrical lanterns—until then, these would remain RRDA standard issue.

Getting the candles lit was a performance. The draught kept puffing out match-flames before the wicks caught. Violet took over and mumsily arranged everything, then handed out the candles, showing Ernest how to hold his so wax didn't drip on his fingers.

"Metal's hot," said Ernest.

"Perhaps we should leave you here as look-out," said Dick. "You can warn us in case any *dogs* come along."

The metal apparently wasn't *too* hot, since Ernest now wanted to continue. He insisted on being first into the dark, in case there were monsters.

Once they were inside, the door swung shut.

They were in a space carved out of the rock and shored up with timber. Empty barrels piled nearby. A row of fossil-smashing hammers arranged where Violet could spit at them. Smooth steps led upwards, with the rusted remains of rings set into the walls either side.

"'Brandy for the parson, 'baccy for the clerk,'" said Violet.

"Indubitably," responded Dick. "This is clear evidence of smuggling."

"What do people smuggle these days?" asked Violet. "Brandy and tobacco might have been expensive when we were at war with France and ships were slow, but that was ages ago."

Dick was caught out. He knew there was still contraband, but hadn't looked into its nature.

"Jewels, probably," he guessed. "And there's always spying."

Ernest considered the rings in the wall.

"I bet prisoners were chained here," he said, "until they turned to skellytones!"

"More likely people hold the rings while climbing the slippery stairs," suggested Violet, "especially if they're carrying heavy cases of… jewels and spy-letters."

Ernest was disappointed.

"But they *could* be used for prisoners."

Ernest cheered up.

"If I was a prisoner, I could 'scape", he said. He put his hand in a ring, which was much too big for him and for any grown-up too. Then he pulled and the ring came out of the wall.

Ernest tried to put it back.

Dick was tense, expecting tons of rock to fall on them.

No collapse happened.

"Be careful touching things," he warned his friends. "We were lucky that time, but there might be deadly traps."

He led the way up.

# IV

## DH *JTIFBSQQS*

The steps weren't steep, but went up a long way. The tunnel had been hewn out of rock. New timbers, already bowed and near-cracking, showed where the passage had been shored after falls.

"We must be under the Priory," he said.

They came to the top of the stairs, and a basement-looking room. Wooden crates were stacked.

"Cover your light," said Dick.

Ernest yelped as he burned his hand.

"Carefully," Dick added.

Ernest whimpered a bit.

"What do you suppose is in these?" asked Violet. "Contraband?"

"Instruments of evil?" prompted Ernest.

Dick held his candle close to a crate. The slats were spaced an inch or so apart. Inside were copies of *Omphalos Diabolicus*.

"Isn't the point of smuggling to bring in things people *want*?" asked Violet. "I can't imagine an illicit market for unreadable tracts."

"There could be coded spy messages in the books," Dick suggested hopefully.

"Even spies trained to resist torture in the dungeons of the Tsar wouldn't be able to read through these to get any message," said Violet. "My *deduction* is that these are here because Sellwood can't get anybody to buy his boring old book."

"*Maybee* he should change his name to Sellwords."

Dick had the tiniest spasm of impatience. Here they were, in the lair of an undoubted villain, having penetrated secret defenses, and all they could do was make dubiously sarky remarks about his name.

"We should scout further," he said. "Come on."

He opened a door and found a gloomy passageway. The lack of windows suggested they were still underground. The walls were panelled, wood warped and stained by persistent damp.

The next room along had no door and was full of rubble. Dick thought the ceiling had fallen in, but Violet saw at once that detritus was broken-up fossils.

"Ammonites," she said, "also brachiopods, nautiloids, crinoids, plagiostoma, coroniceras, gryphaea *and* calcirhynchia."

She held up what looked like an ordinary stone.

"This could be the knee-bone of a *scelidosaurus*. One was discovered in Charmouth, in Liassic cliffs just like these. The first near-complete dinosaur fossil to come to light. This might have been another find as important. Sellwood is a vandal and a wrecker. He should be hit on the head with his own hammers."

Dick patted Violet on the back, hoping she would cheer up.

"It's only a knee," said Ernest. "Nothing interesting about knees."

"Some dinosaurs had *brains* in their knees. Extra brains to do the thinking for their legs. Imagine if you had brains in your knees."

Ernest was impressed.

"If *I'd* found this, I wouldn't have broken it," said Violet. "I would have *named* it. *Biolettosaurus*, Violet's Lizard."

"Let's try the next room," said Dick.

"There might still be useful fragments."

Reluctantly, Violet left the room of broken stone bones.

Next was a thick wooden door, with iron bands across it, and three heavy bolts. Though the bolts were oiled, it was a strain to pull them—Dick and Violet both struggled. The top and bottom bolts shifted, but the middle one wouldn't move.

"Let me try," said Ernest. "Please."

They did, and he didn't get anywhere.

Violet dipped back into the fossil room and returned with a chunk they used as a hammer. The third bolt shot open.

The banging and clanging sounded fearfully loud in the enclosed space.

They listened, but no one came. *Maybee*, Dick thought—recognizing the Ernestism—Sellwood was up in his tower, scanning the horizon for spy-signals, and his Brethren were taking afternoon naps.

The children stepped through the doorway, and the door swung slowly and heavily shut behind them.

This room was different again.

The floor and walls were solid slabs which looked as if they'd been in place a long time. The atmosphere was dank, slightly mouldy. A stone trough, like you see in stables, ran along one wall, fed by an old-fashioned pump. Dick cupped water in his hand and tasted it. There was a nasty, coppery sting, and he spat.

"It's a *dungeon*," said Ernest.

Violet held up her candle.

A winch-apparatus, with handles like a threshing machine, was fixed to the floor at the far side of the room, thick chain wrapped around the drum.

"Careful," said Violet, gripping Dick's arm.

Dick looked at his feet. He stood on the edge of a circular Hole, like a well. It was a dozen feet across, and uncovered.

"There should be a cap on this," announced Dick. "To prevent accidents."

"I doubt if Sellwood cares much about accidents befalling intruders."

"You're probably right, Vile. The man's a complete rotter."

Chains extended from the winch unto a solid iron ring in the ceiling and then down into the Hole.

"This is an *oubliette*," said Violet. "It's from the French. You capture your *prisonnier* and *jeté* him into the Hole, then *oublié* them—forget them."

Ernest, nervously, kept well away from the edge. He had been warned about falling into wells once, which meant that ever since he was afraid of them.

Violet tossed her rock-chunk into the pool of dark, and counted. After three counts—thirty feet—there was a thump. Stone on stone.

"No splash," she said.

Up from the depths came another sound, a gurgling groan—something alive but unidentifiable. The noise lodged in Dick's heart like a fish-hook of ice. A chill played up his spine.

The cry had come from a throat, but hardly a human one.

Ernest dropped his candle, which rolled to the lip of the pit and fell in, flame guttering.

Round, green eyes shone up, fire dancing in the fish-flat pupils.

Something grey-green, weighted with old chains, writhed at the bottom of the Hole.

Ernest's candle went out.

Violet's grip on Dick's arm hurt now.

"What's *that*?" she gasped.

The groan took on an imploring, almost pathetic tone, tinged with cunning and bottomless wrath.

Dick shrugged off his shiver. He had a moment of pure joy, the *click* of sudden understanding that often occurs at the climax of a case, when clues fit in the mind like jigsaw pieces and the solution is plain and simple.

"That, my dear Vile, is your French spy!"

# V

## *OBDIJFBNTP GDMBQBGS*

"Someone's coming," said Ernest.

Footfalls in the passageway!

"Hide," said Dick.

The only place—aside from the Hole—was under the water-trough. Dick and Violet pinched out their candles and crammed in, pulling Ernest after them.

"They'll see the door's not bolted," said Ernest.

Violet clamped her hand over her cousin's mouth.

In the enclosed space, their breathing seemed horribly loud.

Dick worried. Ernest was right.

*Maybee* the people in the passage weren't coming to *this* room. *Maybee* they'd already walked past, on their way to smash fossils or get a copy of Sellwood's book.

The footsteps stopped outside the door.

*Maybee* this person didn't know it was usually bolted. *Maybee* this dungeon was so rarely visited they'd *oublié* whether it had been bolted shut after the last time.

*Maybee...*

"Fessel, Fose, Milder, Maulder," barked a voice.

The Reverend Mr. Daniel Sturdevant Sellwood, calling his Brethren.

"And who's been opening *my* door," breathed Violet.

It took Dick long seconds to recognize the storybook quotation.

"Who was last here?" shouted Sellwood. "This is inexcusable. With the Devil, one does not take such risks."

"En cain't git ouwt of thic Hole," replied someone.

"Brother Milder, it has the wiles of an arch-fiend. That is why only *I* can be trusted to put it to the question. Who last brought the slops?"

There was some argument.

*Maybee* they'd be all right. Sellwood was so concerned with stopping an escape that he hadn't thought anyone might break *in*.

One of the Brethren tentatively spoke up, and received a clout round the ear.

Dick wondered why anyone would *want* to be in Sellwood's Church Militant.

"Stand guard," Sellwood ordered. "Let me see what disaster is so narrowly averted."

The door was pushed open. Sellwood set a lantern on a perch. The children pressed further back into shrinking shadow. Dick's ankle bent the wrong way. He bit down on the pain.

He saw Sellwood's shoes—with old-fashioned buckles and gaiters—walk past the trough, towards the Hole. He stopped, just by Dick's face.

There was a pumping, coughing sound.

Sellwood filled a beaker.

He poured the water into the Hole.

Violet counted silently, again. After three, the water splashed on the French spy. It cried out, with despair and yearning.

"Drink deep, spawn of Satan!"

The creature howled, then gargled again. Dick realized it wasn't making animal grunts but *speaking*. Unknown words that he suspected were not French.

The thing had been here for over a hundred years!

"Fose, Milder, in here, now. I will resume the inquisition."

Brethren clumped in. Dick saw heavy boots.

The two bruisers walked around the room, keeping well away from the Hole. Dick eased out a little to get a better view. He risked a more comfortable, convenient position. Sellwood had no reason to suspect he was spied upon.

Brother Fose and Brother Milder worked the winch.

The chains tightened over the Hole, then wound onto the winch-drum.

The thing in the *oubliette* cursed. Dick was sure "*f'tagn*" was a swear-word. As it was hauled upwards, the creature struggled, hissing and croaking.

Violet held Dick's hand, pulling, keeping him from showing himself.

A head showed over the mouth of the Hole, three times the size of a man's and with no neck, just a pulpy frill of puffed-up gill-slits. Saucer-sized fish-eyes held the light, pupils contracting. Dick was sure the creature, eyes at floor-level, saw past the boots of its captors straight into his face. It had a fixed maw, with enough jagged teeth to please Ernest.

"Up," ordered Sellwood. "Let's see all of the demon."

The Brethren winched again, and the thing hung like Captain Kidd on Execution Dock. It was man-like, but with a stub of fishtail protruding beneath two rows of dorsal spines. Its hands and feet were webbed, with nastily curved yellow nail-barbs. Where water had splashed, its skin was rainbow-scaled, beautiful even. Elsewhere, its hide was grey and taut, cracked, flaking or mossy, with rusty weals where the chains chafed.

Dick saw the thing was missing several finger-barbs. Its back and front were striped across with long-healed and new-made scars. It had been whipping boy in this house since the days when Boney was a warrior way-aye-aye.

He imagined Jacob Orris trying to get Napoleon's secrets out of the "spy". Had old Orris held up charts and asked the man-fish to tap a claw on hidden harbours where the invasion fleet was gathered?

Ernest was mumbling "sea-ghost" over and over, not frightened but awed. Violet hissed at him to hush.

Dick was sure they'd be caught, but Sellwood was fascinated by the creature. He poked his face close to his captive's, smiling smugly. A cheek muscle twitched around his fixed sneer. The man-fish looked as if it would like to spit in Sellwood's face but couldn't afford the water.

"So, *Diabolicus Maritime*, is it today that you confess? I have been patient. We merely seek a statement we all know to be true, which will end this sham once and for all."

The fish-eyes were glassy and flat, but moved to fix on Sellwood.

"You are a *deception*, my infernal guest, a lure, a living trick, a lie made flesh, a creature of the Prince of Liars. Own that Satan is your maker, imp! Confess your evil purpose!"

Sellwood touched fingertips to the creature's scarred chest, scraping dry flesh. Scales fluttered away, falling like dead moths. Dick saw Sellwood's fingers flex, the tips biting.

"The bones weren't enough, were they? Those so-called 'fossils', the buried lies that lead to blasphemy and disbelief. No, the Devil had a second deceit in reserve, to pile upon the Great Untruth of 'Pre-History'. No mere dead dragon, but a live specimen, one of those fabled 'missing links' in the fairy tale of 'evolution'. By your very existence, you bear false witness, testify that the world is older than it has been proved over and over again to be, preach against creation, tear down mankind, to drag us from the realm of the angels into the festering salt-depths of

Hell. The City of the Damned lies under the Earth, but you prove to my satisfaction that it extends also under the sea!"

The man-fish had no ears, but Dick was certain it could hear Sellwood. Moreover, it *understood*, followed his argument.

"So, own up," snapped the Reverend. "One word, and the deception is at an end. You are not part of God's Creation, but a sea-serpent, an monstrous forgery!"

The creature's lipless mouth curved. It barked, through its mouth. Its gills rippled, showing scarlet inside.

Sellwood was furious.

Dick, strangely, was excited. The prisoner was *laughing* at its captor, the laughter of a patient, abiding being.

Why was it still alive? Could it be killed? Surely, Orris or Sellwood or some keeper in between had tried to execute the monster?

In those eyes was a promise to the parson. *I will live when you are gone.*

"Drop it," snapped Sellwood.

Fose and Milder let go the winch, and—with a cry—the "French spy" was swallowed by its Hole.

Sellwood and his men left the room, taking the lantern.

Dick began breathing properly again. Violet let Ernest squirm a little, though she still held him under the trough.

Then came a truly terrifying sound, worse even than the laughter of the fish-demon.

Bolts being drawn. Three of them.

They were trapped!

# VI

## WSFF IMJTURQ-TK BH M'FYSR

Now was the time to keep calm.

Dick knew Violet would be all right, if only because she had to think about Ernest.

For obvious reasons, the children had not told anyone where they were going, but they would be missed at tea-time. Uncle Davey and

Aunt Maeve could easily overlook a skipped meal—both of them were liable to get so interested in something that they wouldn't notice the house catching fire—but Cook kept track. And Mr. and Mrs. Borrodale were sticklers for being in by five o'clock with hands washed and presentable.

It must be past five now.

Of course, any search party wouldn't get around to the Priory for days, maybe weeks. They'd look on the beaches first, and in the woods.

Eventually, his uncle and aunt would find the folder marked *Qrs Ndps ja qrs Dggjhbqs Dhhbrbfdqjm*. Aunt Maeve, good at puzzles, had taught him how to cipher in the first place. She would eventually break the code and read Dick's notes, and want to talk with Sellwood. By then, it would probably be too late.

They gave the Brethren time enough to get beyond earshot before creeping out from under the trough. They unbent with much creaking and muffled moaning. Violet lit her candle.

Dick paced around the cell, keeping away from the Hole.

"I'm thirsty," said Ernest.

"Easily treated," said Violet.

She found the beaker and pumped water into it. Ernest drank, made a face, and asked for more. Violet worked the pump again.

Water splashed over the brimful beaker, into the trough.

A noise came out of the Hole.

The children froze into mannequins. The noise came again.

"Wah wah… *wah wah…*"

There was a pleading tone to it.

"Wah wah…"

"'Water,'" said Dick, snapping his fingers. "It's saying 'water.'"

"Wah wah," agreed the creature. "Uh, wah wah."

"'Water. Yes, water.'"

"Gosh, Dick, you *are* clever," said Violet.

"Wat war," said the creature, insisting. "Gi' mee wat war, i' oo eese…"

"'Water,'" said Dick, "'Give me—'"

"'—water, if you please,'" completed Violet, who caught on swiftly. "Very polite for a sea-ghost. Well brought-up in Atlantis or Lyonesse or R'lyeh, I imagine."

"Where?" asked Dick.

"Sunken cities of old, where mer-people are supposed to live."

More left-overs from Violet's myths and legends craze. Interesting, but not very helpful.

Ernest had walked to the edge of the Hole.

"This isn't a soppy mer-person," said Ernest. "This is a Monster of the Deep!"

He emptied the beaker into the dark.

A sigh of undoubted gratitude rose from the depths.

"Wat war goo', tanks. Eese, gi' mee moh."

Ernest poured another beakerful. At this rate, they might as well be using an eye-dropper.

Dick saw the solution.

"Vile, help me shift the trough," he said.

They pulled one end away from the wall. It was heavy, but the bolts were old and rusted and the break came easily.

"Careful not to move the other end too much. We need it under the pump."

Violet saw where this was going. Angled down away from the wall, the trough turned into a sluice. It didn't quite stretch all the way to the *oubliette*, but pulling up a loose stone put a notch into the rim which served as a spout.

"Wat war eese," said the creature, mildly.

Dick nodded to Violet. She worked the pump.

Water splashed into the trough and flowed down, streaming through the notch and pouring into the pit.

The creature gurgled with joy.

Only now did Dick wonder whether watering it was a good idea. It might not be a French spy or even a maritime demon, but it was definitely one of Granny Ball's sea-ghosts. If Dick had been treated as it had been, he would not be well disposed towards land-people.

But the water kept flowing.

Violet's arm got tired, and she let up for a moment.

"I' oo eese," insisted the creature, with a reproachful, nannyish tone. "Moh wat war."

Violet kept pumping.

Dick took the candle and walked to the edge of the Hole. Ernest sat there, legs dangling over the edge, fingers playing in the cool cascade.

The boys looked down.

Where water fell, the man-fish was changed—vivid greens and reds and purples and oranges glistened. Its spines and frills and gills and webs were sleek. Even its eyes shone more brightly.

It turned, mouth open under the spray, letting water wash around it, wrenching against its chains.

"Water makes the Monster strong," said Ernest.

The creature looked up at them. The edges of its mouth curved into something like a smile. There was cunning there, and a bottomless well of malice, but also an exultation. Dick understood: when it was wet, the thing felt as he did when he saw through a mystery.

It took a grip on one of its manacles and squeezed, cracking the old iron and casting it away.

"Can I stop now?" asked Violet. "My arm's out of puff."

"I think so."

The creature nodded, a human gesture awkward on the gilled, neckless being.

It stood up unshackled, and stretched as if waking after a long sleep in an awkward position. The chains dangled freely. A clear, thick, milky-veined fluid seeped from the weals on its chest. The man-fish carefully smoothed this secretion like an ointment.

There were pools of water around its feet. It got down on its knees—did it have spare brains in them?—and sucked the pools dry. Then it raised its head and let water dribble through its gills and down over its chest and back.

"Tanks," it said.

Now it wasn't parched, its speech was easier to understand.

It took hold of the dangling chains, and tugged, testing them.

Watering the thing in the Hole was all very well, but Dick wasn't sure how he'd feel if it were up here with them. If he were the creature, he would be very annoyed. He ought to be grateful to the children, but what did anyone know about the feelings of sea-ghosts? Violet had told them the legend of the genie in the bottle: at first, he swore to bestow untold riches upon the man who set him free, but after thousands of years burned to make his rescuer suffer horribly for waiting so long.

It was too late to think about that.

Slick and wet, the man-fish moved faster than anything its size should. No sooner had it grasped the chains than it had climbed them, deft as a sailor on the rigging, quick as a lizard on the flat or a salmon in the swim.

It held on, hanging just under the ring in the ceiling, head swiveling around, eyes taking in the room.

Dick and Ernest were backed against the door, taking Violet with them.

She was less spooked than the boys.

"*Bonjour, Monsieur le Fantôme de la Mer*," she said, slowly and clearly in the manner approved by her tutor, M. Duroc. "*Je m'appelle Violette Borrodale... permettez-moi de presente a vous mon petit cousin Ernest... et Rishard Riddle, le detective juvenile celebré.*"

This seemed to puzzle the sea-ghost.

"Vile, I don't think it's really French," whispered Dick.

Violet shrugged.

The creature let go and leaped, landing frog-like, knees stuck out and shoulders hunched, inches away from them. This close, it stank of the sea.

Dick saw their reflections in its huge eyes.

Its mouth opened. He saw row upon row of shark-like teeth, all pointed and shining. It might not have had a proper meal in a century.

"Scuze mee," it said, extending a hand, folding its frill-connected fingers up but pointing with a single barb.

The wet thorn touched Richard's cheek.

Then it eased the children aside, and considered the bolted door.

"Huff... puff... blow," it said, hammering with fish-fists. The door came off its hinges and the bolts wrenched out of their sockets. The broken door crashed against the opposite wall of the passage.

"How do you know the 'Three Little Pigs'?" asked Violet.

"Gur' nam 'Ooth," it said, "ree' to mee..."

"A girl read to him," Dick explained.

So not all his captors had been tormentors. Who was 'Ooth? Ruth?

Someone called Ruth fit into the story. The little girl lost with the *Sophy Briggs*. Sellwood's niece.

The sea-ghost looked at Violet. Dick deduced all little girls must look alike to it. If you've seen one pinafore, you've seen them all.

" 'Ooth," it said, with something like fondness. "'Ooth kin' to mee. Ree' mee story-boos. *Liss in Wonlan… Tripella Liplik Pik… Taes o Eh Ah Po…*"

"What happened to Ruth?" Violet asked.

"Sellwoo' ki' 'Ooth, an' hi' bro tah Joh-jee," said the creature, cold anger in its voice. "Tey wan let mee go sea, let mee go hom. Sellwoo' mak shi' wreck, tak ever ting, tak mee."

Dick understood. And was not surprised.

This was the nature of Sellwood's villainy. Charges of smuggling and espionage remained unproven, but he was guilty of the worst crime of all—murder!

People were coming now, alerted by the noise.

The sea-ghost stepped into the passage, holding up a hand—fingers spread and webs unfurled—to indicate that the children should stay behind.

They kept in the dark, where they couldn't see what was happening in the passage.

The man-fish leaped, and landed on someone.

Cries of terror and triumph! An unpleasant, wet crunching… followed by unmistakable chewing.

More people came on the scene.

"The craytur's out o' thic Hole," shrieked someone.

A very loud bang! A firework stink.

The man-fish staggered back past the doorway, red blossoming on its shoulder. It had more red stuff around its mouth, and scraps of cloth caught in its teeth.

It roared in rage and threw itself at whoever had shot it.

Something detached from something else and rolled past the doorway, leaving a trail of sticky splashes.

Violet kept her hand over Ernest's eyes, though he tried to pick at her fingers.

"Spawn of Satan, you show your true colours at last!"

It was Sellwood.

"Milder, Fessel, take him down."

The Brethren grunted. The doorway was filled with struggling bodies, driving the children back into the cell. They pressed flat against the wet cold walls.

Brother Milder and Brother Fessel held the creature's arms and wrestled it back, towards the Hole.

Sellwood appeared, hefting one of his fossil-breaking hammers.

He thumped the sea-ghost's breast-bone with all his might, and it fell, sprawling on the flagstones. Milder and Fessel shifted their weight to pin the creature down.

Still, no one noticed the children.

The creature's shoulder-wound closed like a sea anemone. The bruise in the middle of its chest faded at once. It looked hate up at the Reverend.

Sellwood stood over the wriggling man-fish. He weighed his hammer.

"You're devilish hard to kill, demon! But how would you like your skull pounded to paste? It might take a considerable while to recover, eh?"

He raised the hammer above his head.

"You there," said Violet, voice clear and shrill and loud, "stop!"

Sellwood swivelled to look.

"This is an important scientific discovery, and must not be harmed. Why, it is practically a living dinosaur."

Violet stood between Sellwood and the pinned man-fish. Dick was by her side, arm linked with hers. Ernest was in front of them, fists up like a pugilist.

"Don't you hurt my friend the Monster," said Ernest.

Sellwood's red rage showed.

"You see," he yelled, "how the foulness spreads! How the lies take hold! You see!"

Something snapped inside Milder. He rolled off the creature, limbs loose, neck flopping.

The sea-ghost stood up, a two-handed grip on the last of Sellwood's Brethren, Fessel.

"Help," he gasped. "Children, help…"

Dick had a pang of guilt.

Then Fessel was falling into the *oubliette*. He rattled against chains, and landed with a final-sounding crash.

The sea-ghost stepped around the children and took away Sellwood's hammer, which it threw across the room. It clanged against the far wall.

"I am not afraid of you," announced the Reverend.

The creature tucked Sellwood under its arm. The Reverend was too surprised to protest.

"Shouldn' a' ki' 'Ooth a' Joh-jee, Sellwoo'. Shouldn' a' ki.'"

"How do you know?" Sellwood was indignant, but didn't deny the crime.

"Sea tol' mee, sea tel' mee all ting."

"I serve a greater purpose," shouted Sellwood.

The sea-ghost carried the Reverend out of the room. The children followed.

The man-fish strode down the passage, towards the book-room. Two dead men—Maulder and Fose—lay about.

"Their heads are gone," exclaimed Ernest, with a glee Dick found a little disturbing. At least Ernest wasn't picking up one of the heads for the office wall.

Sellwood thumped the creature's back. Its old whip-stripes and poker-brands were healing.

Dick, Violet and Ernest followed the escapee and its former gaoler.

In the book-room, Sellwood looked with hurried regret at the crates of unsold volumes and struggled less. The sea-ghost found the steps leading down and seemed to contract its body to squeeze into the tunnel. Sellwood was dragged bloody against the rock ceiling.

"Come on, detectives," said Dick, "after them!"

# VII

## *DHQRMJKJP BNQRYJP IBJFFSQQD*

They came out under Ware Cleeve. Waves scraped shingle in an eternal rhythm. It was twilight, and chilly. Well past tea-time.

The man-fish, burden limp, tasted the sea in the air.

"Tanks," it said to the children, "tanks very mu."

It walked into the waves. As sea soaked through his coat, Sellwood was shocked into consciousness and began to struggle again, shouting and cursing and praying.

The sea-ghost was waist-deep in its element.

It turned to wave at the children. Sellwood got free, madly striking *away* from the shore, not towards dry land. The creature leaped completely out of the water, dark rainbows rippling on its flanks, and landed heavily on Sellwood, claws hooking into meat, pressing the Reverend under the waves.

They saw the swimming shape, darting impossibly fast, zigzagging out into the bay. Finned feet showed above the water for an instant and the man-fish—the sea-ghost, the French spy, the living fossil, the snare of Satan, the Monster of the Deep—was gone for good, dragging the Reverend Mr. Daniel Sturdevant Sellwood with him.

"...to Davey Jones's locker," said Ernest.

Dick realized Violet was holding his hand, and tactfully got his fingers free.

Their shoes were covered with other people's blood.

"*Anthropos Icthyos Biolletta*," said Violet. "Violet's Man-Fish, a whole new *phylum*.

"I pronounce this case closed," said Dick.

"Can I borrow your matches?" asked Violet. "I'll just nip back up the tunnel and set fire to Sellwood's books. If the Priory burns down, we won't have to answer questions about dead people."

Dick handed over the box.

He agreed with Violet. This was one of those stories for which the world was not yet ready. Writing it up, he would use a double cipher.

"Besides," said Violet, "some books deserve to be burned."

While Violet was gone, Dick and Ernest passed time skipping stones on the waves. Rooting for ammunition, they found an ammonite, not quite as big and nice as the one that was smashed, but sure to delight Violet and much easier to carry home.

# INNSMOUTH CLAY

*by* H. P. LOVECRAFT AND AUGUST DERLETH

THE FACTS RELATING to the fate of my friend, the late sculptor, Jeffrey Corey—if indeed 'late' is the correct reference—must begin with his return from Paris and his decision to rent a cottage on the coast south of Innsmouth in the autumn of 1927. Corey came from an armigerous family with some distant relationship to the Marsh clan of Innsmouth—not, however, such a one as would impose upon him any obligation to consort with his distant relatives. There were, in any case, rumours abroad about the reclusive Marshes who still lived in that Massachusetts seaport town, and these were hardly calculated to inspire Corey with any desire to announce his presence in the vicinity.

I visited him a month after his arrival in December of that year. Corey was a comparatively young man, not yet forty, six feet in height, with a fine, fresh skin, which was free of any hirsute adornment, though his hair was worn rather long, as was then the custom among artists in the Latin quarter of Paris. He had very strong blue eyes, and his lantern-jawed face would have stood out in any assemblage of people, not alone for the piercing quality of his gaze, but as much for the rather strange, wattled appearance of the skin back from his jaws, under his ears and down his neck a little way below his ears. He was not ill-favoured in looks, and a queer quality, almost hypnotic, that informed his fine-featured face had a kind of fascination for most people who met him. He was well settled in when I visited him, and had begun work on a statue of Rima, the Bird-Girl, which promised to become one his finest works.

He had laid in supplies to keep him for a month, having gone into Innsmouth for them, and he seemed to me more than usually loquacious, principally about his distant relatives, about whom there was a considerable amount of talk, however guarded, in the shops of Innsmouth. Being reclusive, the Marshes were quite naturally the object of some curiosity; and since that curiosity was not satisfied, an impressive lore and legendry had grown up about them, reaching all the way back to an earlier generation which had been in the South Pacific trade. There was little definite enough to hold meaning for Corey, but what there was suggested all manner of arcane horror, of which he expected at some nebulous future time to learn more, though he had no compulsion to do so. It was just, he explained, that the subject was so prevalent in the village that it was almost impossible to escape it.

He spoke also of a prospective show, made references to friends in Paris and his years of study there, to the strength of Epstein's sculpture, and to the political turmoil boiling in the country. I cite these matters to indicate how perfectly normal Corey was on the occasion of this first visit to him after his return from Europe. I had, of course, seen him fleetingly in New York when he had come home, but hardly long enough to explore any subject as we were able to do that December of 1927.

Before I saw him again, in the following March, I received a curious letter from him, the gist of which was contained in the final paragraph, to which everything else in his letter seemed to mount as to a climax—

You may have read of some strange goings-on at Innsmouth in February. I have no very clear information about it, but it must surely have been in the papers somewhere, however silent our Massachusetts papers seem to have been. All I can gather about the affair is that a large band of Federal officers of some kind descended upon the town and spirited away some of the citizens—among them some of my own relatives, though which I am at a loss to say since I've never troubled to ascertain how many of them there are—or were, as the case may be. What I can pick up in Innsmouth has reference to some kind of South Pacific trade in which certain shipping interests in the town were still evidently engaged, though this seems to be pretty far-fetched, insofar as the docks are all but abandoned, and actually largely useless for the ships now plying the Atlantic, most of which go to the larger and more modern ports. Quite apart from the reasons for the Federal action—and considerably of more importance to me, as you will see—is the indisputable fact that, coincident with the raid on Innsmouth, some naval vessels appeared off the coast in the vicinity of what is known as Devil Reef, and there dropped a power of depth charges! These set off such turmoil in the depths that a subsequent storm washed ashore all manner of debris, of which a peculiar blue clay came in along the water's edge here. It seemed to me very much like that moulding clay of similar colour found in various parts of interior America and often used for the manufacture of bricks, particularly years ago when more modern methods of brick-making were not available to builders. Well, what is important about all this is that I gathered up the clay I could find before the sea took it back again, and I have been working on an entirely new piece I've tentatively titled "Sea Goddess"—and I am wildly enthusiastic about its possibilities. You will see it when you come down next week, and I am certain you will like it even more than my "Rima".

Contrary to his expectations, however. I found myself oddly repelled at my first sight of Corey's new statue. The figure was lissome, save for rather heavier pelvic structure than I thought fitting, and Corey had chosen to alter the feet with webbing between the toes.

"Why?" I asked him.

"I really don't know," he said. "The fact is I hadn't planned to do it. It just happened."

"And those disfiguring marks on the neck?" He was apparently still at work in that area.

He gave an embarrassed laugh, and a strange expression came into his eyes. "I wish I could explain those marks to my own satisfaction, Ken," he said. "I woke up yesterday morning to find that I must have been working in my sleep, for there were slits in the neck below her ears—on both sides—slits like—well, like gills. I'm repairing the damage now."

"Perhaps a 'sea goddess' ought to have gills," I said.

"I'd guess it came about as a result of what I picked up in Innsmouth day before yesterday when I went in for some things I needed. More talk of the Marsh clan. It boiled down to the suggestion that members of the family were reclusive by choice because they had some kind of physical deformity that related to a legend tying them to certain South Sea islanders. This is the kind of fairy tale that ignorant people take up and embellish—though I grant that this one is more unusual than the kind one commonly picks up, related to the Judaeo-Christian morality pattern. I dreamed about it that night— and evidently walked in my sleep and worked out some part of the dream on my 'Sea Goddess.'"

However strange I thought it, I made no further comments on the incident. What he said was logical, and I confess that I was appreciably more interested in the Innsmouth lore than in the disfigurement of the "Sea Goddess".

Moreover, I was somewhat taken aback at Corey's evident preoccupation. He was animated enough when we were in conversation, no matter what the subject, but I could not help noticing an air of abstraction whenever we were not—as if he had something on his mind of which he was reluctant to speak, something that vaguely troubled him, but of which he had no certain knowledge himself, or knowledge insufficient to permit him to speak. This showed itself in various ways—a distant look in his eyes, an occasional expression of bafflement, a far gazing out to sea, and now and then a bit of wandering in his talk, an edging off the subject, as were some more demanding thought intruding upon the subject under discussion.

I have thought since that I ought to have taken the initiative and explored the preoccupation so manifest to me; I deferred doing so because I thought it did not concern me and to have done so seemed to me an invasion of Corey's privacy. Though we were friends of long standing, it did not seem that it should be incumbent upon me to intrude upon matters that were patently his alone, and he did not offer to introduce the subject himself, which, I felt, precluded my doing so.

Nevertheless, if I may digress here and leap forward to that period after Corey's disappearance, when I had come into possession of his estate—as directed by him in a formally drawn-up document—it was at about this time that Corey began to jot down disturbing notes in a journal or diary he kept, one that had begun as a commonplace book relating solely to his creative life. Chronologically, these jottings fit at this point into any account of the facts about Jeffrey Corey's last months.

*March 7.* A very strange dream last night. Something impelled me to baptise "Sea Goddess". This morning found the piece *wet* about the head and shoulders, as if I had done it. I repaired the damage, as if no alternative were offered me, though I had planned to crate "Rima". The *compulsion* troubles me.

*March 8.* A dream of swimming accompanied by shadowy men and women. Faces, when seen, hauntingly familiar—like something out of an old album. This undoubtedly took rise in the grotesque hints and sly innuendos heard at Hammond's Drug Store today—about the Marshes, as usual. A tale of great-grandfather Jethro *living* in the sea. Gilled! The same thing said of some members of the Waite, Gilman and Eliot families. Heard the identical stuff when I stopped to make an enquiry at the railroad station. The natives here have fed upon this for decades.

*March 10.* Evidently sleep-walked in the night, for some slight alterations had been made in "Sea Goddess". Also curious indentations as if someone's arms had been around the statue, which was yesterday far too hard to take any sort of impression not made by a chisel or some such tool. The marks bore the appearance of having been *pressed into soft clay*. The entire piece *damp* this morning.

*March 11.* A really extraordinary experience in the night. Perhaps the most vivid dream I've ever had, certainly the most erotic. I can hardly even now think of it without being aroused. I dreamed that a woman, *naked*, slipped into my bed after I had gone to sleep, and remained there all night. I dreamed that the night was spent at love—or perhaps I ought to call it lust. Nothing like it since Paris! And as real as those many nights in the Quarter! Too real, perhaps, for I woke exhausted. And I had undoubtedly spent a restless night, for the bed was much torn up.

*March 12.* Same dream. Exhausted.

*March 13.* The dream of swimming again. In the sea-depths. A sort of city far below. Ryeh or R'lyeh? Something named "Great Thooloo"?

Of these matters, these strange dreams, Corey said very little on the occasion of my March visit. His appearance at that time seemed to me somewhat drawn. He did speak of some difficulty sleeping; he was not, he said, getting his "rest"—no matter when he went to bed. He did ask me then if I had ever heard the names "Ryeh" or "Thooloo"; of course, I never had, though on the second day of my visit, we had occasion to hear them.

We went into Innsmouth that day—a short run of less than five miles—and it was evident to me soon that the supplies Corey said he needed did not form the principal reason for going to Innsmouth. Corey was plainly on a fishing expedition; he had come deliberately to find out what he could learn about his family, and to that end the way from one place to another, from Ferrand's Drug Store to the public library, where the ancient librarian showed an extraordinary reserve on the subject of the old families of Innsmouth and the surrounding countryside, though she did at last mention two names of very old men who might remember some of the Marshes and Gilmans and Waites, and who might be found in their usual haunt, a saloon on Washington Street.

Innsmouth, for all that it had much deteriorated, was the kind of village that must inevitably fascinate anyone with archaeological or architectural interests, for it was well over a century old, and the majority of its buildings—other than those in the business-section, dated back many decades before the turn of the century. Even though many were now deserted, and in some cases fallen into ruin, the architectural features of the houses reflected a culture long since gone from the American scene.

As we neared the waterfront, on Washington Street, the evidence of catastrophe was everywhere apparent. Buildings lay in ruins—"Blown up," said Corey, "by the Federal men, I'm told"—and little effort had been made to clean up anything, for some side streets were still blocked by brick rubble. In one place an entire street appeared to have been destroyed, and all the old buildings once used as warehouses along the docks—long since abandoned—had been destroyed. As we neared the sea shore, a nauseating, cloying musk, icthyic in origin, pervaded everything; it was more than the fishy odour often encountered in stagnant areas along the coast or, too, in inland waters.

Most of the warehouses, Corey said, had once been Marsh property; so much he had learned at Ferrand's Drug Store. Indeed, the remaining members of the Waite and Gilman and Eliot families had suffered very little loss; almost the entire force of the Federal raid had fallen upon the Marshes and their holdings in Innsmouth, though the Marsh Refining Company, engaged in manufacturing gold ingots, had not been touched, and still afforded employment to some of the villagers who were not engaged in fishing, though the Refining Company was no longer directly controlled by members of the Marsh clan.

The saloon, which we finally reached, was plainly of nineteenth-century origin; and it was equally clear that nothing in the way of improvement had been done to the building or its interior since it had gone up, for the place was unbelievably rundown and shabby. A slovenly middle-aged man sat behind the bar reading a copy of the *Arkham Advertiser*, and two old men, one of them asleep, sat at it, far apart.

Corey ordered a glass of brandy, and I did likewise.

The bartender did not disguise a cautious interest in us.

"Seth Akins?" asked Corey presently.

The bartender nodded toward the customer who slept at the bar.

"What'll he drink?" asked Corey.

"Anything."

"Let's have a brandy for him."

The bartender poured a shot of brandy into an ill-washed glass and put it down on the bar. Corey took it down to where the old man slept, sat down beside him, and nudged him awake.

"Have one on me," he invited.

The old fellow looked up, revealing a grizzled face and bleary eyes under tousled grey hair. He saw the brandy, grabbed it, grinning uncertainly, and drank it down.

Corey began to question him, at first only establishing his identity as an old resident of Innsmouth, and talking in a general fashion about the village and the surrounding country to Arkham and Newburyport. Akins talked freely enough; Corey bought him another drink, and then another.

But Akins' ease of speech faded as soon as Corey mentioned the old families, particularly the Marshes. The old man grew markedly more cautious, his eyes darting longingly toward the door, as if he would have liked to escape. Corey, however, pressed him hard, and Akins yielded.

"Guess thar ain't no harm sayin' things naow," he said finally. "Most o' them Marshes is gone since the guv'mint come in last month. And no one knows whar to, but they ain't come back." He rambled quite a bit, but, after circling the subject for some time, he came at last to the "East Injy trade" and "Cap'n Obed Marsh—who begun it all. He had some kind a truck with them East Injuns—brung back some o' thar women an' kep' 'em in that big haouse he'd built—an' after that, the young Marshes got that queer look an' took to swimmin' aout to Devil Reef an' they'd be gone fer a long time—haours—an' it wan't natural bein' underwater so long. Cap'n Obed married one o' them women—an' some o' the younger Marshes went aout to the East Injys an' brung back more. The Marsh trade never fell off like the others'. All three o' Cap'n Obed's ships—the brig *Columby*, an' the barque *Sumatry Queen* an' another brig, *Hetty*—sailed the oceans for the East Injy an' the Pacific trade withaout ever a accident. An' them people—them East Injuns an' the Marshes—they begun a new kind a religion—they called it the Order o' Dagon—an' there was a lot o' talk, whisperin' whar nobuddy heerd it, abaout what went on at their meetin's, an' young folk—well, maybe they got lost, but nobuddy ever saw 'em again, an' thar was all that talk about sacreefices—*human* sacreefices—abaout the same time the young folks dropped aout o' sight—none o' them Marshes or Gilmans or Waites or Eliots, though, none o' thar young folk ever got lost. An' thar was all them whispers abaout some place called 'Ryeh' an' somethin' named 'Thooloo'— some kin't Dagon, seems like..."

At this Corey broke in with a question, seeking to clarify Akins' reference; but the old man knew nothing, and I did not understand until later the reason for Corey's sudden interest.

Akins went on. "People kep' away from them Marshes—an' the others, too. But it was the Marshes that had that queer look mostly. It got so bad some o' them never went aout o' the house, unless it was at night, an' then it was most o' the time to go swimmin' in the ocean. They cud swim like fish, people said—I never saw 'em myself, and nobuddy talked much cuz we noticed whenever anybuddy talked a lot he sort o' dropped aout o' sight—like the young people—and were never heerd from again.

"Cap'n Obed larnt a lot o' things in Ponape an' from the Kanakys— all abaout people they called the 'Deep Ones' that lived under the water—an' he brought back all kinds o' carved things, queer fish things and things from under the water that wan't fish-things—Gawd knows what them things wuz!"

"What did he do with those carvings?" put in Corey.

"Some as didn't go to the Dagon Hall he sold—an' fer a good price, a real good price they fetched. But they're all gone naow, all gone— an' the Order of Dagon's all done an' the Marshes ain't been seen hereabaouts ever since they dynamited the warehaouses. An' they wan't all arrested, neither—no, sir, they do say what was left o' them Marshes jist walked daown't the shore an' aout into the water an' kilt themselves." At this point he cackled mirthlessly. "But nobuddy ain't seen a one o' them Marsh bodies, thar ain't been no corp' seen all up an' daown the shore."

He had reached this point in his narrative when something extremely odd took place. He suddenly fixed widening eyes on my companion, his jaw dropped, his hands began to shake; for a moment or two he was frozen in that position; then he shrugged himself up and off the barstool, turned, and in a stumbling run burst out of the building into the street, a long, despairing cry shuddering back through the wintry air.

To say that we were astonished is to put it mildly. Seth Akins' sudden turning from Corey was so totally unexpected that we gazed at each other in astonishment. It was not until later that it occurred to me that Akins' superstition-ridden mind must have been shaken by the sight of the curious corrugations on Corey's neck below his ears—for in the course of our conversation with the old man, Corey's thick scarf, which had protected his neck from the still cold March air, had loosened and fallen to drape over his chest in a short loop, disclosing the indentations and rough skin which had always been a part of Jeffrey Corey's neck, that wattled area so suggestive of age and wear.

No other explanation offered itself, and I made no mention of it to Corey, lest I disturb him further, for he was visibly upset, and there was nothing to be gained by upsetting him further.

"What a rigmarole!" I cried, once we were again on Washington Street.

He nodded abstractedly, but I could see plainly that some aspects of the old fellow's account had made an impression of sorts—and a not entirely pleasant one—on my companion. He could smile, but ruefully, and at my further comments he only shrugged, as if he did not wish to speak of the things we had heard from Akins.

He was remarkably silent throughout that evening, and rather noticeably preoccupied, even more so than he had been previously. I recall resenting somewhat his unwillingness to share whatever burdened his thoughts, but of course this was his decision to make, not mine, and I suspect that what churned through his mind that evening must have seemed to him far-fetched and outlandish enough to make him want to spare himself the ridicule he evidently expected from me. Therefore, after several probing questions which he turned off, I did not again return to the subject of Seth Akins and the Innsmouth legends.

I returned to New York in the morning.

Further excerpts from Jeffrey Corey's *Journal.*

*March 18.* Woke this morning convinced that I had not slept alone last night. Impressions on pillow, in bed. Room and bed very *damp*, as if someone wet had got into bed beside me. I know intuitively it was a woman. But *how?* Some alarm at the thought that the Marsh madness may be beginning to show in me. *Footprints* on the floor.

*March 19.* "Sea Goddess" gone! The door open. Someone must have got in during the night and taken it. Its sale value could hardly be accounted as worth the risk! Nothing else taken.

*March 20.* Dreamed all night about everything Seth Akins said. Saw Captain Obed Marsh under the sea! Very ancient. *Gilled!* Swam to far below the surface of the Atlantic off Devil Reef. Many others, both men and women. The queer Marsh look! Oh, the power and the glory!

*March 21.* Night of the equinox. My neck throbbed with pain all night. Could not sleep. Got up and walked down to the shore. How the sea draws me! I was never so aware of it before, but I remember now how as a child I used to fancy I *heard*—way off in mid-continent!—the sound of the sea, of the seas' drift and the windy waves!—A fearful sense of anticipation filled me all night long.

Under this same date—March 21—Corey's last letter to me was written. He said nothing in it of his dreams, but he did write about the soreness of his neck.

It isn't my throat—that's clear. No difficulty swallowing. The pain seems to be in that disfigured area of skin—wattled or wart-like or fissured, whatever you prefer to call it—beneath my ears. I cannot describe it; it isn't the pain one associates with stiffness or friction or a bruise. It's as if the skin were about to break outward, and it goes deep. And at the same time I cannot rid myself of the conviction that something is about to happen—something I both dread and look forward to, and all manner of *ancestral awarenesses*—however badly I put it—obsess me!

I replied, advising him to see a doctor, and promising to visit him early in April.

By that time Corey had vanished.

There was some evidence to show that he had gone down to the Atlantic and walked in—whether with the intention of swimming or of taking his life could not be ascertained. The prints of his bare feet were discovered in what remained of that odd clay thrown up by the sea in February, but there were no returning prints. There was no farewell message of any kind, but there were instructions left for me directing the disposal of his effects, and I was named administrator of his estate—which suggested that some apprehension did exist in his mind.

Some search—desultory at best—was made for Corey's body along the shore both above and below Innsmouth, but this was fruitless, and a coroner's inquest had no trouble in coming to the conclusion that Corey had met his death by misadventure.

No record of the facts that seemed pertinent to the mystery of his disappearance could possibly be left without a brief account of what I saw off Devil Reef in the twilight of the night of April 17th.

It was a tranquil evening; the sea was as of glass, and no wind stirred the evening air. I had been in the last stages of disposing of Corey's effects and had chosen to go out for a row off Innsmouth. What I had heard of Devil Reef drew me inevitably toward its remains—a few jagged and broken stones that jutted above the surface at low tide well over a mile off the village. The sun had gone down, a fine afterglow lay in the western sky, and the sea was a deep cobalt as far as the eye could reach.

I had only just reached the reef when there was a great disturbance of the water. The surface broke in many places; I paused and sat quite still, guessing that a school of dolphins might be surfacing and anticipating with some pleasure what I might see.

But it was not dolphins at all. It was some kind of sea-dweller of which I had no knowledge. Indeed, in the fading light, the swimmers looked both fish-like and squamously human. All but one pair of them remained well away from the boat in which I sat.

That pair—one clearly a female creature of an oddly clay-like colour, the other male—came quite close to the boat in which I sat, watching with mixed feelings not untinged with the kind of terror that takes its rise in a profound fear of the unknown. They swam past, surfacing diving, and, having passed, the lighter-skinned of the two creatures turned and distinctly flashed me a glance, making a strange guttural sound that was not unlike a half-strangled crying-out of my name: "Jack!" and left me with the clear and unmistakable conviction *that the gilled sea-thing wore the face of Jeffrey Corey!*

It haunts my dreams even now.

# THE ARCHBISHOP'S WELL

*by* REGGIE OLIVER

**M**Y FATHER NEVER spoke about his war experiences. That was quite common for men of his generation, but what is strange is that he hardly ever said anything to me about his life before it. I knew his academic career as a medieval historian had begun in the 1930s and that was all. It was only after his death a decade ago that I discovered the diaries that he had kept during this period, and a sort of explanation for his reticence started to emerge.

Reading them was an odd experience for me in many ways, chiefly because the person in these diaries was not at all like the one I knew. It was hard to reconcile this lively young man with my father, the dour, sarcastic Oxford don who seldom had any time for me. Only a few characteristic quirks and turns of phrase suggested that they were the same person at all.

The journals begin in late 1936 when, at twenty-five, my father, Dr. Charles Vilier, was appointed to a lectureship in Medieval History at the new University of Wessex. Its campus occupies land just outside the town of Bartonstone, some ten miles south-west of Morchester. My father's first years there seem to have been carefree and happy. He was a great giver and frequenter of sherry parties, then a popular form of entertainment for those who were not quite smart enough for cocktails. By 1938, the year of the Munich Crisis, my father was beginning to be faintly aware that the world around him was darkening, but it was not until September that his own personal crisis began.

## SEPTEMBER 2ND, 1938

Bertie Winship drove down from Morchester in his old banger. I gave him dinner at the Crown, the only half-decent hostelry in Bartonstone, and we imbibed not a few glasses of Amontillado, followed by a bottle of the best claret mine host could provide. I have barely seen young Bertie since varsity days, but he is the same cheery idiot who once introduced a python into the Master of Balliol's lodgings, causing much consternation and merriment thereby. It is strange to think of him now as a man of the cloth, a Canon of Morchester Cathedral no less, and a master at the choir school.

He regaled me with stories of Cathedral Life which seems to be by no means as dull as one might think. The Bishop, a gouty old sport called Bulstrode, is completely under the thumb of the Dean who goes by the name of the Very Reverend Herbert Grice. Grice is, according to Bertie, a holy terror, all for change and doing what he calls "meeting the challenges of the modern world". Needless to say, this does not go down too well with some of his colleagues who call him "*Il Duce*" behind his back because he is so fearfully keen on efficiency and making the Cathedral services start and finish on time. His main opponent is the Venerable Thaddeus Hill, the Archdeacon, a white-bearded old patriarch who has been at Morchester since the Ark. All this would be very amusing but not worth recording were it not for the business of the Archbishop's Well.

According to Bertie, this well has stirred up a veritable hornet's nest. It's hard at first to conceive why. I have of course visited the Cathedral and seen it. It stands in the middle of the cloister garth, a patch of greensward on the south side of the Cathedral. The cloisters that enclose it are the oldest part of the Cathedral, dating back to the eleventh century, being the only surviving portion of the original Abbey Church of Morchester. The well, by all accounts, is even older, but it is extremely unimpressive to look at.

It is a roughly circular enclosure of irregular stones which have been frequently repaired over the years with ugly slatherings of mortar. The opening is capped with a heavy circular lid of oak, bound with elaborately arabesqued iron bands and attached to the stone surround by heavy iron rings and padlocks. No one knows quite why it is called the Archbishop's Well, except of course that the Cathedral itself is St. Anselm's, named after Anselm, the eleventh-century Archbishop of Canterbury and inventor of the celebrated Ontological Argument for the existence of God.

Well—the pun is purely accidental—the long and short of it is that Bishop Bulstrode, at Dean Grice's prompting of course, wants to do away with this ancient relic and replace it with something useful and "up to date". A drinking fountain for the benefit of visitors to the Cathedral has been suggested. A drinking fountain, forsooth! No doubt one of those polished granite monstrosities that rich "philanthropists" are in the habit of inflicting on our public parks. Oddly enough, says Bertie, the Bishop's proposal has met with quite a bit of support, but there is also some vehement opposition, most notably from old Archdeacon Hill. Bertie, to his credit, is with the old boy, but his voice counts for very little.

Bertie says there was a fearful row about it at the last meeting of the Dean and Chapter a couple of days ago. The Archdeacon said that the well went back quite possibly to pre-Christian times and that to remove it would be a sacrilege. To which Dean Grice smartly replies that if the well is pre-Christian it could not possibly count as sacrilege to dispose of it.

It was then that Bertie had what he is pleased to call his "brain wave". He proposed that an independent expert be called in to pronounce on the historic and architectural importance of said well. When asked, in sarcastic tones by the Dean, where that expert might be found, Bertie replied that there was a just such a blighter with all the correct qualifications lecturing on things medieval only up the road at the University of Wessex, to wit, yours truly.

I don't know whether to feel flattered or to knock young Bertie about the mazzard for being an infernal, interfering pill. I expect nothing will come of it, though.

## SEPTEMBER 5TH

A letter arrived this morning with the Morchester Cathedral crest embossed on the back of the envelope. Everything about it is stiff: the envelope, the note-paper within and the wording typed thereon. It is from Dean Grice inviting me over to Morchester to consult about the well and proposing a date for the meeting. The final paragraph reads as follows:

> I must earnestly entreat you to say nothing about this commission to friends or colleagues and *on no account* to inform the press. I cannot emphasise too strongly that the utmost confidentiality is essential. You will receive an adequate honorarium for the benefit of your expertise and any researches that might be required. However, should you breach the seal of discretion in any way, no such remuneration will be forthcoming.

It all seemed unnecessarily pedantic to me, perhaps even a little "neurotic", as the followers of Dr. Freud would say. What had got the wind up? Anyway, I wrote back agreeing to his terms as I must admit to being rather intrigued.

## SEPTEMBER 10TH

This morning I took the train into Morchester, arriving shortly before ten. It was a fine, balmy day, so I walked the quarter-mile to the Deanery which is in the south-west corner of the Cathedral close. The Deanery is a pretty little three-storey Queen Anne house of mellow red brick with, over the front door, an elegant little pedimented portico made out of the local limestone. There is no bell-push, but there is a bronze knocker on the door of curious design. I believe it to have been modelled from one of the gargoyles on the Cathedral roof. (Morchester Cathedral, of course, is famous for its grotesque carvings.) It was in the shape of the head of some sort of beast. The eyes were large and saucer-like and there was little in the way of a nose, apart from a rather ugly cavity for a nostril. Where the mouth should have been there was a mass of strands or tentacles that seemed to writhe snakelike as if each one had a life of its own. It was a finely crafted piece, but all the more distasteful to handle because of it.

Nevertheless I grasped the thing and rapped on the door which was opened by a tall, elderly, angular woman who looked as if her morning bath had had an iceberg in it. She scrutinised me with some disdain, then, pointing imperiously to her right, told me that all hawkers, vagrants and people seeking assistance from the diocese should apply at the tradesman's entrance.

I had on an old pair of grey flannel bags and a heavily patched tweed sports coat, but I didn't think that I looked that disreputable. Perhaps the fact that I had no tie on and wear sandals at all times of the year gave me a bohemian or even—oh horror!—a socialist look.

I explained that I was Dr. Vilier and had an appointment to see the Dean. The lady still regarded me with suspicion.

"My husband is *not* unwell," she said indignantly.

Before I could explain to her that my doctorate was in History not Medicine, she had disappeared into the dark bowels of the Deanery. After a while she re-emerged from the gloom to tell me that the Dean would see me now in his study, indicating the second door on the left of a dingy corridor that passed right through the house. I smiled and tried to thank her warmly but the frost on her upper slopes failed to thaw.

I knocked and was bidden to enter the Dean's study. The room I came into was lit only by the light from a window which faced onto a back garden. At the bottom of the garden I could just see, through the willows, the glitter of a stream.

I have to say that Dean Grice's welcome was not much cheerier than his wife's. He greeted me by rising from behind his desk and favouring me with a handshake that felt like a long-dead haddock. He has a narrow face, parchment skin, and little round, silver-rimmed spectacles that glinted in the dimness of the study, occasionally turning his eyes into blank discs of reflected light. Having obtained from me the solemn assurance that I had told no one about my visit, he suggested briskly that we should walk over together to the Cathedral and take a look at the well.

As we stepped out of the deanery a cool breeze blew up. The rooks, who inhabit a stand of elms at the west end of the Cathedral close suddenly all flew as one from their "buildings" (as I believe their nests are called) in the trees and began to wheel around screeching, making their characteristic *kaa, kaa* sound. Once across the road and onto the green, the Dean and I took a diagonal paved path which leads directly to the West door of the Cathedral. I stared in awe at the rooks as they circled and cried. I could not get it out of my head that they were, for purposes unknown, putting on a demonstration of some kind. The Dean, evidently well accustomed to this curious animal behaviour, took no notice whatsoever.

While I was looking around me I noticed that someone was on the path behind us and trying to attract our attention. It was a tallish man wearing a cloak and a battered sombrero hat. He appeared somewhat eccentric, but as he was a hundred and fifty yards away I could not make out his features. He waved a thin arm and said "Hi!" so I alerted the Dean to his presence. The Dean, without breaking his stride, turned round to look, then almost immediately turned back and began to walk even more determinedly towards the Cathedral. I had seen a look of disgust, perhaps even of fear, pass across his ascetic features.

"We wish to have no intercourse with that man," said the Dean.

"Who is he?"

"He is called Felix Cutbirth."

"Unusual surname."

"It is a variant of Cuthbert, an Anglo-Saxon name. He comes from a very old family which has lived in Morsetshire since before the Norman Conquest. Unhappily, in his case, ancient lineage is no guarantee of respectability. The Cutbirths have long had an evil reputation."

"What does he want with us?"

"I cannot possibly imagine," said the Dean dismissively. We were now at the West Door. "Come! Let us go into the Cathedral. He will not follow us in there, I fancy."

Once we were inside, I was conscious of a certain relaxation in the Dean. He became almost animated. Clearly he loved the place, and his knowledge of medieval architecture was intelligent and extensive. My own complemented his, so we enjoyed each other's company as we walked down the great Early English nave, like an avenue of tall and stately trees. Weak sunlight filtered through the high windows and few people were about. I glanced quickly behind me. The Dean's surmise was correct: Cutbirth had not followed us into the Cathedral. After this brief interlude, the Dean took me out into the cloisters to survey the well.

Though I had seen it before I had not examined it at close quarters because, as notices proclaimed, it was forbidden for ordinary mortals to tread the lawn of the cloister garth. The Dean led me boldly across it.

"There you see," he said. "Not a thing of beauty and a joy forever."

I had to admit he was right. The "thing" had been built, rebuilt and repaired over centuries. There was no unity in this strange circular wall. Some of the stones were large, some small, some rough-hewn, a few dressed. I noticed that there was a section at the base on the south side that was not made of stone at all, but brick, and Roman bricks at that. I recognised their flat shape and the excellent quality of the mortar. I mentioned my discovery to the Dean, who merely nodded.

"Yes. That is known. Quite late Roman, I believe. Fourth or fifth century." He seemed unimpressed. I also noticed that some of the Roman bricks had a crude drawing of an eye scratched on them: a so-called "apotropaic eye" of the kind you see on the sides of Greek fishing vessels, designed to ward off evil. This I did not mention to the Dean.

When the Dean asked my opinion, I told him that the well was of no architectural but of great archaeological interest. I said that there would need to be a thorough archaeological survey of the well before anything was done to it and that, to expedite matters, I would, with his permission, discover all I could about the well from the Cathedral archives.

The Dean took all this in with a kind of weary resignation, as I suppose it was the answer he was expecting. The cloisters had been deserted when we entered them, but just as we were about to leave we heard a voice.

"I see you!" It said. The voice was a man's; the tone was mocking with a hint of menace about it.

We looked around. Finally we saw a face poking over the wall of one of the open Gothic arcades. On the head was a battered sombrero. It was Cutbirth.

The Dean started violently when he saw him, executing a little involuntary jump which made Cutbirth laugh as he got up off his knees, lifted a long leg over the cloister wall and stepped through the arcade onto the cloister garth.

"You may not walk on this grass!" yapped the Dean.

"Why not? You do."

"What are you doing here?"

Cutbirth began to walk lazily towards us over the manicured lawn, removing his hat as he did so. He must have been about forty, but age with such a strange creature was hard to assess. He was long and loosely built, with abnormally large hands. His skin was a yellowish colour, coarse and porous in texture. His head was a large, virtually hairless oval, but the features were small, strangely caught together in the middle of his face, like those of a horrible baby. He was trying to exude an air of insouciant mockery, but the eyes—green, I think— were full of rage.

"I might ask you the same question," said Cutbirth. His accent was odd. He spoke with the languid drawl of the upper classes, but some of his vowels were pure rural Morsetshire.

"It is none of your business," said the Dean raising his voice and sounding petulant.

"I think it is, Mr. Dean. You do realise that this has been a sacred spot long before your psalm-singing milk-white Christians started erecting their pious monstrosities over it? I know what you want to do. You want to obliterate the sanctity of centuries. You want to banish the Old Gods forever. And for what? For some damned, provincial little water trough to slake the putrid tongues of cheap charabanc tourists!"

"Who told you that?"

"Never you mind, Mr. Dean." Then turning to me, with disdainful a glance at my sandals, he said: "And what's your little game, my Communist Friend?"

"Don't answer him!" said the Dean. To tell the truth, I was so shocked at being denounced as a Communist on account of my footwear that I was incapable of speech. "Will you kindly leave forthwith, or I shall be forced to summon assistance and have you thrown off."

Cutbirth laughed harshly: "I warn you, Dean Grice—" he pronounced it *grease* "—the House of Dagon will suffer wrong no more! The Old Gods are awaking from their long sleep and you would do well not to despise their help in the gathering storm. Soon the rivers of Europe will run with blood. You will bleat for the Nazarene to help you, but he will not come, and the tide of blood will advance till it engulfs even Morchester. I warn you, Grice!"

With that he turned and left us, jamming his sombrero down on his head as he did so. Despite this faintly ludicrous gesture we were both stunned—I might almost say impressed—by his speech. For nearly a minute we stood there silent, motionless. Though, objectively, I have nothing but contempt for Cutbirth, I had been made aware of a certain power in him, or about him.

The Dean finally broke the silence: "Come, Dr. Vilier. Let me show you the library where you will be conducting your researches."

"What was that about the House of Dagon?"

"Oh, just his usual nonsense," said the Dean irritably. Then he paused, hesitating whether to confide in me. At last he said: "Felix Cutbirth is by way of being an artist. I had the misfortune to see some of his paintings at an exhibition in Morchester not so long ago. They are vile things, vile… But not without accomplishment. He studied at the Slade in London, I believe. While there, he became involved with something called the Order of the Golden Dawn, an occult society. You remember: Yeats, Crowley, Machen, Mathers—?" I nodded. "Well, after a while he became dissatisfied with them and broke away to found his own little magical sect called the Order of Dagon. I am happy to say it failed miserably. On his return to Morchester, Cutbirth tried to set up the Order here. He had a temple for a while at the back of a Turkish Restaurant in Morchester High Street, but neither the temple nor the restaurant prospered. He still has a few devotees among the credulous of this city, but they may be counted on the fingers of one hand. That is all we need to know about Mr. Cutbirth!"

And with that we proceeded to the library.

\* \* \*

## SEPTEMBER 13TH

This is my second day in the library and I have made some progress. There is surprisingly little information to be had on the well other than the rather surprising fact that it has not been used as such since the early twelfth century. A date of 1107 or 1108 is usually given for the closing of the well, but no explanation is given. I presume that it became contaminated in some way, but I could not understand why the whole structure was not destroyed.

Today, however, I have made a discovery. Of course the real story will, I suspect, remain hidden, but at least we have the legend. Legends are revealing in their own way.

One of the oldest volumes in the library is a kind of scrapbook, an untidy binding together of all sorts of early manuscripts to do with the Cathedral. Most of these are deeds and charters and inventories, not very interesting, but towards the end of the book I found what I recognised as a very early—perhaps even the original—manuscript of William of Morchester's *Gesta Anselmi*.

In the 1160s Archbishop Thomas Becket was, no doubt for his own political purposes, pressing the Pope to make a former Archbishop of Canterbury, Anselm (1033–1109) a saint. To this end he commissioned William of Morchester to write a life of Anselm, praising him and listing all his miracles: a hagiography in other words. This William called the *Gesta Anselmi* or "The Deeds of Anselm".

It is a typical work of the period, with very little of historical value in it. It deals in the kind of absurd legends and miracles that the Medievals loved: Anselm restores sight to a blind man; he revives a dead child; a barren woman prays at the tomb of Anselm and soon finds herself with child, and so on. I had seen copies of it before, but this manuscript seemed fuller and older than the others.

Towards the end of the MS I came across a passage that I had certainly never previously encountered. Several lines had been drawn through it, as if the scribe had deemed it unsuitable for further publication, but I was able to read it quite easily. It began:

*Anselmus cum in Priorium Benedictinum Morcastri advenerat monachos valde perturbatos de puteo suo vidit...*

When Anselm came to the Benedictine Priory at Morchester he saw the monks in much distress on account of their well. For they had built their cloister around an ancient well which had been there for many centuries and where in time past many foul and blasphemous ceremonies had been enacted to worship the ancient Gods and Demons of the Pagans. For, it was said, in the depths of this ancient well were many caverns and paths beneath the earth which connected with sea caverns on the southern shores. [In the eleventh and twelfth centuries the sea was much closer to Morchester than it is now.] And it was said that these demons came out of the sea and through the caverns to the well where they had been worshipped as gods in former times.

Now certain of the monks, hoping to draw greater quantities of the sweet water to be found in the well, had descended into its depths to dig deeper and uncover new springs. But in so doing they had awakened the demons who had lain dormant in caverns beneath the well for many centuries. They had troubled their unholy sleep and awakened their anger. And these demons had arisen from the well to bring destruction on the monks and the people of Morchester. The monks were tormented by ill dreams and by odours as of fish putrefying. Women of the town began to give birth to all manner of abominations: infants with two heads, and mouths in their fundaments, horns upon their head, many arms but without hands; and one had the face of a great serpent. Such was their consternation that the whole people cried out to Anselm to deliver them from terrors by night and abominations by day.

Then did the Blessed Anselm pronounce absolution for the sins of the whole people. Having done so, the Archbishop, taking his staff of office which contained a reliquary holding a fragment of the true cross and a thumbnail of St. Paul, ordered the monks to let him down into the depths of the well. There Blessed Anselm remained for seven days and seven nights alone wrestling with the spawn of Hell and in particularly the chief of these demons whose name was—[Here the manuscript has been corrected, scratched out and altered several times so that the name is unclear. My best guess is *Dagonus.*]

After seven days and seven nights Blessed Anselm commanded that he be lifted out of the well for he had vanquished the demons therein. Thereupon he commanded that a lid of oak bound with iron be placed over the well and that no person should thereafter remove it, and that new wells be dug to the north of the Abbey. And moreover, Anselm blessed the waters of the Orr [the river that flows past Morchester] so that water might be drawn from it in safety. And he commanded that a great cathedral be erected in place of the Abbey Church for all the people, and that this cathedral be consecrated to St. Michael the Archangel, the vanquisher of demons, and St. George, the slayer of dragons.

It was only after Anselm's official canonisation in 1494 that the Cathedral was rededicated to him. This was not such a radical act as it might seem because it was simply sanctioning local practice. The building had long been known by the inhabitants of Morchester as "Anselm's Cathedral".

I suspect that there is a tiny core of truth in this absurd fable: namely that the well is very old indeed, which the presence of Roman brickwork confirms. It is just possible also that, as the text suggests, the well had at some stage become contaminated by seawater from an underground source. Hence also the stench of rotting fish?

I cannot help being intrigued by the coincidence—and it is only a coincidence!—that Cutbirth's little sect is called the Order of Dagon, and Anselm's main adversary in the well was *Dagonus.*

## SEPTEMBER 15TH

I have given the Dean a précis of my findings and he has agreed that the well should be opened up and surveyed. Bertie is in a state of high excitement and jumping up and down at the prospect of what he insists on calling "an archaeological dig". I remind him that no digging will be involved, just the descent into a well which may, after all, be filled with rubbish, but nothing dampens Bertie. He clamours to be part of the "adventure".

A strange thing happened today. While I was in the cloister

discussing the opening of the well with the Clerk of Works, a boy came up to me and handed me a letter. It was one of the town boys, I think, certainly very scruffy, and before I could speak to him he had run off.

Inside the envelope was a piece of stiff card, like an invitation. It had been expensively engraved with the heading: ORDO TEMPLI DAGONIS (*Order of the Temple of Dagon*). Below this was an elaborate design, rather well executed but curiously unpleasant. Within a fancy baroque cartouche was a drawing of a figure crouched on a throne. I say figure because it was not wholly human nor wholly bestial, but something in-between. It seemed to be in an attitude of deep and trancelike thought, but its outward appearance was savage. Curious tentacles drooped over its mouth-parts. It reminded me somewhat of the Dean's knocker, but I did not study it long. Below it in capitals was written:

**DO NOT MEDDLE WITH THE ANCIENT AND INFINITE.
YOU HAVE BEEN WARNED.**

The sender can only be Cutbirth.

## SEPTEMBER 21ST

Troubling rumours from Europe. A cloudy day. The Clerk and his workmen set up equipment to raise the lid of the well and, if necessary, let me down into it. Bertie was there whenever he could to watch progress, which was painfully slow. In the first place nobody could find the keys to the padlocks which secured the wooden lid to the wall, so they had to be smashed off by main force. It was beginning to get dark before the lid was raised.

The first of our surprises when the well was finally uncovered was the smell. A faint but still unpalatable odour, as of rotten fish, wafted up to us from the bottom of the well which was so deep that my torch could not penetrate its abysses. I noticed, however, that the well was skilfully made with dressed stone forming a perfect cylinder. The walls were virtually black and covered with a thin layer of darkish slime like the tracks of a thousand snails. We had not rope enough to let me down to the bottom, but I noticed that, some thirty feet below, steps had been built into the wall. They descended in an elegant spiral into the unseen depths and looked manageable.

Bertie, like the ass he is, dropped a stone down the well. No splash was heard. Instead there was a sort of cracking sound that reverberated in an odd way. Perhaps the *Gesta* was right and there are caverns down there. That blighter Bertie then decided to try out the echo with his voice and sang what he assured me was an E flat above Middle C. The echo lasted a good ten seconds after he had stopped singing and was strange. Once it was over and I had started to tell Bertie off for his fat-headed behaviour, we both heard another sound come from the well which was most certainly not Bertie's voice. It lasted only for a second or so, but it sounded distinctly as if some thing or things down there were scratching or fluttering about.

Bertie was all for investigating, but I told him not to be an idiot. It was late, it was getting dark and we had done enough for the day. I told the workmen to replace the lid over the well, and it was then that we received our last surprise of the day. On the underside of the lid I noticed that something black had been nailed to the wood. A quick examination showed it to be a crucifix of heavily tarnished silver, early twelfth century and of the finest Norman workmanship.

But what was it doing nailed to the wood, facing downwards into the blackness with nothing and no one to see it?

I decided to leave that and other questions till a later date. I am staying at the Dean's tonight, so as to start bright and early tomorrow. As I was walking back from the Cathedral towards the Deanery, I noticed that the rooks were making more than their usual fuss. They were wheeling around their elms, cawing away, apparently quite unable to settle for the night. A few distant dogs seemed to have caught their mood and began to howl.

Dinner at the Deanery with the Grices was, as I had rather expected, not a lively occasion. Dean Grice is given to rather pontifical remarks on general subjects and sees himself as having very "up-to-date" opinions. He talked with some pride of his time as a chaplain in the trenches during the Great War and gave me his opinion that it had been "the war to end all wars" and that that sort of thing should on no account ever happen again. Then he asked me what I thought of "Mr. Hitler". It took me a second or two to understand whom he was referring to. He sounded as if he were talking about an erring member of his congregation.

Mrs. Dean has no conversation at all. Occasionally she will break her silence by simply repeating what her husband has just said. Needless to say I have retired early. I must try to get some sleep, but there seem to be an awful lot of barking or howling dogs about.

## SEPTEMBER 22ND

I passed a pretty restless night. In addition to the dogs there were the cats. Everywhere they seemed to be out and about howling and screeching. One climbed up the sloping roof outside my window and started scrabbling at the window-pane. I tried to shoo it away several times, but it was persistent and plaintive. Finally I let it in and it made straight for my bed. I tried to push it off, but it mewed pathetically and curled itself up in the crook of my arm. There it stayed all night and, apart from purring rather too loudly, caused me no further trouble.

But that was not the end of it. The next assault on my ears came from a most unexpected quarter. My bedroom is next to that of the Dean and his wife. It being an old house, the partition walls are quite thin, no more than lath and plaster sandwiched in between wooden panelling. At about two o'clock my fitful slumbers were disturbed by what I can only describe as a bout of amorous activity from the next room. I hesitate to write it down. I could barely believe my ears at the time. To judge from the cries made by the two contenders, the event appeared to be violent and not wholly consensual on the part of Mrs. Grice. Neither can be less than sixty years of age.

At breakfast the following morning, Mr. and Mrs. Dean were more than usually taciturn. I noticed that at different times they looked at me enquiringly. Mrs. Dean's hair was in quiet disarray. Fortunately I had an excellent excuse to leave as soon as possible. I needed to supervise the means whereby I was to be let down into the body of the well.

To cut a long story short, it was well into the afternoon before all was ready for the descent. A rope ladder had been found to let me down as far as the spiral steps. The idea was that, once I had reached the steps, further equipment, including a long rope, would be let down to me and I would attach the rope to the wall by means of a metal staple knocked into it. This rope would be there as a safeguard in case the steps proved treacherous. Then I was to walk down the steps into the unknown abyss. With me, in a knapsack, I had two electric torches, a tape measure, a notebook and pencils, and a small camera with flash bulb attachments.

Bertie, needless to say, was on hand and bursting with excited enthusiasm. I asked him if he had had a disturbed night but he had, apparently, slept like a baby.

Before I began my descent, I was suddenly seized with apprehension. I checked everything was secure and told the Clerk of Works that at least two of his men should be on hand at the well-head while I was conducting my investigations. A look was exchanged between the Clerk and his men that I did not understand, but he agreed.

The first part of the descent was made easily. I climbed down the rope ladder to the spiral steps which were rather rough-hewn but not, as I had feared, very slippery. There the workmen let down some tools and the rope. I managed to drive a metal staple into the wall and secure a rope to it. Then, taking my electric torch, I began my descent.

I flashed my torch into the depths but could see no bottom, only the spiral staircase endlessly revolving into the blackness. The masonry that clad the walls was smooth and its composition was what is called "Cyclopean"—that is, huge irregular slabs of stone had been dressed and fitted together, making the wall look like a gigantic piece of crazy-paving on the vertical.

The whole, including the spiral steps, was an astonishing feat of construction and certainly not, in my view, medieval. Anglo-Saxon, then? Even less likely. Roman? I had never seen Roman work that remotely resembled this.

Soon the top of the well had become a little white disc, no bigger than the moon. I trudged downwards, taking care not to touch the walls if I could avoid it. They were covered with a thin layer of something dark and glistening, sticky to the touch, that left a dark brown stain on the hands, like half-dried blood. My dear old tweed jacket was already ruined.

I had entered a world of silence, and if silence can be said to echo, then it did. I suppose what I am saying is that the slightest scrape of my feet on the stone steps came back to me in echoes a thousand fold. Once I coughed and it was like a fusillade of rifle shots. The scent of something decaying and fishlike was getting stronger.

Then I heard a faint pattering sound behind and above me. I looked around and saw a light flickering and flashing, then further pattering, then what sounded like a stifled oath. I shone my torch upwards. Something was coming down the stairway towards me.

It was that infernal ass Bertie Winship! He was carrying a tiny little toy electric torch that was about as much use down there as a paper bag in a thunderstorm.

I gave the blighter a good piece of my mind and told him in no uncertain terms to go back up at once, but he was unrepentant.

"Sorry, old fellow," he said, "I simply couldn't resist it. Anyway, I thought you could do with the company."

I was barely able to admit it to myself, but he was right. The ancient solitude was beginning to oppress me. I told him sharply to put away his stupid little flashlight and take the other of my two torches. I also told him to remain silent as we made our way down.

I don't know how long we had been going, but the entrance to the well was only a pinpoint of light above us—no more than a distant star on a dark night—when we came across the carvings.

The first of them was a frieze carved into the stone, about a foot and a half in depth that ran the whole of the way around the well, broken only by the run of the staircase. It was a continuous key pattern, or, if you like, a set of interlinked swastikas. Apart from anything else it was astonishing to find workmanship like this at such a depth. What possible purpose could it serve?

I could only conjecture that its presence suggested that an early civilisation, probably of Aryan origin, had been at work here and created the descent for ritual purposes. I began to speculate that it might have been used to commune with spirits of the dead, or some Chthonic deity of the underworld. This structure could be an early monument to a mystery religion, perhaps the earliest in these islands, predating Mithraism by hundreds, even thousands of years.

My thoughts were beginning to run away with me when Bertie gave an odd little yelp. His torch had strayed onto a panel carved in low relief, just opposite him. The artist was skilled and the execution showed no signs of imprecision or crudity. The manner was vaguely reminiscent of those to be found on Babylonian and Assyrian monuments: precise, but stylised.

It showed a group of figures huddled together, one of which was wearing a kind of crown or diadem and seemed to be dominating the others. The figures were not human, nor recognisably animal. They looked like some strange miscegenation between a sea creature, of an octopoid kind, and a human or ape. By one of them I was rather unpleasantly reminded of the figure engraved on Felix Cutbirth's card.

"By Jove," said Bertie, "I wouldn't like to meet one of those on a dark night."

I told Bertie to stop making idiotic remarks and we continued our descent. There were several more of these relief sculptures, each one stranger than the last. One depicted a group of human beings kneeling in homage, heads touching the ground like Moslems at prayer, before a strange lopsided creature with a head far too big for its body. In another further down, four men in profile were carrying a rigid human body horizontally. They appeared to be feeding it to one of the strange half-fish creatures; in fact most of the body's head had already entered the beast's vast open mouth.

Shortly after that my foot encountered not another stone step but soft, muddy soil. We were at the bottom of the well. I commanded Bertie to stop and tried the ground. I was afraid it was a quagmire into which we might sink, never to be recovered, but the soil, though moist and soft, appeared to be solidly founded.

I then noticed a strange thing. The aperture at the well-head was almost exactly ten feet across, but the chamber at its base was wider. I measured it with the tape I had brought for the purpose and discovered that we were in a circular space slightly over twenty-three feet in diameter.

We must have been walking down a funnel that slowly tapered

towards the top, but the widening (or narrowing, depending which way you look at it) had been done so gradually and with such cunning that we had never noticed.

The air at the bottom was not free of the odour of rotten fish, but it was not rank or stuffy, and it was almost as if a breeze was coming from somewhere. I noticed that at opposite ends of the circular wall were two black spaces with pointed arches, just wide and tall enough for a man of average height to walk through them. I shone my torch into one of them and it revealed a long, narrow tunnel leading into more blackness.

By this time Bertie had reached the bottom too, and was talking his usual nonsense. He had got it into his head that the whole thing was connected with King Arthur and Merlin, or some such twaddle. He said that the two apertures were bound to lead to "treasure chambers" and that we should explore them at once. I was resolved to do no such thing. We had had quite enough excitement for one day, but just then Bertie let out a cry.

"I say, look at this!" he said.

I prepared myself for yet another inanity, but Bertie had actually found something. He had been idly pushing his foot about in the mud and flashing his torch at it when he had come across something shiny. He pulled it out of the mud and we did our best to clean it up with our pocket-handkerchiefs.

It shone still because it was made of some incorruptible metal or metals, pale yellow in colour. I suspected an alloy of gold and platinum, but this was highly improbable for such an obviously ancient artefact. The workmanship was very fine, but when I say fine, I do not exactly mean beautiful.

It was circular and in the shape of a coronet or diadem, but if it *was* a sort of crown, then the head it had enclosed was monstrous, at least twice the size of an ordinary adult human head. The pattern was one of intricately entwined whorls and concentric circles which, when you looked closely at them, resolved themselves into the coiling limbs of strange creatures whose bulging eyes were represented by some sort of milky-white semiprecious stone. They were not pearls, but could have been white jade, though this seemed unlikely for England. The lowest band or border was composed of the interconnecting key pattern of swastikas that we had seen on the walls above us.

While Bertie was babbling on about how he had found King Arthur's crown, I took out the camera from my knapsack and put a flash bulb into the attachment. I only had a few bulbs so I had to choose my subjects carefully. I took one of the area we stood in as a whole to give an impression of the remarkable structure we had found. I took another, at Bertie's earnest request, of him holding the giant diadem. I then decided that I should point the camera down the two tunnels that projected from our central chamber.

I took one without any effect, but when my camera flashed down the other tunnel I thought I saw through my viewfinder something move at the end of the passageway I was photographing: a pale grey-green something that was smooth and glistening. The next moment I heard a noise, halfway between a groan and a retching cough, but cavernous and hugely magnified. I turned sharply round to see if it was Bertie playing some stupid joke, but he was staring back at me, white and horrified.

The next minute we were storming up those spiral stairs as fast as we could go. Bertie, who was ahead of me, stumbled several times. Each time I picked him up and on we went. By the time we had reached the end of the steps and the rope ladder we were both gasping for breath. It was at least five minutes before we made the final ascent.

As we came out of the well the sun was setting in a clear evening sky, but for a few seconds it seemed impossibly bright to us. I ordered the rope ladder to be drawn up and the lid of the well to be replaced.

I had my camera with me. I turned and asked Bertie if he still had the crown with him, but he said he had dropped it on the way up. I believed him; I think I believed him, but he had his arms folded across his jacket in an odd way.

Bertie had recovered from his fright amazingly quickly and was soon chattering away to the Clerk of Works about the well's "amazing archaeological importance". I noticed, though, that he was very unspecific about our discoveries and for that, I suppose, I should be grateful.

I returned to the Deanery exhausted, and at dinner, I am afraid, proved very unforthcoming about the day's events. Fortunately the Dean was in a very talkative mood. He was full of Mr. Chamberlain's flight to see "Mr. Hitler" and pacify him over the Sudetenland Crisis. He sees the Prime Minister's mission as the epitome of modern statesmanship and diplomacy. I am too weary and confused to agree or disagree openly, but I do not share his confidence in a peaceful outcome. Mrs. Dean remained entirely mute and he barely looked at her.

The Dean then told me he had just heard the melancholy news that during the previous night the Archdeacon, the Venerable Thaddeus Hill, had died, of a "seizure". When the Dean said the word "seizure" I noticed that his wife looked at him very sharply indeed, and I think I saw the Dean's pale skin flush with embarrassment.

## SEPTEMBER 23RD

In the early hours of this morning I was rudely awakened by the Dean. No, not like the night before. He entered my room and shook me awake. There were intruders in the Cathedral, he said: lights had been seen in the cloisters. I told him to alert the police; it was nothing to do with me, but he was insistent. I had never seen the Dean so animated.

I dressed rapidly and grabbed my torch. The Dean was waiting for me downstairs in the hall with a heavy old revolver and some cartridges. Handing me the gun, he said: "Take this, my boy. My old service revolver from the Trenches. We have not a moment to lose." I thought he must be mad.

From the top of the stairs his wife in her night-gown stared down at us, wild and bewildered.

We gained access by the West door but, finding nothing amiss in the Cathedral itself, we hurried on to the cloisters. There, by the light of our torches we could see the lid had been removed from the well and we could hear distant cries. Once we got to the well we could hear the cries clearly, albeit distorted by the well's weird echo. Someone was screaming for help and I could swear the voice was Bertie's.

I loaded the revolver and put it in my pocket, then tucked the torch into my belt. The Dean helped me over the parapet and onto the rope ladder. So I began the descent into the well yet again. The cries from below had not stopped, but they seemed muffled and more distant than before.

I reached the steps and began to hurry down them far more rapidly than I would have wished. Once or twice I tripped and nearly fell into the black abyss. I reached the bottom and flashed my torch about. There was nobody, nothing.

I stood quite still, trying not to breathe too hard, the blood pounding in my head. Bertie—or whoever it was—must have gone through one of the two tunnels, but which one?

I decided to try the one where my flash photography had surprised something. I switched off my torch and entered the Stygian blackness of the narrow tunnel. Darkness and silence enveloped me. I felt my way, along smooth, slimed walls.

Then I began to hear something. It was like a chant, but the tune and the language were alien to me. I could see something red flicker against the glistening black walls of the tunnel. It was no more than a whisper of light, but it spoke terror to me.

The tunnel bent slightly, then suddenly debouched into a vast cavern, over a hundred feet high. Naphtha flares, spurting naturally from the rock, lit the space with a pinkish glare from a thousand crevices. I was in an area at least as vast as the Cathedral somewhere far above me. Parts of the rock vault had been carved into strange shapes, parts had been left in their natural state, rugged and glistening.

Again I heard the chanting and, though clearer, it was still alien to my ears:

*"Iä-R'lyeh! Cthulhu fhtagn! Iä! Iä!"*

About fifty feet from me across a smooth Cyclopean pavement stood a naked man, his back to me. His hands were raised in the air, his almost hairless head thrown back in an ecstasy of adoration. At his feet lay a crumpled form in black. As I approached them across the pavement I recognised the fallen figure. It was Bertie Winship, still in his clerical cassock.

These two were between me and a third figure who stood, or crouched, some yards in front of them. Even now I cannot, or will not describe it fully. Its colour was a greyish-green and its form was stooped with a vast elephantine head on which reposed the coronet that Bertie had discovered at the bottom of the well. Its superabundant flesh, which seemed to disintegrate into a thousand liquid limbs, quivered with infernal energy. It appeared to sway and stoop to the naked man's chant—or was it the chant that swayed to its movement?

I drew and cocked the Dean's service revolver. The naked man must have heard this or my footsteps approaching, because he turned and saw me.

"Get out, you damned fool!" he shrieked. "How dare you interfere?" It was Cutbirth, his evil baby features contorted with rage.

"I have come to take Bertie back," I said.

"You cannot have him! He is already given to the gods. Go back, I tell you!"

At this, the creature let out a groaning screech which filled the cathedral cavern with hellish sound. Cutbirth turned his back on me and again addressed the monster:

"*Ph'nglui mglw'nafh Cthulhu R'lyeh, wgah-nagl fhtagn—*"

Having uttered his cry, he stooped and picked up from the ground something shining and curved like an oriental knife. Then, with his other hand, he gathered up the unconscious form of Bertie by the collar. Bertie's head lolled back, unwittingly presenting his white throat to Cutbirth's blade.

"Put him down or I shoot," I said.

Cutbirth laughed. "You wouldn't dare, you damned sandal-wearing, psalm-singing socialist!"

I pulled the trigger, but the wretched gun jammed. It was a heavy, clumsy old thing. I pulled the trigger again and the gun fired, but the shot went wide and the recoil nearly threw me onto my back. The echoes of the shot filled the cavern with a clatter like machine-gun fire.

Then, gripping the gun in both hands, I steadied myself and took aim at Cutbirth's head. I fired again. The bullet missed Cutbirth by quite a margin, but it hit the creature which loomed before him. It went into one of its huge, milky eyes. The eye seemed to explode with the impact, spraying out torrents of green bile in the process. A hideous shriek filled the cavern.

Cutbirth dropped the knife and turned again towards me with

rage and hatred in every knotted vein of his face. It was a fatal mistake. The beast, assuming that Cutbirth had been the perpetrator of the outrage against its eye, launched one of its great tentacle limbs against him, lashing him to the ground. Cutbirth scrambled to his feet and tried to make a run for it, but the beast was onto him with more of his limbs. A terrible unequal struggle ensued.

Meanwhile I ran towards the unconscious form of Bertie. I was glad to find he was not dead, just heavily drugged from some hideous narcotic that Cutbirth had pumped into him. I picked him up in a fireman's lift and ran towards the little cavern entrance.

There I put Bertie down because there was not room enough to carry him on my back through the tunnel. I would have to drag him by the feet.

I took one last look into the cavern. The creature had Cutbirth wrapped in its limbs and their two heads were very close together. It looked horribly like a lover's embrace. As the creature bent its head towards Cutbirth's, I saw the man's face for the last time. It was full of agonised fear, but also a wondering ecstasy, as if he half-welcomed the devouring kiss of his deity.

I heard a rustling and saw that the cavern was beginning to fill with other creatures, some bigger, some smaller than the one that was now feasting on Cutbirth. They were all piscine, shambling, unearthly, imbued with some sort of mind and power that was beyond my capacity to comprehend.

I took Bertie's feet and began to drag him through the passage. As I was doing so he started to groan. Consciousness of a kind was returning to him, but he was still impossibly weak.

We reached the bottom of the well, and then I had to half-drag, half-carry him up the spiral staircase. It took an age.

When we reached the rope ladder I was faced with a problem. He was still too doped and feeble to climb it himself and I could not carry him up it on my back. Then I remembered the rope that I had tied to the staple at the bottom of the rope ladder.

I detached the rope from the staple and tied one end of the rope securely around Bertie's waist. Then, taking the other end of the rope, I climbed with it to the top of the rope ladder. Dawn was breaking over the Cathedral as I clambered over the well parapet. Fortunately the Dean was still there.

With much heaving on the rope we managed to pull young Bertie to the top. He was just revived enough by this time to scramble over the well enclosure and flop exhausted onto the dewy lawn of the cloister garth.

Over the next few hours I managed to get some sort of a story out of him. The silly young blighter *had* still got the coronet with him when we had come out of the well the previous evening. He had then done something which exceeded even my estimation of his fat-headedness. He had taken it to show Felix Cutbirth.

Apparently, Bertie had struck up a weird sort of friendship with Cutbirth, owing to a mutual interest in folklore and local legend. It was undoubtedly Bertie who had alerted him to our schemes with regard to the well.

To cut a long story short, Cutbirth, no doubt with promises of "treasure chambers" and the like, persuaded young Bertie to take him to the well and make another descent in the small hours. Bertie's memory collapses at this point, but one can guess the remainder.

We are both in a state of shock, and no doubt the reaction will hit us more heavily later on. Meanwhile, the Dean has given orders that the lid is to be put back on the well and the padlocks restored. But has the genie been put back in the bottle? I doubt it.

## OCTOBER 5TH, 1938

This is the first time I have written in my journal for some days. I am recovering at Margate and my sister is with me. She takes me down to the front every day, puts me on a bench and tucks a plaid travelling rug around my knees, as if I were an elderly aunt with arthritis. I feel such a fool because there is really nothing wrong me, but every time I close my eyes they come. I can barely sleep, and when I do it is not long before I wake up screaming.

So I sit here watching the sea as it makes its slow gestures of advance and retreat upon the sand, like a sluggish invading army. Sometimes I fancy I see shapes forming themselves in the waves. I wait for them to resolve themselves into the monsters I once glimpsed, but mercifully they never do. One day beasts will come out of the waves, beasts of iron and steel, but not today.

I have just heard news of Bertie Winship. He had it worse than I did. He is in some sort of special Church of England nuthouse, but they tell me he makes a little progress. Bertie will recover, I feel sure of it, but he will never be the same Bertie he once was. Just as well, you may say, the perishing little pill! All the same, a part of me will regret the passing. By the end of it all we'll none of us be the same.

I know now what I am going to do. I am going to resign my lectureship at Wessex and enlist in the South Morsetshire. Chaos is coming, rivers of blood will flow, and I feel it is better to be in the midst of chaos, than on the edge of it looking down into the black hole…

I must stop this.

It was St. Anselm himself who said: *credo ut intelligam*—"I believe so that I may understand". I wish I did not believe. I wish to God I did not understand.

# YOU DON'T WANT TO KNOW

*by* ADRIAN COLE

**D**AWN HAD JUST started to edge the clouds behind the blocked silhouettes across the river, a white-grey mist. For a few moments the Manhattan skyline looked alien, like something Cyclopean, a hundred suns away. But the two men hardly registered the change in the light. Engrossed in their thoughts, they sat on a bench, focused on the shared inner dilemma that had occupied them throughout the night and previous evening.

The man wearing the distinctive blue of the NYPD, a sergeant, leaned back and yawned: he looked exhausted. Beside him, no less tired, the police detective watched the cold water thoughtfully. From the pocket of his raincoat he pulled a small audio tape, idly turning it over in his fingers. The other looked at it uneasily, hands shoved deep in his own pockets, as though a sudden chill breeze had ruffled him.

"So what's the deal, Hal?" said the detective, though his eyes were still on the river. "You want to hear this again before I turn it over to the chief?"

The other considered a moment. "I guess we'll all look pretty stupid. It's not just the private dick that'll sound like a fruitcake. Me most of all. I was the one who went in after him."

"You think anyone will believe this stuff?"

"Do you, Ed? You've known me a long time. You think I'm cracking up?"

The detective shook his head. "Nah. If you say you saw something, then you saw it. But you're *certain*? It was late, Hal. You were tired. The light wasn't good, that's what they'll say. It's not the sort of thing people want to hear. You know?"

"Yeah, sure. Let me think about it."

"Okay, but we don't have much time. They'll expect us back at the precinct pretty soon. One way or the other, we have to decide on our story."

Again he flipped the tape recording.

As the dawn dragged itself skywards, they mentally went over the tape's contents one last time.

Transcript of the interview recorded by Detective Sergeant Ed Mullins, NYPD. October 14th, 2002. In attendance, police sergeant Hal Vanner.

The voice is that of Mr. N. Stone, a private investigator.

In my line of business, you can't afford to be picky. Some days, some months, you have to take the rough, as there's no smooth. Putting it bluntly, these days there's not a lot of smooth. Smooth is something I get from a whisky bottle. Okay, I draw the line at some stuff: I don't do divorce cases, snooping on some sucker who's screwing around, or some wife who's looking for a new life away from her loaded husband. You can keep that kind of grime. Otherwise I'll take on the more obscure stuff and brother, I've seen some bizarre things. There may be a Hell waiting in the afterlife, but I've been there already, more times than I care to mention.

I know a lot of the guys in this town call me Nick Nightmare, usually when I'm out of earshot. That's about all you need to know about me. You'll have a file on me. There's always a file, right? Nick Stone, Private Eye, Public Fist. Tackles the cases other dicks won't touch, kind of like that beer ad.

So anyway, you want to know about this case. Yeah, well, it's pretty weird, I'll give you that.

It started with a phone call. I was workin' late the night before last, catchin' up on some paperwork. I'd had a lean week, so I shut myself away to get on with it. I don't have a secretary. They'd only go nuts tryin' to work for me. Anyway, this phone call was from some guy who sounded like he was talkin' through a hole in his throat. Maybe he was, given the kind of crap he was mixed up in.

Wanted me to find a man. Here in New York. Wouldn't be easy, said the guy. The man he was after was an illegal immigrant, gone to ground. They had a few clues about where he might be, a trail.

I asked for some details, but gravel-voice didn't want to stay on the phone. Maybe he thought my wire was tapped. It's not, I promise you. I like my privacy and I have some good contacts for that kind of wire work.

The guy said, was I free now. This was 2:00 a.m. But it suited me. Especially when he told me how much he would pay. You don't need to know that. So I said, come on over.

Less than an hour later they were knockin' on the office door. Three of them. I know it's October, but these guys were done up like they were headin' for the Russian Front. I thought maybe they had at least three trench coats on, they were so god-dammed *broad*. And the slouched hats were classics. What little I saw of their faces were white. Not pale, but *white*. I'm not sayin' they were zombies, but they did not look healthy. And they never showed their hands. Just kept them at their sides, deep down in their pockets. Shooters, I guessed. Why be different from everyone else in the neighborhood?

Only one of them spoke: the batteries on the other two must have run down. I guess he was the guy I'd spoken with on the phone. His voice was a gargle, foreign, maybe Eastern bloc, like he was full of runny cold. I know the light in my office was pretty poor, but his eyes were colourless. No emotion. Flat. Very cold fish.

He didn't give me much to go on. The guy they were after, last calling himself Stefan Zeitsheim, had stepped off a boat out of Odessa that had arrived here in New York a few days ago. He had no papers, but had given everyone the slip. He was being hunted. So my job was to find him first.

I may not have the quickest brain this side of the Atlantic, but I figured out pretty sharply that if these handsome guys were good buddies of Mr. Zeitsheim, he would have made a beeline for them once he'd slipped the ship. But obviously he was looking forward to meeting them with as much enthusiasm as a vampire would greet a priest. So he'd gone to ground. Lookin' at them, I'd say Zeitsheim had his head screwed on.

"We don't want to meet him," gurgled my new employer. For the one and only time he took his hand out of his coat. Thick black glove, so no surprise there. He also had a thin black file, which he dropped on my desk. Taped to the front of it was a key. I recognized it: safety deposit box, Grand Central Station.

"Your pay. Half of it. The rest when the job is completed, Mr. Stone." He shoved his hand back in his pocket, as if it had already been exposed to the air too long.

"So what do I do when I find him? Buy him lunch? Show him around the Big Apple?"

No hint of a smile. "It's all in the file, Mr. Stone. You kill him."

That was it, no frills. Just simply, you kill him.

"He is *persona non grata*. Find him quickly. No one need know."

Yeah, except for whoever the hell else was hunting him. Like the law, or more likely the KGB, or whatever they call themselves these days.

"You have a suitable weapon?" growled the overcoat.

"If you mean a gun, yeah. Or is this a knife job? Or maybe a glass of something very strong?"

"We leave the means to you, Mr. Stone. But once you have killed him, and this is vital, you must incinerate him."

There was what the poet once called a pregnant pause. *Incinerate* him?

"You would rather not accept this commission?"

Oh yeah, with these three monoliths looming over me, like I was going to refuse? I said not.

"Everything you need is in the file. We will contact you again, one week from now, at the same time. Be alone. Provided you have completed the task, the rest of the money will be in the same deposit box."

I decided not to waste any time. My initial stop was Grand Central. The first helping of money was in the box all right. I could have moved out of town and set up on the West Coast right there and then, but I had this feeling that the three goons wouldn't take too kindly to it. I read through the file. I have it safely tucked away. You guys are welcome to it when you want it. It's not the snappiest read since Spillane. Just a few details about Stefan Zeitsheim, coupla mug shots so's I'd know him. Looked like he'd spent a month or two in a jail, fed on bread and water once a week.

I grabbed a few hours' sleep then decided to check out the docks. It was nearly 6:00 a.m. when I got there. Zeitsheim was supposed to have come in on one of the huge rust buckets, with some tongue-twisting Russian name. Easy enough to find the tub, but it would have been a needle-in-a-haystack job finding out from someone where he took off from. Yet already the quayside was crawling with unaccustomed life. Your boys in blue were out in force—maybe you know which ones?

I saw someone I knew over in the shadows of a warehouse. Never mind who: just a bum who tips me off from time to time. In a job like mine, you need eyes and ears everywhere. These guys are my lifeblood.

I eased over to him and slipped him a smoke. "So what's the story?"

"Hi, Nick. Some guy left that big tub last night and walked straight into the next world. Cut himself up. No kiddin'. Real messy. Seems a long way to come to end it all."

*Suicide?* That didn't make any sense. "Don't tell me. Name of Zeitsheim?"

"You knew him?"

"Of him. You?"

"All I know is, some of the boys got word there were some weird characters on the waterside. Expensive suits. You know, not regulars.

Not the Mob either. They must have been waiting for the guy. He didn't want to meet them, big time."

I described the three uglies that had visited me.

"Nah. These were slick. More like FBI. But they weren't quick enough to stop the Russkie toppin' himself. See, over there." He pointed to a group of shadows, men cleaning up the quayside. "Bled a river before they hauled his carcass out of here."

"Who took him away?"

"Meat wagon. Down to the morgue. The slicks didn't hang around. I guess they'll be on the other side of the state by now."

So my work was already done for me. Or it seemed like it. But this whole thing stank. Like my man had said, why come halfway across the world to cut yourself up?

"Get me any information you can on the suits. Where they went, who they spoke to," I said and started for the local morgue. I needed to tie up some loose ends before I collected the second half of my takings.


No one takes too much interest in the comings and goings of a mortuary at 6:00 a.m., not unless something really big has gone down, so when I got there, it was quiet. Zeitsheim's suicide would have been no great shakes here. I knew the guy on the desk, Raglo. I won't say I'm a regular, but we'd played poker together a few times. He's the worst poker player I know, but I let him win more than lose. That way I don't always have to pry information out of him with a crowbar.

"Much happenin'?" I asked him.

"Quiet night, Nick. Three or four heart attacks, one drunk fished out the Hudson, brawl victim. Usual intake. What's your angle?"

I flashed him a glimpse of Zeitsheim. "Fresh off the night boat from Odessa."

He knew the case, of course, but his face clouded and he pulled back. "No, I don't think so. You got the wrong morgue."

"Don't go cold on me, Raglo. He's here."

My man was sweating. "I don't know nothin'."

I smiled my horrible smile and leaned over the counter. "I know that. But tell me anyway."

He knew what I was like when someone upset me. "Three guys came in, flashing badges at me."

"Let me guess. FBI?"

He looked appalled. "You know about them?"

"A little. So what did they want, apart from a peek at Zeitsheim?"

He looked even worse, like he had acute guts ache. His face was like chalk. "They wanted more than that. They wanted his *corpse*. I mean, they wanted to take it away."

I started sliding notes across the counter, lots of them.

"Listen, I saw the guy when we unzipped his bag and put him in the locker," said Raglo, face even whiter.

"A mess, right?"

"You got that right. Nick. Used a long knife on himself. You know I ain't squeamish, but this was about as bad as it gets. The guy was *dead*, right. You don't get no deader. Think I don't know a stiff when I seen one? Jimmy and me slid him home into a locker and turned the key."

I straightened up. "So?"

"When I took the three suits back there and Jimmy unlocked it—*jeeze*, it was crazy. The smell was like nothin' I ever smelled before. I tell ya, I've known every kind of horror in this place, Nick. Makes you thick-skinned and you can take anything, sights, smells, whatever. But this was one stench. Like a drain outta Hell itself."

"The body?"

"*Body?* Shit, there was no body. Just a pool of… what the hell can I call it? Green slime. Yeah, slime. Inch deep in the locker."

"You're telling me that the body had decomposed that quickly? Turned into a pool of green slime in—what, minutes?"

He shook his head. "No. Weirder than that, pal. Jimmy spotted the rest of it. You want to see? Only you betta be quick. The dicks'll be here in a minute."

"Lead on." I followed him out through the back into the cold room. Jimmy, his attendant, was slumped at a desk, head down, snoring. We didn't wake him. Sounded like he'd had enough for one night.

"This is the locker. But look, that's what Jimmy noticed." He pointed to the polished floor. Going across it was a kind of trail. I went over to look at it and bent down. Green slime was right. Like some big fat slug had dragged itself across the room. I got up and walked through an open door to a small washroom out back.

"I haven't touched anything," avowed Raglo. "The Feds told me not to. They said they'd be back."

I nodded. "I haven't been here, okay? And you were right about the stink." It made me cough. It was, not to put too fine a point on it, vile. But if you guys have been down there, you'll know that.

Raglo pointed to the window. It was busted, like something far too bulky had been shoved through it, hard. More slime.

"Nick, what in hell is goin' on? Who's done this? Jimmy says no one could have got in here. No one could have gotten that body out of the locker without him knowin'."

I shoved some more dollar notes into his shaking hand. "I guess you're right. So we have to consider the other possibility. Well, *you* don't, but I do."

He gaped at me like a beached guppy.

"The guy was alive," I said. "He crawled out. Where does the window lead to?"

I left him to it and none too soon. Minutes after I quit the morgue, a couple of police wagons drew up. At least I had a short head start on them.

Round the back of the building I found the alley system that was fed by the window from which Stefan Zeitsheim (or whatever had consumed him) had made his escape. I was beginning to see the attraction this guy had for his various pursuers. My current employers had told me that Stefan was hunted. No wonder. FBI? I had no contacts there. My guess was that they wanted him alive, while my employers wanted him dead. Maybe he had the dirt on them.

I picked up the slime trail, but it wound its way through a dozen alleys and petered out. After that there was nothing much to go on. So what was I looking for now? The mother of all maggots, or Houdini's older brother? If this was a trick, a fake suicide and a weird escape to follow, it had taken some pulling off.

I went back to more familiar haunts and pored over what I knew so far with a pot of coffee and a fried breakfast at Fat Duke's. Halfway through the bacon, a guy came in, noticed me in the corner and helped himself to the chair opposite me. I chewed slowly, waiting. This was no chance encounter. Another nice suit. The mountain had come to Mohammed.

"Mr. Stone." Nice voice. Nice salary too, I guessed.

"You want a coffee?"

He shook his head. "We have a mutual friend. I think you know to whom I am referring."

"Yes, I think I know to whom you are referring. Tell me something, is this friend of ours dead or still wandering the streets of our fair city?"

"I was hoping you could tell me that, Mr. Stone."

"So why are you interested in him?"

"It's rather a complicated story."

"Isn't it always?"

He sort of smiled, but he made it look like he had the gripe. "Our friend is wanted for questioning. Not just by us. It's an international matter. Security. And he is a very dangerous character. I can't tell you how dangerous."

I carried on chewing, occasionally breaking to sip my coffee. "I guess a man like that makes more than a few enemies."

"It doesn't pay to get mixed up with this sort of people."

Ah, did I detect a chill note creeping into the voice? A coldness of expression? I grunted.

"So what is your interest, Mr. Stone?"

"Let's just call it curiosity."

"If you say so, Mr. Stone. Is the payload worth the trouble?"

"A man's got to eat."

"You know who I represent? It's a powerful outfit."

It was taking him a long time to get round to the threat. But this had to be it. "Sure."

"How much would it take to eliminate your curiosity?"

"Like I said, a man's got to eat."

He named a figure that would have fed a sell-out at the Yankee Stadium. "You want me to forget about our mutual friend."

"Completely."

"Somebody might be disappointed if I did that. Somebody with a bad attitude. It could affect my health."

"We can take care of that for you. If you help us."

The idea of the FBI and my three employers going head to head was an interesting one. I just didn't want to get mashed in the middle of it. "I'll think about it."

He nodded and got up, pushing the chair back slowly. "Good. We'll talk again, Mr. Stone. I'll be in touch. I know where you live," he added, with a grin.

I forgot to shudder and just did my casual wave. But the fact was, I was deep in the mire. Whatever I did now, someone was going to be very upset.


Later in the day, one of my sewer rats came up with a lead. He'd been in and out of the wharf cafés, bumming smokes and a crust or two, when he'd tuned in on an intriguing conversation. Now this guy, a dropout called Shivers, is a real pro. He can blend in with the walls, or the furniture, or the garbage. You wouldn't know he was there. He lives by the skin of his teeth and traffics in gossip. And he makes a point of knowing his market. So he knew that Nick Nightmare had an ear out for anything to do with the dockside "suicide". Word had already got around.

In another bar, tucked away in a thick wooden booth, the air hung with smoke as thick as curtains, he spilled his news. He'd overheard two guys. One of them was a major link in an illegal immigrant chain, a man who could arrange to shift people from place to place with no questions asked. I knew the guy by reputation. Let's call him BoBo.

According to Shivers, BoBo was talking to a weird guy—I interrupted him to show him the mug shot of Zeitsheim.

"Jeeze, Nick, that's him, I tell ya! That's the guy. White as a corpse."

"You don't know the half of it."

"He was lookin' for passage along the coast. Not by any normal channels. He kept turnin' round as if Satan himself was blowin' hot air down his neck, so I guess he was on the run."

"How did he smell?"

Shivers nearly choked on his beer. "What the—? You know about that? Real bad, Nick. I mean, *real* bad. Fish gone off. I been in some places, but man, this guy was stinkin' fit to make a guy retch."

I merely nodded. Sailor Stefan it was, then.

"He spoke low and with a weird kind of voice, like he had a mother of a cold. But I heard him mention one of them old Massachusetts seaports. Innsmouth. He wanted to get to Innsmouth. BoBo took his time about answerin'. Sounded like Innsmouth was bad news to him. But he agreed. The fish guy gave him a wad of notes, must've been a fortune. BoBo told him it would take a few days to sort out. The guy would have to hole up until then."

"You know where he is now?"

"Yeah." He gave me the address of an old warehouse down by the docks. Good place to hide a needle. "Want me to take you?"

"Not yet. But keep an eye on him. I don't want him leaving New York before I get a chance to meet him."

My man was living up to his name, shivering like it was snowing out. Maybe it wasn't just the cold and maybe the beer and the fug hadn't done enough to warm him. I'd already given him some money, but I dragged my coat from the chair beside me. It had had its day. "Here, keep this. You need it more than I do." If this panned out the way I hoped, I'd be picking up a dozen new coats before this affair was closed. Maybe even get myself a slick suit.

He struggled into the coat like it was something alien, but grinned a crack-toothed grin. You could have got two of him inside it. "Thanks, Nick," he muttered. Then he was gone.

I was left to chew over what he'd told me. Innsmouth. Meant nothing to me. So it was library time, for a bit of research.


It took some digging out. I spend half my life glued to old newspapers: the good ladies at the library are getting used to me. I think they find me kinda romantic. Must be my old-fashioned charm. Whatever, they came up trumps on Innsmouth. And I had my connection.

Years ago, way back in the winter of 1927–28, it seems that the Government had investigated some pretty weird goings-on in the port, following complaints about demon worship and likewise subversive cults. The Feds had gone as far as to blow up or burn down whole parts of the town. There had been a lot of arrests. One report referred to a submarine diving down into the deep waters off the port to a reef known as Devil's Reef, where something had been torpedoed. There had obviously been some sort of lunatic cult based around the area. And it seemed like overkill for bootlegging. Whatever they had really been up to would probably remain a mystery, but the Government had obviously taken it seriously enough to send in their heavies.

It had been a long time ago and I couldn't find out anything more, but maybe there was still life left in the place and Stefan Zeitsheim wanted a piece of the action.

Evening was drawing on. Time to look up the errant sailor. In spite of my instructions, I didn't plan on killing him. I reckoned he'd be worth more alive.

I knew where to find the warehouse Shivers had told me about. I parked a few blocks away, checked my Beretta and used the thickening shadows to mask my approach. Shivers wouldn't be far away. He'd see me when others wouldn't.

I was within a hundred yards of the building, when I heard a commotion up ahead. And I knew in my guts it was going to be bad news. I wasn't wrong.

There was a mob. These streets were usually dead at this time of the day. Something had stirred them up, like a kicked hornets' nest. They were crowding round the sidewalk, opposite the warehouse.

I moved in, looking down.

"Hey, Nick," breathed a voice beside me. Another of the local dropouts.

"What gives?"

"It's Shivers. Some punk shot him."

I started muscling people aside. Sure enough, Shivers was sprawled across the edge of the sidewalk. I bent down to him. He was alive, but only just. His face was grey, his expression a mixture of agony and disbelief. I felt his chest. It was a mess.

Only one bullet, but it had done the job. I felt the fury rising up in me, but fought it down.

"A car," he breathed through teeth clenched on pain. "The gun… silencer. Jeeze, I'm so cold, Nick. So *cold*."

I pulled the coat tighter around him. The coat, goddam it. *My* coat. He was wearing the coat I'd given him. The bullet had been meant for me.

"Who did this, Shivers?"

He managed only half a word before he died. But it was enough. *Suit*. It had been some guy in a suit. It figured. The Feds had warned me off. They really had meant business.

"Cops are on the way," someone above me said. I got up and stood aside. In a minute or two I'd slipped to the back of the crowd. No one paid me any attention, all eyes on the curled-up form of Shivers.

I made my way along the street and crossed it where I thought I'd be least noticed. I guessed the Feds would have gone, thinking they'd taken me out of the picture. It was the one advantage I had on them. I was going to find Zeitsheim before they did, so help me.

At the far end of the warehouse there was an alley running alongside it. The light was fading away, but I could just about see enough to ease my way down it. It suited me. I flattened against the wall and moved forward by inches. Shivers would have known exactly where Zeitsheim was holed up inside, but now I was going to have to flush him out. I had a feeling it was going to be damn tough. My quarry had already shown his credentials in the hide-and-seek stakes.

I was about halfway down the alley when I noticed the breeze. Nothing unusual about a breeze, especially in these city canyons. They come and go. But there was something about this breeze that made my skin crawl, like it was the breath of some huge beast, crouched back there in the darkness.

Something scratched along the alley. A ball of newspaper. The breeze stiffened and in a minute, other bits of lightweight garbage came tumbling along. Couple of paper cups. More paper. Discarded bags.

I heard something far overhead, a distant roar. Maybe there was a storm brewing up. Very sudden. But what the hell, it was October.

I had my Beretta out, catch off. My nerves were dancing. More scraping sounds behind me. I swung round, aiming the gun. A tin can rolled, followed by more paper, a crushed cardboard box. The breeze was a light wind now. I could feel its strength growing, cold on the face. It kept cuffing stuff down the alley like it was a wind tunnel.

At the end of the alley was a mesh fence, eight feet high, beyond it a pile of crates and other junk, heaped up so that the fence bulged at its base, fit to burst. There were broken tea chests and tumbled stacks of newspaper this side of the fence. The wind was driving more captive garbage towards them, a growing procession.

Moving on down the alley, I fetched up against some metal bins, beyond which was a door into the warehouse. It didn't look like it had been opened in a long time. I reached for the rusting handle.

"You don't want to go in there, Mr. Stone," called a soft voice from across the alley. I recognized it. The Fed from Fat Duke's.

I was instantly down on one knee, partially masked by the bins, gun trained at the shadows across the way. I could already imagine the slug smashing into me.

"Easy, Mr. Stone." He was well hidden, but I could see half of him. And a gun. Either he or one of his companions had killed Shivers. "I told you we would take care of this."

I shifted back a little, getting more of me behind the bins. I was getting angry again.

The wind abruptly rose a tone or two, gusting down the alley, rolling another wave of litter forward. It struck me for the first time that there was something freakish about the moving garbage. There seemed to be an unusual amount of it.

"There's still time for you to leave," came the voice.

Sure, and take a bullet like Shivers had. I wasn't planning on making the first move. And I wasn't going to make polite conversation.

"You've no idea what you're dealing with, Mr. Stone."

"Suppose you enlighten me."

"I can't do that. It's a case of—"

He didn't get to finish. Near to the shadows that hid him, a pile of the litter seemed to erupt upward, cartons and cans and paper all bursting every which way. The Fed swung his gun arm round as if he would start pumping shots into the mass of paper. It was all I needed.

My Beretta spat once. At that range I don't miss, never mind the poor vision. I heard the bullet smack into flesh and bone across the alley. The Fed's gun spun from his grasp and clanked as it hit the ground. He gasped, his forearm shattered, and crashed back into the recess behind him.

The pile of garbage revealed itself to be some poor wino whose drunken stupor had been interrupted by the arrival of the Fed and me. Arms flapping like a scarecrow, he gabbled and shrieked something unintelligible and sat down hard among the huge pile of garbage that was his home. A half-full bottle of something rolled from his fingers into the middle of the alley. A few thin beams of light played on the moving contents inside it.

I was across the alley quickly, picking up the Fed's gun and pocketing it. I was risking that he only carried one. He'd gone quiet. I guessed he'd passed out.

The wino suddenly started to blubber, shouting something crazy about the garbage trying to eat him. I watched as the wino, no more than a filthy bundle of old rags, leapt to his feet, beat at himself as if he was on fire, then tried to run off back up the alley. Paper clung to him like a cloud of huge moths.

I looked down at the bottle. The wino must've been totally freaked out to leave it.

I pulled out my lighter and snapped it on. I needed to see the Fed. Cautiously I went toward him. In the flickering glow I could just make him out. He was conscious, his good arm tightly clutching his bad, very bad, one. That was no flesh wound. He'd need attention pretty soon.

But I was in no hurry. Obviously I didn't want his death on my hands, but there would be time yet to call the medics.

I held my gun up, aimed at his forehead. "You want to tell me why you tried to kill me? Why a man is dead instead of me?"

He shook his head, eyes shutting and opening against the pain in his shattered arm.

"You're going to have to talk to somebody. If not me, the cops. I'm a man who likes to trade. Tell me about Zeitsheim and you can go back to your buddies in one piece."

The wind was now howling overhead. I hadn't been taking any notice. But again I got the feeling something was really freakish about it. More litter came rolling and tumbling down the alley, like a paper wave breaking on a beach. I turned to the Fed, about to step up our little chat. But something even more weird was going on.

The garbage. It had heaped itself around the Fed and, just like it had with the wino, it started to heave and bulge upward. Not another goddam wino!

But it wasn't. The Fed started to scream. No exaggeration. He *screamed*. The wind was shrieking around us now, like a banshee, but the Fed's scream tore right through it. I shuffled back, my gun aimed at the garbage pile. I swear to God it was *bunching* itself together. Shaping itself into something. And *the wind* was doing it. Like a potter kneading clay. All that garbage that had come rolling down into the alley was now gathering itself.

And the Fed went on screaming. The garbage shape raised itself. It now looked about the size of a man, hunched over, neck-less, its rounded, incomplete head a massive paper blob on huge shoulders.

I fired twice at it. Trust me, those bullets went right into its guts. But it didn't make any difference. I stepped back, but my heel came down carelessly on the wino's discarded bottle. I was over on my back before I knew it, the air punched out of me by the landing, Beretta spinning away. I could just about see the garbage-thing bending over the Fed.

A few seconds later the screaming stopped. And the thing turned round to look for me. I say look for me, but it had no face, no eyes. Like a dried papier-mâché golem gone wrong, it shambled forward, spurred on by the wind, which seemed like it was howling with glee, encouraging its malformed offspring. The contorted arms that reached out for me were wet and dark with the Fed's blood.

No time to think. Just do. Whatever. Instinct took over.

My left hand was inches from the bottle that had betrayed me. I grabbed it. The limbs of the thing above me were a couple of feet from my face. I was still holding my lighter in my right hand: I stuck it in my teeth. I rolled aside, snatched up some sheets of paper, made crude spills of them and rammed them down the neck of the bottle. Still on my back, I faced the oncoming shape again. I used the lighter to ignite my impromptu touch paper. Please God it was meths or something like it in that bottle.

I shoved the bottle up into where the mouth should have been. Something soft and pulpy gave, like I was punching a bowl of jelly. But the wine bottle stuck firm. I rolled over a few times, just in time to avert the sudden *whoosh* of fire as the spirits ignited. The mock arms that had been about to grab my face were suddenly beating at the head and chest of my assailant. With all that tinder at its disposal, the fire caught on fast. It crackled and snapped and the shape swung aside, blundering into the mound of debris by the fence, an instant bonfire. I watched as the bulging head dissolved into smoke and the upper torso streamed red fire.

I was on my feet fast, picking up my gun. I would just have a moment to look at the Fed. He was slumped down, but alive. His good arm groped for me. I yanked him to his feet and he almost swung round into the garbage and an early cremation. But I dragged him away. The smoke was coming in dense clouds. There was going to be one helluva conflagration in no time.

I put my arm round the groaning Fed, straining to get him across the alley. I could feel my eyebrows singeing in the ferocious heat. Nothing for it now but to get through the door into the warehouse. We made it across and I yanked at the handle so hard that it snapped off. But the door swung open. I pushed the Fed in, took one last look at the inferno behind me and got the door as near shut as I could.

He grunted, something clutched tightly in his good hand. It was a mobile phone. I prized it loose, but it was thankfully useless, squashed like an empty can, I guess by the paper monstrosity. But that suited me fine: I didn't want the Fed calling up a swarm of his buddies. I flung the phone aside.

There were stone stairs going up. I flipped my lighter on. It would do. I got the Fed up the first flight, turned a corner and let him slump down.

I held the flame close to his face. There was blood on it. The guy was a real mess. But I couldn't tell if mâché-man had drawn more blood or spread what was leaking from the gunshot wound.

"Can you hear me?"

His eyes opened, blinking tears, and he nodded.

"Pal, you have to talk to me," I snapped. "What in hell is going on here?"

As if suddenly coming round to our position, he jerked upright. "Where is it? That thing—"

"Gone up in a blaze of glory," I told him, waving the lighter.

"There may be more—"

"Not from the alley. It'll take a fleet of fire wagons to clear it. So what was it? Tell me I'm not going nuts."

"He sent it. Zeitsheim. He has very strange connections," the Fed gasped, wincing as more agony lanced through his arm. "He's protected. For the love of Mike, don't try going after him, Stone. He's in this warehouse. But you've seen what he can do."

"So he's some kind of magician?"

"He has equally dangerous enemies. You work for them. I doubt if you know who they really are."

"While you obviously do. Explain. You ain't going nowhere. We're stuck here. Once that smoke gets in, we have to enter the warehouse. So talk to me. Tell me about what's happening down at Innsmouth."

It was a long shot, but it hit home. "You know about Innsmouth?"

"Enough."

"Damn diseased place," he coughed. "Zeitsheim is one of its progeny. There are other enclaves in Europe. He's on his way back from there. We have to get to him before he gets back to Innsmouth. It's too far for even one of his kind to swim."

"So the FBI wants him alive?"

"Yeah. Your employers are his own kind. They don't want us to get hold of him. Not outside Innsmouth. Down there, he'd be safe enough. They have ways of protecting the community you wouldn't believe. On his own, here, he's vulnerable. So rather than let him fall into our hands, they want him dead."

"Incinerated," I corrected.

"What?"

"Incinerated. If Zeitsheim burns like that paper zombie out there, there'll be no more than a small pile of ash to interrogate. That was my job. What I was paid to do, anyhow. Which is why, I assume, you guys wanted to remove me. And why a friend of mine ended up bleeding to death on the sidewalk."

The Fed grimaced, but I won't say it was remorse. "You seemed determined not to take a hint."

"So, what did you mean when you said that Zeitsheim *sent* that thing?"

"You won't believe it—"

"After what I saw out there, at least try me."

"Not all of his kind want him dead. Others want to help get him back to Innsmouth. Whatever transpired in Europe, they want to know about it. So they send him help when he calls for it. Did you notice the wind? How freakish it was?"

"Sure." The wind that had sculpted the garbage man.

"Does the name Ithaqua mean anything to you? Or the Wendigo?"

I nodded at the latter. "Indian spirit." I was combing my mental files for a reference. "Walker on the winds." Ah, illumination, of a sort.

"That's it, Mr. Stone," the Fed grunted. "The winds. But it was around long before the Indians called it the Wendigo. Zeitsheim and his kind call it Ithaqua. They worship it and other very strange gods. Gods that have been around longer than the solar system."

"They wouldn't be gods otherwise," I said flippantly.

"Doesn't pay to laugh at them."

"No. I wasn't laughing when that thing came at me. So you're telling me that Zeitsheim *summoned* the wind—the wind-walker? And it moulded the garbage thing?" But I'd *seen* it, goddam it. It had happened right in front of me. That was no illusion. For the moment I was going to have to go along with all this bullshit.

The Fed started coughing and I noticed the air getting thick. The damn smoke was seeping in fast. We had to get up into the warehouse. I dragged the Fed to his feet, pulled his gun out of my pocket and stuck it into his left hand.

"You may need this. But forget about taking me out of the equation, pal. Next time I shoot at you, it'll be here." And I tapped him lightly between the eyes. He knew I wasn't kidding.

We made our way up the stairs. The stairwell was filling with smoke now. I guessed the fire outside had really got going. Maybe the whole block would end up in flames. Well, it's what my employers wanted, assuming Zeitsheim ended up on the pyre. We went through some doors onto a floor of the warehouse.

My night vision isn't bad, but I wouldn't have seen anything if it hadn't been for the fire below in the alley. Waving red light danced on the walls opposite, so that we could see around us. The place was lit in dull, wavering orange, the deserted spaces like an alien landscape. Which was appropriate, I guess.

"How do you know Zeitsheim is still here?" I said softly.

The Fed leaned on one of the iron columns. "We've got all the exits covered. Cellars are shut down. He can't walk through walls."

"Sewers? Seems to me if a guy stinks like he does, a little excrement isn't going to make a lot of difference."

"He couldn't get into the system. Sealed a while ago for safety."

I nodded. "He knows you're after him and he knows his mock suicide didn't work. How did he do that, by the way? The word is, he was dead. Down at the morgue, they do know a dead body when they see one."

"You don't want to know."

"Oh, but I do. One more impossibility isn't going to spoil my day."

"All right. Can't do any harm to tell you. No one would believe you. He's not human. Not completely. None of them are in that damn seaport. They spend most of their lives in the sea, god damn it. The *sea*!"

A momentary reflection came to me, something I'd read in the papers I'd been researching. "Isn't there some kind of reef?"

"Devil's Reef? Yeah, you've been doing your homework, Mr. Stone."

"Your mob torpedoed it some seventy-five-odd years ago. I guess they didn't finish the job."

He shook his head. "Guess you're right. They've spawned anew. And we can't just go in, guns blazing. We've sent investigative bodies in to Innsmouth, but they cover themselves. We have nothing to go on. No shred of evidence that would hold up in court. But if we could take Zeitsheim…" He suddenly gripped my arm, his face knotted in pain.

"Stone, I'm going to need medical attention soon. Lost a lot of blood. Listen to me. You have to keep away from Zeitsheim. You have to let our men take him. Never mind what you're being paid. We'll treble it."

"Yeah, yeah. Just stay cool. But I think I know where our man will be."

He looked as if he was going to slip into unconsciousness, but he managed to nod. I let him down, resting his back against the column. His lap was full of blood. He'd be lucky if his arm survived this. But he was luckier than Shivers had been.

I left him there and went back to the stairs. But they were thick with smoke. Instead I crossed the huge, empty floor and found another stair. If Zeitsheim could talk to the wind, the best place to do it would be up on the roof. I went up after him, though I had no concrete plan.

The roof was several flights up, beyond a half-dozen empty floors that offered no hint as to where Zeitsheim was. I went up the last steps very slowly. There was still enough of a glow from below to show me the terrain here. Beyond it, opposite where the fire was, the dark waters of the Hudson stretched on either side.

Zeitsheim could have been hiding behind any number of vents up here. The fire was roaring away noisily below and I could hear sirens. This whole block was in danger of going up if they didn't control it soon. But the wind had died down, back to what it had been during the day.

I ducked and weaved between vents, using the shadows to cover me. Then I found what I was looking for, or rather, my nose did. It was that stench again, the one I'd first encountered at the morgue. And sure enough, the green slime. I picked up a length of wood that had come away from the vent housing and dipped the end of it in the slime, holding it up before me. It was no illusion. Whatever it was, it was real. Like the viscous oozing of a snail, only a human-size one.

The slime trail led to another opening in the roof and more stairs. Carefully I peered down and, as I did so, I heard shots—several of them—a few floors below. It could only be the Fed. Dammit, Zeitsheim had conned me. He's gone back down after him. Divide and conquer.

I hurtled down the stairs, practically breaking my neck in the process. When I reached the floor where I'd left the Fed, the whole area was lit up by the bonfire below. I could see the slumped form of the Fed. But Zeitsheim had made himself scarce again. My guess now was that he'd be making for the water. The Fed said these people had an affinity for the sea, so maybe that was where Zeitsheim would have to end up.

I reached the Fed. He gazed up at me like a beached fish, his gun hanging from limp fingers.

"It was here. I emptied the gun into it," he croaked.

"Looks like you missed."

He shook his head weakly. "Bullets don't hurt them."

"Crap. You missed him."

He shook his head more emphatically. "No, Stone. That's the point. They've been working on something. Their breeding program. Zeitsheim is back from Europe. The enclave over there must be more advanced. They've had years to develop, hidden away deep in the Eastern bloc. They morph. From their true form. At best I may have wounded it, but it's still alive."

"Heading for the river?"

"It'll dive in. It'll have to swim out to sea. Try for another ship to get it up to Innsmouth. It's desperate to get there, to pass on what it can do. Leave me here. Find it. Stop it. If it gets to Innsmouth and starts breeding—"

"Tell me again why my employers want it incinerated? Don't they want its secrets themselves?"

"They are terrified of the possibility of us taking Zeitsheim alive. Nothing is worth that risk to them. And, God help us, Stone, there will be others coming over. They have been patient. Time means nothing to these creatures. Zeitsheim is just the forerunner." He sank back, exhausted.

I left him again, making for the far side of the warehouse and steps that would lead down to the wharf-side. I was being cautious about my descent but even so, I nearly slipped and went headlong. More slime, so I was on the right track. I could just make out the ground floor below me. There was a door, which must lead out on to the wharf.

I kept very still. If Zeitsheim was there, he would have heard me. I had one last card I could play. I held the Beretta tightly, even though the Fed had told me its bullets would be useless.

"Zeitsheim!" I hissed. I repeated the name a couple of times. "I'm from BoBo. He told me you'd be here. You hear me? I'm from BoBo."

I inched my way down the slippery stair. The light below was very poor, but something shifted in the shadows. I called him again. Then at last I saw him, though he was no more than a blur. He was on the next landing down, halfway between me and the floor!

"Zeitsheim. That you? I'm from BoBo. You can't stay here. We gotta find you another bolt-hole until the ship for Innsmouth is ready."

He eased out from cover. From here, he looked human enough, though I couldn't see his face properly. I kept my gun out of sight.

"The Feds are lookin' for you," I told him, easing down another step. "Can't stay here, pal. BoBo has a better place."

He didn't look hostile, so maybe he was buying it. But I wasn't about to find out. The outside door opened, letting in a pale shaft of streetlight. Zeitsheim swung round and over his massive shoulder I saw a figure slide into the building only to take immediate cover in the pitch darkness behind the door.

"Don't move up there!" barked a voice. "NYPD! I have a gun trained on you. One move and I will shoot. You hear me. I will shoot. Now, come down the stairs very slowly with your hands on your head."

The cop edged forward and I could just make him out. He had his weapon held in both hands, trained like he said on Zeitsheim.

Impasse. What the hell was I supposed to do now?

But Zeitsheim made up my mind for me. He swung round and hauled himself up the stairs, his shape blurring for a moment as he did so. Like I said, the light was very poor, the whole place one mass of shadows. But Zeitsheim was changing. His trunk thickened, his neck disappearing. In that darkness, he was just like a single mass rising up the stairs. And he meant to burst past me. Or *over* me.

Down below, the cop opened fire. I was too mesmerized to turn and make a bolt for it. I took out my own gun and let the Zeitsheim-thing have it. I didn't miss and I guess the cop's bullets found their mark, too. At any rate, the combined force of the bullets achieved something, because the shape crashed into the steel rail at one side of the stair, snapped it clean off like it was made of balsa wood and then went tumbling out into space.

It landed with a sickening smack on the cement floor, making a sound like a huge sack of eggs bursting. I was grateful for the darkness, because the thing *exploded*. It's the only word for it.

And the shafts of light from the open door picked out the details in appalling, gory splendor. Like a bathful of slime. One very big bathful.

The cop staggered back against the door, pretty shaken up, his gun hanging at his side. He hardly noticed me as I began a slow climb down.

But the fun was only just beginning. As I looked down at the widespread remains of Zeitsheim, I realized that they were moving. *Rippling*, to be precise. The extremities of that slick pool were beginning to *flow* towards the door. And gradually the whole mass started to shiver and edge forward, like fluid running off toward a drain.

The sea! That was it. This damn thing was flowing back to the water beyond the wharf outside the door, no more than a few yards away.

The cop was just gaping, rigid as stone.

"Shut the door!" I yelled. "For Chrissake, shut the door!"

It snapped him awake, but panic swept over him and he blasted away with his last couple of rounds. The bullets whanged off the floor and walls, powerless against the moving slime. But one of them clanged into a pile of oil drums that had been stacked beyond the shadows. Faintly I could hear the *glug, glug* of oil that had been released.

I flicked on my lighter and held it up. Sure enough, oil was leaking out over the floor, running thickly to the edge of the pool of moving slime.

I had my instructions.

I tossed the lighter floor-ward. It bounced and came to a halt in the widening oil slick. For a moment I thought nothing would happen. But the oil caught. And I had my second blaze of the night.

Without another glance, I raced down the last of the stairs. The oil had really caught now and fingers of flame were reaching out across the floor. The cop didn't know which way to look, like a man in a dream.

Almost beside us, the slime suddenly rose up, seemingly in an attempt to reshape itself into a human form, the fire engulfing its base as though the slime were as combustible as the oil. A wild, wide mouth formed somewhere where the head was supposed to be and a dreadful hissing, an agonized shriek, emerged.

"What the—?" gasped the cop.

"Don't ask," I told him, gripping him by the elbow and marshalling him to the door. Behind us, Zeitsheim was swaying to and fro, his shape completely distorted now, like someone trying to break its way out of a thick cellophane shroud. But the flames just roared into it. It would be over in seconds.

I pushed the cop out on to the wharf, which was easy enough given his stupefaction, and dragged the door shut behind me. I turned round—to find myself looking into the mouths of three more guns.

"FBI," said one of the gunmen, holding up a badge briefly.

I'd already put my empty Beretta away out of sight. "You better go quickly if you want to pull your buddy out," I told them, jerking my thumb up at the warehouse. "He's gonna need medical help."

The first of them swore, speaking urgently into his mobile phone.

"What about Zeitsheim?" another of them growled, almost in my ear.

I looked down. A smear of something dark had oozed out from under the door. I was about to comment, when a small tongue of fire licked out and covered it possessively. There was a brief crackle, like fat on a fire, then it was over.

"He's all yours," I told them.

They were far too interested in their quarry to pay the cop and me any more attention. So we simply walked away.

The Feds had parked their car along the wharf. Just behind it, another cop was leaning against the bonnet of a patrol car. "What's all the fuss, sarge?" he said to the cop beside me. "I heard shooting, but the Feds told me to keep my nose out of it." It didn't look like it had bothered him.

The cop with me just shook his head, like a man in a dream.

"If you don't mind, I think I'll just leave you boys to it," I drawled, making a move to do just that.

But the cop beside me finally came to. "Hold it, pal. You're not going anywhere until we've cleared this mess up. We have arson—

two fires, dammit—we have Feds crawlin' about the place—we have that… thing in there. There's a whole lot of questions that need answering, down at the precinct."

I shrugged in resignation. It was going to be a long night.

The cop looked out again at the river, shaking his head. "I know what I saw, Ed. It's just like Stone says on the tape. He didn't make that up. Not the last bit anyway. *Damn*, I saw it!"

"We can't hold him forever. We have to charge him, or let him go."

"What about the Feds?"

"If they found any trace of this illegal immigrant, they're saying nothing. And they're not filing any charges against Stone for shooting up their pal. And by the time that fire's finally done with, there'll be nothing left of that warehouse worth sifting through."

"So all we have is that tape," said the cop, eyeing the audio dubiously, "and my statement. Joe didn't see anything. First sound of shooting and he'd have ducked under the dashboard. The Feds'll deny all knowledge of involvement. They'll want this covered up, whatever the hell was goin' on. And I'll tell you what else. I for one don't want to go snoopin' round that Innsmouth place. Back of hell and beyond."

"You got that right. And I'll tell you another thing, Hal. This is one case that ain't gonna win you promotion."

Hal nodded slowly. "So what the hell did I see?"

"Beats me. But maybe setting it alight was the best thing for it."

Hal took the tape, considered it for a moment, then flung it far out into the river. "Let Stone go. No charges."

"A wise decision, Hal."

"What was it that dick called himself?"

"Stone?"

"Nightmare. Nick Nightmare."

"That about says it all."

Hal nodded again, watching the river. Suddenly he felt very tired.

# FISH BRIDE

*by* CAITLÍN R. KIERNAN

**W**E LIE HERE together, naked on her sheets which are always damp, no matter the weather, and she's still sleeping. I've lain next to her, watching the long cold sunrise, the walls of this dingy room in this dingy house turning so slowly from charcoal to a hundred successively lighter shades of grey. The weak November morning has a hard time at the window, because the glass was knocked out years ago and she chose as a substitute a sheet of tattered and not-quite-clear plastic she found washed up on the shore, held in place with mismatched nails and a few thumbtacks. But it deters the worst of the wind and rain and snow, and she says there's nothing out there she wants to see, anyway. I've offered to replace the broken glass, a couple of times now I've said that, but it's just another of the hundred or so things that I've promised I would do for her and haven't yet gotten around to doing; she doesn't seem to mind. That's not why she keeps letting me come here. Whatever she wants from me, it isn't handouts and pity and someone to fix her broken windows and leaky ceiling. Which is fortunate, as I've never fixed anything in my whole life. I can't even change a flat tyre. I've only ever been the sort of man who does the harm and leaves it for someone else to put right again,

131

or simply sweep beneath a rug where no one will have to notice the damage I've done. So, why should she be any different? And yet, to my knowledge, I've done her no harm so far.

I come down the hill from the village on those interminable nights and afternoons when I can't write and don't feel like getting drunk alone. I leave that other world, that safe and smothering kingdom of clean sheets and typescript, electric lights and indoor plumbing and radio and window frames with windowpanes, and follow the sandy path through gale-stunted trees and stolen, burned-out automobiles, smouldering trash-barrel fires and suspicious, under-lit glances.

They all know I don't belong here with them, all the other men and women who share her squalid existence at the edge of the sea, the ones who have come down and never gone back up the hill again. I call them her apostles, and she gets sullen and angry.

"No," she says, "it's not like that. They're nothing of the sort."

But I understand well enough that's exactly what they are, even if she doesn't want to admit it, either to herself or to me. And so they hold me in contempt, because she's taken me into her bed— me, an interloper who comes and goes, who has some choice in the matter, who has that option because the world beyond these dunes and shanty walls still imagines it has some use for me. One of these nights, I think, her apostles will do murder against me. One of them alone, or all of them together. It may be stones or sticks or an old filleting knife. It may even be a gun. I wouldn't put it past them. They are resourceful, and there's a lot on the line. They'll bury me in the dog roses, or sink me in some deep place among the tide-worn rocks, or carve me up like a fat sow and have themselves a feast. She'll likely join them, if they are bold enough and offer a few scraps of my charred, anonymous flesh to complete the sacrifice. And later, much, much later, she'll remember and miss me, in her sloppy, indifferent way, and wonder whatever became of the man who brought her beer and whiskey, candles and chocolate bars, the man who said he'd fix the window, but never did. She might recall my name, but I wouldn't hold it against her if she doesn't.

"This used to *be* someplace," she's told me time and time again. "Oh, sure, you'd never know it now. But when my mother was a girl, this used to be a town. When I was little, it was still a town. There were dress shops and a diner and a jail. There was a public park with a bandshell and a hundred-year-old oak tree. In the summer, there was music in the park, and picnics. There were even churches, *two* of them, one Catholic and one Presbyterian. But then the storm came and took it all away."

And it's true, most of what she says. There was a town here once. Half a century's neglect hasn't quite erased all signs of it. She's shown me some of what there's left to see—the stump of a brick chimney, a few broken pilings where the waterfront once stood—and I've asked questions around the village. But people up there don't like to speak openly about this place, or even allow their thoughts to linger on it very long. Every now and then, usually after a burglary or before an election, there's talk of cleaning it up, pulling down these listing, clapboard shacks and chasing away the vagrants and squatters and winos. So far, the talk has come to nothing.

A sudden gust of wind blows in from off the beach, and the sheet of plastic stretched across the window flaps and rustles, and she opens her eyes.

"You're still here," she says, not sounding surprised, merely telling me what I already know. "I was dreaming that you'd gone away and would never come back to me again. I dreamed there was a boat called the *Silver Star*, and it took you away."

"I get seasick," I tell her. "I don't do boats. I haven't been on a boat since I was fifteen."

"Well, you got on this one," she insists, and the dim light filling up the room catches in the facets of her sleepy grey eyes. "You said that you were going to seek your fortune on the Ivory Coast. You had your typewriter, and a suitcase, and you were wearing a brand new suit of worsted wool. I was standing on the dock, watching as the *Silver Star* got smaller and smaller."

"I'm not even sure I know where the Ivory Coast is supposed to be," I say.

"Africa," she replies.

"Well, I know that much, sure. But I don't know *where* in Africa. And it's an awfully big place."

"In the dream, you knew," she assures me, and I don't press the point further. It's her dream, not mine, even if it's not a dream she's actually ever had, even if it's only something she's making up as she goes along. "In the dream," she continues, undaunted, "you had a travel brochure that the ticket agent had given you. It was printed all in colour. There was a sort of tree called a bombax tree, with bright red flowers. There were elephants, and a parrot. There were pretty women with skin the colour of roasted coffee beans."

"That's quite a brochure," I say, and for a moment I watch the plastic tacked over the window as it rustles in the wind off the bay. "I wish I could have a look at it right now."

"I thought what a warm place it must be, the Ivory Coast," and I glance down at her, at those drowsy eyes watching me. She lifts her right hand from the damp sheets, and patches of iridescent skin shimmer ever so faintly in the morning light. The sun shows through the thin, translucent webbing stretched between her long fingers. Her sharp nails brush gently across my unshaven cheek, and she smiles. Even I don't like to look at those teeth for very long, and I let my eyes wander back to the flapping plastic. The wind is picking up, and I think maybe this might be the day when I finally have to find a hammer, a few ten-penny nails, and enough discarded pine slats to board up the hole in the wall.

"Not much longer before the snow comes," she says, as if she doesn't need to hear me speak to know my thoughts.

"Probably not for a couple of weeks yet," I counter, and she blinks and turns her head towards the window.

In the village, I have a tiny room in a boarding house on Darling Street, and I keep a spiral-bound notebook hidden between my mattress and box springs. I've written a lot of things in that book that I shouldn't like any other human being to ever read—secret desires, things I've heard, and read; things she's told me, and things I've come to suspect all on my own. Sometimes, I think it would be wise to keep the notebook better hidden. But it's true that the old woman who owns the place, and who does all the housekeeping herself, is afraid of me, and she never goes into my room. She leaves the clean linen and towels in a stack outside my door. Months ago, I stopped taking my meals with the other lodgers, because the strained silence and fleeting, leery glimpses that attended those breakfasts and dinners only served to give me indigestion. I expect the widow O'Dwyer would ask me to find a room elsewhere, if she weren't so intimidated by me. Or, rather, if she weren't so intimidated by the company I keep.

Outside the shanty, the wind howls like the son of Poseidon, and, for the moment, there's no more talk of the Ivory Coast or dreams or sailing gaily away into the sunset aboard the *Silver Star*.

Much of what I've secretly scribbled there in my notebook concerns that terrible storm that you claim rose up from the sea to steal away the little park and the bandshell, the diner and the jail and the dress shops, the two churches, one Presbyterian and the other Catholic. From what you've said, it must have happened sometime in September of '57 or '58, but I've spent long afternoons in the small public library, carefully poring over old newspapers and magazines. I can find no evidence of such a tempest making landfall in the autumn of either of those years. What I can verify is that the village once extended down the hill, past the marshes and dunes to the bay, and there was a lively, prosperous waterfront. There was trade with Gloucester and Boston, Nantucket and Newport, and the bay was renowned for its lobsters, fat black sea bass, and teeming shoals of haddock. Then, abruptly, the waterfront was all but abandoned sometime before 1960. In print, I've found hardly more than scant and unsubstantiated speculations to account for it, that exodus, that strange desertion. Talk of over-fishing, for instance, and passing comparisons with Cannery Row in faraway California, and the collapse of the Monterey Bay sardine canning industry back on the 1950s. I write down everything I find, no matter how unconvincing, but I permit myself to believe only a very little of it.

"A penny for your thoughts," she says, then shuts her eyes again.

"You haven't got a penny," I reply, trying to ignore the raw, hungry sound of the wind and the constant noise at the window.

"I most certainly do," she tells me, and pretends to scowl and look offended. "I have a few dollars, tucked away. I'm not an indigent."

"Fine, then. I was thinking of Africa," I lie. "I was thinking of palm trees and parrots."

"I don't remember any palm trees in the travel brochure," she says. "But I expect there must be quite a lot of them, regardless."

"Undoubtedly," I agree. I don't say anything else, though, because I think I hear voices, coming from somewhere outside her shack—urgent, muttering voices that reach me despite the wind and the flapping plastic. I can't make out the words, no matter how hard I try. It ought to scare me more than it does. Like I said, one of these nights, they'll do murder against me. One of them alone, or all of them together. Maybe they won't even wait for the conspiring cover of nightfall. Maybe they'll come for me in broad daylight. I begin to suspect my murder would not even be deemed a crime by the people who live in those brightly painted houses up the hill, back beyond the dunes. On the contrary, they might consider it a necessary sacrifice, something to placate the flotsam and jetsam huddling in the ruins along the shore, an oblation of blood and flesh to buy them time.

Seems more likely than not.

"They shouldn't come so near," she says, acknowledging that she too hears the whispering voices. "I'll have a word with them later. They ought to know better."

"They've more business being here than I do," I reply, and she silently watches me for a moment or two. Her grey eyes have gone almost entirely black, and I can no longer distinguish the irises from the pupils.

"They ought to know better," she says again, and this time her tone leaves me no room for argument.

There are tales that I've heard, and bits of dreams I sometimes think I've borrowed—from her or one of her apostles—that I find somewhat more convincing than either newspaper accounts of depleted fish stocks or rumours of a cataclysmic hurricane. There are the spook stories I've overheard, passed between children. There are yarns traded by the half dozen or so grizzled old men who sit outside the filling station near the widow's boarding house, who seem possessed of no greater ambition than checkers and hand-rolled cigarettes, cheap gin and gossip. I have begun to believe the truth is not something that was entrusted to the press, but, instead, an ignominy the town has struggled, purposefully, to forget, and which is now recalled dimly or not at all. There is remaining no consensus to be had, but there *are* common threads from which I have woven rough speculation.

Late one night, very near the end of summer or towards the beginning of fall, there was an unusually high tide. It quickly swallowed the granite jetty and the shingle, then broke across the seawall and flooded the streets of the harbour. There was a full moon that night, hanging low and ripe on the eastern horizon, and by its wicked reddish glow men and women saw the things that came slithering and creeping and lurching out of those angry waves. The invaders cast no shadow, or the moonlight shone straight through them, but was somehow oddly distorted. Or, perhaps, what came out of the sea that night glimmered faintly with an eerie phosphorescence of its own.

I know that I'm choosing lurid, loaded words here—*wicked, lurching, hungry, eerie*—hoping, I suppose, to discredit all the cock and bull I've heard, trying to neuter those schoolyard demons. But, in my defence, the children and the old men whom I've overheard were quite a bit less discreet. They have little use, and even less concern for the sensibilities of people who aren't going to believe them, anyway. In some respects, they're almost as removed as she, as distant and disconnected as the other shanty dwellers here in the rubble at the edge of the bay.

"I would be sorry," she says, "if you were to sail away to Africa."

"I'm not going anywhere. There isn't anywhere I want to go. There isn't anywhere I'd rather be."

She smiles again, and this time I don't allow myself to look away. She has teeth like those of a very small shark, and they glint wet and dark in healthy pink gums. I have often wondered how she manages not to cut her lips or tongue on those teeth, why there are not always trickles of drying blood at the corners of her thin lips. She's bitten into me enough times now. I have ugly crescent scars across my shoulders and chest and upper arms to prove that we are lovers, stigmata to make her apostles hate me that much more.

"It's silly of you to waste good money on a room," she says, changing the course of our conversation. "You could stay here with me. I hate the nights when you're in the village and I'm alone."

"Or you could go back with me," I reply. It's a familiar sort of futility, this exchange, and we both know our lines by heart, just as we both know the outcome.

"No," she says, her shark's smile fading. "You know that I can't. You know they'd never have me up there," and she nods in the general direction of the town.

And yes, I do know that, but I've never yet told her that I do.

The tide rose up beneath a low red moon and washed across the waterfront. The sturdy wharf was shattered like matchsticks, and boats of various shapes and sizes—dories and jiggers, trollers and Bermuda-rigged schooners—were torn free of their moorings and tossed onto the shivered docks. But there was no storm, no wind, no lashing rain. No thunder and lightning and white spray off the breakers. The air was hot and still that night, and the cloudless sky blazed with the countless pin-prick stars that shine brazenly through the punctured dome of Heaven.

"They say the witch what brought the trouble came from someplace up Amesbury way," I heard one of the old men tell the others, months and months ago. None of his companions replied, neither nodding their heads in agreement, nor voicing dissent. "I heard she made offerings every month, on the night of the new moon, and I heard she had herself a daughter, though I never learned the girl's name. Don't guess it matters, though. And the name of her father, well, ain't nothing I'll ever say aloud."

That night, the cobbled streets and alleyways were fully submerged for long hours. Buildings and houses were lifted clear of their foundations and dashed one against the other. What with no warning of the freakish tide, only a handful of the waterfront's inhabitants managed to escape the deluge and gain the safety of higher ground. More than two hundred souls perished, and for weeks afterwards the corpses of the drowned continued to wash ashore. Many of the bodies were so badly mangled that they could never be placed with a name or a face, and went unclaimed, to be buried in unmarked graves in the village beyond the dunes.

I can no longer hear the whisperers through the thin walls of her shack, so I'll assume that they've gone, or have simply had their say and subsequently fallen silent. Possibly, they're leaning now with their ears pressed close to the corrugated aluminium and rotting clapboard, listening in, hanging on her every syllable, even as my own voice fills them with loathing and jealous spite.

"I'll have a word with them," she tells me for the third time. "You should feel as welcome here as any of us."

The sea swept across the land, and, by the light of that swollen, sanguine moon, grim approximations of humanity moved freely, unimpeded, along the flooded thoroughfares. Sometimes they swam, and sometimes they went about deftly on all fours, and sometimes they shambled clumsily along, as though walking were new to them and not entirely comfortable.

"They weren't men," I overheard a boy explaining to his friends. The boy had ginger-coloured hair, and he was nine, maybe ten years old at the most. The children were sitting together at the edge of the weedy vacant lot where a travelling carnival sets up three or four times a year.

"Then were they women?" one of the others asked him.

The boy frowned and gravely shook his head. "No. You're not listening. They weren't women, neither. They weren't *anything* human. But, what I heard said, if you were to take all the stuff gets pulled up in trawler nets—all the hauls of cod and flounder and eel, the dogfish and the skates, the squids and jellyfish and crabs, *all* of it and whatever else you can conjure—if you took those things, still alive and wriggling, and could mush them up together into the shapes of men and women, *that's* exactly what walked out of the bay that night."

"That's not true," a girl said indignantly, and the others stared at her. "That's not true at all. God wouldn't let things like that run loose."

The ginger-haired boy shook his head again. "They got different gods than us, gods no one even knows the names for, and that's who the Amesbury witch was worshipping. Those gods from the bottom of the ocean."

"Well, I think you're a liar," the girl told him. "I think you're a blasphemer *and* a liar, and, also, I think you're just making this up to scare us." And then she stood and stalked away across the weedy lot, leaving the others behind. They all watched her go, and then the ginger-haired boy resumed his tale.

"It gets worse," he said.

A cold rain has started to fall, and the drops hitting the tin roof sound almost exactly like bacon frying in a skillet. She's moved away from me, and is sitting naked at the edge of the bed, her long legs dangling over the side, her right shoulder braced against the rusted iron headboard. I'm still lying on the damp sheets, staring up at the leaky ceiling, waiting for the water tumbling from the sky to find its way inside. She'll set jars and cooking pots beneath the worst of the leaks, but there are far too many to bother with them all.

"I can't stay here forever," she says. It's not the first time, but, I admit, those words always take me by surprise. "It's getting harder being here. Every day, it gets harder on me. I'm so awfully tired, all the time."

I look away from the ceiling, at her throat and the peculiar welts just below the line of her chin. The swellings first appeared a few weeks back, and the skin there has turned dry and scaly, and has taken on a sickly greyish-yellow hue. Sometimes, there are boils, or seeping blisters. When she goes out among the others, she wears the silk scarf I gave her, tied about her neck so that they won't have to see. So they won't ask questions she doesn't want to answer.

"I don't have to go alone," she says, but doesn't turn her head to look at me. "I don't want to leave you here."

"I can't," I say.

"I know," she replies.

And this is how it almost always is. I come down from the village, and we make love, and she tells me her dreams, here in this ramshackle cabin out past the dunes and dog roses and the gale-stunted trees. In her dreams, I am always leaving her behind, buying tickets on tramp steamers or signing on with freighters, sailing away to the Ivory Coast or Portugal or Singapore. I can't begin to recall all the faraway places she's dreamt me leaving her for. Her nightmares have sent me round and round the globe. But the truth is, *she's* the one who's leaving, and soon, before the first snows come.

I know it (though I play her games), and all her apostles know it, too. The ones who have come down from the village and never gone back up the hill again. The vagrants and squatters and winos, the lunatics and true believers, who have turned their backs on the world, but only after it turned its back on them. Destitute and cast away, they found the daughter of the sea, each of them, and the shanty town is dotted with their tawdry, makeshift altars and shrines. She knows precisely what she is to them, even if she won't admit it. She knows that these lost souls have been blinded by the trials and tribulations of their various, sordid lives, and *she* is the soothing darkness they've found. She is the only genuine balm they've ever known against the cruel glare of the sun and the moon, which are the unblinking eyes of the gods of all mankind.

She sits there, at the edge of the bed. She is always alone, no matter how near we are, no matter how many apostles crowd around and eavesdrop and plot my demise. She stares at the flapping sheet of plastic tacked up where the windowpane used to be, and I go back to watching the ceiling. A single drop of rainwater gets through the layers of tin and tarpaper shingles and lands on my exposed belly.

She laughs softly. She doesn't laugh very often any more, and I shut my eyes and listen to the rain.

"You can really have no notion how delightful it will be, when they take us up and throw us, with the lobsters, out to sea," she whispers, and then laughs again.

I take the bait, because I almost always take the bait.

"But the snail replied 'Too far, too far!' and gave a look askance," I say, quoting Lewis Carroll, and she doesn't laugh. She starts to scratch at the welts below her chin, then stops herself.

"In the halls of my father," she says, "there is such silence, such absolute and immemorial peace. In that hallowed place, the mind can be still. There is serenity, finally, and an end to all sickness and fear." She pauses, and looks at the floor, at the careless scatter of empty tin cans and empty bottles and bones picked clean. "But," she continues, "it will be lonely down there, without you. It will be something even worse than lonely."

I don't reply, and in a moment, she gets to her feet and goes to stand by the door.

# THE HAG STONE

*by* CONRAD WILLIAMS

## I

### A DICEY FLIGHT · I ARRIVE SAFELY AT FORT REQUIN

IT WAS MY first trip anywhere in an aeroplane.

I know that must sound absurd coming from a man in his seventies, especially in this day and age when cheap flights are so freely available and people hop on and off aircraft as if they were buses; but I (nor my wife for that matter) had never entertained the thought to go travelling, let alone sight-seeing. My idea of hell was a hot beach in a land where English was not spoken, and endless hours were spent chasing away flies from whatever inedible repast might be put in front of me at a less-than-reputable restaurant.

No, my heart (though recently damaged) was meant to remain in England. However, the best-laid plans, and all that.

How was I to know I would suffer a heart attack? I say that with the lack of foresight we all of us are cursed with in regard to the proclivities of health, but the question really ought to have been: how could I have expected anything *but* a heart attack? For the seat of all my passion and feeling had been under assault for two weeks, since my darling wife, my beautiful Clarissa, succumbed to the persistent and aggressive cancer in her spine.

Though the likelihood is that I don't have much time left on this Earth, what time I do have will no doubt be shadowed by the memories of her final months and the pathetic attempts by the medical staff to arrest the inevitable. Clarissa had quite reconciled herself to that long sleep; I, less so, and I'm afraid I was something of a quivering wreck whenever I sat with her in her hospital bed.

She seemed to be shrinking by the day, but her smile remained a constant, as warm and as inviting as it had been on the first day I was favoured with it, over fifty years previously. And the grip of her warm, smooth hand retained its urgency.

Alas, a sure touch and a ready smile are not enough to repel death, and she succumbed one rainy Tuesday afternoon while I was failing to persuade one of the vending machines in the corridor to yield a hot chocolate.

A fortnight later, not sleeping well, drinking rather more than I ought and in a constant mither of wringing hands and regret, I suffered, in the lobby of a city-centre hotel, what my doctor called a heart seizure. Arrhythmia, apparently: the chaotic spasming of the muscle. I was rescued by the smart thinking of a receptionist who had first-aid training and knew where the nearest defibrillating device could be found.

I was in hospital for a week, and then happily discharged with a hefty arsenal of pills to take every day for the rest of whatever life I had left. I was warned, before leaving, about depression, and that a number of renowned foundations were available for me to consult, but I would not have it. I'd never felt happier. I was convinced that the seizure had marked the return of my wife as something living, and within me, to provide succour and prevent me from falling into a funk of loneliness. Any murmurs from now on I would attribute to her, geeing me up, reminding me to take my medicine, or prompting me to remember her.

Though it was my first journey through the air, it was a notable one, or so I was assured, by my fellow passengers on the flight down to Guernsey from Heathrow, and the pilot of the little Aurigny Trislander, a propeller plane that took us from Guernsey to Alderney.

The weather was atrocious—a knot or two harder and the flight, apparently, would have been cancelled. We were buffeted like a favourite toy in the hands of a clumsy child. I must say, I found it tremendous fun, like being on a fairground ride, although the three other people sitting near me—a man and woman and (presumably) their young son—were a little green around the gills and spent much of their time clutching at sick bags and groaning at each other.

The sea was a riot of white breakers and I could not see any boats braving the swells. That said, I did see something moving against the waves, but at this distance I could not be sure what it was. A seal of some sort, perhaps. Whatever it was, it was alone, and moving fairly quickly.

Then all too soon we were coming in to land at the tiny airstrip. It was a little bumpy, but the pilot knew what he was doing and within a minute we were unfastening our seatbelts and being guided out of the aircraft towards the baggage claim and the single counter that served as passport control.

Soon, trusty suitcase in hand, I was in a taxi headed for my destination. I felt excited and childish, my head twisting this way and that as I took in the sweep of the land, and the houses nestled within it. Gulls were fastened to the sky—it was as if they need never flap their wings again. I was hoping for something exotic, I suppose, but this was only the Channel Islands after all. Even my taxi driver was from Manchester!

He was pleasant enough, and I chatted with him about this and that before the road suddenly gave way to a dirt track along the coast—a precipitous drop to our right on to jags of rock causing me to lean obviously to my left, as if that might help us from slipping down. The taxi driver moved with extreme caution; there were deep potholes here, he explained, and notwithstanding the cliff, he didn't want to damage the car, or cause it to become stuck.

It took an age, but once we'd rounded the bluff, I saw our destination for the first time: Fort Requin, a beautiful old citadel built into and, somehow, out of a series of huge rocks that were like a final attempt by the island to reach as far as possible into the sea. Built around the advent of steam power, the fort was seen as a necessary bulwark against any possible naval attack by the French. Later it was seized by Hitler as a stepping-stone in his desire for British invasion. Once more I mentally thanked my sons, Brian and Gordon, for arranging and paying for this little holiday for me. They were fine boys and I was lucky to have them.

The taxi driver steered us down an incline and across a causeway to another slight rise which took us to the entrance to the fort. He parked and retrieved my bags from the boot and wished me a pleasant stay.

As I reached the gateway, the door swung open to reveal a tall man in half-moon spectacles and a bottle-green raincoat. This was the caretaker, a Mr. Standish, who briskly showed me to my rooms and gave me a map outlining the other accommodations that comprised Fort Requin.

"Here is the communal dining room," he pointed out, "and here is a recreation room. No television, I'm afraid. Just books and some board games."

I told him I was here for long walks and that while I might pick up a book or two, the only other activity likely to be given its head was plenty of sleep.

"Very good too," he said, with a smile. "Now I must be away. Your food will be delivered some time in the next hour or so—we tried to get everything on your list, but we might have had to mix and match in some cases. The Cotterhams, the family sharing the facilities with you this week, have already arrived and are unpacking in the Officer's Quarters."

He put his finger to his forehead as if to help himself remember some important piece of information. "Two more things before I go. There is a Union Jack, neatly folded in the recreation room. It's purely optional, but we invite our guests to hoist it on the flagpole to announce the fort is occupied—you'll find it on top of the Upper Magazine, it's on the map. There's a bugle too, if you fancy blasting out reveille or taps. Now, the other issue is the Outpost. It's no longer used because it's inaccessible. Well, what I mean is that you can get to where there used to be a walkway across to it, but that's all collapsed into the sea now. We have a danger sign and some metal fencing in place, but the determined will find a way around it. I'd respectfully ask that you steer clear of it, and do what you can to ensure young Ralph—he's about twelve or so—steers clear of it too. I know it's his parents' responsibility, but you know what happens. They might oversleep, as parents of older children are wont to do, and he might nip off on his own. We've got a chap coming in to completely seal off the archway with bricks and mortar, but for this week, I ask that you keep a sea-faring eye open for potential mishaps."

I told him he could rely on me while I was here and that was that. I closed the door behind him and, turning, took a deep breath of the salty, crisp air before heading down to the German Casement, which was to be my home for the next six nights.

# II

## THE COTTERHAMS · THE FISHERMAN · THE OUTPOST (I)

What a queer place this was! I was in a room with two beds, and racks on the wall showing where the original bunks had been positioned for the German soldiers of the Third Reich—imagine it!—to lay their weary, English-hating heads. I knew Alderney's citizens had been given the option to evacuate at the start of the war, when the British government decided they held no military significance and would not be defended.

After the German occupation in 1940, four concentration camps built on the island—the only camps of their kind to exist on British soil—housed around 6,000 slave labourers helping to build fortifications, shelters and gun emplacements. What a desolate, lonely island this must have been for those stationed or imprisoned here.

The view from my window was staggering. The ocean and the surrounding rocks—including Les Etacs, an island turned white by the thousands of northern gannets that had colonised it—and miles of thunderous sky. Once more my eye was drawn to the churning sea, and the compulsion that something was swimming within it, against its currents, creating a wake as it moved just beneath the surface.

I kept my eye on it, praying to see the tail of a whale, or the joyous leap of a dolphin, but it remained submerged and, after a few seconds, the wake receded, as whatever it was finned to depths that were only imaginable.

It was slightly on the chilly side in the room, despite the presence of a cast-iron Duchess radiator, and there was a faint smell of oil, as if the grease from the Germans' guns, or the oil from their lamps, had left indelible traces of itself behind.

I unpacked, hanging my clothes in one of the pair of handsome oak wardrobes, then I took a brief, refreshing shower and dressed for dinner. I reached the kitchen just as the last of the supplies were being delivered. A box on the long dining table had my name pinned to it. A woman was putting the last of the groceries away from her own three boxes. She was the kind of woman who wears a faint smile no matter how laborious the task being undertaken, and went about her work briskly, no-nonsense. She'd have been the kind of woman depicted on those old DIG FOR VICTORY posters that were produced during the war.

"Mrs. Cotterham?" I said, and she looked up, startled.

"Oh my!" she said. "You did surprise me. I think we took that earlier flight together."

"You're right," I said, recognising her now that the colour was back in her cheeks. Her hair was tied neatly back from her face too. "I do hope you feel better?"

"Much better, thank you, Mr...." she eyed my grocery crate, "Stafford?"

"Adrian, please," I said.

"You're alone?"

"I'm afraid so. This is meant to be a convalescence of sorts. I'm recovering from illness."

"Oh dear, I'm sorry to hear it," she said. "I hope you don't mind that we're here too."

"I wasn't expecting to be here by myself," I said. "And, truth be told, I'm glad there is someone else. I imagine this place would be a little alarming for the lone visitor."

"You're right there," she said. "Especially if this weather carries on."

The wind groaned as if in agreement, and it heralded the arrival of

Mr. Cotterham and his son. We shook hands and exchanged names (Penny and Alastair; young Ralph I'd already heard about) and Penny invited me to dine with them. We all mucked in together, peeling vegetables, uncorking wine, setting the table and, before long, we were tucking into excellent pork chops and trading tales as if we had been known to each other for months as opposed to minutes.

By pudding (pears poached in red wine, delicious) I had learned Alastair (a tousle-haired, portly gentleman with a somewhat out-of-fashion moustache—he reminded me of the playwright Colin Welland) was a technical writer who specialised in the history of British military jets since World War II. He already had three books under his belt regarding decommissioned fighters, bombers and reconnaissance aircraft. I liked the self-deprecatory way in which he brushed off his achievements as so many dry accounts, and liked even more Penny's leaping to his defence.

Penny was visibly older than Alastair, but she was slim and healthy-looking, so it came as no surprise to find out she was a yoga teacher. Ralph was polite enough, I suppose, but a victim to that dislocated air that afflicts many children on the cusp of teen-hood. I'm sure he'd rather have been anywhere else than that table with its collection of ageing adults talking about their obsessive, exclusive little interests.

Sure enough, when we'd put down our spoons, he asked to be excused and that was the last I saw of him that night.

We adjourned to the sitting room.

"Comics and Nintendo," his father said, dismissively, as we sat down.

"At least he's reading," I reasoned. "Comics didn't do too badly for me when I was a lad."

"That was then," he said. "Your comics were filled with text. His comics are just excuses for a slew of jokes about burps, farts and bogeys."

"There are worse things to pore over."

"Oh, he does, believe me. Do you know a boy who isn't fascinated by blood and death?"

"Ah," I said. "But, there's something you can exercise control over at least, no?"

Penny sniffed at that. "We can stop him from playing violent games, or watching video nasties, or whatever they're called nowadays—"

"Barbaric Blu-Rays!" Alastair interjected.

"—but," continued Penny, "we can't, I won't, censor the news. Even now." She poured out the last of the wine.

I stared at her blankly. I hadn't seen a front page or a news bulletin since Clarissa's death. "What's happened?"

"The Fisherman," said Alastair, ominously.

I drained my glass. "The fisherman? What's this, a quota story? I don't see how that could possibly—"

"The Fisherman is a killer. He's been preying on women for the past month. Always women. Always on or near beaches. Never inland. Their bodies are often found dumped in beds of seaweed." Here Alastair lowered his voice and craned his neck as if he could ascertain whether Ralph was properly out of earshot. "And always, their wombs have been removed."

"How ghastly," I cried, and wished there was some of the wine left so I could rinse away the terrible, claggy feeling of dread at the back of my throat.

"Yes," Penny said. She seemed a little pale, although that might have been down to the bleaching effect of the nearby lamp. "What's worse is that these murders have not just been confined to one area."

I spluttered some disbelieving grunt in response, but Alastair was nodding.

"It's true," he said. "The first body was discovered in Morecambe Bay. Two days later there was a body, same *modus operandi*, washed up on the beach in Oban, and then, where was the next one, Pen?"

"They've found them all over. Scarborough, Southwold, Newquay… the last one was in Portsmouth. Yesterday."

The conversation had knocked the stuffing out of me. Silence seemed to have been enforced by the gravity of the story. Their wombs? What could they possibly—I sighed. I was a seventy-four-year-old man trying to understand the machinations of a world I'd outgrown. It was beyond me. And a part of me was glad.

The weather had died down a little and I didn't want to go to bed with a thick head, so I bid them a good night and, availing myself of one of the torches by the front door, stepped out into the courtyard. Samphire and mesembryanthemum were growing wildly on the rocks across from the stairwell. I gently ran my hands over the foliage while my attention was drawn to the black cauldron of the sea, faintly visible beneath the ice-white frosting of light edging the clouds.

My curiosity had been piqued in regard to the Outpost Mr. Standish had done his best to scare me away from. No longer tired (in fact, I was rejuvenated by the sea air and the prospect of a little adventure), I skipped on to the greensward and picked a route up through the broken collars of rock to a channel carved into the face of the cliff. Here it was that I saw the first barrier to my progress, but it was little more than a wire-mesh fence, unattached, and I was able to lift and reposition it to allow me through.

Warning signs: DANGER. STEEP DROP. DO NOT ENTER. The torch showed me where to put my feet. Suddenly I was there, standing before an arch that did little more than frame a precipitous drop to the fangs of rock below. The walkway connecting the Outpost to the mainland was gone, destroyed by nature most likely. I imagined it had existed as a crow's nest kind of place—the view of the sea was unhindered.

Perhaps a radio operator would have spent time there, ready to send an urgent telegram to the Wolf's Lair at the first sign of aggression from His Majesty's fleet. From here it looked like a tiny space, enough for one man and a rickety little bunk. I wished I could get across to satisfy my curiosity, but it was impossible.

Reluctantly, I turned back, but I had been re-energised and I fancied I'd need more of a walk to coax tiredness back into my limbs. Also, I'd been somewhat unnerved by Alastair's revelations regarding The Fisherman (not to mention the lascivious glee he divined from relating the story) and I wanted to erase it, or at least remove it for the time being, from my thoughts. No man could entertain the prospect of sleep with that kind of nastiness flitting around his head.

Making sure I had a key to the front gate, I let myself out on to the causeway, and angled down to the beach.

\* \* \*

## III

### LATE-NIGHT CONSTITUTIONAL · A CURIOSITY · THE OLD MAN · A BAD NIGHT'S SLEEP

Bliss! In all my time, even while I was courting Clarissa and we'd spent the odd weekend in Blackpool, I'd never taken a midnight stroll along the seashore. What I'd been missing!

I saw—or rather, heard—bats, and even felt their tiny wings changing the currents of the air close to my face. I saw phosphorescence in the waves—glimmering green beads of light strung out like a discarded necklace. I was convinced I felt the tremor of the sea as a whale crashed into it, playing deliriously and celebrating its freedom. I thought I might have heard it too, that wildly exciting, but strangely comforting sequence of moans and squeals, both mordant and uplifting in the same breath.

My feet crunched satisfyingly on the shingle beach, a melange of ancient pebbles, shells, polished fragments of glass and what have you, and my spirits were replenished. I trained the torch upon my intended route, to ensure I didn't sprain an ankle on any rogue lengths of driftwood, but I needn't have bothered—the ambient light cast by the concealed moon was sufficient to navigate by.

After a good half an hour, I was starting to feel properly tired, that good, ache-filled enervation that comes from honest endeavour. I knew I would sleep well, despite the oily smell of the Quarters and the thoughts of the ghosts of German soldiers who had visited any and all kinds of unpleasantness on the island's prisoners. *That was over seventy years ago*, I admonished myself. *You've lived your life in the span since then.* Spilled milk, and all that.

I was about to turn in when the torchlight picked something out that caused my mind to snag for a second. That's funny, I thought. Some anomaly in the pattern of the beach. I know that sounds a little strange, given that a beach of shingle can't really lay claim to any sort of pattern, or logic, but there you have it. I felt a difference in the stones. And there it was. A pebble that was larger than the others (about the size of a lime, but flatter), highly polished, and with a hole bored right through, off-centre. It looked like something you might wear on a length of chain or leather.

It was a handsome chunk of stone, and I pocketed it immediately. I poked around for a few minutes more, thinking I might find another like it, but the beach had retained its anonymity. It was then, as I began the slow march back up to the causeway, that I was given another surprise.

I saw thrashing limbs breaking the surface of the sea, and a furious foaming as something came fast towards the shore. I caught my breath and staggered backwards, almost tripping in the shingle. The limbs disappeared, submerging, and the relative calm returned, but then a great column of white rose as whatever it was resurfaced, this time head-first.

The water cascaded off it to reveal a naked man. I laughed out loud with relief and consternation. He seemed more stunned than I, however, and halted his progress from the water mid-stride, almost shying away from me as I padded through the shingle to greet him.

"Are you all right?" I called. I was dressed in thick layers but I could still feel the chill in the air. This man must have been swimming in temperatures close to freezing. He didn't say anything and I thought, My God, he's in shock. He's been washed ashore from a ship run aground on the rocks. But then he seemed to find his voice and I realised his hesitation was down to a lack in his English—he was obviously from distant shores. Perhaps Scandinavian. Perhaps Slav.

"I apologise," he said, "if I startle you."

"It's not a problem," I assured him. "You just don't expect to see people swimming at this time of night, at this time of the year."

"I am swimming every day," he said. "All year round."

"Do you live on the island?"

"This area has been in my family's blood for centuries."

"My name's Adrian," I said, and extended my hand. He seemed nonplussed, as if he had never been taught the rituals of introduction.

"Gluckmann," he said, finally, but he left my hand dangling.

I nodded, withdrew my arm, suddenly struck by the farcical situation I was in: chatting at midnight with a naked man of my own age—if not older—in the freezing cold.

"Well," I said. "It was nice to meet you."

I left him on the shore and picked my way back up to the causeway, pausing at the top to look back. He was still standing there, staring after me. There was no evidence of any clothes, or even a towel, nearby. I felt giddy. I felt as though I wanted to run away, as fast as I could.

We had not shaken hands, yet I felt as though my skin was greasy from his touch. And there was a smell in my clothes, though it hadn't been there before I met him—a fishy smell, but not the clean, marine piquancy one knows from clean seawater; this was the days-old odour of tainted things, of rotting prawns and mussels gone bad. And hadn't his skin been a little strange? Was it just that he was old that it seemed spongy and loose, with the texture of raw tripe? Was it merely the slackening of tissue from the piling on of years that gave his fingers a webbed appearance?

Nonsense, I told myself, over and over, as I fumbled to get the key in the lock with fingers that felt thick and unresponsive with fear. I was close to crying out, but I must not. If I disturbed the Cotterhams from their slumber I'd have some explaining to do, and I had nothing to offer beyond the unhinging of my own sanity.

Once I had the door closed on the world, I leaned my head against the wood and tried to calm my laboured heart. I felt his scrutiny through the stone ramparts. Was that who I'd seen earlier? Both from the window of the plane, and while taking in the view from the Soldier's Quarters? Nonsense, nonsense. But the conviction would not be dissolved, no matter how much I tried to reason with myself.

You would die if you spent too much time in that water. Exposure, hypothermia... yet he had looked as unbothered by the perilous temperatures as an elephant seal, his flesh retaining a healthy pinkness despite its saggy constitution.

I stumbled towards bed, making sure I locked the door of the Soldier's Quarters. The cold had not been vanquished by that old radiator. Fully clothed, I slid between the sheets of my bed and fell into a tortuous sleep populated by an impossible creature, born from the silly discomfort that Gluckmann had instilled in me, yet blown up into a thing of terror so alarming I could barely credit how my mind had come to fashion it.

My imagination was that of a normal human being, a dull old man if I was being honest. I had never been a fan of the kind of films that were popular among the young: films about death and blood, full of monsters that hunted for human meat. Not my cup of tea. And yet here was a beast that would not look out of place in such a feature.

I dreamed of the old man standing at the sea's edge, and changing... His horribly soft skin hung in swags around him like discarded clothes. Beneath this thin film that kept his shape vaguely human thrashed an oily roil of cartilaginous limbs, a knot of furious movement like that of an overdue infant impatient to be born. I saw the shudder of his head as his jaws reared back, carrying such a great cargo of teeth that they ought not be able to fit in a human mouth. He was making awful *gluk-gluk* noises in his throat, which was blocked, crammed with food he had not chewed properly.

His eyes bulged as he worked this mass, but even as he struggled to swallow whatever it was, he was raising more fistfuls of dinner to mash between his fangs—what looked like filthy carrot tops, but which resolved themselves into the hair of dismembered men, women and children, burst and broken between his fingers. He was gigantic, then, though my dream up until that point had not given me a frame of reference against which he could be measured.

I felt myself, in that sickly incapable way one has in nightmares, try to turn and run as his bloodshot eyes found me, but he was upon me within one stride. I could smell the high, ammoniac reek of his breath, feel the chill of his body assault me like hammering waves at a weather-beaten shoreline. I knew his name, though it made my brain bleed from every aperture to think it, let alone say it, if indeed I had the tongue for such a conglomeration of alien sounds.

*Uhogguath. Uhogguath.*

It sounded like the kind of wet, stertorous breathing a predator does when it is head-deep in carrion. His hand closed around me. I felt his fingers squeeze the life from my lungs. Red filled my vision. I felt the grind of bones as he pulverised my body, felt the furnace of his lungs as they churned carious breath around the target of my head.

When I woke up, my nails having dug into the palms hard enough to draw blood, the name was so much air hissing from between my teeth and I could barely remember it, only that my speaking of it in the dream had caused the oceans to yawn open to their beds, where pregnant things struggled and palpated and razored each other with claws, foul and black like something found rotting at the bottom of a fruit bowl. Things that were not for the sane to alight upon.

The wind was howling once more at the edges of the room and, had I not been reassured that the rock and the living quarters were almost one and the same, I would have believed that the weather could tear open the face of the cliff and deliver me to this churning sea where its bedevilled, unnatural population would devour me in a trice.

## IV

### THE DISAGREEABLE MATTER OF THE HARE · FISH AND CHIPS · AN UNFORTUNATE ACCIDENT · THE CORNER OF MY EYE

After a shower, and a modest breakfast—a handful of nuts mixed with Greek yoghurt and honey—I felt emboldened enough to share the dream with my fellow guests. Penny blanched somewhat when I told her about the realisation that the fistful of carrot-tops was nothing of the sort.

"I think that's easily the most dreadful thing I've ever heard," she said.

"Oh come," protested her husband. "There are worse things every night on the news. This is a dream, a confection of the brain, that's all." I could see that he was unhappy with me. I hadn't thought this through, convinced only that it would make for an amusing anecdote. All it had done was upset Penny, position Alastair against me as a result, and remind me of the whole sordid evening. Ralph was the only one who seemed impressed by my narrative.

"I found this on the beach," I said, rooting in my pocket, desperate to claw back some vestige of respect. I held up the stone like a trophy. "Pretty little thing, isn't it?"

And it was, even more so in daylight. The stone had been washed smooth by countless millennia of tidal movement, the hole perhaps created by centuries of focused boring by a channel of water when it had become trapped in one position. Penny was suitably impressed, and I felt the mood change for the better.

She took the stone from me—I felt a sudden pang of resentment at that—and cooed over the striations in the stone, the little glints and glimmers of silica or quartz. I found my resentment deepen when she started to lecture me about what it was called.

"An adder stone," she said, "or a hag stone. They're meant to possess magical properties. Some would have it that they're made from the hardened saliva of a nest of dragons or serpents, the hole made by the stabbing of their tongues. They work like charms, warding off curses or disease. And if you look through the hole, you can detect traps, or see the true identity of witches or other supernatural creatures."

"Thank you for that lesson," I said, somewhat tartly, and extended my hand. Penny returned the stone and I slipped it into my pocket. "There are others, I'm sure, if you do a little hunting." I felt awkward now that the stone was back in my possession, as if I'd humiliated a child. There remained a stiltedness in the atmosphere that would not be relieved.

I decided to do the honourable thing and retreat for a few hours. The wind was stiff still, but not quite so savage as it had been first thing and anyway, its bark, especially in the exposed knuckle of the Soldier's Quarters, was much worse than its bite. The clouds were torn to shreds by it, allowing a bright, wintry sun to have some say in the matter.

I decided to unlock one of the guest bicycles and take a ride to Bray beach via the coastal road. If I found a windbreak, I could warm up over the newspaper for an hour or two before a spot of lunch.

The romantic notion I had of myself pedalling gaily along a picturesque coastline was swiftly banished once I found myself travelling against the wind. I was breathing heavily by the time I reached the end of the causeway, and I stopped to button my jacket closed in a bid to lessen its drag quotient.

As I did so, I nervously eyed the surf, searching for a glimpse of Mr. Gluckmann. But surely he would be at work today? I tried to imagine what sort of job he did, but could not shake the unpleasant images of him picking his teeth with the splintered bones of something he'd just consumed. He looked like the type of person who entertained vast appetites. When he wasn't swimming, I imagined him eating— his wide, fleshy mouth enveloping tidbits like some ravenous sucking loach at the bottom of a fish tank.

I set myself against the wind once more and wobbled upright, but then my eye was distracted by something on the causeway, blocking my route, and I almost fell from the saddle. Covering my mouth with my hand, I pushed the bicycle to the edge of an apron of blood. It was dried into the causeway rock, but it possessed a lighter shade, suggesting it had not been long since it had been spilled.

At the centre of this was a hare, or the remains of a hare—all I could discern amid the twisted, denuded limbs, was a pair of matted ears and a few dried, salt-encrusted organs that were either inedible or a mouthful too far for whatever had destroyed the poor thing. The chewed, grey foreleg bones poked from the shredded sleeves of its fur like knitting needles freighted with an aborted garment. I guessed it must have been picked clean by seagulls, but what had done for it in the first place, and why had it been left here, like some warning?

I shuddered to imagine Penny or Ralph seeing this (I was in no doubt that they would consider me a dreadful person for leaving it in full view of them, or anybody else who should come this way), so I toed it off the causeway, into a rock pool where the crabs could undress it further at their leisure.

I went on my way, struggling up the hill, negotiating potholes and puddles, cursing the painful, self-inflicted wounds in my palms, until I reached a level surface where I could get a little speed up. It was hard work. The blanketing of many years played its part, but I had to accept that I was not the fit man of even ten years previously.

Eventually I hit a downward slope and freewheeled for the best part of a mile, pretty much all the way to the harbour. I slowly levered myself off the bicycle and locked it against the drainpipe of the harbour inn. My shirt was glued to my back, and I was having trouble calming my breath down. I felt a little panicky for a moment, wondering if I really ought to have been doing this at all, considering my reasons for being here in the first place, but gradually the dials all started to swing back to normal.

There were no suitable hiding places to get away from the wind that hadn't already been snaffled by families and lovers, so I decided I had deserved a drink and settled myself in a corner of the inn's beach-view patio.

I had an interminable wait until some young thing with more tattoos than wit came to take my order. I asked for a pint of bitter and a newspaper, and she trotted off, leaving me to wonder if she'd poured herself into those skin-tight satin trousers.

An hour passed pleasantly enough. Putting some distance between me and the fort (and, by extension, the hare and Mr. Gluckmann) had done wonders for my mood. The beer had something to do with it too, I'm sure, but for the first time I felt as though I was relaxing, that I didn't feel the need to be anywhere or to be doing something. Time was redundant (other than helping me to decide when I should order my lunch) and there were no appointments to fret about. I wrote a couple of postcards to my sons, then leaned back to try to allow as much vitamin D as possible into my skin, and opened the newspaper.

People began to drift into the patio and the tables filled up around me. I asked the waitress for fish and chips and took a break from the cryptic crossword to watch the activity on the beach.

The breakwater was host to a bunch of teenagers in swimming costumes performing bombs and swan dives off the edge. Older people wrapped up against the chill stood along the railing, watching, shaking their heads. It was busy, despite the cold—fun-seekers desperate to eke out one last day of larks on the beach, no matter how distant and weak the sun was becoming.

The waves creamed against the bank of dark, damp sand, pushing before it a line of debris—driftwood, seaweed—that failed to settle. It was turning out to be a lovely day, but my eye was drawn to a haze of dark cloud far away to the east. There was rain in that—you could tell by the faintest teased-away columns within it, darker, grainier, like pleats of shadow in a lace wedding dress.

Ah, Clarissa, you would have loved it here.

I ordered another drink; my meal came. It was good and fresh, if a little on the large side for a person whose appetites had shrunk somewhat in the preceding decade. But as I got to the end of what I presumed was a fillet of battered cod, my teeth crunched into something that was certainly no shell of deep fried flour and egg. Its taste contained the sharp tang of rot. Discreetly, I spat the mouthful back on to my plate, and with a fork I prodded the bolus of semi-chewed fish.

I was appalled to see a mangled conglomeration of piscine body parts reveal themselves on its tines. There were fish-bones, but these were black and oily; an eyeball, larger than one might expect from a cod, made opaque by the process of cooking, and most horrible of all, a fractured beak from an octopus, with a tiny green, decayed fish trapped within. Whatever had happened, this beast had been caught and killed while it was in the process of consuming a meal. Lord only knew why the chef hadn't seen it while he was battering fillets in the kitchen.

I pushed the plate away and pressed a napkin to my lips. It's all right, I thought to myself. I didn't swallow any of that.

The first spots of rain came down, as if in sympathy with my mood. That rain front had whipped in double-quick to dissolve the furthest curve of the beach—about half a mile away—and send packing, in an ecstasy of flapping towels, the people from the sand.

The waitress returned and I told her what had happened. She seemed unimpressed by my story—more put out by the fact that I had regurgitated my meal. She cleared the table without the merest hint of remorse and asked me if I wanted anything else.

"Just the bill," I retorted, and turned my attention back to the breakwater in time to see a man and woman locking their bikes against the railing, while a young boy of around three or four leaned against the lowest bar. I felt my guts loosen.

I've always hated heights, especially seeing others display a fearlessness of them such as those old photographs of men hopping around girders at the top of unfinished skyscrapers in New York.

The divers on the breakwater had decided to call it a day—one of them, a teenage girl in flip-flops and long blonde hair seemed lost, she walked up and down it as if she'd misplaced something.

The bay was emptying quite rapidly now as the grey deepened and the rain—an unpleasant driving mist—enveloped the whole of the beach and set the parasols fluttering. Lights came on.

The little boy fell.

I felt the thump of his body through my feet as he hit the sand. My heart skittered. He was still for a while, but then he began to move like someone coming out of deep sleep—squirming, flinching. His parents were still absorbed by their lock and had not seen the accident occur.

The sea was coming in—I could see it lapping at the boy's feet, like something tasting him. The image—prompted by the unpleasant affair of my meal—disgusted me and I leapt upright, gesturing wildly at the couple on the breakwater. Nobody else had witnessed this. The boy could be lying there with a punctured lung, drowning on his own fluids while Mum and Dad bickered about how best to lock a bicycle to a post.

Now the boy found his voice and let out a cry. He was clearly hurt. The sound did not reach his parents. I hurried down the steps from the patio to the sand, ignoring the bleats of the waitress who had returned to present me with my bill.

As I rounded the first set of steps, a shoulder of the patio blocked out the view to the beach. In my peripheral vision—I was concentrating on my descent and did not want to follow the boy into A&E with a pratfall of my own—I saw a diabolically large shadow separate itself from the surface of the sea, close to where he was lying. It was muscular, gunmetal grey, carrying the sheen of something alive and purposeful.

I began to scream and shout, hollering like a madman, and the faces of the boy's parents were tilted down to me as I rounded the final flight and reached the sand. As I had disturbed them from their obsession with the bike lock, so I had disturbed whatever it was that had risen from the sea.

Now there was just the boy, getting wetter as the tide foamed at his back. I yelled at the dozy idiots to get down to their poor child, and they whirled around like pantomime actors on a stage. Mum started wailing; Dad shouted "Billy! Billy!" in a desperate voice. I suddenly felt bad about raising my voice at them. A momentary loss of concentration and a child's life was in the balance.

I got to him first, moments before the father.

"Don't touch him!" I snapped, and he favoured me with a gaze to cook the skin off my bones. "He might have a bad break. If you lift him up it could be catastrophic."

"He was right next to me," the father said. "He was an inch away."

"It's these railings," I said. "Fine for you and me, but they look like a climbing frame for children."

We crouched by Billy and managed to get him to tell us if he hurt anywhere. It soon became apparent that the relatively dampening effect of the sand and a child's natural "bounciness" had resulted in little more than a bad fright.

"I'll call an ambulance, if you want me to," I offered.

"It's okay," said the mother, as she rocked her son and repeatedly kissed the top of his head. "We'll drop by the hospital and get him seen to."

They thanked me fulsomely and traipsed up to the main road. I felt the occasional pang I got when I see children playing, or being cuddled by their parents. A wishfulness, a wistfulness. The faint memory of tender, unconditional, filial love. And then it was gone, and I turned back to the ocean, which was being whipped into large combers of seething white.

I stared into it for some time, trying to convince myself that what I'd seen was strange shadow-play, a collision of the last glint of sunlight and the enveloping dark of the squall.

"You're bitter," a voice said.

"I beg your pardon?" I turned to see the waitress standing a few feet away, holding out a piece of paper.

"Your bitter," she said. "You just have to pay for your bitter. No charge for the food."

I went back to my bicycle and unlocked it. As I pedalled towards the village centre I caught sight of the blonde teenage girl wrapped in a dark blue towel. She was standing at the end of the breakwater and calling in a tiny, fragmented voice that was pulled this way and that by the wind: "Harry? Harry?"

# V

## MRS. COTTERHAM · THE POLICE MAKE SOME ENQUIRIES · AN INVITATION

I stopped in the village to buy stamps and to send my postcards. I spotted Mr. Gluckmann while I waited in the post office queue— he was talking animatedly to a man in a dark suit who held a clipboard. They were standing in front of an estate agent's window. Mr. Gluckmann was wearing a long, grey raincoat, a hat, scarf and gloves. He looked like someone trying to conceal himself, and I wondered if that was what I would do if I suffered his skin condition or whether I would consider it a problem for the public to have to deal with. My attention was gradually drawn away from that strange old man to a conversation two women ahead of me in the queue were having about the Fisherman. Something had happened on the island, it transpired, that morning.

One of the women, whose hair was so white you'd be forgiven for expecting a light dusting of talc to spring from it at every movement she made, was pale with shock. "On your own doorstep," she said. "Who would countenance such a thing?"

The other woman was more fatalistic. "Why should we be immune? You hear people say 'Why me, why us?' all the time and you have to ask the question, 'Why *not* me, why *not* us?'"

Apparently a group of teenage revellers having a bonfire near the cliffs on the southern edge of the island had spotted a woman in the rocks, close to the airport. Her bright orange umbrella marked her out among the black teeth where she had been discarded, otherwise she might never have been discovered at all. A post-mortem was being carried out that afternoon, but everyone was convinced she would be the next notch on the Fisherman's tally stick.

I was feeling tired by now; within an hour it would be dark and I didn't want to be navigating those treacherous roads with the small, ineffectual lights on the bike. I set off back along the coastal road thinking of Clarissa, and the events of the day, and wondering if, after all, my dead wife would have liked it here.

Thanks to the weird, cruel way of the world, my journey back was just as tough and rigorous as the first leg, the wind having changed direction to beat me in the face as I fought against that long incline to the disintegration of the road, where the slope would turn in my favour, but the poor surface would keep me at a crawl until I reached the causeway. The light had turned gloomy by then, full of mud, so I could no longer see a clear break between the sky and the sea.

I returned the bike to the lean-to inside the gate and hurried back to my room, hoping to avoid the Cotterhams, but Alastair must have been waiting for me because he shot out of the door, his face wild, his normally well-groomed hair antic.

"Have you seen Penny?" he demanded. He said it in such a way as to make any denial seem redundant, yet deny it I had to.

"Not since this morning, when I left," I said. "Why?"

Alastair studied me as if I must be lying, concealing something, and I thought: *The Fisherman. No. No. Surely not.*

"She's missing," he said. "She left this morning to go for a walk, clear her head—she suffers from these awful migraines—and I told her I would have breakfast ready for her return, but an hour went by, then two, and she didn't come back."

"Have you contacted the police? The coast guard?"

He looked suddenly close to tears, as if my saying this had somehow confirmed what he was fearing. "No," he said. "I wanted to wait as long as possible. I wanted to ask you…" His voice tapered off, perhaps as he realised how pathetic he sounded.

"Allow me," I said, and swept past him, into the Officer's Quarters. Ralph was sitting on one of the sofas, his knees drawn up to his chin, trying not to allow the little boy through, but failing miserably. He looked alarmed, forlorn, lost. I tried to smile at him, but the muscles in my face were still stiff from the journey—I must have looked anything but optimistic to him; he turned away.

I managed to get through to the island police office and informed them briefly of the situation and our whereabouts. They told me to stay where we were, and that an officer would be with us within the half-hour.

I went straight to my suitcase and pulled out the small bottle of

Jura I'd brought with me to help keep the nip from my bones. I poured two glasses and handed one to Alastair. He eyed the whisky with suspicion but swallowed it down in one gulp. He sighed. "Thanks," he said. "That was good."

I sipped my own drink in a more leisurely fashion, perched on the edge of the kitchen table while he sat with Ralph and tried to comfort him. When I'd finished I pulled on my coat and went up to the gate and peered through the hatch, trying to make out any kind of movement on the causeway, or the hills leading off in the direction of Bray. After about five minutes I saw headlights following the ruined road towards the causeway.

Ambient light, most probably from the fort's floodlights, picked out the reflective stripes on the side of the car. I unlocked the gate as it pulled up in the small parking space and two uniformed officers climbed out.

We didn't speak. I merely led the way and indicated Alastair's whereabouts. The officers thanked me with the kind of sad, formal smile that heralds no good news.

I listened, a hand over my mouth, as the officers went through the motions. *We're very sorry to have to inform you… terrible news… your wife, Penelope, was found this morning… she died as a result of her injuries…*

It was decided that he and Ralph should leave immediately in order to identify the body. I told Alastair that I would help in any way possible and he thanked me, though I imagine he barely heard what I said to him. I gave Ralph a pat on the back and told him to be strong and look after his dad, but he was in a terrible state, unable to hold the tears back any longer.

What a terrible, terrible ordeal. Losing my own wife had no bearing on this whatsoever. We'd both had time to come to terms with what was happening and Clarissa's demise, though premature, was as near to what one might term a 'good' death as one could hope. I wished Alastair and his boy might find some form of closure. It was pale comfort, I suppose, but at least a body had been found. If the rocks had not snagged her, she might never have been seen again.

I had another glass of whisky in a bid to ward off the maudlin thoughts jostling for attention, and to blunt my senses against the realisation that I was now alone in this remote outcrop. My skin prickled with the thought of Mr. Gluckmann emerging from the water like a sponge that has been chewed beyond recognition. I thought I still smelled the residue of our meeting the previous night in the tips of my fingers and felt my gorge rising. I managed to reach the bathroom before I was sick, and I was bizarrely grateful for the hot stink of whisky fumes to mask that other odour.

Back in the Soldier's Quarters I showered and brushed my teeth, and fell into a weak, feverish sleep invaded by Gluckmann, who was once again naked, his skin looped and pale like something molten. What looked like organic baskets were stitched into the flesh around his waist and slung over his shoulders like bandoliers. Each basket was topped by a scalp, to keep covered whatever lay inside.

He came out of the shadows and the moonlight, where it touched him, made him translucent, and I discerned shadowy joins in the skin, like little blisters. They shimmered in a peristaltic motion, chasing each other over the immense surface area of his body like shoals of fish jinking this way and that to confuse a pursuer. The 'baskets' I noticed were translucent too. Each contained something craven in attitude, hunched in on itself as if trying to hide. Something limbless, yet budding, with a network of veins feeding, and leaving, a soft, red heart beating at the centre. Something unformed, vaguely human, yet riddled with teeth and spines.

I woke up cold and frightened and close to tears. I had wet the bed.

Angry with myself, I stripped the sheets and took another shower. It was a couple of hours until dawn, but I didn't want to court sleep again, not with that poor woman dead and the spectre of Gluckmann so fresh in my thoughts. There would be no refreshing slumber now.

So I dressed and made tea and I took it up to the flagpole, where a cannon the best part of a hundred years old had been left to rust away, a reminder and perhaps a warning of what had occurred on this island during the war. The Union Jack whipped and smacked under assault from the wind. The Cotterhams must have been up to perform the ceremony. I imagined Penny trying to coax a tune from the bugle, the family laughing together at whatever squeaks and squawks flew into the night.

There was no sign of any lone swimmer in the ocean.

The hot drink inside me, I felt much happier. Despite the terror of the dream and the unpleasantness of the previous evening I felt buoyed, optimistic even. I was on the mend and not feeling any deleterious side effects from my hours cycling, beyond a slight rash and a not unpleasurable ache on the tops of my thighs.

I went down to the kitchen to find that at some time in the night Alastair had packed away the family things and vacated their rooms. There were two letters on the kitchen table addressed to me. One was from him, thanking me for my help and wishing me well, the other was from Mr. Standish, hoping that the unfortunate incident had not put me off the island, and asking whether I would like to accompany him—weather permitting—on a kayaking expedition that afternoon.

# VI

## MADMAN'S WOUND · STRIKING TRANSIT AND AN UNEXPECTED HAZARD · THE BONE BOOK

To ensure I spent my energies best on the paddle rather than the pedal, Mr. Standish had arranged for a car to pick me up. Nigel, his son, took me on the brief drive to Murène Bay, a broad beach with a half-mile crescent of sand and a protective wall that Nigel told me had been built during the German Occupation. Mr. Standish ("Call me Trevor, please") was waiting, looking very keen and professional in what I'm led to believe is called a shorty wetsuit. No such apparel for me, but then I wasn't intending to go in the water, as he was.

I was given a life jacket and a paddle and shown to my boat, a handsome thing with a transparent base, to better enjoy any marine life we might espy.

"Very sturdy, very stable boats, these," Trevor assured me. "Honestly, you could do an Irish jig in it and it would barely move. The only problem is that, as a result, it's a bit of a bugger to steer, so you have to work hard to turn left or right."

I told him not to worry. I had done quite a bit of canoeing in the Bristol Channel when younger (a lot younger), but I felt confident in a boat (especially when I'd checked my pocket to make sure the hag stone was safely accompanying me) and once we'd set off and I got the feel of the vessel beneath me, we started making good time heading around the coast to investigate the many caves that ate into the sides of the island.

We were lucky with the wind. Where it had been savage during the nights, now it barely registered, and what sun there was licked my bare arms and felt good on my face. Streams of silver fish darted beneath the boat and it was all I could do to keep my attention on the rocks to make sure I didn't come a cropper and put a hole in a very expensive bit of kit.

"Over here!" called Trevor.

I dutifully paddled over to him and he showed me a deep crevice channelling into the cliff-face. "Madman's Wound," he yelled (the gravelly, rasping cry of the gannets gliding around us was near deafening). "So-called because for a period of about twenty years in the eighteenth century it actually sealed itself shut, healed itself, you might say—some weird realignment of the rocks, tectonic shifting, minor earth tremor, nobody knows for sure—until about seventy years ago, when it mysteriously reappeared."

"Is it safe to go in?"

"Today, yes, I think so. Usually no, because of the swift tides around here and the choppy waters."

"Shall we?"

"If you're feeling intrepid enough, of course."

And so it was that we braved the currents and the rocks to breach that horrible aperture in the cliff-face which looked—I hesitate to say it in case it should make me appear downright strange—vaguely sexual, and travelled through a claustrophobically narrow and low tunnel (having to duck our heads on numerous occasions) until we reached a broadening space that bounced the echoes of the lapping waves and our wondrous voices back at us, along with the eye-watering stench of bat guano.

I felt myself become rather faint—there was no obvious vent in the interior to allow the air in here to be recycled—and had to bring the boat to a stop alongside a low outcrop of rock in order to hold myself steady. To lose consciousness here, in near darkness, was to invite a swift drowning.

The shock of that thought helped revive me a little; but not as much as the inadvertent placing of my hand on something both horrible and yet strangely familiar. I thought I'd simply touched a pile of waste—more of that stinking ordure, most probably, or the body of a bat that had reached the end of its life and was settling into putrescence. But this possessed uniform shape, despite its revolting, organic yield beneath my fingers.

Before I knew what I was doing, I'd scooped up the queer artefact and hidden it beneath the seat of my boat. My heart was drumming—I felt as though I'd committed a crime. I heard Trevor yap on about the cave without taking any of it in, beyond the mention of it being rumoured to be a location for ceremonies involving pagans making sacrifices to the sea.

When his lecture had run its course, we navigated a route back out into open water and wearily paddled back to shore. I was tuckered out, but I felt good. Fresh sea air and honest exertion had repaired me, I believed.

"Look!" called Trevor. I followed the trajectory of his pointing finger and saw what at first glance looked like a lighthouse striped black and white on a promontory of rock fronting one of the smaller islands. But it was far too small and at the top, where there ought to have been a light, was more like a turret.

"Striking transit," Trevor explained. "If you line that up with the white tower behind, so it's blocked from sight, it means you're in the vicinity of a hazard. Underwater rocks that will tear a hole in a ship like a witch's claw through a pair of tights."

We paddled carefully over to the area the striking transit was warning us about. "See?" Trevor yelled, his face intent on the transparent base of his boat. I stared down at the seemingly limitless green-grey sea and felt a twinge of vertigo at the thought of all that depth.

"What am I looking at?" I asked.

"You'll see it in a minute, just keep drifting this way."

I used the paddle as a rudder to steer closer to Trevor's position, and flinched in shock as a cluster of sharp black jags of rocks appeared like thrusting fingers, inches away from the hull.

"Impressive, no?" As he made for shore, Trevor was grinning like a schoolboy who had found a rude magazine. I nodded and began to paddle to catch up with him. A glint of light caught my eye; no natural play of sunlight this… It was a soft, strangely *greasy* light coming from within the water—not a reflection, or a glint of scales on the silver flank of a mackerel.

I'd never seen its like before. It seemed to be some freak conglomeration of limbs and fins and, yes, *mouths*. A hideous collision of terrifying sea creatures, as if many different breeds had somehow managed to find a way to make the worst of their genes apparent in their offspring. It was devilish, unholy. Massive. And it was coming towards me.

It was finning its way around the treacherous columns of rock, moving much more swiftly than its awkward bulk should have allowed. The light came from odd, fleshy baskets arranged around and across its torso, similar to those I'd seen on Gluckmann in my dreams. Scraps of hairy skin—weird 'lids'—flapped back and forth on top of them, allowing a view of what lay coiled inside: wet, dark things with grinning jaws that flashed in deep, layered triangles of silver. Shark mouths on human embryos—my nightmares given oxygen. I hadn't been dreaming. I'd predicted this, or been channelled some hellish vision after meeting Gluckmann that night.

The speed of it.

It changed direction with the dizzying immediacy of a shoal of herring. I saw a strange mix of fin and hand rise up momentarily, splayed as a brake was applied to its progress, and it was like a pale starfish, webbed, peppered with tiny barnacles. It stared up at me with ancient, anemone-encrusted eyes, then at the thing I'd stolen from the cave, and I felt my knees began to shake uncontrollably with fear—they began spanking uncontrollably against the side of the kayak. What had I done?

Trevor was ahead of me now, so did not see me reach down to

pick up my find. I thought my capacity for surprise had been blunted over the past few days, but here was another shock. I felt the wind belted from me as I beheld what could only be described as a book fashioned from the sea—its covers a melange of fish-skin, scales, fins and needle-bones. An eye stared lifeless, opaque, from one corner. The whole had been varnished with some kind of foul-smelling lacquer; it shone like the creamy, nacreous innards of an oyster shell.

I turned the 'pages' and a rotten *nam pla* odour assaulted me like slaps across the face. Mashed, dried fish, teeth and tentacles. Crushed octopus beaks. Frills and gills and suckers. No words. I felt each page as if there might be some braille-like sense to be gleaned from them, but I received nothing for my labour but the stomach-turning reek of decay and the jab of spines into my skin.

How long had it been there in the oily shadows of the cave?

The creature beneath the surface had changed its posture. It had assumed some sort of attitude of attack—everything sharp on its body curved towards me. I tossed the 'book' into the surf and wiped my hands against my jacket. Just some oddity created by a personage with too much time on their hands and an unhealthy relationship with things best left below the surface of the sea.

Nevertheless, the creature was besotted by it: I watched it follow the book as it sank to the shadows. The only thing to suggest any kind of living being had been within my vicinity was a stream of silver bubbles torrenting up from the deep.

Back at shore Trevor helped me drag the boat on to the sand.

"Are you okay, old chap?" he asked.

I nodded, incapable of speech. If I'd tried to say anything, I would have been violently sick. Eventually I was able to thank Trevor for allowing me to accompany him on his adventure (though I wanted to do anything but), blaming my pallor on my age. I'd been overdoing it, despite my overall feelings of good health. He drove me back to Fort Requin and I was horrified to see the sea lapping at the causeway, the beach where I had walked and unearthed the hag stone now covered completely by water.

"High tides," he explained, unnecessarily. "But you'll be quite all right inside those thick walls. The sea will have retreated by morning."

He drove expertly through the surf, knowing instinctively where the road was, though I could see nothing beneath that shifting, hungry body. He dropped me off and waved goodbye, and I watched him churn through the water back to St. Anne.

Darkness was coming on and I suddenly felt very alone, and utterly certain that I wanted to leave. I should have asked him to take me to the airport. At the very least I might have asked him to stay with me that night, to provide company and beggar the fact he'd have thought me a nervous ninny.

I locked and bolted the gate, ditto the door to the kitchen. I was determined to spend the night in there rather than the chilly Soldiers' Quarters with its unfettered vista of the ocean. I'd had quite a bellyful of the sea. I was looking forward to getting back to the dry, landlocked interior of Leicestershire.

I made myself a cup of tea and carried it to the sofa, where I made a den from the blankets and pillows from the bed Ralph had vacated (I found one of his comics that had fallen down the side; it upset me disproportionately). A long, sound sleep and then in the morning I would see about making preparations for my departure. Trevor Standish could have no qualms about reimbursement—my convalescence was predicated upon calm and rest. I'd encountered neither. I'm sure he would not like to have a heart attack as well as a murdered guest on his hands.

I turned out the light and wriggled down into my shelter—the sofa was long and deep. Rain rattled briefly at the windowpanes like the nails of someone demanding entry. I willed sleep to come. I did not want another night of anxiety. Usually, when I wanted slumber to envelop me, I thought of water. I imagined myself as a smooth, dark pebble thrown into deep water. By the time I hit the ground I would be snoozing contentedly.

Water, though, was the thing I least wanted to think about. I didn't like what it concealed here. I didn't appreciate the way it had erased the concourse and trapped me in this cold, forbidding place. They could dress it up as much as they liked—pretty curtains, fancy soaps in the dish by the bath—it was still a place where soldiers had marched, with their guns and their knives and grenades, death on their minds.

At least, I comforted myself, I was in a place that had been designed to be well-nigh impregnable. The walls in parts of this structure were almost twenty feet thick. Do your worst, Mr. Gluckmann, I thought. Do your damnedest.

# VII

## THE OUTPOST (II) · THE EYE OF THE STONE

"The hag stone, it finds you. You do not find it."

I felt my neck snap as I jerked upright at the deep, clotted voice. Mr. Gluckmann was standing knee-deep in the surf, his baskets hanging glutinously around his hips like oilcloth canteens. What hair remained on his head hung limp and grey. His mouth was much wider than I had initially thought, the corners slack and encrusted with dried salt. His lips glistened, pursing obscenely. It was a mouth that looked like something big and meaty you might unlock from the seized shell of a bivalve.

His eyes, round and black, were fast upon my pocket. I felt the stone within cold against my thigh, as if it were the intensity of his gaze that was reducing its temperature.

"You know," he said, "there are a lot of fishermen around here who invest great stock in the idea of holy stones protecting their boats? They tie them to nails hammered into the bows, near the gunwale. It is believed these stones ward off the approach of witches, or witch-directed spirits. Those that decide not to tie a stone to their vessel, or do not position it carefully, might not land as many fish. If they're lucky. If they're unlucky? Well, there are a lot of wrecks in these waters. A lot of unrecovered fishermen swaying in time to those deep ocean currents."

Something flopped over the lip of one of the baskets. Long, spiny feelers, or, God forbid, fingers. As far removed from human as you could pray for. They clacked together, stiff but with some yield to them, and they were wet with some kind of slime, like the thick, bubbled spit worked up within the maws of crabs or lobsters. Mr. Gluckmann slapped at them with his hand and they retreated.

"How is your house-hunting going?" I asked. All of the baskets were rattling now—I saw movement within each one. Some were being stretched as whatever squirmed inside extended itself. The membrane thinned, whitening as claw or pincer or tooth became embossed against it.

Mr. Gluckmann rubbed at his cheek and the layers of flab there shivered. I wouldn't have been surprised, had he teased them open, to see a set of gills arranged across the flesh. "We walk among you now," he said. "It has been so long."

Behind him the sea began to boil. I forced myself to look away, certain that my meagre faculties would not be able to cope with the sight of the thing—beyond massive—that could cause such a churning. I pulled the stone from my pocket and Mr. Gluckmann began to jangle and jerk like a marionette. Those baskets—those *wombs*—which I now saw were not merely looped over and around his body, but *attached* to Gluckmann's skin, were swelling by the minute. Soon they would not be able to contain their inhabitants.

A shadow fell across the world, and the odour of something unimaginably old hit me like a wall. I felt the coil and slither of gigantic tentacles test my limbs from all angles. And slowly, inexorably, I was drawn towards the sea. At my back I felt the heat of jaws I refused to countenance.

The last thing I saw was Mr. Gluckmann carrying his crowning babies as he waddled towards the town and its unsuspecting population. "You are no threat to us," he said, "damned as you are by the cage of your own mortality."


Somehow I had become tangled in the blankets and sheets that formed my temporary bed. I was hot and sweaty, the stone in my hand threatening to slip from my grasp. It took a moment to orient myself, but in the end I was just glad to be anywhere other than in the grip of some terrible, benthic creature eager on adding me to the contents of its belly.

What a nightmare. The most horrible, the most vivid I have ever encountered in my three score years and ten.

What was worse was that only two hours had gone by since deciding to go to bed. Muscles aching, but sleep now as likely as Clarissa's return, I padded to the kitchen and set about making myself a mug of hot milk.

The weather remained squally—spits of rain (or maybe even fragments of shingle and surf tossed up by the tantrum winds) clattered against the windows. I shrugged on my coat and, hot drink in hand, unbolted the door.

It was piercingly cold; within seconds my milk had been cooled to a drinkable temperature.

*We walk among you now.*

I shuddered. What was that dream all about? Some weird idea, fuelled by too much red wine and seafood, of a world being gradually overtaken by an army of amphibious Mr. Gluckmanns? Utterly preposterous, yet I felt vaguely proud of the breadth of my imagination. Surely my ongoing fear of dementia was a long way off yet.

I thought about the object I'd found in the cave. That weird, fishy book, if it could be called such a thing. I found myself thinking I was lucky to have thrown it back to the sea. It seemed unthinkable now that I might have taken it for good.

At the hatch in the gate I peered down towards the causeway and saw, with dismay, that the sea had completely cut me off from the mainland. Waves crashed up against the car park where I had trundled my cycle not twelve hours previously. I eyed that dark stretch feverishly, but there was nothing in it, or of it, that caught my attention. Nor would there be beyond limpets, seaweed and crabs. The most exotic thing found at these latitudes were conger eel and smooth-hound. Perhaps the odd seal.

I set my jaw against the weather and the water and drew an imaginary line under my fear. Come dawn, I would be shot of the place.

Turning back to the promise of warmth, I heard a sound under the racket of the sky and ocean that gave me pause. It sounded like crumbling masonry, but the walls here were sound as far as I could see. Rocks then? Peeling away from the cliff-face under scrutiny from the buffeting wind?

I tried leaning over the parapet in the courtyard fronting the quarters, but I could see nothing untoward. Then I remembered the Outpost, and the more expansive view the disintegrated walkway allowed of the bay. I put down my mug and clambered back up through the samphire to the narrow corridor and negotiated once more the mesh barriers and warning signs.

A shadow moved across the open doorway of that separated room.

I stared, barely able to breathe, and tried to convince myself I had not seen it. But then terrible sounds came to me from the black shadows of the open window and that gaping doorway. The tiny room ought not to have been able to produce the kind of acoustics that caused the sounds to carry, but here they came—moist, tearing noises. And beneath them, muttered, but with a kind of religious intensity, I heard words. They were words I'd never heard before— and never want to hear again—but I couldn't replicate them here. They sounded foreign, wildly alien even, but somehow rooted to reality, an Earth I knew from folklore, or race memory or some-such.

Forgive me if I ramble, but it's difficult for me to explain. I come from a modest background, a family that lived on the breadline for many years, after the hardships of World War II. I didn't see a banana until I was in my teenage years. So this kind of peculiarity left me stunned, scared. It didn't fit into any pattern I recognised.

Furthermore, I didn't *want* to recognise. I wanted to block it out, forget it, refuse to acknowledge that anything like this could occur in a world I thought I'd got the hang of during my time in it. But I stood there and I listened and I cringed under the weight of those impossible words and the crimson sounds in which they were couched. There was injury and death and meanness in every plosive, fricative and aspiration.

Without realising it I had started crying. I felt like a child who had strayed into a room where grown-ups were fighting, or making violent love. I didn't understand.

I began to edge back from the gap in the rock. I didn't trust myself not to give away my position via some pathetic whimper, or pratfall.

I'd like to think, as I turned and plunged back towards that lockable fortified room, that cell of mine, that the stink coming off the waves was being pushed from Les Etacs, where the gannets turned the rock white in more ways than one, but I knew the odour was pulsing from the Outpost.

And I had to keep thinking of the smell, otherwise my mind would fasten on to the sight of something loose, like a grey sack, flopping across the doorway and being dragged away. A sack unfit for any kind of business, it was so full of holes. A sack, after all, though, yes. A sack it was.

I fought with the urge to try to escape, to cast my luck upon the depth of water on the causeway, and the hope that the current was not as keen as it looked. Come dawn, not three hours away, the waters would have retreated and I would be able to cross to the mainland and leave this wretched place for good.

I sat on my bed, fully dressed, gripping a bar from one of the loose bunk rails, my eyes glued to the handle of the door. I didn't move for the rest of the night and, because the light came back to the room so stealthily, did not realise it was morning until, yawning, I felt my back crackle as if my spine had been taken from me during those cold, lonely hours, and replaced with a giant icicle. I was stiff all over, my neck bright with pain whenever I turned my head.

I put down the bar and went to the window, pulled back the curtains. Grey sky, grey sea. Les Etacs was engulfed with wings. The waves were topped with scimitars of foam, as if the sea were trying to copy the shape of the birds it stared at all day. Against my better judgement, I unlocked the door and stepped outside.

The wind was little more than playful this morning, exhausted from last night's violence. I stared up at the little mound that prefaced the corridor to the Outpost and, though I desperately wanted to assuage my suspicion, my legs simply would not carry me back up there.

The beeping of a car horn.

I went back to my room and grabbed my packed suitcase. In that moment I felt my heart beating, but I was kidded into thinking it was a strong, healthy pulse—rather it was the flesh that carried it, grown weak over the decades, amplifying every pathetic rinse and suck of blood. Yet strangely, I was no longer afraid of that tardy muscle, sitting withered and wounded in its cage.

*You are no threat to us...*

I realised there were lots of other things to be fearful of in this world, and, in many ways, thank God, it had taken me a lifetime to discern it.

I shut the gate and struggled to remain upright on the slippery rock as I headed down to where the taxi was parked. The driver, my friend from Manchester, helped me to get the suitcase in the boot and then I was safely in the back seat and we were trundling over the causeway, now dry, the withdrawn tide collected in the surrounding rock pools, serene, all threat in abeyance; you'd be forgiven for thinking there was no such thing as high-tide here.

I felt in my pocket for the hag stone, momentarily panicked by the possibility I'd left it in the bed, but it was there, smooth and warm, and I clasped it as we headed towards the airport.

The heat in the taxi was thick and restful. I felt it seep into my bones.

Movement.

I jerked my head up and the muscles in my neck yelled at me. The sea was flat and relatively calm. No boats. But closer, down on a track beneath the road, what was that? It was Mr. Gluckmann, walking with his hands deep in his pockets, his wispy hair flailing around his head like seaweed lacing a submersed rock. He looked up as we slowly went by and his shaded eyes were shark-black. He smiled. I nodded, glad to see him fall behind us as the road improved and the taxi driver leaned on the accelerator.

Gluckmann raised his hand and I mirrored him. The hag stone was in my fingers. As I withdrew it, my view of the diminishing Gluckmann was impeded until he appeared within its hole, as he returned his arm to his overcoat pocket. And I had to close my eyes against the thrash in my chest and force myself over and over to believe that what I had seen in that ancient frame was skin and bone, and not the sinuous curve of a tentacle.

# ON THE REEF

## by CAITLÍN R. KIERNAN

*Man is least himself when he talks in his own person.*
*Give him a mask, and he will tell you the truth.*
OSCAR WILDE (1891)

THERE ARE RITES that do not die. There are ceremonies and sacraments that thrive even after the most vicious oppressions. Indeed, some may grow stronger under such duress, stronger and more determined, so that even though devotees are scattered and holy ground defiled, the rituals will find a way. The people will find a way back, down long decades and even centuries, to stand where strange beings were summoned—call them gods or demons or numina; call them what you will, as all words only signify and may not ever define or constrain the nature of these entities. Temples are burned and rebuilt. Sacred groves are felled, but new trees take root and flourish.

And so it is with this ragged granite skerry a mile and a half out from the ruins of a Massachusetts harbour town that drew its final, hitching breaths in the winter of 1928. Cartographers rarely take note of it, and when they do, it's only to mark the location for this or that volume of local hauntings or guides for legend-trippers. Even the teenagers from Rowley and Ipswich have largely left it alone, and the crumbling concrete walls are almost entirely free of the spray-painted graffiti that nowadays marks their comings and goings.

Beyond the lower falls of the Castle Neck (which the Wampanoag tribes named Manuxet), where the river takes an abrupt south-eastern turn before emptying into the Essex Bay, lies the shattered waste that once was Innsmouth. More than half-buried now by the tall advancing dunes sprawls this tumbledown wreck of planks weathered grey as oysters, a disarray of cobblestone streets and brick sidewalks, the stubs of chimneys, and rows of warehouses and docks rusted away to almost nothing. But the North Shore wasteland doesn't end at the shore, for the bay is filled with sunken trawlers and purse seiners, a graveyard of lobster pots and steel hulls, jute rope and oaken staves, where sea robins and flounder and spiny blue crabs have had the final word.

However, the subject at hand is not the fall of Innsmouth town, nor what little remains of its avenues and storefronts. The subject at hand is the dogged persistence of ritual, and its tendency to triumph over adversity and prejudice. The difficulty of forever erasing belief from the mind of man. We may glimpse the ruins, as a point of reference, but are soon enough drawn back around to the black granite reef, its rough spine exposed only at low tide. Now, it's one hour after sundown on a Halloween night, and a fat harvest moon as fiery orange as molten iron has just cleared the horizon. You'd think the sea would steam from the light of such a moon, but the water's too cold and far too deep.

On this night, there's a peculiar procession of headlights along the lonely Argilla Road, a solemn motorcade passing all but unnoticed between forests and fallow fields, nameless streams and wide swaths of salt marsh and estuary mudflat. *This* night, because this night is one of two every year when the faithful are drawn back to worship at their desecrated cathedral. The black reef may have no arcade, gallery, or clerestory, no flying buttresses or papal altar, but it *is* a cathedral, nonetheless. Function, not form, makes of it a cathedral.

The cars file down to the ghost town, the town which is filled only with ghosts. They park where the ground is firm, and the drivers and passengers make their way by moonlight, over abandoned railroad tracks and fallen telegraph poles, skirting the pitfalls of old wells and barbed-wire tangles. They walk silently down to this long stretch of beach, south of Plum Island and west of the mouth of the Annisquam River and Cape Ann.

Some have come from as far away as San Francisco and Seattle, while others are locals, haling from Boston and Providence and Manhattan. Few are dwellers in landlocked cities.

Each man and each woman wears identical sturdy cloaks sewn from cotton velveteen and lined with silk, cloth black as raven feathers. Most have pulled the hoods up over their heads, hiding their eyes and half-hiding their faces from view. On the left breast of each cape is an embroidered symbol, which bears some faint resemblance to the *ikhthus*, secret sign of early Christian sects, and before that, denoting worshippers at the shrines of Aphrodite, Isis, Atargatis, Ephesus, Pelagia and Delphine. Here, it carries other connotations.

There are thirteen boats waiting for them, a tiny flotilla of slab-sided Gloucester dories that, hours earlier, were rowed from Halibut Point, six miles to the east. The launching of the boats is a ceremony in its own right, presided over by a priest and priestess who are never permitted to venture to the reef out beyond the ruins of Innsmouth.

As the boats are filled, there's more conversation than during the walk down to the beach; greetings are exchanged between friends and more casual acquaintances who've not spoken to one another since the last gathering, on the thirtieth of April. News of deaths and births is passed from one pilgrim to another. Affections are traded like childhood Valentines. These pleasantries are permitted, but only briefly, only until the dories are less than a mile out from the reef, and then all fall silent in unison and all eyes watch the low red moon or the dark waves lapping at the boats. Their ears are filled now with the wind, wild and cold off the Atlantic and with the rhythmic slap of the oars.

There is a single oil lantern hung upon a hook mounted on the prow of each dory, but no other light is tolerated during the crossing from the beach to the reef. It would be an insult to the moon and to the darkness the moon pushes aside. In the boats, the pilgrims remove their shoes.

By the time the boats have gained the rickety pier—water-logged and slicked with algae, its pilings and boards riddled by the boring of shipworms and scabbed with barnacles—there is an almost tangible air of anticipation among these men and women. It hangs about them like a thick and obscuring cowl, heavy as the smell of salt in the air. There's an attendant waiting on the pier to help each pilgrim up the slippery ladder. He was blinded years ago, his eyes put out, that he would never glimpse the faces of those he serves; it was a mutilation he suffered gladly. It was a small enough price to pay, he told the surgeon.

Those who have come from so far, and from not so far, are led from the boats and the rotting pier out onto the reef. Each must be mindful of his or her footing. The rocks are slippery, and those who fall into the sea will be counted as offerings. No one is ever pulled out, if they should fall. Over many thousands of years, since the glaciers retreated and the seas rose to flood the land, this raw spit of granite has been shaped by the waves. In the latter years of the eighteenth century, and the early decades of the nineteenth—before the epidemic of 1846 decimated the port—the reef was known as Cachalot Ledge, and also Jonah's Folly, and even now it bears a strong resembles to the vertebrae and vaulted ribs of an enormous sperm whale, flayed of skin and muscle and blubber. But after the plague, and the riots that followed, as outsiders began to steer clear of Innsmouth and its harbour, and as the heyday of New England whaling drew to a close, the rocks were re-christened Devil Reef. There were odd tales whispered by the crews of passing ships, of nightmarish figures they claimed to have seen clambering out of the sea and onto those rocks, and this new name stuck and stuck fast.

Late in the winter of 1927–28, the submarine *U.S.S. 0-10* was deployed to these waters, from the Boston Navy Yard. The 173-foot vessel's tubes were armed with a complement of twenty-nine torpedoes, all of which were discharged into an unexpectedly deep trench discovered just east of Devil Reef. The torpedoes detonated almost a mile down, devastating a target that has never been publicly disclosed. But the pilgrims know what it was, and that attack is to them no less a blasphemy than the destruction of synagogues and cathedrals during the firestorms of the two World Wars, no less a crime than the razing of Taoist temples by Chinese communists, or the devastation of the Aztec Templo Mayor by Spaniard conquistadors after the fall of Tenochtitlan in 1521. And they remember the benthic mansions of Y'ha-nthlei and the grand altars and the beings murdered and survivors left dispossessed by those torpedoes. They remember the gods of that race, and the promises, and the rites, and so they come this night. They come to honour the Mother and the Father, and all those who died and who have survived, and all those who have yet to make the passage, but yet may. The old blood is not gone from the world.

Two are chosen from among the others. A box carved from jet is presented, and two lots are drawn. On each lot is graven the true name of one of the supplicants, the names bestowed in dreamquests by Father Dagon and Mother Hydra. One male and one female, or two female, or two male. But always the number is two. Always only a single pair to enact the most holy rite of the Order. There is no greater honour than to be chosen, and all here desire it. But, too, there is trepidation, for one may not become an avatar of gods without the annihilation of self, to one degree or another. And becoming the avatars of the Mother and the Father means utter and complete annihilation. Not physical death. Something far more destructive to both body and mind than mere death. The jet box is held high and shaken once, and then the lots are drawn, and the names are called out loudly to the pilgrims and the night and the waters and the glaring, lidless eye of the moon.

"The dyad has been determined," declares the old man who drew the lots, and then he steps aside, making way for the two women who have been named. One of them hesitates a moment, but only a moment, and only for the most fleeting of moments. They have names, in the lives they have left behind, lives and families and careers and histories, but tonight all this will be stripped away, sloughed off, just as they now remove their heavy black cloaks to reveal naked, vulnerable bodies. They stand facing one another, and a priestess steps forward. She anoints their foreheads, shoulders, bellies, and vaginas with a stinking paste made of ground angelica and mandrake root, the eyes and bowels of various fish, the aragonite cuttlebones of Sepiidae, foxglove, amber, frankincense, dried kelp and bladderwrack, the blood of a calf, and powdered molybdena. Then the women join hands, and each receives a wafer of dried human flesh, which the priestess carefully places beneath their tongues. Neither speaks. Even the priestess does not speak.

Words will come soon enough.

And now it is the turn of the Keeper of the Masks, and he steps forward. The relics he has been charged with protecting are swaddled each in yellow silk. He unwraps them, and now all the pilgrims may look upon the artefacts, shaped from an alloy of gold and far more precious metals, some still imperfectly known (or entirely unknown) to geologists and chemists, and some which have fallen to this world from the gulfs of space. To an infidel, the masks might seem hideous, monstrous things. They would miss the divinity of these divine objects, too distracted by forms they have been taught are grotesque and to be loathed, too unnerved by the almost inexplicable angles into which the alloy was shaped long, long ago, geometries that might seem "wrong" to intellects bound by conventional mathematics. Sometime in the early 1800s, these hallowed relics were brought to Innsmouth by the hand of Captain Obed Marsh himself, delivered from the Windward Islands of French Polynesia and ferried home aboard the barque *Sumatra Queen*.

The Keeper of Masks makes the final choice, selecting the face of Father Dagon for one of the two women, and the face of Mother Hydra for the other. The women are permitted to look upon the other's mortal countenance one last time. And then the Keeper hides their faces, fitting the golden masks and tying them tightly in place with cords woven from the tendons of blood sacrifices, hemp, and sisal. When it is certain that the masks are secure, only then does the Keeper step back into the his place among the others. And the two women kneel bare-kneed on stone worn sharp enough to slice leather.

"*Iä!*" cries the priestess, and then the Keeper of the Masks, and, finally, the man who drew the lots. Immediately, the pilgrims all reply, "*Iä! Iä! Rh'típd! Cthulhu fhtagn!*" And then the man who drew the lots, in a sombre voice that barely is more than an awed whisper, adds: "*Ph'nglui mglw'nafh Cthulhu R'lyeh wgah'nagl fhtagn. Rh'típd qho'tlhai mal.*" His words are lost on the wind, which greedily snatches away each syllable and strews them to the stars and sinks them to that immemorial city far below the waves, its spires broken and crystalline roofs splintered by naval munitions more than eighty years before this night.

"You are become the Mother and the Father," he says. "You are become the living incarnation of the eternal servants of R'lyeh. You are no more what you were. Those former lives are undone. You are become the face of the deep and the eyes of the heavens. You are on this night forever more wed."

The two kneeling women say nothing at all. But the wind has all at once ceased to blow, and around the reef the water has grown still and smooth as glass. The moon remains the same, though, and leers down upon the scene like a jackal waiting for its turn at someone else's kill, or Herod Antipas lusting after dancing Salomé. But no one among the pilgrims looks away from the kneeling women. No one ever looks away, for to avert their eyes from the sacrament would be unspeakable offence. They watch, as the moon watches, with great anticipation, and some with envy, that their names were not chosen from the bag of lots.

To the west—over the wooded hills beyond Essex Bay and the vast estuarine flats at the mouth of the Manuxet River—there are brilliant flashes of lighting, despite the cloudless sky. And, at this moment, as far away as Manchester-by-the-Sea, Wenham and Topsfield, Georgetown and Byfield, hounds have begun to bay. Cats only watch the sky in wonder and contemplation. The waking minds of men and women are suddenly, briefly, obscured by thoughts too wicked to ever share. If any are asleep and dreaming, their dreams turn to hurricane squalls and drownings and impossible beasts stranded on sands the colour of a ripe cranberry bog. In this instant, the land and the ocean stand in perfect and immemorial opposition, and the kneeling women who wear the golden masks are counted as apostates, deserting the continent, defecting to brine and abyssal silt. The women are tilting the scales, however minutely, and on this night the sea will claim a victory, and the shore may do no more to protest their desertion than sulk and drive the tides much further out than usual.

No one on the reef turns away. And they don't make a sound. There's nothing left for the pilgrims but to bear silent witness to the transition of the anointed. And that change is not quick, nor is it in any way merciful; neither woman is spared the least bit of agony. But they don't give voice to their pain, if only because their mouths have been so altered that they will nevermore be capable of speech or any other utterance audible to human ears. The masks have begun to glow with an almost imperceptible phosphorescence, and will shortly drop away, shed skins to be retrieved later by the Keeper.

Wearing now the mercurial forms of Mother Hydra and Father Dagon, the lovers embrace. Their bodies coil tightly together until there's almost no telling the one from the other, and the writhing knot of sinew and organs and rasping teeth glistens wetly in the bright moonlight. The two are all but fused into a single organism, reaffirming a marriage first made among the cyanobacterial mats of warm paleoarchean lagoons, three and a half billion years before the coming of man. There is such violence that this coupling looks hardly any different from a battle, and terrible gaping wounds are torn open, only to seal themselves shut again. The chosen strain and bend themselves towards inevitable climax, and the strata of the reef shudders repeatedly beneath the feet of the pilgrims. Several have to squat or kneel to avoid sliding from the rocks to be devoured by the insincere calm of the sea. In the days to come, none of them will mutter a word about what they've seen and heard and smelled in the hour of this holy copulation. This is a secret they guard with their lives and with their sanity.

No longer sane, the lovers twist, unwind and part. The Father has already bestowed his gift, and now it is the Mother's turn. A bulging membrane bursts, a protuberance no larger than the first of a child, and she weeps blood and ichor and a single black pearl. It is *not* a pearl, but by way of the roughest sort of analogy or approximation. One may as well call it a pearl as not. The true name for the Mother's gift is forbidden. It drops from her and lies quivering in a sticky puddle, to be claimed as the masks will be claimed. And then they drag themselves off the steep eastern lip of the reef, slithering from view and sinking into the ocean as the waves and wind return. They will spend the long night spiralling down and down, descending into that same trench the Ø-10 torpedoed eighty-two Februaries ago. And by the time the sun rises, and Devil Reef is once more submerged, they will have found the many-columned vestiges of the city of Y'ha-nthlei, where they will be watched over by beings that are neither fish nor men nor any amphibious species catalogued by science.

By then, the cars parked above the ghost town will have gone away, carrying the pilgrims back to the drab, unremarkable lives they will live until the end of April and the next gathering. And they will all dream their dreams, and await the night they may wear the golden masks.

# THE SONG OF SIGHS

*by* A N G E L A   S L A T T E R

## I

### FEBRUARY 12TH

*The song of Sighs, which is his.*
*Let him kiss me with his mouths:*
*for his love is better than ichor.*

**T**HE TRANSLATION IS coming along, but ponderously.

It takes so long to get the languages to agree, the tongues to collude. But it is close. Some days, though, I wonder why I don't adopt an easier hobby, like knitting or understanding string theory. I tap on the thick folio with nails marred by chipped polish. I remind myself this is for fun and stare at the creamy slab of bound pages, let my eyes lose focus so all the notations of my pen look like so many chicken scratches. So they all cease to make sense. If I stare long enough, perhaps I might see through time, see the one who wrote *this* and ask, perhaps, for its greater meaning.

A polite cough interrupts my reverie. I look up and find twenty pairs of eyes fixed upon me. I realise that I heard the buzzer a full minute ago, that my class has quietly packed up their texts and pads, pens and pencils.

"Doctor Croftmarsh?" says one of them, a handsome manly boy, tall for his age, dreamy blue eyes. I cannot remember his name. "Doctor, may we go? Only, Master Thackeray gets annoyed when we're late."

I nod, pick his name from the air. "Yes, Stephen, sorry. Offer my apologies to the Master and tell him I will make amends. Read chapter seven of the Roux, we will discuss what he says about Gilgamesh tomorrow."

Thackeray will expect expensive whisky in recompense; he does not miss an opportunity to drink on another's tab. His forgiveness is dearly bought, but it is easier to keep him sweet than make an enemy of him. There is the scrape and squawk of chair legs dragged across wooden floorboards, and desk lids clatter as students check they've not forgotten anything.

As they file out, I offer an afterthought, "Those of you wishing to do some extra study for next week's exams, don't forget your translations. The usual time."

"Yes, Doctor Croftmarsh," comes the chorus. There will be at least six of them, the brightest, the most ambitious, those desiring ever so ardently to get ahead. This is what the academy specialises in, propelling orphans *upward*. Idly, I make a bet with myself: Tilly Sanderson will be the first to knock at 6:30.

The door closes softly behind the last of the students and the space is silent, properly silent for the first time today, no *whoosh* of breath in and out, no nasal snorts or adenoidal whistles, no sneezes, no sighs, no surreptitious farts, no whispered conversations they think I cannot hear simply because they don't want me to. Dust specks cartwheel in the shafts of light coming through the windows. I close my eyes, enjoying the sensation of not being scrutinised for however brief a time. A band of tension is tightening across my forehead. Beneath my fingers, the substantial cushion of journal pages is strangely warm.

* * *

## II

### FEBRUARY 13TH

*Because of thy savour*
*thy name is as fear poured forth,*
*And thus do virgins fear thee.*

The refectory is awash with polite noise, the clatter of cutlery against crockery, the *ting* of glasses and water jugs meeting. Students and teachers, all at their allotted tables, talk quietly to one another, all in their own class groups.

The academy is a large place, a great building in the Gothic style, four long wings joined to make a square, with a broad green quadrangle in the middle. Two sides of the structure face the sea, looking out over the epic cliff drop; the other two are embraced by the woods and the well-tended grounds. The nearest town is ten miles distant. There is a teaching staff of twenty, three cooks, four cleaners, two gardeners and a cadre of two hundred-odd students.

As a child, I was occasionally sent to stay with an acquaintance of my parents, here in this very house, before its owners' dipping fortunes made a change of hands essential, and it became a school for exceptional orphans. I recollect very little about those visits, having but dim impressions of many rooms, large and dust-filled, corridors long and portrait-lined, and bed chambers stuffed with canopied beds, elaborate dressers and wardrobes that loomed towards one in the night like trolls creeping from beneath bridges. I remember waking from nightmares of the place, begging my mother and father not to be sent there again.

It was only after they were gone, when I was grown and qualified, seeking employment and a quiet retreat after the accident, that I saw an advertisement for a history teacher. It seemed like the perfect opportunity. I have been here for a year.

This is what I'm told I remember.

I'm assured it's one of those things, this kind of amnesia that takes away some recollections and leaves others—I retain everything I must know in order to teach. I keep every bit of study I ever undertook tucked under my intellectual belt. I memorised the things that have happened since I came here. I may even recall the car accident—or at least, I have a sense of an explosion, of flying through the air, of terrible, intense pain—but I'm never quite sure what I can actually *invoke* of that time.

I suppose I am fortunate to be alive when my parents are not. I've been promised that many people I once knew are dead, but I'm uncertain whether I actually *feel* a loss. There are no remnants of that old life, no photos of my parents and me. No holiday snaps, no foolish playing-around in the backyard photos. I have no box of mementoes, no inherited jewellery, no ancient teddy bear with its fur loved off. Nothing that might provide proof of my growing up, of my youth, of my *being*.

I fear I have no true memory of who I am.

In the same notebook where I make my translations, in the very back pages are the scribbles I write to remind myself of who I am supposed to be. I read them over and again: I am Vivienne Croftmarsh. I have a Ph.D. I teach at the academy. I am an only child and now an orphan. I translate ancient poetry as a pastime.

This is who I am.

This is what I tell myself.

But I cannot shake the feeling that something is working loose, that the world around me is softening, developing cracks, threatening to crumble. I can't say why. I cannot deny a sense of formless dread. My hands are beginning to ache; I rub at the slight webbing between the fingers, massaging the tenderness there.

"Wake up, dreamy-drawers." Fenella Burrows is the closest thing I have to a friend here; she plants herself and her lunch tray across from me at the deserted end of the table I've chosen. Most of the faculty take the hint and stay away, but not her, and I don't mind. She tells me we went to school together, but isn't offended when I am unable to reminisce. She jerks her head towards the journal and my ink-stained fingers. "How's it going?"

"Getting there. Second verse."

"Second verse, same as the first," she snorts. Fenella throws back her head when she laughs, all the mouse-brown curls tumbling down her back like a waterfall. She leans in close and says, "Don't look now, but Thackeray is watching you."

I pull a face, don't turn my head. "Thackeray's always watching."

"Oh, don't tell me you don't think he's attractive."

Yes, he is attractive, but he stares too much, seems to see too much, seems to dig beneath my skin with his gaze and pull out secrets I didn't know were there. That's the sense I get anyway, but I don't tell Fenella because it sounds stupid and *she* clearly finds him appealing. Her smile is limned with the pale green of jealousy. "He's all yours," I say.

She sighs. "If only. No one wants the plain bridesmaid."

"How were your classes this morning?" I ask.

"Tilly Sanderson out-Frenched me."

"That sounds appalling and punishable by a jail term."

"Grammar-wise, you fool." She adds more salt to the unidentifiable vegetarian mush on her plate. I can't really bear to look at it. Fenella insists it's an essential tool in her diet plan. I see no evidence: her face is still as round as a pudding and so is she.

"Well, she's very smart."

"Yes, but I hate it when the little beasts are smarter than us." She shovels the mess from her plate to her mouth and seems to chew for a long time.

"Honestly, don't you think eating is meant to be, if not fun, then at least easy? How much mastication does that require?"

"It's good for you; it's just a bit… fibrous."

"It looks like the wrong end of the digestion process."

"You're an unpleasant creature. Don't know why I talk to you." She steals a chip off my plate.

I stare up at the head table, frown. "Have you seen the Principal lately?"

"A day or so ago," she says. "Why?"

"Just feel like they haven't been around for ages."

"That'd be your dodgy memory. Old trout will be here somewhere," she says dismissively. "You can always talk to Candide, if it's urgent."

"No, nothing really. Just curious. Also, I don't want to get trapped by the Deputy Head—last time I ended up listening to him recounting his thesis from 1972 on the evils of the Paris student uprisings of '68." Candide's about sixty, but he seems older and dustier than he should. Fenella hooks her thumbs under the front facing of her academic gown, tucks her chin into her neck and looks down her nose at me, adopting a sonorous intonation.

"'Bloody peasants, disrespecting their betters. It's all one can expect from a nation that murdered its own royalty and has far too many varieties of cheese.'"

"Don't make the mistake of mentioning Charles I and the thud his head made on the scaffolding. I learned that the hard way."

We laugh until we're gasping, and the older teachers are looking at us disapprovingly. We'll be spoken to later about the dangers of hilarity in front of the students and letting our dignity visibly slip. Causes the natives to become restless if they think we're human and we lose our grip on the moral high ground.

### III

#### FEBRUARY 14TH

*Lead me, I will wait for thee:*
*the King once summoned me into his chambers:*
*and I was glad and rejoiced,*
*I remember thy love more than life:*
*All tremble before thee.*

There are two kinds of people in this world: those who, when faced with a window two floors up, will immediately accept the limitations it places upon them; and those who instantly look for a way to subvert both the height and the threatened effects of gravity. This room is full of the latter. It's one of the reasons I love teaching: the opportunity to find those who would chance a fall in the attempt to fly, rather than stay safely within bounds.

The buzz of conversation in my oak-panelled rooms washes over me. Stephen and Tilly are arguing about whether Ishtar is more or less powerful as a profligate prostitute goddess, or is simply a male wish-fulfilment fantasy; the other five watch the back and forth of a teen intellectual tennis match. The tipple of port has made them aggressive and I imagine sex will be the result at some point. Time to nip that in the bud. I give a slow blink, to moisten my dry eyeballs, and clap my hands.

"Enough, enough. You're not talking history any more, you've slid into pop culture, which is Doctor Burrows' area, not mine," I say. "Look at the time. Off you all go."

"Goodnight, Doctor Croftmarsh," they say. The closing of the door and then the one student left, the one who always waits behind; the one who stands out, and frequently apart from, her fellows. Tilly, who thinks herself special, and is, I suppose. So much talent, so clever; she will do well when she goes out into the world.

"How are you?" she asks and I am a bit taken aback. She steps close, takes my hands in hers, begins stroking the palms, an intimate, invasive gesture. I don't think she knows she's doing it. "Do you feel it yet? Has it begun?"

"Do I feel *what*, Tilly?"

Her face changes, the avid expression painted over by one of uncertainty, perhaps fear. What does the child mean?

"Tilly." Thackeray's voice is low but seems to affect the girl like the crack of a whip. She starts and looks guilty. I didn't even hear the door open. "Tilly, don't bother Doctor Croftmarsh. It's late and time for you to be getting back to your room."

Tilly drops my hands, and dips her head, blonde curls covering her blush-red face. She makes for the exit, then looks back over her shoulder before she leaves, smiling a sunburst at me and then throwing an odd glance at Thackeray, which I cannot interpret.

"Sleep well. Don't forget to read the Roux," I say after her as the door closes and Thackeray leans his back against it.

He grins, his thick lips smug, then he moves into the room without invitation and helps himself to the whisky waiting on the shelf, knocking one of the heavy crystal glasses against the other. He raises the bottle at me, and I nod. Beneath his black woollen academic robe he is still a rugby player, but slowly going soft and bloating in parts. His pale cheeks are shadowed with ebony stubble; the ruffian's posture hides an acute, albeit lazy intelligence; sometimes I wonder how he came to teach at a place as exclusive as this.

"So, young Tilly Sanderson," he begins, handing me one of the tumblers. His own measure is far more generous. He slumps into the chair I recently vacated, drapes himself across it, long legs stretched forward, one arm hanging down almost to the carpet, the other hand clutching his drink. His voice is low, trying for levity, but there's a dark edge that tells me to tread carefully. "Not teaching her something new, are you?'

"Don't be ridiculous." I sip at the whisky, feel it burn down my throat then take up residence in my belly, heating me surely as a fire. From a chest at the foot of my writing desk, I pull an unopened bottle and hold it out to him.

"What? Can't want me gone so soon, surely." But he gets to his feet and reaches out. He wraps his large hand around not just the neck, but my hand as well, trapping me unless I want to sacrifice forty-year-old Scotch. His breath is hot and malt-rich on my face; I can feel the warmth radiating off his body, and my cheeks flame with a dim memory of drunken fumbling. I'm not sure how far it went. "Surely we could indulge ourselves once again… Who's to know?"

I would know. And so would he. And it would give him something else to use against me in a school where fraternisation of any kind is reason for dismissal. I know how the world works; he would receive a slap on the wrist and I would be gone without references. "Good night, Thackeray."

I pull away and he has to juggle to save his prize. He gives a slow smile, takes his defeat well, throws back the amber in his glass and returns the empty to the shelf.

He leaves and I feel as if I can breathe for the first time in an age. From the corridor, I hear the whisper and scuffle of boots. My heart clenches at the idea that any of the other teachers might have seen him coming out of my room. I creep over and crack the door, putting my eye to the sliver.

Thackeray and Tilly stand close, oh so close. His free hand is roaming up one thigh, over her hip, then cupping her backside roughly. Her face is hidden from me, pressed into his chest.

I step back. The headache that's been with me all day worsens; I feel as if the bones of my skull are pushing against each other. I rub my palms across my face, hoping to hold the pieces in place, to press the pain back.

# IV

## FEBRUARY 15TH

*I am hidden, but lovely, O ye daughters of darkness,*
*as the dreams of Great Old Ones,*
*as the drowned houses of R'lyeth.*

The office door, with its frosted glass panel reading simply PRINCIPAL, is unlocked, and there is no sign of the watchdog, Mrs. Kilkivan. The Tilly–Thackeray situation gave me a restless night and I thought I might approach the Head before class.

Inside, the floor is covered with an enormous rug that stretches almost to the boundaries of the enormous office. The walls are covered by bookshelves, neatly stacked with hardbacks, decorative spines showing off silver lettering. Three display cases take up one corner, each with a series of ancient gold jewellery, marked with carefully hand-written labels and histories: this one found in ancient Babylon, this one from a well in Kish, yet another dug up from the depths of Nineveh, this from Ashur, these from Ur and Ebla. Artefacts excavated from the cradle of civilisation; I seem to recall the Head had been active in archaeological digs in early life, and that father and mother, uncles and aunts, had all spent time in the Middle East.

Beneath the broad tall window is a desk roughly the width of the office, with just enough space to walk around, if you've slim hips. The desk is neat and tidy, a notepad on the blotter which is perfectly aligned with the edge of the mahogany edifice, the bases of the two banker's lamps also carefully placed, one on the left corner, the other one the right. The pens, fine things, are in individual cases on the polished surface; a sturdy pewter letter opener lies next to them, protected in a bronze enamelled sheath.

Some of the shelves are bereft of books, but stand instead as habitations for busts of Greek and Roman philosophers, statuettes of gods and demons, strange twisted things that would not be out of place in a museum.

Unable to resist the impulse, I step around the desk, plant myself in the ample leather seat and try one of the drawers. Locked. All of them. I rub at my forearms; the skin is dry, thickening, irritated. The grandfather clock strikes the hour and I will be late for class. I snatch a piece of paper from the notebook and scribble a message to the Principal that I need a word. I place it in the centre of the blotter, where it cannot be missed. I carefully put the pen back in its case, only after trying to wipe off any finger marks.

Here is my problem: Tilly seemed willing. She is almost eighteen—yes, we keep them here longer, if they wish. Eighteen, nineteen, twenty. Some stay on and become staff, studying, learning from the teachers here, which gives them a far better training than they would find elsewhere. Here is my other problem: the possibility of Thackeray revealing what may have happened between us, but which I am unsure even took place. And Tilly, she is a child, easily influenced.

Who do I protect? Myself or the child?

I don't know what I will tell the Head. Candide will be useless; he will simply give me a slow blink and ask *whatever do you mean*? The Principal is the key. When we meet I will know what to say.

# V

## FEBRUARY 16TH

*Look not upon me, because I am disguised,*
*because the sun hath burned me:*
*Earth's children were angry with me;*
*they stole what was mine;*
*They kept him from me.*

The west wing houses the library; it's stacked with shelving and desks overrun by computer terminals and printers. A wooden set of card-index drawers stands lonely and lost in the middle of the room—the young librarian doesn't know quite what to do with it and is too afraid of the ghosts of librarians past to throw it out. Curiosities abound: a giraffe's skeleton, a giant cephalopod, spears and shields and helmets of disappeared empires, bronze horse statuettes, elephant tusks and rhinoceros horns, all take up space on walls, shelves, nooks and alcoves. There are portraits, too: long-dead educators staring down with what might be disapproval or hauteur or both.

The only wall unencumbered by shelves or display items is covered by a tapestry. A woman sits enthroned on a stone seat, a staff in one hand, a snake in the other. Her eyes are wide, almost too much so: icthyoid and protuberant; her lips pouting, her nose somewhat flat; hair a mess of black; yet there is a kind of beauty to her, a compelling strangeness that draws the observer in. She wears a simple green robe, something that seems almost armoured, perhaps scaled, and at her slippered feet, a field of blossoms: black, silver, red, yellow and richest chestnut petals on stalks of green. She sits most closely to the left of the tapestry—or rather, to the right—and to the right, or rather her left, nothing more than a verdant tangle of forest. Branches and trunks, undergrowth and vines, all twist together to form a dense curtain, seemingly without uniformity or plan, utterly wild and overgrown, curled around the stony ruins of a building crushed by the foliage.

In a quiet corner of the room sits Fenella, surrounded and almost concealed by a fortress of books built on the desk in front of her. At one of the tables are Tilly and Stephen and their various acolytes; I note the blonde curly head turn towards me, offering a smile, but I pretend not to see her, keep myself aimed directly at my friend.

"Have you seen the Head?" I ask, *sotto voce*, as I scratch at the sides of my throat, trying to get rid of the terrible itching there. She jumps, pulled from her concentration by my question, both hands thumping on the tabletop in fright.

"Don't you knock?" One of the book towers wobbles and begins a slow slide. She tries to stop it, then gives up and lets the tomes fan out, domino-like, until the final one teeters on the edge and falls. It marks the end of its descent with a noise like a shot that stops the library for a few moments.

Fenella folds her arms and looks at me.

I ask again, "Have you seen the Head?"

"This morning," she says. "What is *wrong* with you?"

And she's right, I'm jumpy, sweating, twitching at the slightest noise, the tiniest hints of something moving in the corner of my eye. There's still the headache: as if someone is trying to crack my skull open. And I cannot shake the accompanying sense that success will result in a dark river, a black tide flowing out of me. I blink, hard, eyes dry.

"I don't feel well," I say. "And…"

She puts a hand on my forehead—the cool flesh is a shock against my hot skin. "Go and lie down. You don't have any classes this afternoon."

"Thackeray," I say, the words becoming harder to force out, the hurt pressing in on my head. "Thackeray and Tilly, were…"

She tilts; the whole room tilts and I can't figure out why. I wonder that the books aren't falling from the shelves; then I realise I'm the one who's on an angle. I'm the one who's falling. I hit the floor, head bouncing against the polished parquetry.

There's a burble of noise around me; I see figures looming above, blurring. Beneath my head, I feel a beat. A thudding, ever so gentle, a mere echo of a vibration, a rhythm, a pulse, a song, but it will grow stronger, of that I have no doubt. It travels up me like a tremor, a whisper of motion. It moves me and shakes me and lulls me all at once. I close my eyes, for I have no choice, and everything is blocked out.

The last thing I hear is Fenella swearing at the crowd to stand back and let me have some air. I try to smile, but cannot feel my face.

# VI

## FEBRUARY 17TH

*Tell me, O thou whom my soul loveth, where thou waitest,*
*where thou sleepest:*
*for I shall not be as one turned aside*
*by the rise and fall of aeons.*

Sound, unclear, as if heard through water. I swim up, slowly, ignoring the yearning pain in my bones. Voices. It's voices: male and female.

All I can feel beneath me now are the soft crisp linens of my bed;

no more subtle rhythm, no more gentle beat. Clear-headed at last, but I keep my eyes closed, for they still retain an echo of the ache. And I listen.

"How is she?" Thackeray, subdued.

"The same as she always is at this point." Fenella, cool. They've been arguing.

"No. It seems different—she's never struggled like this."

Fenella is silent.

"What if she's—?"

"You're an idiot." Fenella, angry. "*She* saw you. You can't just fuck about for the better part of a year. You put us all in danger. We're not completely invisible here."

"We've been over this already. What does it matter? She'll be gone soon."

"We go to all the trouble of choosing, of making each one think they're special."

"So? I just made her feel a little bit extra special."

"Everyone else here is *careful*. Goes out of their way to keep us all secret and safe." Her voice drops. "I will tell her, when this one is gone and *she's* back."

"You worry too much, Burrows. Her time is short," he sneers.

"She won't need long."

That shuts him up, then there is a shuffling, his heavy steps moving away, the door opening and closing. I crack an eyelid and see Fenella, hands over her face, shoulders slumped. I know my vision is still wrong because she seems to have only three fingers. She sighs, throws back her shoulders, takes a deep breath. I focus.

She leans over me without really looking at me, touches my face. Five digits, of course; stupidity. I do not react, keep my breathing steady, slow. She steps away and leaves the room.

I wait, counting down seconds, counting down until I feel safe. I sit up, throw back the covers, swing my legs out of bed. Through the window I can see the sky, blue-black, dotted with stars, buttoned-down with a full moon. 11:30 says the bedside clock. I have slept long.

My legs tremble, I straighten. My hands spasm, the base of my skull feels... stretched. I shake my head, leave the room, uncaring that my pink flannel pyjamas are not the best attire for sneaking through corridors.

The dust and darkness are heavy in the Principal's office. The moonlight streams in and on the broad expanse of the desk I can see a piece of paper. My note. Untouched, unmoved, unread.

Once again, I pull at the drawers, knowing they'll still be locked. I take the letter opener from its place and jam it into the keyhole, then into the thin space between the bottom of one drawer and the top of another, jiggle it, jemmy it and to my surprise the lower one grinds open with a protest. The fine dark wood splinters, exposing its pale naked inside. The drawer slides on reluctant runners.

There is a sewing-box, a padded embroidered thing, quite large, a silver toggle slid through the loop on the front to keep it closed. I unclasp it and flip it open. Inside, threads. So many threads, all twisted into figures of eight, their middles cinched in by the end of the very same thread. Tens, twenties, fifties, hundreds? So many: black, silver, red, yellow, richest chestnut. On the padded silk inside the lid, an array of needles, sentinels pinned through the fabric, all fine and golden, some thicker than others, fit for all manner of work, for varying thicknesses of material, canvas, skin, hide, what-have-you. I reach in, prick my index finger, watch the blood well and drip onto the pale blue silk, clotting bundles of thread.

I suck on the injured digit and notice, behind the casket, a creamy wad of pages. I draw them forth. Each one has a ragged edge as if torn from a journal. Each one is filled with scribbles, ancient cuneiforms of text, amateurish translations beside those obtuse scratchings:

*I am hidden, but lovely, O ye daughters of darkness. They kept him from me. I remember thy love more than life. Let him kiss me with his mouths. Thy name is as fear poured forth. Lead me, I will wait for thee.*

Each page dated; I can see a series of different years. How many? Oh, God, how many?

The grandfather clock interrupts me as I kneel there on the floor.

It chimes the quarter-hour and I watch the hands move. The office door opens and Tilly's soft voice, rich with anticipation, a little fear, calls "Doctor Croftmarsh? It's time."

"Tilly. Tilly, you have to get away from here." I scramble up off my knees, try to move towards her at the same time, stumble twice before I stand and manage to get a hand on her arm. The touch is as much to steady me as to underline my point to her. "There's something going on. We have to go—we'll go out through the kitchens, no one will see us—"

"Doctor Croftmarsh, don't be ridiculous," she says, barely concealing disdain. I tighten my fingers around her wrist. She jerks her arm away.

"No, Tilly, I'm not being silly. Something is happening and you're in danger."

"No," she says, smiling, but I can't quite fathom the demeanour. "I'm not in danger—*He* has called my name and I will heed him. He will know me and choose me for I am *new*."

And all at once I know that inimitable combination of tone and expression: triumph and malice, jealousy and hope. The child thinks she is part of a greater mystery. She thinks Thackeray will—will what? Despair and desperation well up inside me as rhythmic pulses of pain.

We stare at each other, time seemingly marching in place until, at last, there is the sound of the final *flick* of the clock hands shifting into place. Mechanisms begin to sing *midnight* and all of my agonies fall away. I smile at the girl and offer my hand in conciliation.

# VII

## FEBRUARY 18TH

*If thou know not, O thou greatest among beasts,*
*Send me dreams so I might guess,*
*and kill the flock by the shepherds' tents.*

With my free hand I hook the edge of the tapestry and pull. The right half of it hangs from a rail separate to that for the left, so, when drawn across, the picture changes, the forest folded back upon itself becomes a creature, muscular, tentacled, winged; the broken stones become a second throne and the lord's limbs, now seen true, caress his bride in lewd love.

More importantly, this redecoration shows a door in the wall behind the arras, a door which leads down to the academy's rarely used chapel; to the undercroft more precisely. I wrench it open and a whiff of dust puffs out. Dust and something else, like long-dead fish.

"Come, Tilly," I say. There is no answer. I turn to look at her; she is staring at the hanging. I take her face in my hands, run my fingers through her hair, tender as a mother. I kiss her on the forehead, a chaste embrace, and say, "You were right: you have been called, Tilly, and you are needed. You are anointed, the *coming one*. And *He* will know your name and I shall see you covered in the throes of glory before this night is out."

In the darkness, I can see with the unerring stare of a creature from the deep. In her gaze is my reflection, my features rewritten by my memories, my *true* memories: eyes set wide and angled up, icthyoid and protuberant, pouting lips, flattened nose. And the hair, a waving tangle of green-black tentacles, a-shiver with a life of their own. I stretch, my bones cracking. I am taller.

The girl's expression is stunned. "Doctor Croftmarsh?"

I nod and smile, my teeth sharp and liberally spaced. The girl shudders. Some panic at this moment, the imminence of death shaking them from the enchantment of being chosen; some go quietly. Tilly, I suspect, is beginning to realise that she did not take note of the fine print in the deal that was struck. I lock a webbed hand around her wrist and pull her towards her destiny.

My head is full of things long-forgotten, long set aside so that I— we—might hide and survive. Today, this anniversary of the Fall of Innsmouth, of my Lord's terrible injuries and afflictions, of his everdying, this day the memories are whole. They do not *afflict* me. They are *mine* and they rest easy in the pan of my skull.

"Never fear, Tilly." The language feels strange in my mouth, the words seemingly square, not sibilant, not long and serpentine, but blocky. I persist, dragging the girl behind me, down into the darkness of the cold stone staircase and the crushing blackness of the undercroft and the tomb. The space is just large enough to fit the rest of the staff, teaching and domestic, all changed, all re-made like me; all clustered in a tenebrous group at the far end of the crypt. "Know that you are a part of something great."

Here she will breathe her last, her soul, her blood given so that my Lord may heal. A process oh-so-slow, but only on this one day is the barrier between his death and my life thin enough for this service.

In my haste I am clumsy.

In her terror she is strong.

When she kicks at me, I loosen my grip and she pulls away, races in the shadows, back towards the stairs, towards freedom. All the trouble gone to, to cut her from the herd, to groom her, to make her feel special—and she runs. There is the sound of a slap, a grunt.

"Careless," says Thackeray. "You are not what you were." He holds the girl still, carries her as a child does a reluctant cat, her back against his chest, her limbs splayed, belly exposed. She no longer struggles. Thackeray offers her to me. I stare into her moon-wide eyes and whisper, "All will be well."

The talons of my right hand open up her chest, the nightgown then the skin. A silver mist bursts from the hole, followed by a gush of blood, and both are drawn down to the stone of the tomb, then immediately begin to seep through the porous surface.

I hear, as her life pours out, the great booming rhythm of my Lord's heart, strengthened across aeons, across life and death and the space in between. Such a slow healing.

From the gloom steps Fenella, a broad smile on her plain face. "We must talk, before you grow forgetful again," she says.

I don't answer, merely look at the shell of Tilly Sanderson sprawled across my husband's resting place where Thackeray discarded her. The rhythm of his renewal is loud and I think: *If one can do this, then surely a legion…*

"You will lose yourself once more," Fenella continues. "We must discuss matters for the coming year."

"Tomorrow's forgetting will be but a dream," I say, skittering my nails across the top of my Lord's tomb, finding not a skerrick of blood left there.

I am so tired of waiting.

How many years between Innsmouth and now? How many times have I taken filaments from young heads and selected a fine needle so I may embroider a new flower into the weave of the tapestry, its border growing with each passing sacrifice? How many years have I sat beside a *rock* and told my Lord, my liege, my love the same tale, of the patient queen who hides away, protecting her beloved from his enemies? The tale of a wife who loses herself for his very sake, who folds the cloak of Vivienne Croftmarsh around her recollections, her histories, and suppresses everything she is, so hunters may not track him through the power of her memory. A woman who sings him his song, his hymn, his dirge, and waits and waits and waits.

A woman who is weary of waiting.

From beneath, from across, I hear him sigh.

"Bring them," I say to Burrows and Thackeray, who give me blank stares. My voice is thunder when next I speak, and they cringe with the power of my rage. "Bring them all!"

"But—" begins Thackeray and I grab the front of his shirt and lift him off his feet, revelling in the strength of my arm, myself; and knowing, at last, that I am unwilling to once again give up this self. I shake him for good measure.

"Bring them, by twos and threes. Bring them here and we shall see my Lord awake before too many more cycles have passed. I am tired of waiting."

A new tomorrow is about to dawn on the Esoteric Order's Orphans Academy. And then, when my Lord shall finally rise again, I shall take my proper place at *His* side…

# THE SAME DEEP WATERS AS YOU

*by* BRIAN HODGE

T HEY WERE DOWN to the last leg of the trip, miles of iron-grey
ocean skimming three hundred feet below the helicopter, and
she was regretting ever having said yes. The rocky coastline of
northern Washington slid out from beneath them and there they
were, suspended over a sea as forbidding as the day itself. If they
crashed, the water would claim them for its own long before anyone
could find them.

Kerry had never warmed to the sea—now less than ever.

Had saying no even been an option? *The Department of Homeland
Security would like to enlist your help as a consultant,* was what the
pitch boiled down to, and the pair who'd come to her door yesterday
looked genetically incapable of processing the word no. They couldn't
tell her what. They couldn't tell her where. They could only tell her to
dress warm. Better be ready for rain, too.

The sole scenario Kerry could think of was that someone
wanted her insights into a more intuitive way to train dogs, maybe.
Or something a little more out there, something to do with birds,
dolphins, apes, horses… a plan that some questionable genius had
devised to exploit some animal ability that they wanted to know

how to tap. She'd been less compelled by the appeal to patriotism than simply wanting to make whatever they were doing go as well as possible for the animals.

But this? No one could ever have imagined this.

The island began to waver into view through the film of rain that streaked and jittered along the window, a triangular patch of uninviting rocks and evergreens and secrecy. They were down there.

Since before her parents were born, they'd always been down there.


It had begun before dawn: an uncomfortably silent car ride from her ranch to the airport in Missoula, a flight across Montana and Washington, touchdown at Sea-Tac, and the helicopter the rest of the way. Just before this final leg of the journey was the point they took her phone from her and searched her bag. Straight off the plane and fresh on the tarmac, bypassing the terminal entirely, Kerry was turned over to a man who introduced himself as Colonel Daniel Escovedo and said he was in charge of the facility they were going to.

"You'll be dealing exclusively with me from now on," he told her. His brown scalp was speckled with rain. If his hair were any shorter, you wouldn't have been able to say he had hair at all. "Are you having fun yet?"

"Not really, no." So far, this had been like agreeing to her own kid-napping.

They were strapped in and back in the air in minutes, just the two of them in the passenger cabin, knee-to-knee in facing seats.

"There's been a lot of haggling about how much to tell you," Escovedo said as she watched the ground fall away again. "Anyone who gets involved with this, in any capacity, they're working on a need-to-know basis. If it's not relevant to the job they're doing, then they just don't know. Or what they think they know isn't necessarily the truth, but it's enough to satisfy them."

Kerry studied him as he spoke. He was older than she first thought, maybe in his mid-fifties, with a decade and a half on her, but he had the lightly lined face of someone who didn't smile much. He would still be a terror in his seventies. You could just tell.

"What ultimately got decided for you is full disclosure. Which is to say, you'll know as much as I do. You're not going to know what you're looking for, or whether or not it's relevant, if you've got no context for it. But here's the first thing you need to wrap your head around: what you're going to see, most of the last fifteen presidents haven't been aware of."

She felt a plunge in her stomach as distinct as if their altitude had plummeted. "How is that possible? If he's the Commander-in-Chief, doesn't he…?"

Escovedo shook his head. "Need-to-know. There are security levels above the office of president. Politicians come and go. Career military and intelligence, we stick around."

"And I'm none of the above."

It was quickly getting frightening, this inner-circle business. If she'd ever thought she would feel privileged, privy to something so hidden, now she knew better. There really were things you didn't want to know, because the privilege came with too much of a cost.

"Sometimes exceptions have to be made," he said, then didn't even blink at the next part. "And I really wish there was a nicer way to tell you this, but if you divulge any of what you see, you'll want to think very hard about that first. Do that, and it's going to ruin your life. First, nobody's going to believe you anyway. All it will do is make you a laughingstock. Before long, you'll lose your TV show. You'll lose credibility in what a lot of people see as a fringe field anyway. Beyond that… do I even need to go beyond that?"

*Tabby*—that was her first thought. Only thought, really. They would try to see that Tabitha was taken from her. The custody fight three years ago had been bruising enough, Mason doing his about-face on what he'd once found so beguiling about her, now trying to use it as a weapon, to make her seem unfit, unstable. *She talks to animals, your honour. She thinks they talk back.*

"I'm just the messenger," Colonel Escovedo said. "Okay?"

She wished she were better at conversations like this. Conversations in general. Oh, to not be intimidated by this. Oh, to look him in the eye and leave no doubt that he'd have to do better than that to scare her. To have just the right words to make him feel smaller, like the bully he was.

"I'm assuming you've heard of Guantanamo Bay in Cuba? What it's for?"

"Yes," she said in a hush. Okay, this was the ultimate threat. Say the wrong thing and she'd disappear from Montana, or Los Angeles, and reappear there, in the prison where there was no timetable for getting out. Just her and 160-odd suspected terrorists.

His eyes crinkled, almost a smile. "Try not to look so horrified. The threat part, that ended before I mentioned Gitmo."

Had it been that obvious? How nice she could amuse him this fine, rainy day.

"Where we're going is an older version of Guantanamo Bay," Escovedo went on. "It's the home of the most long-term enemy combatants ever held in US custody."

"How long is long-term?"

"They've been detained since 1928."

She had to let that sink in. And was beyond guessing what she could bring to the table. Animals, that was her thing, it had always been her thing. Not POWs, least of all those whose capture dated back to the decade after the First World War.

"Are you sure you have the right person?" she asked.

"Kerry Larimer. Star of *The Animal Whisperer*, a modest but consistent hit on the Discovery Channel, currently shooting its fourth season. Which you got after gaining a reputation as a behavioural specialist for rich people's exotic pets. You *look* like her."

"Okay, then." Surrender. They knew who they wanted. "How many prisoners?" From that long ago, it was a wonder there were any left at all.

"Sixty-three."

Everything about this kept slithering out of her grasp. "They'd be over a hundred years old by now. What possible danger could they pose? How could anyone justify—"

The colonel raised a hand. "It sounds appalling, I agree. But what you need to understand from this point forward is that, regardless of how or when they were born, it's doubtful that they're still human."

He pulled an iPad from his valise and handed it over, and here, finally, was the tipping point when the world forever changed. One photo, that was all it took. There were more—she must've flipped through a dozen—but really, the first one had been enough. Of course it wasn't human. It was a travesty of human. All the others were just evolutionary insult upon injury.

"What you see there is what you get," he said. "Have you ever heard of a town in Massachusetts called Innsmouth?"

Kerry shook her head. "I don't think so."

"No reason you should've. It's a little pisshole seaport whose best days were already behind it by the time of the Civil War. In the winter of 1927–28, there was a series of raids there, jointly conducted by the FBI and US Army, with naval support. Officially—remember, this was during Prohibition—it was to shut down bootlegging operations bringing whiskey down the coast from Canada. The truth..." He took back the iPad from her nerveless fingers. "Nothing explains the truth better than seeing it with your own eyes."

"You can't talk to them. That's what this is about, isn't it?" she said. "You can't communicate with them, and you think I can."

Escovedo smiled, and until now, she didn't think he had it in him. "It must be true about you, then. You're psychic after all."

"Is it that they can't talk, or won't?"

"That's never been satisfactorily determined," he said. "The ones who still looked more or less human when they were taken prisoner, they could, and did. But they didn't stay that way. Human, I mean. That's the way this mutation works." He tapped the iPad. "What you saw there is the result of decades of change. Most of them were brought in like that already. The rest eventually got there. And the changes go more than skin deep. Their throats are different now. On the inside. Maybe this keeps them from speaking in a way that you and I would find intelligible, or maybe it doesn't but they're really consistent about pretending it does, because they're all on the same page. They do communicate with each other, that's a given. They've been recorded extensively doing that, and the sounds have been analysed to exhaustion, and the consensus is that these sounds have their own syntax. The same way bird songs do. Just not as nice to listen to."

"If they've been under your roof all this time, they've spent almost a century away from whatever culture they had where they came from.

All that would be gone now, wouldn't it? The world's changed so much since then they wouldn't even recognise it," she said. "You're not doing science. You're doing national security. What I don't understand is why it's so important to communicate with them after all this time."

"All those changes you're talking about, that stops at the seashore. Drop them in the ocean and they'd feel right at home." He zipped the iPad back into his valise. "Whatever they might've had to say in 1928, that doesn't matter. Or '48, or '88. It's what we need to know *now* that's created a sense of urgency."

Once the helicopter had set down on the island, Kerry hadn't even left the cabin before thinking she'd never been to a more miserable place in her life. Rocky and rain-lashed, miles off the mainland, it was buffeted by winds that snapped from one direction and then another, so that the pines that grew here didn't know which way to go, twisted until they seemed to lean and leer with ill-intent.

"It's not always like this," Escovedo assured her. "Sometimes there's sleet, too."

It was the size of a large shopping plaza, a skewed triangular shape, with a helipad and boat dock on one point, and a scattering of outbuildings clustered along another, including what she assumed were offices and barracks for those unfortunate enough to have been assigned to duty here, everything laced together by a network of roads and pathways.

It was dominated, though, by a hulking brick monstrosity that looked exactly like what it was—a vintage relic of a prison—although it could pass for other things, too: an old factory or power plant, or, more likely, a wartime fortress, a leftover outpost from an era when the west coast feared the Japanese fleet. It had been built in 1942, Escovedo told her. No one would have questioned the need for it at the time, and since then, people were simply used to it, if they even knew it was there. Boaters might be curious, but the shoreline was studded at intervals with signs, and she imagined that whatever they said was enough to repel the inquisitive—that, and the triple rows of fencing crowned with loops of razor wire.

Inside her rain slicker, Kerry yanked the hood's drawstring tight and leaned into the needles of rain. October—it was only October. Imagine this place in January. Of course it didn't bother the colonel one bit. They were halfway along the path to the outbuildings when she turned to him and tugged the edge of her hood aside.

"I'm not psychic," she told him. "You called me that in the helicopter. That's not how I look at what I do."

"Noted," he said, noncommittal and unconcerned.

"I'm serious. If you're going to bring me out here, to this place, it's important to me that you understand what I do, and aren't snickering about it behind my back."

"You're here, aren't you? Obviously somebody high up the chain of command has faith in you."

That gave her pause to consider. This wouldn't have been a lark on their part. Bringing in a civilian on something most presidents hadn't known about would never have been done on a hunch—see if this works, and if it doesn't, no harm done. She would've been vetted, extensively, and she wondered how they'd done it. Coming up with pretences to interview past clients, perhaps, or people who'd appeared on *The Animal Whisperer*, to ascertain that they really were the just-folks they were purported to be, and that it wasn't scripted; that she genuinely had done for them what she was supposed to.

"What about you, though? Have you seen the show?"

"I got forwarded the season one DVDs. I watched the first couple episodes." He grew more thoughtful, less official. "The polar bear at the Cleveland Zoo, that was interesting. That's 1,500 pounds of apex predator you're dealing with. And you went in there without so much as a stick of wood between you and it. Just because it was having OCD issues? That takes either a big pair of balls or a serious case of stupid. And I don't think you're stupid."

"That's a start, I guess," she said. "Is that particular episode why I'm here? You figured since I did that, I wouldn't spook easily with these prisoners of yours?"

"I imagine it was factored in." The gravel that lined the path crunched underfoot for several paces before he spoke again. "If you don't think of yourself as psychic, what is it, then? How *does* it work?"

"I don't really know." Kerry had always dreaded the question, because she'd never been good at answering it. "It's been there as far back as I can remember, and I've gotten better at it, but I think that's just through the doing. It's a sense as much as anything. But not like sight or smell or taste. I compare it to balance. Can you explain how your sense of balance works?"

He cut her a sideways glance, betraying nothing, but she saw he didn't have a clue. "Mine? You're on a need-to-know basis here, remember."

Very good. Very dry. Escovedo was probably more fun than he let on.

"Right," she said. "Everybody else's, then. Most people have no idea. It's so intrinsic they take it for granted. A few may know it has to do with the inner ear. And a few of them, that it's centred in the vestibular apparatus, those three tiny loops full of fluid. One for up, one for down, one for forward and backward. But you don't need to know any of that to walk like we are now and not fall over. Well… that's what the animal thing is like for me. It's there, but I don't know the mechanism behind it."

He mused this over for several paces. "So that's your way of dodging the question?"

Kerry grinned at the ground. "It usually works."

"It's a good smokescreen. Really, though."

"Really? It's…" She drew the word out, a soft hiss while gathering her thoughts. "A combination of things. It's like receiving emotions, feelings, sensory impressions, mental imagery, either still or with motion. Any or all. Sometimes it's not even that, it's just… pure knowing, is the best way I know to phrase it."

"Pure knowing?" He sounded sceptical.

"Have you been in combat?"

"Yes."

"Then even if you haven't experienced it yourself, I'd be surprised if you haven't seen it or heard about it in people you trust—a strong sense that you should be very careful in that building, or approaching that next rise. They can't point to anything concrete to explain why. They just know. And they're often right."

Escovedo nodded. "Put in that context, it makes sense."

"Plus, for what it's worth, they ran a functional MRI on me, just for fun. That's on the season two DVD bonuses. Apparently the language centre of my brain is very highly developed. Ninety-eighth percentile, something like that. So maybe that has something to do with it."

"Interesting," Escovedo said, and nothing more, so she decided to quit while she was ahead.

The path curved and split before them, and though they weren't taking the left-hand branch to the prison, still, the closer they drew to it, darkened by rain and contemptuous of the wind, the greater the edifice seemed to loom over everything else on the island. It was like something grown from the sea, an iceberg of brick, with the worst of it hidden from view. When the wind blew just right, it carried with it a smell of fish, generations of them, as if left to spoil and never cleaned up.

Kerry stared past it, to the sea surging all the way to the horizon. This was an island only if you looked at it from out there. Simple, then: *Don't ever go out there.*

She'd never had a problem with swimming pools. You could see through those. Lakes, oceans, rivers… these were something entirely different. These were *dark* waters, full of secrets and unintended tombs. Shipwrecks, sunken airplanes, houses at the bottom of flooded valleys… they were sepulchres of dread, trapped in another world where they so plainly did not belong.

Not unlike the way she was feeling this very moment.


As she looked around Colonel Escovedo's office in the administrative building, it seemed almost as much a cell as anything they could have over at the prison. It was without windows, so the lighting was all artificial, fluorescent and unflattering. It aged him, and she didn't want to think what it had to be doing to her own appearance. In one corner, a dehumidifier chugged away, but the air still felt heavy and damp. Day in, day out, it must have been like working in a mine.

"Here's the situation. Why now," he said. "Their behaviour over there, it's been pretty much unchanged ever since they were moved to this installation. With one exception. Late summer, 1997, for about a month. I wasn't here then, but according to the records, it was like…" He paused, groping for the right words. "A hive mind. Like they were a single organism. They spent most of their time aligned to a precise angle to the south-west. The commanding officer at the time mentioned in his reports that it was like they were waiting for something. Inhumanly patient, just waiting. Then, eventually, they stopped and everything went back to normal."

"Until now?" she said.

"Nine days ago. They're doing it again."

"Did anybody figure out what was special about that month?"

"We think so. It took years, though. Three years before some analyst made the connection, and even then, you know, it's still a lucky accident. Maybe you've heard how it is with these agencies, they don't talk to each other, don't share notes. You've got a key here, and a lock on the other side of the world, and nobody in the middle who knows enough to put the two together. It's better now than it used to be, but it took the 9/11 attacks to get them to even *think* about correlating intel better."

"So what happened that summer?"

"Just listen," he said, and spun in his chair to the hardware behind him.

She'd been wondering about that anyway. Considering how functional his office was, it seemed not merely excessive, but out of character, that Escovedo would have an array of what looked to be high-end audio-video components, all feeding into a pair of three-way speakers and a subwoofer. He dialled in a sound file on the LCD of one of the rack modules, then thumbed the PLAY button.

At first it was soothing, a muted drone both airy and deep, a lonely noise that some movie's sound designer might have used to suggest the desolation of outer space. But no, this wasn't about space. It had to be the sea, this all led back to the sea. It was the sound of deep waters, the black depths where sunlight never reached.

Then came a new sound, deeper than deep, a slow eruption digging its way free of the drone, climbing in pitch, rising, rising, then plummeting back to leave her once more with the sound of the void. After moments of anticipation, it happened again, like a roar from an abyss, and prickled the fine hairs on the back of her neck—a primal response, but then, what was more primal than the ocean and the threats beneath its waves?

*This* was why she'd never liked the sea. This never knowing what was there, until it was upon you.

"Heard enough?" Escovedo asked, and seemed amused at her mute nod. "*That* happened. Their hive-mind behaviour coincided with that."

"What *was* it?"

"That's the big question. It was recorded several times during the summer of 1997, then never again. Since 1960, we've had the oceans bugged for sound, basically. We've got them full of microphones that we put there to listen for Soviet submarines, when we thought it was a possibility we'd be going to war with them. They're down hundreds of feet, along an ocean layer called the sound channel. For sound conductivity, it's the Goldilocks zone—it's just right. After the Cold War was over, these mic networks were decommissioned from military use and turned over for scientific research. Whales, seismic events, underwater volcanoes, that sort of thing. Most of it, it's instantly identifiable. The people whose job it is to listen to what the mics pick up, 99.99 per cent of the time they know exactly what they've got because the sounds conform to signature patterns, and they're just so familiar.

"But every so often they get one they can't identify. It doesn't fit any known pattern. So they give it a cute name and it stays a mystery. This one, they called it the 'Bloop'. Makes it sound like a kid farting in the bathtub, doesn't it?"

She pointed at the speakers. "An awfully big kid and an awfully big tub."

"Now you're getting ahead of me. The Bloop's point of origin was calculated to be in the South Pacific… maybe not coincidentally, not far from Polynesia, which is generally conceded as the place of origin for what eventually came to be known in Massachusetts as 'the Innsmouth look'. Some outside influence was brought home from Polynesia in the 1800s during a series of trading expeditions by a sea captain named Obed Marsh."

"Are you talking about a disease, or a genetic abnormality?"

Escovedo slapped one hand onto a sheaf of bound papers lying on one side of his desk. "You can be the judge of that. I've got a summary here for you to look over, before you get started tomorrow. It'll give you more background on the town and its history. The whole thing's a knotted-up tangle of fact and rumour and local legend and God knows what all, but it's not my job to sort out what's what. I've got enough on my plate sticking with facts, and the fact is, I'm in charge of keeping sixty-three of these proto-human monstrosities hidden from the world, and I know they're cued into something anomalous, but I don't know what. The other fact is, the last time they acted like this was fifteen years ago, while those mics were picking up one of the loudest sounds ever recorded on the planet."

"How loud was it?"

"Every time that sound went off, it wasn't just a local event. It was picked up over a span of five thousand kilometres."

The thought made her head swim. Something with that much power behind it… there could be nothing good about it. Something that loud was the sound of death, of cataclysm and extinction events. It was the sound of an asteroid strike, of a volcano not just erupting, but vaporising a land-mass—Krakatoa, the island of Thera. She imagined standing here, past the north-western edge of the continental US, and hearing something happen in New York. Okay, sound travelled better in water than in air, but still—*three thousand miles*.

"Despite that," Escovedo said, "the analysts say it most closely matches a profile of something alive."

"A whale?" There couldn't be anything bigger, not for millions of years.

The colonel shook his head. "Keep going. Somebody who briefed me on this compared it to a blue whale plugged in and running through the amplifier stacks at every show Metallica has ever played, all at once. She also said that what they captured probably wasn't even the whole sound. That it's likely that a lot of frequencies and details got naturally filtered out along the way."

"Whatever it was… there have to be theories."

"Sure. Just nothing that fits with all the known pieces."

"Is the sound occurring again?"

"No. We don't know what they're cueing in on this time."

He pointed at the prison. Even though he couldn't see it, because there were no windows, and now she wondered if he didn't prefer it that way. Block it out with walls, and maybe for a few minutes at a time he could pretend he was somewhere else, assigned to some other duty.

"But *they* do," he said. "Those abominations over there know. We just need to find the key to getting them to tell us."

She was billeted in what Colonel Escovedo called the guest barracks, the only visitor in a building that could accommodate eight in privacy, sixteen if they doubled up. Visitors, Kerry figured, would be a rare occurrence here, and the place felt that way, little lived in and not much used. The rain had strengthened closer to evening and beat hard on the low roof, a lonely sound that built from room to vacant room.

When she heard the deep thump of the helicopter rotors pick up, then recede into the sky—having waited, apparently, until it was clear she would be staying—she felt unaccountably abandoned, stranded with no way off this outpost that lay beyond not just the rim of civilisation, but beyond the frontiers of even her expanded sense of life, of humans and animals and what passed between them.

Every now and then she heard someone outside, crunching past on foot or on an all-terrain four-wheeler. If she looked, they were reduced to dark, indistinct smears wavering in the water that sluiced down the windows. She had the run of most of the island if she wanted, although that was mainly just a licence to get soaked under the sky. The buildings were forbidden, other than her quarters and the admin office, and, of course, the prison, as long as she was being escorted. And, apart for the colonel, she was apparently expected to pretend to be the invisible woman. She and the duty personnel were off-limits to each other. She wasn't to speak to them, and they were under orders not to speak with her.

They didn't know the truth—it was the only explanation that made sense. They didn't know, because they didn't need to. They'd been fed a cover story. Maybe they believed they were guarding the maddened survivors of a disease, a genetic mutation, an industrial accident or something that had fallen from space and that did terrible things to DNA. Maybe they'd all been fed a different lie, so that if they got together to compare notes they wouldn't know which to believe.

For that matter, she wasn't sure she did either.

First things first, though: she set up a framed photo of Tabitha on a table out in the barracks' common room, shot over the summer when they'd gone horseback riding in the Sawtooth Range. Her daughter's sixth birthday. Rarely was a picture snapped in which Tabby wasn't beaming, giddy with life, but this was one of them, her little face rapt with focus. Still in the saddle, she was leaning forward, hugging the mare's neck, her braided hair a blonde stripe along the chestnut hide, and it looked for all the world as if the two of them were sharing a secret.

The photo would be her beacon, her lighthouse shining from home.

She fixed a mug of hot cocoa in the kitchenette, then settled into one of the chairs with the summary report that Escovedo had sent with her.

Except for its cold, matter-of-fact tone, it read like bizarre fiction. If she hadn't seen the photos, she wouldn't have believed it: a series of raids in an isolated Massachusetts seaport that swept up more than two hundred residents, most of whose appearances exhibited combinations of human, ichthyoid, and amphibian traits. 'The Innsmouth look' had been well known to the neighbouring towns for at least two generations—"an unsavoury haven of inbreeding and circus folk", according to a derisive comment culled from an Ipswich newspaper of the era—but even then, Innsmouth had been careful to put forward the best face it possibly could. Which meant, in most cases, residents still on the low side of middle-age… at least when it came to the families that had a few decades' worth of roots in the town, rather than its more recent newcomers.

With age came change so drastic that the affected people gradually lost all resemblance to who they'd been as children and young adults, eventually reaching the point that they let themselves be seen only by each other, taking care to hide from public view in a warren of dilapidated homes, warehouses and limestone caverns that honeycombed the area.

One page of the report displayed a sequence of photos of what was ostensibly the same person, identified as Giles Shapleigh, eighteen years old when detained in 1928. He'd been a handsome kid in the first photo, and if he had nothing to smile about when it was taken, you could at least see the potential for a roguish, cockeyed grin. By his twenty-fifth year, he'd visibly aged, his hair receded and thinning, and after seven years of captivity he had the sullen look of a convict. By thirty, he was bald as a cue ball, and his skull had seemed to narrow. By thirty-five, his jowls had widened enough to render his neck almost non-existent, giving him a bullet-headed appearance that she found all the more unnerving for his dead-eyed stare.

By the time he was sixty, with astronauts not long on the moon, there was nothing left to connect Giles Shapleigh with who or what he'd been, neither his identity nor his species. Still, though, his transformation wasn't yet complete.

He was merely catching up to his friends, neighbours and relatives. By the time of those Prohibition-era raids, most of the others had been this way for years—decades, some of them. Although they aged, they didn't seem to weaken and, while they could be killed, if merely left to themselves, they most certainly didn't die.

They could languish, though. As those first years went on, with the Innsmouth prisoners scattered throughout a handful of remote quarantine facilities across New England, it became obvious that they didn't do well in the kind of environment reserved for normal prisoners: barred cells, bright lights, exercise yards... *dryness*. Some of them developed a skin condition that resembled powdery mildew, a white, dusty crust that spread across them in patches. There was a genuine fear that, whatever it was, it might jump from captives to captors, and prove more virulent in wholly human hosts, although this never happened.

Thus it was decided: they didn't need a standard prison so much as they needed their own zoo. That they got it was something she found strangely heartening. What was missing from the report, presumably because she had no need to know, was *why*.

While she didn't want to admit it, Kerry had no illusions—the expedient thing would've been to kill them off. No one would have known, and undoubtedly there would've been those who found it an easy order to carry out. It was wartime, and if war proved anything, it proved how simple it was to dehumanise people even when they looked just like you. This was 1942, and this was already happening on an industrial scale across Europe. These people from Innsmouth would have had few advocates. To merely look at them was to feel revulsion, to sense a challenge to everything you thought you knew about the world, about what could and couldn't be. Most people would look at them and think they deserved to die. They were an insult to existence, to cherished beliefs.

Yet they lived. They'd outlived the men who'd rounded them up, and their first jailers, and most of their jailers since. They'd outlived everyone who'd opted to keep them a secret down through the generations… yet for what?

Perhaps morality *had* factored into the decision to keep them alive, but she doubted morality had weighed heaviest. Maybe, paradoxically, it had been done out of fear. They may have rounded up over two hundred of Innsmouth's strangest, but many more had escaped—by most accounts, fleeing into the harbour, then the ocean beyond. To exterminate these captives because they were unnatural would be to throw away the greatest resource they might possess in case they ever faced these beings again, under worse circumstances.

Full disclosure, Escovedo had promised. She would know as much as he did. But when she finished the report along with the cocoa, she had no faith whatsoever that she was on par with the colonel, or that even he'd been told the half of it himself.

How much did a man need to know, really, to be a glorified prison warden?

Questions nagged, starting with the numbers. She slung on her coat and headed back out into the rain, even colder now, as it needled down from a dusk descending on the island like a dark grey blanket. She found the colonel still in his office, and supposed by now he was used to people dripping on his floor.

"What happened to the rest of them?" she asked. "Your report says there were over two hundred to start with. And that this place was built to house up to three hundred. So I guess somebody thought more might turn up. But you're down to sixty-three. And they don't die of natural causes. So what happened to the others?"

"What does it matter? For your purposes, I mean. What you're here to do."

"Did you know that animals understand the idea of extermination? Wolves do. Dogs at the pound do. Cattle do, once they get to the slaughterhouse pens. They may not be able to articulate it, but they pick up on it. From miles away, sometimes, they can pick up on it." She felt a chilly drop of water slither down her forehead. "I don't know about fish or reptiles. But whatever humanity may still exist in these prisoners of yours, I wouldn't be surprised if it's left them just as sensitive to the concept of extermination, or worse."

He looked at her blankly, waiting for more. He didn't get it.

"For all I know, you're sending me in there as the latest interrogator who wants to find out the best way to commit genocide on the rest of their kind. *That's* why it matters. Is that how they're going to see me?"

Escovedo looked at her for a long time, his gaze fixated on her, not moving, just studying her increasing unease as she tried to divine what he was thinking: if he was angry, or disappointed, or considering sending her home before she'd even set foot in the prison. He stared so long she had no idea which it could be, until she realised that the stare *was* the point.

"They've got these eyes," he said. "They don't blink. They've got no white part to them anymore, so you don't know where they're looking, exactly. It's more like looking into a mirror than another eye. A mirror that makes you want to look away. So... how they'll *see* you?" he said, with a quick shake of his head and a hopeless snort of a laugh. "I have no idea *what* they see."

She wondered how long he'd been in this command. If he would ever get used to the presence of such an alien enemy. If any of them did, his predecessors, back to the beginning. That much she could see.

"Like I said, I stick with facts," he said. "I can tell you this much:

When you've got a discovery like *them*, you have to expect that every so often another one or two of them are going to disappear into the system."

"The system," she said. "What does that mean?"

"You were right, we don't do science here. But they do in other places," he told her. "You can't be naïve enough to think research means spending the day watching them crawl around and writing down what they had for lunch."

Naïve? No. Kerry supposed she had suspected before she'd even slogged over here to ask. Just to make sure. You didn't have to be naïve to hope for better.

She carried the answer into dreams that night, where it became excruciatingly obvious that, while the Innsmouth prisoners may have lost the ability to speak in any known language, when properly motivated, they could still shriek.


Morning traded the rain for fog, lots of it, a chilly cloud that had settled over the island before dawn. There was no more sky and sea, no more distance, just whatever lay a few feet in front of her, and endless grey beyond. Without the gravel pathways, she was afraid she might've lost her bearings, maybe wander to the edge of the island. Tangle herself in razor wire, and hang there and die before anyone noticed.

She could feel it now, the channels open and her deepest intuition rising: this was the worst place she'd ever been, and she couldn't tell which side bore the greater blame.

With breakfast in her belly and coffee in hand, she met Escovedo at his office, so he could escort her to the corner of the island where the prison stood facing west, looking out over the sea. There would be no more land until Asia. Immense, made of brick so saturated with wet air that its walls looked slimed, the prison emerged from the mist like a sunken ship.

What would it be like, she wondered, to enter a place and not come out for seventy years? What would that do to one's mind? Were they even sane now? Or did they merely view this as a brief interruption in their lives? Unless they were murdered outright—a possibility—

their life-spans were indefinite. Maybe they knew that time was their ally. Time would kill their captors, generation by generation, while they went on. Time would bring down every wall. All terrestrial life might go extinct, while they went on.

As long as they could make it those last few dozen yards to the sea.

"Have any of them ever escaped from here?" she asked.

"No."

"Don't you find that odd? I do. Hasn't most every prison had at least one escape over seventy years?"

"Not this one. It doesn't run like a regular prison. The inmates don't work. There's no kitchen, no laundry trucks, no freedom to tunnel. They don't get visitors. We just spend all day looking at each other." He paused in the arched, inset doorway, his finger on the call button that would summon the guards inside to open up. "If you want my unfiltered opinion, those of us who pulled this duty are the real prisoners."

Inside, it was all gates and checkpoints, the drab institutional hallways saturated with a lingering smell of fish. *Them*, she was smelling *them*. Like people who spent their workdays around death and decay, the soldiers here would carry it home in their pores. You had to pity them that. They would be smelling it after a year of showers, whether it was there or not.

Stairs, finally, a series of flights that seemed to follow the curvature of some central core. It deposited them near the top of the building, on an observation deck. Every vantage-point around the retaining wall, particularly a trio of guard posts, overlooked an enormous pit, like an abandoned rock quarry. Flat terraces and rounded pillows of stone rose here and there out of a pool of murky seawater. Along the walls, rough stairways led up to three tiers of rooms, cells without bars.

This wasn't a prison where the inmates would need to be protected from each other. They were all on the same side down there, prisoners of an undeclared war.

Above the pit, the roof was louvred, so apparently, although closed now, it could be opened. They could see the sky. They would have air and rain. Sunshine, if that still meant anything to them.

The water, she'd learned from last night's briefing paper, was no stagnant pool. It was continually refreshed, with drains along the bottom and grated pipes midway up the walls that periodically spewed a gusher like a tidal surge. Decades of this had streaked the walls with darker stains, each like a ragged brush stroke straight down from the rusty grate to the foaming surface of their makeshift sea.

Fish even lived in it, and why not? The prisoners had to eat.

Not at the moment, though. They lined the rocks in groups, as many as would fit on any given surface, sitting, squatting, facing the unseen ocean in eerily perfect alignment to one another.

"What do you make of it?" he asked.

Kerry thought of fish she'd watched in commercial aquariums, in nature documentaries, fish swimming in their thousands, singularly directed, and then, in an instantaneous response to some stimulus, changing directions in perfect unison. "I would say they're schooling."

From where they'd entered the observation deck, she could see only their backs, and began to circle the retaining wall for a better view.

Their basic shapes looked human, but the details were all wrong. Their skin ranged from dusky grey to light green, with pale bellies— dappled sometimes, an effect like sunlight through water—and rubbery-looking even from here, as though it would be slick as a wetsuit to the touch, at least the areas that hadn't gone hard and scaly. Some wore the remnants of clothing, although she doubted anything would hold up long in the water and rocks, while others chose to go entirely without. They were finned and they were spiny, no two quite the same, and their hands webbed between the fingers, their feet ridiculously outsized. Their smooth heads were uncommonly narrow, all of them, but still more human than not. Their faces, though, were ghastly. These were faces for another world, with thick-lipped mouths made to gulp water, and eyes to peer through the murky gloom of the deep. Their noses were all but gone, just vestigial nubs now, flattened and slitted. The females' breasts had been similarly subsumed, down to little more than hard bumps.

She clutched the top of the wall until her fingernails began to bend. Not even photographs could truly prepare you for seeing them in the flesh.

*I wish I'd never known,* she thought. *I can never be the same again.*

"You want to just pick one at random, see where it goes?" Escovedo asked.

"How do you see this working? We haven't talked about that," she said. "What, you pull one of them out and put us in a room together, each of us on either side of a table?"

"Do you have any better ideas?"

"It seems so artificial. The environment of an interrogation room, I mean. I need them open, if that makes sense. Their minds, open. A room like that, it's like you're doing everything you can to close them off from the start."

"Well, I'm not sending you down there into the middle of all sixty-three of them, if that's what you're getting at. I have no idea how they'd react, and there's no way I could guarantee your safety."

She glanced at the guard posts, only now registering why they were so perfectly triangulated. Nothing was out of reach of their rifles.

"And you don't want to set up a situation where you'd have to open fire on the group, right?"

"It would be counter-productive."

"Then you pick one," she said. "You know them better than I do."

If the Innsmouth prisoners still had a sense of patriarchy, then Escovedo must have decided to start her at the top of their pecking order.

The one they brought her was named Barnabas Marsh, if he even had a use any more for a name that none of his kind could speak. Maybe names only served the convenience of their captors now, although if any name still carried weight, it would be the name of Marsh. Barnabas was the grandson of Obed Marsh, the ship's captain who, as village legend held, had sailed to strange places above the sea and below it, and brought back both the DNA and partnerships that had altered the course of Innsmouth's history.

Barnabas had been old even when taken prisoner, and by human terms he was now beyond ancient. She tried not to think of him as monstrous, but no other word wanted to settle on him, on any of them.

Marsh, though, she found all the more monstrous for the fact that she could see in him the puffed-up, barrel-chested bearing of a once-domineering man who'd never forgotten who and what he had been.

Behind the wattles of his expanded neck, gills rippled with indignation. The thick lips, wider than any human mouth she'd ever seen, stretched downward at each corner in a permanent, magisterial sneer.

He waddled when he walked, as if no longer made for the land, and when the two guards in suits of body armour deposited him in the room, he looked her up and down, then shuffled in as if resigned to tolerating her until this interruption was over. He stopped long enough to give the table and chairs in the centre of the room a scornful glance, then continued to the corner, where he slid to the floor with a shoulder on each wall, the angle where they met giving room for his sharp-spined back.

She took the floor as well.

"I believe you can understand me. Every word," Kerry said. "You either can't or won't speak the way you did for the first decades of your life, but I can't think of any reason why you shouldn't still understand me. And that puts you way ahead of all the rest of God's creatures I've managed to communicate with."

He looked at her with his bulging dark eyes, and Escovedo had been right. It was a disconcertingly inhuman gaze, not even mammalian. It wasn't anthropomorphizing to say that mammals—dogs, cats, even a plethora of wilder beasts—had often looked at her with a kind of warmth. But *this*, these eyes… they were cold, with a remote scrutiny that she sensed regarded her as lesser in every way.

The room's air, cool to begin with, seemed to chill even more as her skin crawled with an urge to put distance between them. Could he sense that she feared him? Maybe he took this as a given. That he could be dangerous was obvious—the closer you looked, the more he seemed covered with sharp points, none more lethal than the tips of his stubby fingers. But she had to trust the prison staff to ensure her safety. While there was no guard in here to make the energy worse than it was already, they were being watched on a closed-circuit camera. If Marsh threatened her, the room would be flooded with a gas that would put them both out in seconds. She'd wake up with a headache, and Marsh would wake up back in the pit.

And nothing would be accomplished.

"I say God's creatures because I don't know how else to think of you," she said. "I know how *they* think of you. They think you're all aberrations. Unnatural. Not that I'm telling you anything you probably haven't already overheard from them every day for more than eighty years."

And did that catch his interest, even a little? If the subtle tilt of his head meant anything, maybe it did.

"But if you exist, entire families of you, colonies of you, then you can't be an aberration. You're within the realm of nature's possibilities."

Until this moment, she'd had no idea what she would say to him. With animals, she was accustomed to speaking without much concern for what exactly she said. It was more how she said it. Like very young children, animals cued in on tone, not language. They nearly always seemed to favour a higher-pitched voice. They responded to touch.

None of which was going to work here.

But Barnabas Marsh was a presence, and a powerful one, radiant with a sense of age. She kept speaking to him, seeking a way through the gulf between them, the same as she always did. No matter what the species, there always seemed to be a way, always something to which she could attune—an image, a sound, a taste, some heightened sense that overwhelmed her and, once she regained her equilibrium, let her use it as the key in the door that would open the way for more.

She spoke to him of the sea, the most obvious thing, because no matter what the differences between them, they had that much in common. It flowed in each of them, water and salt, and they'd both come from it; he was just closer to returning, was all. Soon she felt the pull of tides, the tug of currents, the cold wet draw of gravity luring down, down, down to greater depths, then the equipoise of pressure, and where once it might've crushed, now it comforted, a cold cocoon that was both a blanket and a world, tingling along her skin with news coming from a thousand leagues in every direction—

And with a start she realised that the sea hadn't been her idea at all.

She'd only followed where he led. Whether Marsh meant to or not.

Kerry looked him in his cold, inhuman eyes, not knowing quite what lay behind them, until she began to get a sense that the sea was *all* that lay behind them. The sea was all he thought of, all he wanted, all that mattered, a yearning so focused that she truly doubted she could slip past it to ferret out what was so special about *now*. What they all sensed happening *now*, just as they had fifteen years ago.

It was all one and the same, of course, bound inextricably together, but first they had to reclaim the sea.

And so it went the rest of the day, with one after another of this sad parade of prisoners, until she'd seen nearly twenty of them. Nothing that she would've dared call progress, just inklings of impressions, snippets of sensations, none of it coalescing into a meaningful whole, and all of it subsumed beneath a churning ache to return to the sea. It was their defence against her, and she doubted they even knew it.

Whatever was different about her, whatever had enabled her to whisper with creatures that she and the rest of the world found more appealing, it wasn't made to penetrate a human-born despair that had hardened over most of a century.

There was little light remaining in the day when she left the prison in defeat, and little enough to begin with. It was now a colourless world of approaching darkness. She walked a straight line, sense of direction lost in the clammy mist that clung to her as surely as the permeating smell of the prisoners. She knew she had to come to the island's edge eventually, and if she saw another human being before tomorrow, it would be too soon.

Escovedo found her anyway, and she had to assume he'd been following all along. Just letting her get some time and distance before, what, her debriefing? Kerry stood facing the water as it slopped against a shoreline of rocks the size of piled skulls, her hand clutching the inner fence. By now it seemed that the island was less a prison than a concentration camp.

"For what it's worth," the colonel said, "I didn't expect it to go well the first day."

"What makes you think a second day is going to go any better?"

"Rapport?" He lifted a Thermos, uncapped it, and it steamed in the air. "But rapport takes time."

"Time." She rattled the fence. "Will I even be leaving here?"

"I hope that's a joke." He poured into the Thermos cup without asking and gave it to her. "Here. The cold can sneak up on you out like this."

She sipped at the cup, coffee, not the best she'd ever had but far from the worst. It warmed her, though, and that was a plus. "Let me ask you something. Have they ever bred? Either here or wherever they were held before? Have *any* of them bred?"

"No. Why do you ask?"

"It's something I was picking up on from a few of them. The urge. You know it when you feel it. Across species, it's a great common denominator."

"I don't know what to tell you, other than that they haven't."

"Don't you find that odd?"

"I find the whole situation odd."

"What I mean is, even pandas in captivity manage to get pregnant once in a while."

"I've just never really thought about it."

"You regard them as prisoners, you *have* to, I get that. And the females don't look all that different from the males. But suppose they looked more like normal men and women. What would you expect if you had a prison with a mixed-gender population that had unrestricted access to each other?"

"I get your point, but…" He wasn't stonewalling, she could tell. He genuinely had never considered this. Because he'd never had to. "Wouldn't it be that they're too old?"

"I thought it was already established that once they get like this, age is no longer a factor. But even if it was, Giles Shapleigh wasn't too old when they first grabbed him. He was eighteen. Out of more than two hundred, he can't have been the only young one. You remember what the urge was like when you were eighteen?"

Escovedo grunted a laugh. "Every chance I get."

"Only he's never acted on it. None of them have."

"A fact that I can't say distresses me."

"It's just…" she said, then shut up. She had her answer. They'd never bred. Wanted to, maybe felt driven to, but hadn't. Perhaps captivity affected their fertility, or short-circuited the urge from becoming action.

Or maybe it was just an incredible act of discipline. They had to realise what would happen to their offspring. They would never be allowed to keep them, raise them. Their children would face a future of tests and vivisection. Even monstrosities would want better for their babies.

"I have an observation to make," Kerry said. "It's not going to go any better tomorrow, or the day after that. Not if you want me to keep doing it like today. It's like they have this shell around them." She tipped the coffee to her lips and eyed him over the rim, and he was impossible to read. "Should I go on?"

"I'm listening."

"You're right, rapport takes time. But it takes more than that. Your prisoners may have something beyond human senses, but they still have human intellects. More or less. It feels overlaid with something else, and it's not anything good, but fundamentally they haven't stopped being human, and they need to be dealt with that way. Not like they're entirely animals."

She stopped a moment to gauge him, and saw that she at least hadn't lost him. Although she'd not proposed anything yet.

"If they *looked* more human to you, don't you think the way you'd be trying to establish rapport would be to treat them more like human beings?" she said. "I read the news. I watch TV. I've heard the arguments about torture. For and against. I know what they are. The main thing I took away is that when you consult the people who've been good at getting reliable information from prisoners, they'll tell you they did it by being humane. Which includes letting the prisoner have something he wants, or loves. There was a captured German officer in World War II who loved chess. He opened up after his interrogator started playing chess with him. That's all it took."

"I don't think these things are going to be interested in board games."

"No. But there's something every one of them wants," she said.

"There's something they love more than anything else in the world."

*And why does it have to be the same thing I dread?*

When she told him how they might be able to use that to their advantage, she expected Escovedo to say no, out of the question. Instead, he thought it over for all of five seconds and said yes.

"I don't like it, but we need to fast-track this," he said. "We don't just eyeball their alignment in the pit, you know. We measure it with a laser. That's how we know how precisely oriented they are. And since last night they've shifted. Whatever they're cued in on has moved north."

The next morning, dawn came as dawn should, the sky clear and the fog blown away and the sun an actual presence over the horizon. After two days of being scarcely able to see fifty feet in front of her, it seemed as if she could see forever. There was something joyously liberating in it. After just two days.

So what was it going to feel like for Barnabas Marsh to experience the ocean for the first time in more than eighty years? The true sea, not the simulation of it siphoned off and pumped into the pit. Restrained by a makeshift leash, yes, three riflemen ready to shoot from the shore, that too, three more ready to shoot from the parapet of the prison... but it would still be the sea.

That it would be Marsh they would try this with was inevitable. It might not be safe and they might get only one chance at this. He was cunning, she had to assume, but he was the oldest by far, and a direct descendant of the man who'd brought this destiny to Innsmouth in the first place. He would have the deepest reservoir of knowledge.

And, maybe, the arrogance to want to share it, and gloat.

Kerry was waiting by the shallows when they brought him down, at one end of a long chain whose other end was padlocked to the frame of a four-wheel all-terrain cycle that puttered along behind him—he might have been able to throw men off balance in a tug-of-war, but not this.

Although he had plenty of slack, Marsh paused a few yards from the water's edge, stopping to stare out at the shimmering expanse of sea. The rest of them might have seen mistrust in his hesitation, or savouring the moment, but neither of these felt right. *Reacquainting*, she thought. *That's it.*

He trudged forward then, trailing chain, and as he neared the water, he cast a curious look at her, standing there in a slick blue wetsuit they'd outfitted her with, face-mask and snorkel in her hand. It gave him pause again, and in whatever bit of Marsh that was still human, she saw that he understood, realised who was responsible for this.

Gratitude, though, was not part of his nature. Once in the water, he vanished in moments, marked only by the clattering of his chain along the rocks.

She'd thought it wise to allow Marsh several minutes alone, just himself and the sea. They were midway through it when Escovedo joined her at the water's edge.

"You sure you're up for this?" he said. "It's obvious how much you don't like the idea, even if it was yours."

She glanced over at Marsh's chain, now still. "I don't like to see anything captive when it has the capacity to lament its conditions."

"That's not what I mean. If you think you've been keeping it under wraps that you've got a problem with water, you haven't. I could spot it two days ago, soon as we left the mainland behind."

She grinned down at her flippers, sheepish. Busted. "Don't worry. I'll deal."

"But you still know how to snorkel…?"

"How else are you going to get over a phobia?" She laughed, needing to, and it helped. "It went great in the heated indoor pool."

She fitted the mask over her face and popped in the snorkel's mouthpiece, and went in after Marsh. Calves, knees… every step forward was an effort, so she thought of Tabby. *The sooner I get results, the quicker I'll get home.* Thighs, waist… then she was in Marsh's world, unnerved by the fear that she would find him waiting for her, tooth and claw, ready to rip through her in a final act of defiance.

But he was nowhere near her. She floated facedown, kicking lightly and visually tracking the chain down the slope of the shoreline, until she saw it disappear over a drop-off into a well that was several feet deeper. *There he is.* She hovered in place, staring down at Marsh as he luxuriated in the water. Ecstatic—there was no other word for him. Twisting, turning, undulating, the chain only a minor impediment, he would shoot up near the surface, then turn and plunge back to the bottom, rolling in the murk he stirred up, doing it again, again, again. His joyous abandon was like a child's.

He saw her and stilled, floating midway between surface and sand, a sight from a nightmare, worse than a shark because even in this world he was so utterly alien.

And it was never going to get any less unnerving. She sucked in a deep breath through the snorkel, then plunged downward, keeping a bit of distance between them as she swam to the bottom.

Two minutes and then some—that was how long she could hold her breath.

Kerry homed in on a loose rock that looked heavy enough to counter her buoyancy, then checked the dive compass strapped to her wrist like an oversized watch. She wrestled the wave-smoothed stone into her lap and sat cross-legged on the bottom, matching as precisely as she could the latest of the south-westerly alignments that had so captivated Marsh and the other sixty-two of them. Sitting on the seabed with the Pacific alive around her, muffled in her ears and receding into a blue-green haze, as she half-expected something even worse than Marsh to come swimming straight at her out of the void.

Somewhere above and behind her, he was watching.

She stayed down until her lungs began to ache, then pushed free of the stone and rose to the surface, where she purged the snorkel with a gust of spent air, then flipped to return to the seabed. Closer this time, mere feet between her and Marsh as she settled again, no longer needing the compass—she found her bearing naturally, and time began to slow, and so did her heartbeat in spite of the fear, then the fear was gone, washed away in the currents that tugged at her like temptations.

Up again, down again, and it felt as if she were staying below longer each time, her capacity for breath expanding to fill the need, until she was all but on the outside of herself looking in, marvelling at this creature she'd become, amphibious, neither of the land nor the water, yet belonging to both. She lived in a bubble of breath in an infinite now, lungs satiated, awareness creeping forward along this trajectory she was aligned with, as if it were a cable that spanned the seas, and if she could only follow it, she would learn the secrets it withheld from all but the initiated—

And he was there, Barnabas Marsh a looming presence drifting alongside her. If there was anything to read in his cold face, his unplumbed eyes, it was curiosity. She had become something he'd never seen before, something between his enemies and his people, and changing by the moment.

She peered at him, nothing between them now but the thin plastic window of her mask and a few nourishing inches of water.

*What is it that's out there?* she asked. *Tell me. I want to know. I want to understand.*

It was true—she did. She would wonder even if she hadn't been asked to. She would wonder every day for the rest of her life. Her existence would be marred by not knowing.

*Tell me what it is that lies beyond…*

She saw it then, a thought like a whisper become an echo, as it began to build on itself, the occlusions between worlds parting in swirls of ink and oceans. And there was so *much* of it, this was something that couldn't be—who could build such a thing, and who would dream of finding it *here*, at depths that might crush a submarine—then she realised that all she was seeing was one wall, one mighty wall, built of blocks the size of boxcars, a feat that couldn't be equalled even on land. She knew without seeing the whole that it spanned miles, that if this tiny prison island could sink into it, it would be lost forever, an insignificant patch of pebbles and mud to what lived there—

And she was wholly herself again, with a desperate need to breathe.

Kerry wrestled the rock off her lap for the last time, kicking for a surface as far away as the sun. As she shot past Barnabas Marsh she was gripped by a terror that he would seize her ankle to pull her back down.

But she knew she could fight that, so what he did was worse somehow, nothing she knew that he *could* do, and maybe none of these unsuspecting men on the island did either. It was what sound could be if sound were needles, a piercing skirl that ripped through her like an electric shock and clapped her ears as sharply as a pressure wave. She spun in the water, not knowing up from down, and when she stabilised and saw Marsh nearby, she realised he wasn't even directing this at her. She was just a bystander who got in the way. Instead, he was facing out to sea, the greater sea, unleashing this sound into the abyss.

She floundered to the surface and broke through, graceless and gasping, and heard Colonel Escovedo shout a command, and in the next instant heard the roar of an engine as the four-wheeler went racing up the rock-strewn slope of the island's western edge. The chain snapped taut, and moments later Marsh burst from the shallows in a spray of surf and foam, dragged twisting up onto the beach. Someone fired a shot, and someone else another, and of course no one heard her calling from nearly a hundred feet out, treading water now, and they were all shooting, so none of them heard her cry out that they had the wrong idea. But bullets first, questions later, she supposed.

His blood was still red. She had to admit, she'd wondered.


It took the rest of the morning before she was ready to be debriefed, and Escovedo let her have it, didn't press for too much, too soon. She needed to be warm again, needed to get past the shock of seeing Barnabas Marsh shot to pieces on the beach. Repellent though he was, she'd still linked with him in her way, whispered back and forth, and he'd been alive one minute, among the oldest living beings on the earth, then dead the next.

She ached from the sound he'd made, as if every muscle and organ inside her had been snapped like a rubber band. Her head throbbed with the assault on her ears.

In the colonel's office, finally, behind closed doors, Kerry told him of the colossal ruins somewhere far beneath the sea.

"Does any of that even make sense?" she asked. "It doesn't to me. It felt real enough at the time, but now… it has to have been a dream of his. Or maybe Marsh was insane. How could anyone have even known if he was?"

Behind his desk, Escovedo didn't move for the longest time, leaning on his elbows and frowning at his interlaced hands. Had he heard her at all? Finally he unlocked one of the drawers and withdrew a folder; shook out some photos, then put one back and slid the rest across to her. Eight in all.

"What you saw," he said. "Did it look anything like this?"

She put them in rows, four over four, like puzzle pieces, seeing how they might fit together. And she needed them all at once, to bludgeon herself into accepting the reality of it: stretches of walls, suggestions of towers, some standing, some collapsed, all fitted together from blocks of greenish stone that could have been shaped by both hammers and razors. Everything was restricted to what spotlights could reach, limned by a cobalt haze that faded into inky blackness. Here, too, were windows and gateways and wide, irregular terraces that might have been stairs, only for nothing that walked on human feet. There was no sense of scale, nothing to measure it by, but she'd sensed it once today already, and it had the feeling of enormity and measureless age.

It was the stuff of nightmares, out of place and out of time, waiting in the cold, wet dark.

"They've been enhanced because of the low-light conditions and the distance," Escovedo said. "It's like the shots of the *Titanic*. The only light down that far is what you can send on a submersible. Except the Navy's lost every single one they've sent down there. They just go offline. These pictures… they're from the one that lasted the longest."

She looked up again. The folder they'd come from was gone. "You held one back. I can't see it?"

He shook his head. "Need to know."

"It shows something that different from the others?"

Nothing. He was as much a block of stone as the walls.

"Something living?" She remembered his description of the sound heard across three thousand miles of ocean: *The analysts say it most closely matches a profile of something alive.* "Is that it?"

"I won't tell you you're right." He appeared to be choosing his words with care. "But if that's what you'd picked up on out there with Marsh, then maybe we'd have a chance to talk about photo number nine."

She wanted to know. Needed to know as badly as she'd needed to breathe this morning, waking up to herself too far under the surface of the sea.

"What about the rest of them? We can keep trying."

He shook his head no. "We've come to the end of this experiment. I've already arranged for your transportation back home tomorrow."

Just like that. It felt as if she were being fired. She hadn't even delivered. She'd not told them anything they didn't already know about. She'd only confirmed it. What had made that unearthly noise, what the Innsmouth prisoners were waiting for—that's what they were really after.

"We're only just getting started. You can't rush something like this. There are sixty-two more of them over there, one of them is sure to—"

He cut her off with a slash of his hand. "Sixty-two of them who are in an uproar now. They didn't see what happened to Marsh, but they've got the general idea."

"Then maybe you shouldn't have been so quick to order his execution."

"That was for you. I thought we were protecting you." He held up his hands then, appeasement, time-out. "I appreciate your willingness to continue. I do. But even if they were still in what passes for a good mood with them, we've still reached an impasse here. You can't get through to them on our turf, and I can't risk sending you back out with another of them onto theirs. It doesn't matter that Marsh didn't actually attack you. I can't risk another of them doing what he did to make me think he had."

"I don't follow you." It had been uncomfortable, yes, and she had no desire to experience it again, but it was hardly fatal.

"I've been doing a lot of thinking about what that sound he made meant," Escovedo said. "What I keep coming back to is that he was sending a distress call."


She wished she could've left the island sooner. That the moment the colonel told her they were finished, he'd already had the helicopter waiting. However late they got her home again, surely by now she would be in her own bed, holding her daughter close because she needed her even more than Tabby needed her.

Awake part of the time and a toss-up the rest, asleep but dreaming she was still trying to get there. Caught between midnight and dawn, the weather turning for the worse again, the crack and boom of thunder like artillery, with bullets of rain strafing the roof.

She had to be sleeping some of the time, though, and dreaming of something other than insomnia. She knew perfectly well she was in a bed, but there were times in the night when it felt as if she were still below, deeper than she'd gone this morning, in the cold of the depths far beyond the reach of the sun, drifting beside leviathan walls lit by a phosphorescence whose source she couldn't pin down. The walls themselves were tricky to navigate, like being on the outside of a maze, yet still lost within it, finding herself turning strange corners that seemed to jut outward, only to find that they turned in. She was going to drown down here, swamped by a sudden thrashing panic over her air tank going empty, only to realise…

She'd never strapped on one to begin with.

She belonged here, in this place that was everything that made her recoil.

*Marsh*, she thought, once she could tell ceiling from sea. Although he was dead, Marsh was still with her, in an overlapping echo of whispers. Dead, but still dreaming.

When she woke for good, though, it was as abruptly as could be, jolted by the sound of a siren so loud it promised nothing less than a cataclysm. It rose and fell like the howling of a feral god. She supposed soldiers knew how to react, but she wasn't one of them. Every instinct told her to hug the mattress and melt beneath the covers and hope it all went away.

But that was a strategy for people prone to dying in their beds.

She was dressed and out the door in two minutes, and though she had to squint against the cold sting of the rain, she looked immediately to the prison. Everything on the island, alive or motorised, seemed to be moving in that direction, and for a moment she wondered if she should too—safety in numbers, and what if something was *driving* them that way, from the east end?

But the searchlights along the parapet told a different story, three beams stabbing out over the open water, shafts of brilliant white shimmering with rain and sweeping to and fro against the black of night. *A distress call*, Escovedo had said—had it been answered? Was the island under attack, an invasion by Innsmouth's cousins who'd come swarming onto the beach? No, that didn't seem right either. The spotlights were not aimed down, but out. Straight out.

She stood rooted to the spot, pelted by rain, lashed by wind, frozen with dread that something terrible was on its way. The island had never felt so small. Even the prison looked tiny now, a vulnerable citadel standing alone against the three co-conspirators of ocean, night and sky.

Ahead of the roving spotlights, the rain was a curtain separating the island from the sea, then it parted, silently at first, the prow of a ship spearing into view, emerging from the blackness as though born from it. No lights, no one visible on board, not even any engine noise that she could hear—just a dead ship propelled by the night or something in it. The sound came next, a tortured grinding of steel across rock so loud it made the siren seem weak and thin. The ship's prow heaved higher as it was driven up onto the island, the rest of it coming into view, the body of the shark behind the cone of its snout.

And she'd thought the thunder was loud. When the freighter ploughed into the prison the ground shuddered beneath her, the building cracking apart as though riven by an axe, one of the spotlights tumbling down along with an avalanche of bricks and masonry before winking out for good. She watched men struggle, watched men fall, and at last the ship's momentum was spent. For a breathless moment it was perfectly still. Then, with another grinding protest of metal on stone, the ship began to list, like twisting a knife after sticking it in. The entire right side of the prison buckled and collapsed outward, and with it went the siren and another of the searchlights. The last of the lights reeled upward, aimed back at the building's own roofline.

Only now could she hear men shouting, only now could she hear the gunfire.

Only now could she hear men scream.

And still the ground seemed to shudder beneath her feet.

It seemed as if that should've been the end of it, accident and aftermath, but soon more of the prison began to fall, as if deliberately wrenched apart. She saw another cascade of bricks tumble to the left, light now flickering and spilling from within the prison on both sides.

Something rose into view from the other side, thick as the trunk of the tallest oak that had ever grown, but flexible, glistening in the searing light. It wrapped around another section of wall and pulled it down as easily as peeling wood from rotten wood. She thought it some kind of serpent at first, until, through the wreckage of the building, she saw the suggestion of more, coiling and uncoiling, and a body—or head—behind those.

And still the ground seemed to shudder beneath her feet.

It was nothing seismic—she understood that now. She recalled being in the majestic company of elephants once, and how the ground sometimes quivered in their vicinity as they called to one another from miles away, booming out frequencies so deep they were below the threshold of human hearing, a rumble that only their own kind could decipher.

*This was the beast's voice.*

And if they heard it in New York, in Barrow, Alaska, and in the Sea of Cortez, she would not have been surprised.

It filled her, reverberating through rock and earth, up past her shoes, juddering the soles of her feet, radiating through her bones and every fibre of muscle, every cell of fat, until her vision scrambled and she feared every organ would liquefy. At last it rose into the range of her feeble ears, a groan that a glacier might make. As the sound climbed higher she clapped both hands over her ears, and if she could have turtled her head into her body she would've done that too, as its voice became a roar became a bellow became a blaring onslaught like the trumpets of Judgement Day, a fanfare to split the sky for the coming of God.

Instead, *this* was what had arrived, this vast and monstrous entity, some inhuman travesty's idea of a deity. She saw it now for what it was to these loathsome creatures from Innsmouth—the god they prayed to, the Mecca that they faced—but then something whispered inside, and she wondered if she was wrong. As immense and terrifying as this thing was, what if it presaged more, and was only preparing the way, the John the Baptist for something even worse.

Shaking, she sunk to her knees, hoping only that she might pass beneath its notice as the last sixty-two prisoners from Innsmouth climbed up and over the top of the prison's ruins, and reclaimed their place in the sea.

To be honest, she had to admit to herself that the very idea of Innsmouth, and what had happened here in generations past, fascinated her as much as it appalled her.

Grow up and grow older in a world of interstate highways, cable TV, satellite surveillance, the Internet, and cameras in your pocket, and it was easy to forget how remote a place could once be, even on the continental US, and not all that long ago, all things considered. It was easy to forget how you might live a lifetime having no idea what was going on in a community just ten miles away, because you never had any need to go there, or much desire, either, since you'd always heard they were an unfriendly lot who didn't welcome strangers, and preferred to keep to themselves.

Innsmouth was no longer as isolated as it once was, but it still had the feeling of remoteness, of being adrift in time, a place where businesses struggled to take root, then quietly died back into vacant storefronts. It seemed to dwell under a shadow that would forever keep outsiders from finding a reason to go there, or stay long if they had.

Unlike herself. She'd been here close to a month, since two days after Christmas, and still didn't know when she would leave.

She got the sense that, for many of the town's residents, making strangers feel unwelcome was a tradition they felt honour-bound to uphold. Their greetings were taciturn, if extended at all, and they watched as if she were a shoplifter, even when crossing the street, or strolling the riverwalk along the Manuxet in the middle of the day. But her money was good, and there was no shortage of houses to rent—although her criteria were stricter than most—and a divorced mother with a six-year-old daughter could surely pose no threat.

None of them seemed to recognise her from television, although would they let on if they did? She recognised none of them, either, nothing in anyone's face or feet that hinted at the old, reviled

'Innsmouth look'. They no longer seemed to have anything to hide here, but maybe the instinct that they did went so far back that they knew no other way.

Although what to make of that one storefront on Eliot Street, in what passed for the heart of the town? The stencilled lettering— charmingly antiquated and quaint—on the plate-glass window identified the place as

### THE INNSMOUTH SOCIETY FOR PRESERVATION AND RESTORATION.

It seemed never to be open.

Yet it never seemed neglected.

Invariably, whenever she peered through the window Kerry would see that someone had been there since the last time she'd looked, but it always felt as if she'd missed them by five minutes or so. She would strain for a better look at the framed photos on the walls, tintypes and sepia tones, glimpses of bygone days that seemed to be someone's idea of something worth bringing back.

Or perhaps their idea of a homecoming.

It was January in New England, and most days so cold it redefined the word bitter, but she didn't miss a single one, climbing seven flights of stairs to take up her vigil for as long as she could endure it. The house was an old Victorian on Lafayette Street, four proud storeys tall, peaked and gabled to within an inch of its mouldering life. The only thing she cared about was that its roof had an iron-railed widow's walk with an unobstructed view of the decrepit harbour and the breakwater and, another mile out to sea, the humpbacked spine of rock called Devil Reef.

As was the custom during the height of the Age of Sail, the widow's walk had been built around the house's main chimney. Build a roaring fire down below, and the radiant bricks would keep her warm enough for a couple of hours at a time, even when the sky spat snow at her, while she brought the binoculars to her eyes every so often to check if there was anything new to see out there.

"I'm bored." This from Tabitha, nearly every day. *Booorrrrred*, the way she said it. "There's nothing to do here."

"I know, sweetie," Kerry would answer. "Just a little longer."

"When are they coming?" Tabby would ask.

"Soon," she would answer. "Pretty soon."

But in truth, she couldn't say. Their journey was a long one. Would they risk traversing the locks and dams of the Panama Canal? Or would they take the safer route, around Argentina's Cape Horn, where they would exchange Pacific for Atlantic, south for north, then head home, at long last home.

She knew only that they were on their way, more certain of this than any sane person had a right to be. The assurance was there whenever the world grew still and silent, more than a thought... a whisper that had never left, as if not all of Barnabas Marsh had died, the greater part of him subsumed into the hive mind of the rest of his kind. To taunt? To punish? To gloat? In the weeks after their island prison fell, there was no place she could go where its taint couldn't follow. Not Montana, not Los Angeles, not New Orleans, for the episode of *The Animal Whisperer* they'd tried to film before putting it on hiatus.

She swam with them in sleep. She awoke retching with the taste of coldest blood in her mouth. Her belly skimmed through mud and silt in quiet moments; her shoulders and flanks brushed through shivery forests of weeds; her fingers tricked her into thinking that her daughter's precious cheek felt cool and slimy. The dark of night could bring on the sense of a dizzying plunge to the blackest depths of ocean trenches.

Where else was left for her to go but here, to Innsmouth, the place that time seemed to be trying hard to forget.

And the more days she kept watch from the widow's walk, the longer at a time she could do it, even while the fire below dwindled to embers, and so the more it seemed that her blood must've been going cold in her veins.

"I don't like it here," Tabby would say. "You never used to yell in your sleep until we came here."

How could she even answer that? No one could live like this for long.

"Why can't I go stay with Daddy?" Tabby would ask. *Daddeeeee*, the way she said it.

It really would've been complete then, wouldn't it? The humiliation, the surrender. The admission: *I can't handle it any more, I just want it to stop, I want them to make it stop.* It still mattered, that her daughter's father had once fallen in love with her when he thought he'd been charmed by some half-wild creature who talked to animals, and then once he had her, tried to drive them from her life because he realised he hated to share. He would never possess all of her.

*You got as much as I could give*, she would tell him, as if he too could hear her whisper. *And now they won't let go of the rest.*

"Tell me another story about them," Tabby would beg, and so she would, a new chapter of the saga growing between them about kingdoms under the sea where people lived forever, and rode fish and giant seahorses, and how they had defenders as tall as the sky who came boiling up from the waters to send their enemies running.

Tabby seemed to like it.

When she asked if there were pictures, Kerry knew better, and didn't show her the ones she had, didn't even acknowledge their existence. The ones taken from Colonel Escovedo's office while the rains drenched the wreckage, after she'd helped the few survivors that she could, the others dead or past noticing what she might take from the office of their commanding officer, whom nobody could locate anyway.

The first eight photos Tabby would've found boring. As for the ninth, Kerry wasn't sure she could explain to a six-year-old what exactly it showed, or even to herself. Wasn't sure she could make a solid case for what was the mouth and what was the eye, much less explain why such a thing was allowed to exist.

One of them, at least, should sleep well while they were here.

Came the day, at last, in early February, when her binoculars revealed more than the tranquil pool of the harbour, the snow and ice crusted atop the breakwater, the sullen chop of the winter-blown sea. Against the slate-coloured water, they were small, moving splotches the colour of algae. They flipped like seals, rolled like otters. They crawled onto the ragged dark stone of Devil Reef, where they seemed to survey the kingdom they'd once known, all that had changed about it and all that hadn't.

And then they did worse.

Even if something was natural, she realised, you could still call it a perversity.

Was it preference? Was it celebration? Or was it blind obedience to an instinct they didn't even have to capacity to question? Not that it mattered. Here they were, finally, little different from salmon now, come back to their headwaters to breed, indulging an urge eighty-some years strong.

It was only a six-block walk to the harbour, and she had the two of them there in fifteen minutes. This side of Water Street, the wharves and warehouses were deserted, desolate, frosted with frozen spray and groaning with every gust of wind that came snapping in over the water.

She wrenched open the wide wooden door to one of the smaller buildings, the same as she'd been doing every other day or so, the entire time they'd been here, first to find an abandoned rowboat, and then to make sure it was still there. She dragged it down to the water's edge, ploughing a furrow in a crust of old snow, and once it was in the shallows, swung Tabby into it, then hopped in after. She slipped the oars into the rusty oarlocks, and they were off.

"Mama…?" Tabitha said after they'd pushed past the breakwater and cleared the mouth of the harbour for open sea. "Are you crying?"

In rougher waters now, the boat heaved beneath them. Snow swirled in from the depths overhead and clung to her cheeks, eyelashes, hair, and refused to melt. She was that cold. She was *always* that cold.

"Maybe a little," Kerry said.

"How come?"

"It's just the wind. It stings my eyes."

She pulled at the oars, aiming for the black line of the reef. Even if no one else might've, even if she could no longer see them, as they hid within the waves, she heard them sing a song of jubilation, a song of wrath and hunger. Their voices were the sound of a thousand waking nightmares.

To pass the time, she told Tabby a story, grafting it to all the other tales she'd told about kingdoms under the sea where people lived forever, and rode whales and danced with dolphins, and how they may not have been very pleasant to look at, but that's what made them love the beautiful little girl from above the waves, and welcome her as their princess.

Tabby seemed to like it.

Ahead, at the reef, they began to rise from the water and clamber up the rock again, spiny and scaled, finned and fearless. Others began to swim out to meet the boat. Of course they recognised her, and she them. She'd sat with nearly a third of them, trying trying trying to break through from the wrong side of the shore.

While they must have schemed like fiends to drag her deep into theirs.

*I bring you this gift*, she would tell them, if only she could make herself heard over their jeering in her head. *Now could you please just set me free?*

# THE WINNER

*by* RAMSEY CAMPBELL

UNTIL JESSOP DROVE onto the waterfront he thought most of the wind was racing the moonlit clouds. As the Mini left behind the last of the deserted office buildings he saw ships toppling like city blocks seized by an earthquake. Cars were veering away from the entrance to the ferry terminal. Several minutes of clinging grimly to the wheel as the air kept throwing its weight at the car took him to the gates. A Toyota stuffed with wailing children wherever there was space among the luggage met him at the top of the ramp. "Dublin's cancelled," the driver told him in an Ulster accent he had to strain to understand. "Come back in three hours, they're saying."

"I never had my supper," one of her sons complained, and his sister protested "We could have stayed at uncle's." Jessop retorted inwardly that he could have delayed his journey by a day, but he'd driven too far south to turn back now. He could have flown from London that morning and beaten the weather if he hadn't preferred to be frugal. He sent his windblown thanks after the Toyota and set about looking for a refuge on the dock road. There were pubs in abundance, but no room to park outside them and no sign of any other parking area. He was searching for a hotel where he could linger over a snack, and realising that all the hotels were back beyond the terminal entrance, when he belatedly noticed a pub.

It was at the far end of the street he'd just passed. Enough horns for a brass band accompanied the U-turn he made. He swung into the cramped gap between two terraces of meagre houses that opened directly onto the pavement. Two more uninterrupted lines of dwellings so scrawny that their windows were as narrow as their doors faced each other across two ranks of parked cars, several of which were for sale. Jessop parked outside the Seafarer, under the single unbroken street lamp, and retrieved his briefcase from the back seat before locking the car.

The far end of the street showed him windowless vessels staggering about at anchor. A gust blundered away from the pub, carrying a mutter of voices. The window of the pub was opaque except for posters plastered against the inside: THEME NIGHT'S, SINGA-LONG'S, QUIZ NIGHT'S. He would rather not be involved in any of those, but perhaps he could find himself a secluded corner in which to work. The lamp and the moon fought over producing shadows of his hand as he pushed open the thick shabby door.

The low wide dim room appeared to be entangled in nets. Certainly the upper air was full of them and smoke. Those under the ceiling trapped rather too much of the yellowish light, while those in the corners resembled overgrown cobwebs. Jessop was telling himself that the place was appealingly quaint when the wind used the door to shove him forward and slammed it behind him.

"Sorry," he called to the barman and the dozen or so drinkers and smokers seated at round tables cast in black iron. Nobody responded except by watching him cross the discoloured wooden floor to the bar. The man behind it, whose eyes and nose and mouth were crammed into the space left by a large chin, peered at him beneath a beetling stretch of net. Perhaps the dimness was one reason why his eyes bulged so much that they appeared to be stretched pale. "Here's one," he announced.

"Reckon you're right there, cap'n," growled a man who, despite the competition, would have taken any prize for bulkiness.

"You'd have said it if he hadn't, Joe," his barely smaller partner croaked past a hand-rolled cigarette, rattling her bracelets as she patted his arm.

"I'm sorry?" Jessop wondered aloud.

She raised a hand to smooth her shoulder-length red tresses. "We're betting you went for the ferry."

"I hope you've staked a fortune on it, then."

"He means you'd win another, Mary," Joe said. "He wouldn't want you to lose."

"That's so," Jessop said, turning to the barman. "What do you recommend?"

"Nothing till I know you. There's not many tastes we can't please here, mister."

"Jessop," Jessop replied before he grasped that he hadn't been asked a question, and stared hard at the beer-pumps. "Captain's Choice sounds worth a go."

He surveyed the length of the chipped sticky bar while the barman hauled at the creaking pump. A miniature billboard said WIN A VOYAGE IN OUR COMPETTITTION, but there was no sign of a menu. "Do you serve food?" he said.

"I've had no complaints for a while."

"What sort of thing do you do?"

"Try me."

"Would a curry be a possibility? Something along those lines?"

"What do you Southerners think goes in one of them?"

"Anything that's edible," said Jessop, feeling increasingly awkward. "That's the idea of a curry, isn't it? Particularly on board ship, I should think."

"You don't fancy scouse."

"I've never tried it. If that's what's on I will."

"Brave lad," the barman said and thrust a tankard full of brownish liquid at him. "Let's see you get that down you."

Jessop did his best to seem pleased with the inert metallic gulp he took. He was reaching for his wallet until the barman said "Settle when you're going."

"Shall I wait here?"

"For what?" the barman said, then grinned at everyone but Jessop. "For your bowl, you mean. We'll find you where you're sitting."

Jessop didn't doubt it, since nobody made even a token pretence of not watching him carry his briefcase to the only unoccupied corner, which was farthest from the door. As he perched on a ragged leather stool and leaned against the yielding wallpaper under a net elaborated by a spider's web, a woman who might have been more convincingly blonde without the darkness on her upper lip remarked "That'll be a good few hours, I'd say."

"Can't argue with you there, Betty," said her companion, a man with a rat asleep on his chest or a beard, which he raised to point it at Jessop. "Is she right, Jessop?"

"Paul," Jessop offered, though it made him no more comfortable. "A couple, anyway."

"A couple's not a few, Tom," scoffed a man with tattoos of fish and less shapely deep-sea creatures swimming under the cuffs of his shabby brownish pullover.

"What are they else then, Daniel?"

"Don't fall out over me," Jessop said as he might have addressed a pair of schoolchildren. "You could both be right, either could, rather."

Resentment might have been a reason why Daniel jerked one populated thumb at a wiry wizened man topped with a black bobble cap. "He's already Paul. Got another name so we know who's who?"

"None I use."

"Be a love and fish it up for us."

At least it was Mary who asked in these terms, with a hoarseness presumably born of cigarettes. After a pause Jessop heard himself mumble "Desmond."

"Scouse," the barman said—it wasn't clear to whom or even if it was an order. Hoping to keep his head down, Jessop snapped his briefcase open. He was laying out papers on the table when the street door flew wide, admitting only wind. He had to slap the papers down as the barman stalked to the door and heaved a stool against it. Nobody else looked away from Jessop. "Still a student, are you, Des?" Betty said.

He wouldn't have believed he could dislike a name more than the one he'd hidden ever since learning it was his, but the contraction was worse. Des Jessop—it was the kind of name a teacher would hiss with contempt. It made him feel reduced to someone else's notion of him, in danger of becoming insignificant to himself. Meanwhile he was saying "All my life, I hope."

"You want to live off the rest of us till you're dead," Joe somewhat more than assumed.

"I'm saying there'll always be something left to discover. That ought to be true for everyone, I should think."

"We've seen plenty," Daniel grumbled. "We've seen enough."

"Forgive me if I haven't yet."

"No need for that," said Mary. "We aren't forgivers, us."

"Doesn't it make you tired, all that reading?" Betty asked him.

"Just the opposite."

"I never learned nothing from a book," she said once she'd finished scowling over his words. "Never did me any harm either."

"You'd know a couple's not a few if you'd read a bit," said Joe.

"Lay off skitting at my judy," Tom warned him.

For some reason everybody else but Jessop roared with laughter. He felt as if his nervous grin had hooked him by the corners of his mouth. He was wobbling to his feet when the barman called "Don't let them scare you off, Des. They just need their fun."

"I'm only..." Jessop suspected that any term he used would provoke general mirth. "Where's the..."

"The poop's got to be behind you, hasn't it?" Betty said in gleeful triumph.

Until he glanced in that direction he wasn't sure how much of a joke this might be. Almost within arm's length was a door so unmarked he'd taken it for a section of wall. When he pushed it, the reluctant light caught on two faces gouged out of the wood, carvings of such crudeness that the female was distinguishable from her mate only by a mop of hair. Beyond the door was a void that proved to be a corridor once he located a switch dangling from an inch of flex. The luminous rotting pear of a bulb revealed that the short passage led to an exit against which crates of dusty empties were stacked. The barred exit was shaken by a gust of wind and, to his bewilderment, what sounded like a blurred mass of television broadcasts. He hadn't time to investigate. Each wall contained a door carved with the rudiments of a face, and he was turning away from the Gents before the image opposite alerted him that the man's long hair was a patch of black fungus. He touched as little of the door as possible while letting himself into the Gents.

The switch in the passage must control all the lights. Under the scaly ceiling a precarious fluorescent tube twitched out a pallid glow with an incessant series of insect clicks. There was barely enough space in the room for a pair of clogged urinals in which cigarette butts were unravelling and a solitary cubicle opposite a piebald slimy sink. Beneath the urinals the wall was bearded with green mould. High up beside the cubicle a token window was covered by a rusty grille restless with old cobwebs. Jessop kicked open the cubicle door.

A watery sound grew louder—an irregular sloshing he'd attributed to the cistern. He urged himself to the seatless discoloured pedestal. The instant he looked down, only the thought of touching the encrusted scabby walls restrained him from supporting himself against them. Whatever was gaping wide-mouthed at him from the black water, surely it was dead, whether it had been drowned by someone or swum up the plumbing. Surely it was the unstable light, not anticipation of him, that made the whitish throat and pale fat lips appear to work eagerly. He dragged one sleeve over his hand and wrenched at the handle of the rickety cistern. As a rush of opaque water carried the mouth into the depths, Jessop retreated to the first urinal and kept a hand over his nose and mouth while he filled the mouldy china oval to its lower brim.

He dodged out of the fluttering room and was nearly at the door to the bar when he faltered. A confusion of angry voices was moving away from him. A clatter of furniture ended it, and a hoarse voice he identified as Betty's ordered "Now stay there." He was wishing away the silence as he eased the door open a crack.

The bar seemed emptier than when he'd left it. Two considerable men who'd been seated directly ahead no longer were. The stool hadn't moved from in front of the exit. Could the men be waiting out of sight on either side for him? As he grew furious with his reluctance to know, the barman saw him. "Food's on its way," he announced.

Mary leaned into view, one hand flattening her scalp, to locate Jessop. "Aren't you coming out? This isn't hide and seek."

When embarrassment drove Jessop forward he saw that Daniel

had changed seats. He was penned into a corner by the men from the abandoned table, and looked both dishevelled and trapped. "He was trying to see your papers, Des," Betty said.

"Good heavens, I wouldn't have minded. It isn't important."

"It is to us."

As Jessop resumed his corner Tom said "Got a sweetheart abroad, have you? Was she the lure?"

"His bonnie lies over the ocean," Mary took to have been confirmed, and began to sing.

"No he doesn't," Jessop retorted, but only to himself while he busied himself with his tankard, which had been topped up in his absence. Once the chorus subsided he said guardedly "No, they're over here."

"How many's that?" enquired Joe. "Bit of a ladies' man, are you?"

"A girl in every port," said Tom.

"Not in any really," Jessop said, risking a laugh he hoped was plainly aimed at himself.

"Same with us," Daniel said and gave his fellows an ingratiating look.

The microwave behind the bar rang as if signalling the end of a round, which let Jessop watch the barman load a tray and bring it to him. Once the bowlful of grey stew had finished slopping about, Jessop had to unwrap the fork and spoon from their tattered napkin. He was spooning up a blackened lump when Betty said "What do you make of that then, Des?"

This struck Jessop as the latest of several questions too many. "What would you?"

"Oh, we've had ours. We gobbled it."

"Sup up, Des," Daniel advised. "You'll get plenty of that where you're going."

Was the dish Irish, then? Jessop seemed to have no option other than to raise the dripping lump to his mouth. It was either an unfamiliar vegetable or a piece of meat softened beyond identification, presumably in whatever pot had contained the communal dinner. "Good?" Mary prompted as everyone watched.

"Gum." At least the mouthful allowed him not to answer too

distinctly. He swallowed it as whole as an oyster, only to become aware that his performance had invited however many encores it would take to unload the bowl. He was chewing a chunk that needed a good deal of it when Joe declared "If you're not a student I'm saying you're a teacher."

Jessop succeeded at last in downing and retaining the gristly morsel. "Lecturer," he corrected.

"Same thing, isn't it?"

"I wouldn't say quite."

"Still teach, don't you? Still live off them that works, as well."

"Now, Joe," Mary interrupted. "You'll have our new mate not wanting to stay with us."

Jessop could have told her that had happened some time ago. He was considering how much of his portion he could decently leave before seeking another refuge from the gale, and whether he was obliged to be polite any longer, when Tom demanded "So what do you lecture, Des?"

"Students," Jessop might have retorted, but instead displayed the Beethoven score he'd laid out to review in preparation for his introductory lecture. "Music's my territory."

As he dipped his spoon in search of a final mouthful Mary said "How many marks would our singing get?"

"I don't really mark performances. I'm more on the theory side."

Joe's grunt of disdainful vindication wasn't enough for Tom, who said "You've got to be able to say how good it is if you're supposed to be teaching about it."

"Six," Jessop said to be rid of the subject, but it had occupied all the watching eyes. "Seven," he amended. "A good seven. That's out of ten. A lot of professionals would be happy with that."

Betty gave a laugh that apparently expressed why everyone looked amused. "You haven't heard us yet, Des. You've got to hear."

"You start us off, Betty," Daniel urged.

For as long as it took her to begin, Jessop was able to hope he would be subjected only to a chorus. Having lurched to her feet, she expanded her chest, a process that gave him more of a sense of the inequality of her breasts than he welcomed, and commenced her assault on the song. What was she suggesting ought to be done with the drunken sailor? Her diction and her voice, cracked enough for a falsetto, made it impossible to judge. Jessop fed himself a hearty gulp of Captain's Choice in case it rendered him more tolerant as she sat down panting. "Oh," he said hurriedly, "I think—"

"You can't say yet," Daniel objected. "You've got to hear everyone."

Jessop lowered his head, not least to avoid watching Mary. Betty's lopsidedness had begun to resemble an omen. The sound of Mary was enough of an ordeal—her voice even screechier than her friend's, her answer to the question posed by the song even less comprehensible. "There," she said far too eventually. "Who'll be next?"

As Joe stood up with a thump that might have been designed to attract Jessop's attention, he heaped his spoon with a gobbet of scouse to justify his concentration on the bowl. Once the spoonful passed his teeth it became clear that it was too rubbery to be chewed and too expansive to be swallowed. Before Joe had finished growling his first line, Jessop staggered to his feet. He waved his frantic hands on either side of his laden face and stumbled through the doorway to the toilets.

The prospect of revisiting the Gents made him clap a hand over his mouth. When he elbowed the other door open, however, the Ladies looked just as uninviting. A blackened stone sink lay in fragments on the uneven concrete beneath a rusty drooling tap on a twisted greenish pipe. Jessop ran to the first of two cubicles and shouldered the door aside. Beyond it a jagged hole in the glistening concrete showed where a pedestal had been. What was he to make of the substance like a jellyfish sprawling over the entire rim? Before he could be sure what the jittery light was exhibiting, the mass shrank and slithered into the unlit depths. He didn't need the spectacle to make him expel his mouthful into the hole and retreat to the corridor. He was peering desperately about for a patch of wall not too stained to lean against when he heard voices—a renewal of the television sounds beyond the rear exit and, more clearly, a conversation in the bar.

"Are we telling Des yet?"

"Betty's right, we'll have to soon."

"Can't wait to see his face."

"I remember how yours looked, Mary."

It wasn't only their words that froze him—it was that, exhausted perhaps by singing, both voices had given up all disguise. He wouldn't have known they weren't meant to be men except for the names they were still using. If that indicated the kind of bar he'd strayed into, it had never been his kind. He did his best to appear unaware of the situation as, having managed to swallow hard, he ventured into the bar.

More had happened than he knew. Joe had transferred his bulk to the stool that blocked the street door. Jessop pretended he hadn't noticed, only to realise that he should have confined himself to pretending it didn't matter. He attempted this while he stood at the table to gather the score and return it to his briefcase. "Well," he said as casually as his stiffening lips would allow, "I'd better be on my way."

"Not just yet, Des," Joe said, settling more of his weight against the door. "Listen to it."

Jessop didn't know if that referred to the renewed onslaught of the gale or him. "I need something from my car."

"Tell us what and we'll get it for you. You aren't dressed for this kind of night."

Jessop was trying to identify whom he should tell to let him go— the barman was conspicuously intent on wiping glasses—and what tone and phrasing he should use when Daniel said "You lot singing's put Des off us and his supper."

"Let's hear you then, Des," Joe rather more than invited. "Your turn to sing."

"Yes, go on, Des," Mary shrilled. "We've entertained you, now you can."

Might that be all they required of him? Jessop found himself blurting "I don't know what to perform."

"What we were," Joe said.

Jessop gripped his clammy hands together behind his back and drew a breath he hoped would also keep down the resurgent taste of his bowlful. As he repeated the question about the sailor, his dwarfed voice fled back to him while all the drinkers rocked from side to side, apparently to encourage him. The barman found the glasses he was wiping more momentous than ever. Once Jessop finished wishing it could indeed be early in the morning, if that would put him on the ferry, his voice trailed off. "That's lovely," Betty cried, adjusting her fallen breast. "Go on."

"I can't remember any more. It really isn't my sort of music."

"It will be," Daniel said.

"Take him down to see her," Betty chanted, "and he'll soon be sober."

"Let him hear her sing and then he'll need no drinking," Mary added with something like triumph.

They were only suggesting lyrics, Jessop told himself—perhaps the very ones they'd sung. The thought didn't help him perform while so many eyes were watching him from the dimness that seeped through the nets. He felt as if he'd been lured into a cave where he was unable to see clearly enough to defend himself. All around him the intent bulks were growing visibly restless; Mary was fingering her red tresses as though it might be time to dispense with them. "Come on, Des," Joe said, so that for an instant Jessop felt he was being directed to the exit. "No point not joining in."

"We only get one night," said Tom.

"So we have to fit them all in," Daniel said.

All Jessop knew was that he didn't want to need to understand. A shiver surged up through him, almost wrenching his hands apart. It was robbing him of any remaining control—and then he saw that it could be his last chance. "You're right, Joe," he said and let them see him shiver afresh. "I'm not dressed for it. I'll get changed."

Having held up his briefcase to illustrate his ruse, he was making for the rear door when Mary squealed "No need to be shy, Des. You can in here."

"I'd rather not, thank you," Jessop said with the last grain of authority he could find in himself, and dodged into the corridor.

As soon as the door was shut he stood his briefcase against it. Even if he wanted to abandon the case, it wouldn't hold the door. He tiptoed fast and shakily to the end of the passage and lowered the topmost crate onto his chest. He retraced his steps as fast as silencing the bottles would allow. He planted the crate in the angle under the hinges and took the briefcase down the corridor. He ignored the blurred mutter of televisions beyond the door while he picked up another crate. How many could he use to ensure the route was blocked before anyone decided he'd been out of sight too long? He was returning for a third crate when he heard a fumbling at the doors on both sides of the corridor.

Even worse than the shapeless eagerness was the way the doors were being assaulted in unison, as if by appendages something was reaching out from—where? Beneath him, or outside the pub? Either thought seemed capable of paralysing him. He flung himself out of their range to seize the next crate, the only aspect of his surroundings he felt able to trust to be real. He couldn't venture down the dim corridor past the quivering doors. He rested crate after crate against the wall, and dragged the last one aside with a jangle of glass. Grabbing his briefcase and abandoning stealth, he threw his weight against the metal bar across the door.

It wouldn't budge for rust. He dropped the case and clutched two-handed at the obstruction while he hurled every ounce of himself at it. The bar gave a reluctant gritty clank, only to reveal that a presence as strong as Jessop was on the far side of the door. It was the wind, which slackened enough to let him and the door stagger forward. He blocked the door with one foot as he snatched up the briefcase. Outside was a narrow unlit alley between the backs of houses. Noise and something more palpable floundered at him—the wind, bearing a tangle of voices and music. At the end of the alley, less than twenty feet away, three men were waiting for him.

Wiry Paul was foremost, flanked by Joe and Tom. He'd pulled his bobble hat down to his eyebrows and was flexing his arms like thick stalks in a tide. "You aren't leaving now we've given you a name," he said.

A flare of rage that was mostly panic made Jessop shout "My name's Paul."

"Fight you for it," the other man offered, prancing forward.

"I'm not playing any more games with anyone."

"Then we aren't either. You won."

"Won the moment you stepped through the door," Tom seemed to think Jessop wanted to hear.

Jessop remembered the notice about a competition. It was immediately clear to him that however much he protested, he was about to receive his prize. "You were the quiz," Paul told him as Joe and Tom took an identical swaying pace forward.

Jessop swung around and bolted for the main road. The dark on which the houses turned their backs felt close to solid with the gale and the sounds entangled in it. The uproar was coming from the houses, from televisions and music systems turned up loud. It made him feel outcast, but surely it had to mean there would be help within earshot if he needed to appeal for it. He struggled against the relentless gale towards the distant gap that appeared to mock his efforts by tossing back and forth. He glanced over his shoulder to see Paul and his cronies strolling after him. A car sped past the gap ahead as if to tempt him forward while he strove not to be blown into an alley to his right. Or should he try that route even if it took him farther from the main road? The thought of being lost as well as pursued had carried him beyond the junction when Betty and Mary blocked his view of the road.

They were still wearing dresses that flapped in the wind, but they were more than broad enough to leave him no escape. The gale lifted Mary's tresses and sent them scuttling crabwise at Jessop. "Some of us try to be more like her," Mary growled with a defensiveness close to violence. "Try to find out what'll make her happier."

"Lots have tried," Betty said in much the same tone. "We're just the first that's had her sort on board."

"Shouldn't be surprised if her sisters want to see the world now too."

"She doesn't just take," Betty said more defensively still. "She provides."

Jessop had been backing away throughout this, both from their words and from comprehending them, but he couldn't leave behind the stale upsurge of his dinner. When he reached the junction again he didn't resist the gale. It sent him sidling at a run into the dark until he managed to turn. The houses that walled him in were derelict and boarded up, yet the noise on both sides of him seemed unabated, presumably because the inhabitants of the nearest occupied buildings had turned the volume higher. Why was the passage darkening? He didn't miss the strip of moonlit cloud until he realised it was no longer overhead. At that moment his footsteps took on a note more metallic than echoes between bricks could account for, but his ears had fastened on another sound—a song.

It was high and sweet and not at all human. It seemed capable of doing away with his thoughts, even with his fleeting notion that it could contain all music. Nothing seemed important except following it to its source—certainly not the way the floor tilted abruptly beneath him, throwing him against one wall. Before long he had to leave his briefcase in order to support himself against the metal walls of the corridor. He heard the clientele of the Seafarer tramp after him, and looked back to see the derelict houses rock away beyond Mary and Betty. All this struck him as less than insignificant, except for the chugging of engines that made him anxious to be wherever it wouldn't interfere with the song. Someone opened a hatch for him and showed him how to grasp the uprights of the ladder that led down into the unlit dripping hold. "That's what sailors hear," said another of the crew as Jessop's foot groped downwards, and Jessop wondered if that referred to the vast wallowing beneath him as well as the song. For an instant too brief for the notion to stay in his mind he thought he might already have glimpsed the nature of the songstress. You'd sing like that if you looked like that, came a last thought. It seemed entirely random to him, and he forgot it as the ancient song drew him into the enormous cradle of darkness.

# THE TRANSITION OF ELIZABETH HASKINGS

*by* CAITLÍN R. KIERNAN

LIZABETH HASKINGS INHERITED the old house on Water Street from her grandfather. It would have passed to her mother, but she'd gone away to Oregon when Elizabeth was six years old, leaving her daughter with the old man. She'd said she would come back, but she never did, and after a while the letters stopped coming, and then the postcards stopped coming, too. And now Elizabeth Haskings is twenty-nine, and she has no idea whether her mother is alive or dead. It's not something she thinks about very often. But she does understand *why* her mother left, that it was fear of the broad, tea-coloured water of the Ipswich River, flowing lazily down to the salt marshes and the Atlantic. Flowing down to Little Neck and the deep channel between the mainland and Plum Island, finally emptying into the ocean hardly a quarter of a mile north of Essex Bay. Elizabeth understands it was the ruins surrounding the bay, there at the mouth of the Manuxet River—labelled the Castle Neck River on more recent maps, maps drawn up after the late 1920s.

She's never blamed her mother for running like that. But here, in Ipswich, she has the house and her job at the library, and in Oregon— or *wherever* she might run—she'd have nothing at all. Here she has roots, even if they're roots she does her best not to dwell on. But this is only history, the brief annals of a young woman's life. Relevant, certainly, but only as prologue. What happened in the town that once ringed Essex Bay, the strange seaport town that abruptly died one winter eighty-four years ago, where her grandfather lived as a boy.

It's a Saturday night in June, and on most Saturday nights Elizabeth Haskings entertains what she quaintly thinks of as her "gentleman caller". She enjoys saying, "Tonight, I will be visited by my gentleman caller." Even though Michael's gay. They work together at archives at the Ipswich Public Library, though, sometimes, he switches over to circulation. Anyway, he knows about Elizabeth's game, and usually he brings her a small bouquet of flowers of one sort of another— calla lilies, Peruvian lilies, yellow roses fringed with red, black-eyed susans—and she carefully arranges them in one of her several vases while he cooks her dinner. She feels bad that Michael is always the one who cooks, but, truthfully, Elizabeth isn't a very good cook, and tends to eat from the microwave most nights.

They might watch a DVD afterwards, or play Scrabble, or just sit at the wide dinner table she also inherited from her grandfather and talk. About work or books or classical music, something Michael knows much more about than she does. Truth is, he often makes her feel inadequate, but she's never said so. She loves him, and it's not a simple, platonic love, so she's always kept it a secret, allowed their "dates" to seem like nothing more than a ritual between friends who seem to have more in common with one another than with most anyone else they know in the little New England town (whether that's true or not). Sometimes, she lies in bed, thinking about him lying beside her, instead of thinking about all the things she works so hard *not* thinking about: the river, the sea, her lost mother, the grey, weathered boards and stone foundations where there was once a dingy town, etcetera & etcetera. It's her secret, and she'll never tell him.

Though, Michael knows the most terrible secret that she'll ever have, and she's fairly sure that his knowing it has kept her sane for the five years they've known one another. In an odd way, it doesn't seem fair, the same way his always cooking doesn't seem fair. No, much worse than that. But him knowing this awful thing about her, and her never telling him how she feels. Still, Elizabeth assures herself, telling him that would only ruin their friendship. A bird in the hand being worth two in the bush, and in this instance it really is better not to have one's cake and eat it, too.

They don't always play board games after dinner, or watch movies, or talk. Because there are nights that his just *knowing* her secret isn't enough. There are nights it weighs so much Elizabeth imagines it might crush her flat, like the pressure at the bottom of the deep sea. Those nights, after dinner, they go upstairs to her bedroom, and he runs a porcelain bowl of water from the bathtub faucet. He adds salt to it while she undresses before the tall mirror affixed to one wall, taller than her by a foot, and framed with ornately carved walnut. She pretends that it's only carved with acanthus leaves and cherubs. It's easier that way. It doesn't embarrass her for Michael to see her nude, not even with the disfigurements of her secret uncovered and plainly visible to him. After all, that's why he's returned from the bathroom with the bowl of salty water and a yellow sponge (he leaves the tap running). That's why they've come upstairs, because she can't always be the only one to look at herself.

"It's bad tonight?" he asks.

She doesn't answer straightaway. She's never been one to complain if she can avoid complaining, and it's bad enough that he knows. She doesn't also want to seem weak. After a minute or half a minute she answers, "It's been worse." That's the truth, even if it's also a way of evading his question.

"Betsy, just tell me when you're ready." He always calls her Betsy, never Elizabeth. She's never called him Mike, though.

"I'm ready," she says, leaning her neck to the left or to the right, exposing the pale skin below the ridge of her chin. *But I'm not ready at all. I'm never ready, am I?*

"Okay, then. I'll be as gentle as I can."

He's always as gentle as anyone could be.

"You've never hurt me, Michael. Not even once."

But she has no doubt he can see the discomfort in her eyes when the washcloth touches her skin. She tries hard not to flinch, but, usually, she flinches regardless.

"Was that too hard?"

"No. I'm fine. I'm okay," she tells him, so he continues administering the salt water to her throat, dabbing carefully, and Elizabeth Haskings tries to concentrate on his fingertips, whenever they happen to brush against her. It never takes very long for the three red slits on each side of her throat to appear, and not much longer for them to open. They never open very far, not until later on. Just enough that she can see the barn-red gills behind the stiff, crescent-shaped flaps of skin that weren't there only moments before. That never are there until the salt water. Here, she always loses her breath for a few seconds, and the flaps spasm, opening and closing, and she has to gasp several times to find a balance between the air being drawn in through her nostrils and mouth, and the air flowing across the feathery red gill filaments. Sometimes her legs go weak, but Michael has never let her fall.

"Breathe," he whispers. "Don't panic. Take it slow and easy, Betsy. Just breathe."

The dizziness passes, the dark blotches that swim before her eyes, and she doesn't need him to support her any longer. She stares at herself in the mirror, and by now her eyes have gone black. No irises, no pupils, no sclera. Just inky black where her hazel-green eyes used to be.

"I'm right here," he says.

He doesn't have to tell her that again. He's always there, behind her or at her side.

Unconsciously, she tries to blink her eyes, but all trace of her lids have vanished, and she can only stare at those black, blank eyes. Later, when they begin to smart, Michael will have the eye drops at the ready.

"It's getting harder," she says. He doesn't reply, because she says this almost every time. *All his replies have been used up*, Elizabeth thinks. *No matter how much he might want to calm me or offer surcease, he's already said it all a dozen times over.*

Instead, he asks, "Keep going?"

She nods.

"We don't have too, you know."

"Yes we do. It's bad if we do. It's worse if we don't. It hurts more if we don't." Of course, Michael knows this perfectly well, and there's the briefest impatience that she has to remind him. Not anger, no, but an unmistakable flash of impatience, there and gone in the stingy space of a single heartbeat.

He dips the sponge into the salt water again, not bothering to squeeze it out, because the more the better. The more, the easier. Water runs down his arm and drips to the hardwood floor. Before they're finished, there will be a puddle about her bare feet and his shoes, too. Michael gingerly swabs both her hands with the sponge, and at once the vestigial webbing between her fingers, common to all men and women, begins to expand, pushing the digits further away from one another.

Elizabeth watches, biting her lip against the discomfort, and watches. It doesn't horrify her the same way that the appearance of the gills and the change to her eyes does, but it's much more painful. Not nearly so much as the greater portion of her metamorphosis to come, but enough she *does* bite her lip (careful not to draw blood). Within five minutes, the webbing has grown enough that it's attached at the uppermost joint between each finger, and is at least twice as thick as usual. And the texture of the skin on the backs of her hands and her palms is becoming smoother and faintly iridescent, more transparent, and gradually taking on the faintest tinge of turquoise. She used to think of the colour as *celeste opaco*, because the Italian sounded prettier. But now she settles for *turquoise*. Not as lyrical, no, but it's not opaque, and turquoise is somehow more honest. Monsters should be honest. Before half an hour has passed, most of her skin will have taken on variations of the same hue.

"Yesterday," she says, "during my lunch break, when I said I needed to go to the bank, I didn't."

There are a few seconds of quiet before he asks, "Where did you go, Elizabeth?"

"Choate Bridge," she answers. "I just stood there a while, watching the river." It's the oldest stone-arch bridge anywhere in Massachusetts, built in 1764. There are two granite archways through which the river flows on its easterly course.

"Did it make you feel any better?"

"It made me want to swim. The river always makes me want to swim, Michael. You know that."

"Yeah, Betsy. I know."

She wants to add, *Please don't ask me questions you already know the answers to,* but she doesn't. It would be rude. He means well, and she's never rude if she can help it. Especially not to Michael.

All evidence of her fingernails has completely vanished.

"It terrified me. It always fucking terrifies me."

"Maybe one day it won't. Maybe one day you'll be able to look at the water without being frightened."

"Maybe," she whispers, hoping it isn't true. Pretty sure what'll happen if she ever stops being afraid of the river and the sea. *I can't drown. I can't ever drown. How does a woman who can't drown fear the water?*

*There are things in the water. Things that* can *hurt me. And places I never want to see awake.*

Now he's running the sponge down her back, beginning at the nape of her neck and ending at the cleft between her buttocks. This time, the pain is bad enough she wants to double over, wants to go down on her knees and vomit. But that would be weak, and she won't be weak. Michael used to bring her pills to dull the pain, but she stopped taking them almost a year ago because she didn't like the fogginess they brought, the way they caused her to feel detached from herself, as though these transformations were happening to someone else.

*Monsters should be honest.*

At once, the neural processes of her vertebrae begin to broaden and elongate. She's made herself learn a lot about anatomy: human, anuran, chondrichthyan, osteichthyan, *et al*. Anything and everything that seems relevant to what happens to her on these nights.

*The devil you know,* as her grandfather used to say.

So, Elizabeth Haskings knows that the processes will grow the longest between her third and seventh thoracic vertebrae, and on the last lumbar, the sacrals, and coccygeals (though less so than in the thoracic region), greatly accenting both the natural curves of her back. Musculature responds accordingly. She knows the Latin names of all those muscles, and if there were less pain, she could recite them for Michael. She imagines herself laughing like a madwoman and reciting the names of the shifting, straining tendons. In the end, there won't quite be fins, *sensu stricto*. Almost, but not quite.

*Aren't I a madwoman? How can I possibly still be sane?*

"Betsy, you don't have to be so strong," he tells her, and she hates the pity in his voice. "I know you think you do, but you don't. Certainly not in front of me."

She takes the yellow sponge from him, her hands shaking so badly she spills most of the salt water remaining in the bowl, but still manages to get the sponge sopping wet. Her gums have begun to ache, and she smiles at herself before wringing out the sponge with both her webbed hands so that the water runs down her belly and between her legs. In the mirror, she sees Michael turn away.

She drops the sponge to the floor at her feet (she doesn't have to look to know her toes have begun to fuse one to the next), and gazes into her pitchy eyes until she's sure the adjustments to her genitals are finished. When she does look down at herself, there's a taut, flat place in place of the low mound of the mons pubis, and the labia majora, labia minora, and clitoris—all the intricacies of her sex—have been reduced to the vertical slit of an oviduct where her vagina was moments before. On either side of the slit are tiny, triangular pelvic fins, no more than an inch high and three inches long.

"We should hurry now, Betsy," Michael says. He's right, of course. She has to reach the bathtub full of warm salty water while she can still walk. Once or twice before she's waited too long, and he's had to carry her, and that humiliation was almost worse than all the rest combined. In the tub, she curls almost foetal, and the flaps in front of Elizabeth's gills open and close, pumping in and out again, extracting all the oxygen she'll need until sunrise. Michael will stay with her, guarding her, as he always does.

She can sleep without lids to shield her black eyes, and, *when* she sleeps, she dreams of the river flowing down to the ruined seaport, to Essex Bay, and then out into the Atlantic due south of Plum Island. She dreams of the craggy spine of Devil Reef rising a few feet above the waves and of those who crawl out *onto* the reef most nights to bask beneath the moon. Those like her. And, worst of all, she dreams of the abyss beyond the reef, and towers and halls of the city there, a city that has stood for eighty thousand years and will stand for eighty thousand more. On these nights, changed and slumbering, Elizabeth Haskings can't lie to herself and pretend that her mother fled to Oregon, or even that her grandfather lies in his grave in Highland Cemetery. On these nights, she isn't afraid of anything.

# THE CHAIN

## by MICHAEL MARSHALL SMITH

T HE FIRST DAYS were pleasant. Fun, even. Different from normal life. A break. A *change*—exactly what David needed, and what he'd come there for.

He slept well and rose early, carrying his first herbal tea of the day down to the beach. He took long walks and ate healthy meals, and sometimes when he felt like a cigarette he elected to not have one. He avoided alcohol. He thought about what he might paint, and in the evening sat on the small deck in front of the cottage and read non-taxing fiction or sat gazing calmly into space, nodding affably at people who walked by, as if he really lived here.

Everything flowed. One day led comfortably into the next.

It took a week before the chain began to break.

On Monday he'd arrived by car down from San Francisco and moved into the cottage. This didn't take long. The tiny house was thoughtfully set up for vacation rentals, and provided everything he could possibly need except something to wear and something to do, both of which he'd brought with him in the back seat of his convertible Mini Cooper. Once a source of pride, the car was now battered and prone to malfunction (much like, David occasionally felt, himself).

He put his regular clothes in the drawers in the bedroom. He put his painting clothes in the small garage, along with easel, paints and a stack of canvases. He'd brought ten, a statement of intent. All were three feet square, purely because his supplier in the city happened to have them on sale. Tackling a fixed aspect ratio might be invigorating, and having no choice might also help focus the mind. So he hoped.

The garage had no windows except for a thin frosted strip along the top of the door, but the owner evidently used the space as an occasional workshop and it was artificially well lit via bulbs and fluorescent tubes. It seemed a shame, having driven five hours to such a beautiful part of the coast, to be planning to spend large portions of every day hidden from it—but that was the purpose of being here. To paint. To kick himself back into enjoying his vocation, even caring about it again.

If he really got his groove on, ten canvases wouldn't be nearly enough for three weeks' work—his process was to rough out initial masses quickly, returning at leisure to detail and finesse—but should additional ones be needed then he was confident he'd be able to obtain them. Carmel has a bewildering number of art galleries, and is home to people who fill them. They weren't David's kind of painter, but that was okay. David wasn't sure if he was his kind of painter any more either—or any kind of painter at all.

That was what he was here to find out.


By Wednesday his temporary studio was laid out and ready to go. David was not. This wasn't procrastination—he was wearily familiar with that pissy little demon, alert to its polymorphic disguises and insidious creep. The need to detox from the city and the last year's inactivity, coupled with a desire to explore, seemed a reasonable excuse to postpone sequestering himself on such beautiful fall days.

Carmel is an extremely attractive place to stroll around. It's the first (and rather small) town north of the wilderness of Big Sur, on a ruggedly stunning stretch of coast. There is a craggy cove with a beach, and a great many cypress and eucalyptus and pine trees up and down the narrow streets, at times giving the impression of a village built in a forest. What is most noticeable, however, is the houses.

There are few large dwellings in Carmel—the mansions start further north, on 17 Mile Drive and Pebble Beach and the outskirts of Pacific Grove. Carmel is a collection of cottages, as cute as can be— from perfect little Victorians to jewel-like Gothic and Mission and playful Storybook and Folk Tudor, all cheek-by-jowl, with nothing but narrow strips of intensely manicured garden in between. You wander the streets constantly struck by the dreamlike juxtaposition of styles, stopping to gaze upon one house before realising its neighbour is even more striking, and walking on a few yards to look at it, before having the same realisation about the next dwelling along.

And thus, for David, a few hours would happily pass, and whole mornings and afternoons.

It's a small place—ten streets in one direction, twelve in the other, made cosy and intimate by all the trees, and whichever way you walk you'll get to the centre before long. It's here that (should you somehow have remained in doubt) it becomes clear that Carmel is a place for the wealthy. The centre is quiet and serene, dominated by the sound of birds, the purring of expensive automobiles, the polite chink of silverware. There's an immaculate little bookstore. Patio restaurants, where waiters in white aprons deliver high-spec food and perfectly chilled glasses of local wines to sunglassed patrons in chinos or dresses in muted shades. A charming grocery market. A few coffee houses—mostly hidden down alleys, as if to make the point there are some people who truly live in this paradise, and everyone else is merely a tourist passing through. No Starbucks, God forbid.

And, of course, there are the galleries.

The art wasn't all bad, either. Usually it's axiomatic that the closer a gallery stands to the ocean, the worse its contents will be. The galleries of Carmel are not for enthusiastic amateurs hawking garish sunsets, however. From earliest days the village had been a Mecca for painters who could actually paint, along with poets, writers and free-thinkers of every stripe (though few such could dream of affording to live there now). There's aesthetically lamentable work on sale, naturally—ominously perfect farmhouses in narcotically bucolic country scenes, anthropomorphised dogs, excessively winsome little girls in ballet outfits—but also plenty of serious stores specialising in admirable California painters of the last hundred years, and plenty of contemporary artists who know what they're doing, too, and are capable of keeping on doing it.

Unlike, it might appear, David.

His intention had been to avoid the galleries, in order to avoid provoking the acid churning in the guts that comes from experiencing the work of others, while in the throes of personal non-productivity. This didn't last, and he told himself it was to remind himself that canvases *did* get finished, and hung up, and bought.

As had David's, though not recently. Five years ago he could expect to earn ten to fifteen thousand dollars for a painting, less a gallery's draconian cut, naturally. Then two years ago he'd hit the wall. He'd start work, get as far as blocking out... but a week later realise that he'd never gone back to it. Soon this gap extended to a month, or two, and eventually it got to the point where he'd conceive of a painting and be able to imagine exactly how it might progress, and as a result feel disinclined to even start—knowing it'd be okay, but that there was no real need for it; believing that if he failed to create it, nothing of substance would be lost to the world.

Except, as his bank and other creditors eventually started to remind him, it paid for everything. This information did not help.

It broke the chain.

Finally, on the Friday afternoon, he went into his temporary studio. He put up a canvas. He lifted a 2B pencil from where he'd placed it in readiness, and quickly outlined some shapes. After ten minutes he pulled the iPhone out of his pocket and consulted a shot he'd taken that lunchtime, in the tiny courtyard of a coffee house hidden in the centre of the village. He put the phone back in his pocket—even when working from reference he needed to feel he worked from memory too—and made minor alterations.

He stood back, looked at what he'd done. It seemed okay. He put the pencil back in its place and walked into the house and had a shower.

On Saturday morning he found himself back at the same coffee shop. He sat at the same rickety metal table in the courtyard, watching the light on the opposite wall. The wall was more or less white, the kind of white you see on an exterior surface that was painted white a year or two ago, on top of a previous coat of white, and has since then experienced sun, shade, and only very occasional rain.

To the incurious eye, it looked... white. David's was not an incurious eye, and the wall was what he was hoping to portray. His additions would be shadows. His last successful series of works had involved placing shadows of people on largely featureless walls. A woman sitting, a man standing. A couple together. A suggestion of content through absence. He'd stopped wanting to paint these things, but now he was finding that he did again.

He sat for two hours, drinking three coffees. Usually he'd have one in the course of a morning, two at the most. The brew at Bonnie's was good, though. It had a nutty flavour, a little smoky. While he sat, he eavesdropped and observed a sequence of locals as they passed through, stopping to chat at the other tables. There was talk of planned or recent trips to Europe, the pleasures of a newly acquired boat, upcoming IPOs in Silicon Valley. This was not the kind of content he wished to suggest.

He left and went back to his temporary studio, where he worked all afternoon. It felt good, and as always when it felt good he was baffled why he didn't do this all the time, springing out of bed in the mornings and getting straight to it. Each stroke of the brush seemed to flow from the previous and into the next, urging forward. So why did the chain fall apart so often? Why did it fragment into a series of dull, rusty links that seemed impossible to join together?

Rather than worry at the problem—David did not want to bring activity upon himself by thinking about it, however constructively— he kept working, for once going beyond outlining and starting to actually paint. This wasn't his process, but maybe this was a good thing. Maybe the process itself was flawed. If there's one thing he'd learned over the years it was that if something's working, *you keep doing it*. Don't question, don't second-guess. If you decide later that you don't like what you've done, you can fix it. But you've got to have *done* something first.

So he did.


That evening, to celebrate, he took himself out to dinner. He chose Max's mainly on the basis that it had the most attractive patio, overlooking one of the central streets. He drank two glasses of a very crisp Sauvignon Blanc and ate a ribeye, medium rare. The steak was excellent, of course, accentuated before grilling by some kind of spice rub, smoky and a little sweet.

When the waiter came for his plate David asked what was in the spice mix. The man smiled and said it was a house secret. As usual, David found this irritating. He wasn't going to run off and start his own restaurant on the back of a single recipe.

"Is there coffee in it?"

The waited inclined his head. "You have a good palate."

"Tastes like the brew they have over at Bonnie's," David said.

The waiter smiled again, as if to say that he couldn't possibly confirm or deny such a speculation, and took his plate away.

Back at the cottage, David found himself wishing he'd had one more glass of wine, or else thought to buy a bottle earlier in the day. To distract himself from this line of thinking he went into the studio, though he never normally worked in the evenings. He picked up his brush.

He stopped at midnight, a little confused at how much work he'd done, and the unusual colours in it.


On Sunday morning the work still looked good, but he wasn't inclined to add anything just yet. Instead he went walking again. He remembered to take his proper camera this time, and spent a couple of hours taking pictures of particular houses he'd noticed on previous strolls.

After snapping a series of an especially perfect Storybook cottage, he turned to see a man watching him. Not merely a man, in fact, but a policeman, in khaki shorts and short-sleeved shirt. David felt instinctively defensive.

"Beautiful, huh," the cop said, however. He was young, with short brown hair and a pair of dark glasses. "Always been one of my favourites."

"I can see why," David said, surprised. "Know anything about it?"

It turned out the cop did, from the name of the original builder to its current occupants. Then he seemed to realise there was probably something else he should be doing, and nodded, before starting to leave.

"Lucky place to live," David said. He was speaking largely to himself, but the cop paused.

"Luck doesn't have a lot to do with it," he said, before walking away down the street.

Though he returned to the cottage late morning and spent a couple of hours in the company of his canvas, David did not make any progress. The momentum of the previous day had dissipated. He felt fine. He felt inclined to work. Yet... it wasn't there.

Yesterday's link in the chain was not connected to today's. That happened sometimes. Just as it had once happened, six years ago, that a house he and his wife had wanted very much to purchase had fallen through because the chain of buyers had broken apart. One night it was all in place. By the following lunchtime it was gone. They lost the house.

Often David placed the beginning of the end of their relationship on that morning, that loss. The truth was probably that the chain of I-love-you-I-love-you-too had started to break long before. Even non-events throw shadows. Everything is contingent.

Knowing that the last thing you should do when the work isn't happening is to stand banging your head against it—sometimes you can painfully bore your way through a blockage, but more often you end up tinkering, ruining the freedom of what you've done before— he went downtown for coffee.

He did not sit looking at the wall he was currently trying to portray. He knew enough about it already. What he needed was to clarify his ideas for the shadows he'd be casting upon it. Whose hidden presence did he want to evoke? None of the people he'd observed near it yesterday, that was for sure. Their gilded non-lives didn't speak to him.

He watched the girl behind the counter inside, wondering if she would do. She was young, somewhat attractive, though carrying the extra pounds around the lower half that Californian women often seem to affect, presumably the result of some Scandinavian influence in the genes. She was very affable, dealing with locals and tourists much the same, and presumably had a real life of some kind. David found it hard to imagine what it would be.

He sat drinking another cup of the seductively complex coffee, and failed to come up with anything. He toyed with it being a couple of tourists' shadows. A man and a woman, stopping for refreshment while driving up or down the coast. An air of tension, perhaps. Her wanting to enjoy the drive, him concerned with covering the miles to wherever they were booked for the night. Both of them, in their contradictory—and conflicting—ways, merely wanting the best for each other. Would David be able to evoke that through shadows alone?

It wasn't difficulty that eventually made him go cold on the idea—when it comes to art, difficult is good. It was more the suspicion that no one, himself included, would give a crap when it was done. He needed something with a little more grit.

Finding grit in Carmel—now *there* was a challenge.


As he walked out of the alley onto the main street, he realised that in the six, nearly seven days he'd been in town, he hadn't seen a single person who didn't look as if they would have a perfect credit score. Also, that this was precisely what he'd been looking for. A Carmel wall, but with the imprint of someone who did not belong. *That* was the tension that would make the image worthwhile.

He wandered the central streets, on a mission now. After half an hour he still hadn't seen anyone who stuck out. Everybody dressed the same, spoke the same, walked and shopped the same. It occurred to him that it would make as much sense to stay in one position and keep an eye out for someone passing, and so he did that instead, lighting a cigarette to keep him company.

"You can't do that," a voice said, immediately.

David turned to see a middle-aged woman smiling sternly at him. "Huh?"

"Smoking. On the streets. It's not allowed."

David looked around for a sign. He was used to this kind of restriction, though generally you had to be within twenty feet of an open doorway the public might use, which he currently was not. "Really?"

"Really. Town ordinance."

She smiled again, more tightly, and strode up the street. David flicked the end off his cigarette, stowed the butt in the pack, and watched her go.

He spent the rest of the afternoon looking for grit. He walked a long way. He smoked a cigarette once in a while, careful to cup it in his hand, to hide it from passers-by. This, and the task he'd set himself, made him feel as if he was undercover.

When he gave up at five o'clock, he hadn't seen anyone who looked mildly disadvantaged, never mind actively poor. He'd caught sight of a few Mexicans, engaged in yard-work or carrying sheets to or from vacation rentals, but it wasn't the economic bracket that mattered. He'd seen no one who... he wasn't even sure what the umbrella term would be. No one homeless. No one who looked like they'd ever been on medication stronger than some discrete Prozac, or Xanax to smooth out the bumps.

Living in San Francisco—or pretty much any modern town, he'd have thought—brought you into unavoidable occasional contact with someone who seemed to have been jammed into the world sideways. A corner-shouter. A crazy person. Even a simple down-and-out.

In Carmel, not so much. In fact, not at all.

Maybe there was a town ordinance for that, too.

\* \* \*

On the way back to the cottage he stopped off at the grocery store. He brought a few snacks toward an evening meal at home. He also bought a bottle of wine.

After supper he sat out on the front deck and watched the world go by. It went by, smoothly, and without grit.

He went into the studio early the next morning, though his head did not feel great. He left again after ten minutes and went walking instead. He was more methodical than on the previous day, tracing the streets in a grid pattern. He saw houses he'd never noticed before, though none that looked cheap. He saw a somewhat run-down motor vehicle, but it was vintage rather than simply old.

He still saw no one to disturb the ineffable calm of the locals. No one who smelled. No one sitting with their hand held out, slumped beside a cardboard sign and a patient hound. No one with a battered acoustic guitar on their lap. No one with dreadlocks or dusty clothes.

At one point he thought he saw someone in a long black coat, some distance away, in shadows down a side street. Not just a coat, but wearing a dark and crooked hat, too.

This seemed sufficiently distinctive—and out of keeping with the locals' usual pastel modes of dress—that he hurried down the street to get a better look, but either the person had moved on or had never been more than a trick of the light.

David considered himself no bleeding-heart liberal. He'd volunteered for neither soup kitchen nor shelter in his life. When confronted with such people on his home turf in the city, he experienced the same feelings of discomfort, fear and irritation as everyone else. Here, though… here, it niggled at him. He wasn't sure why.

It wasn't that the town was pissing him off. He liked it well enough, and still hoped to do good work in it. It simply seemed… strange. Could you really have a town in which there were no off-notes, nobody wonky, no misfits? Did such a policy have to be enforced, or was Carmel somehow self-regulating, a delightful painting in which no discordant elements had been incorporated, and for which there was simply no room—a work of living art rendered from a fixed palette in which there were no colors to evoke the discordant?

In the afternoon he went to Bonnie's once more. He hadn't intended to, had in fact grown bored of looking at the wall there, and believed he already knew what he needed to put in front of it. He seemed to have become mildly addicted to their coffee, however, and as he was about to pay, he realised something else might come of his visit.

"Do you live here?" he asked the barista girl.

"All my life."

"Like it?"

"Well… sure."

"There ever been any homeless people here? That you've seen?"

She stared at him for a moment, then laughed.

He went home, but he did not paint.


He'd told himself he put the second bottle in the basket just so he wouldn't have to come by the market again the next day. By the time the first was finished, however, he was no longer that guy. He was the other guy. He knew there must be a link between these two men, some way one flowed into the next, but he'd never been able to spot the point where one ended and the other began.

It wasn't like he had a drinking problem. Sometimes he simply drank too much. It tended to make him cheerful and mischievous rather than depressed or maudlin. The problem lay not with how he was when he was drunk, but how he felt the following day.

If there's anything that breaks the chain of creation, it's a hangover. Try telling that to The Other Guy, though. He won't listen. It may well be from him that inspiration comes in the first place, but he's not the guy who has to stand there making stroke follow stroke in the hours of daylight, and so he just doesn't care.

About a third of the way through the second bottle, the idea dropped into David's head. He could see right away that it was dangerously close to the kind of thing some of his long-ago art college buddies might have undertaken, far too seriously. It was unlike anything he'd ever done. Unlike painting at all, in fact.

This wouldn't be art, though. This would be research. A step towards finishing the painting that was beginning to languish in the temporary studio. Sometimes the artist has to step into his work, after all. Perhaps it is that process that provides the solution in which events float.

He went indoors, colliding with the doorframe on the way, and made the remainder of the wine last as he worked.

As he walked up the street the next morning, David realised that he'd unintentionally added extra touches to his work in progress.

Doesn't matter how long you brush your teeth, when you've consumed two bottles of wine you're going to be exuding it the next morning one way or another. It seeps out of your pores. His head hurt, causing him to squint against the shafts of sunlight that made it down through the trees on his way toward the centre of the village. He'd slept terribly, too—it turned out the floor of the garage was just as uncomfortable as it looked—which conferred valuable extra detail. Often when you create something it's the unintentional or unconscious touches that make all the difference—so long, of course, as the chain is operating.

He got his first sideways glance just as he made it onto the main street. A man wearing immaculate blue shorts, a blue shirt, and a blue cap looked at him, then away, and then back again. He seemed like he wanted to say something.

David looked back and grinned.

The man stayed silent, but walked quickly away.

*Score*, David thought.

He continued up the street, concentrating on shambling. It wasn't hard, given how rough he felt. Just before he turned down the alley toward Bonnie's, he coughed. It was supposed to be merely a throat-clearer, but the vast number of cigarettes he'd smoked the night before elevated it into a consumptive cacophony that lasted twenty seconds, and culminated in hawking a mouthful of beige phlegm into a flowerbed.

Looking up, head swirling, David saw that a middle-aged couple had stopped in their tracks and were staring at him with identical looks on their faces. It was hard to describe their expressions, though if you came home to find the dog had shat in the middle of your bed, you'd probably make something similar.

David waved, and lurched off up the alley.

The girl behind the counter watched his approach. He knew this was going to be an interesting test. She'd seen him the day before. They'd even had a conversation.

He stepped up to the counter, swaying slightly as he peered up at the board.

"Just a coffee," he said. "Twelve ounce."

She reached behind for a cup, not taking her eyes off him. He pulled out the motley handful of loose coins he'd put in his pocket in preparation. It took him quite a while to count out the correct amount. The girl watched, holding back on handing over the cup until he was done.

He filled the cup, added milk and a lot of sugar. Smiled crookedly at the girl as he left. She was still watching, and had not said a single word.

Out in the courtyard he sat at the table in front of the white wall. Had she *really* not recognised David? Hard to tell. Could be that she'd been left speechless by the transformation. He didn't think so, though. He was pretty good at his job. He thought she had no idea who he was, and her reaction had been to what he appeared to be.

It'd taken him five hours. First thing he'd tackled were his clothes. At first he'd thought he might be able to get away with using some of his painting gear, but one glance told him that—to his eye—they were too obviously what they were: clothes someone had used to paint in. The balance and distribution of the colours weren't right.

So he'd gone into the bedroom and found his second pair of jeans and an old-ish shirt. The jeans had always been kind of long in the leg and so the bottoms were ragged and a little dirty, a good start. The shirt was white and in good condition, but he'd worn it on the drive down from San Francisco and it had lain crumpled at the bottom of the linen basket ever since.

Working slowly and methodically—within the confines of the fact that he'd been well on the way to shit-faced drunk by then—he'd tested colours and textures, and then, when satisfied, got to work, layer by layer.

He was a firm believer in the maxim that you can always add but never take away, and so when he was almost done he set the clothes aside and got to work on his face and arms. After a while he hit on a combination of paint, water and dust from the garage floor that seemed to hit the mark. He ran his hands through his hair occasionally, ensuring some of all this got lodged there too.

He finally went back to the clothes and layered in over the creases, then bent and rubbed them against the wall for ten minutes, perfecting the shiny look that comes from dirt and filth that's been lived in for so long it becomes ingrained, part of the garment itself.

He put the clothes on and lurched into the house. He checked the overall impression in the mirror in the bathroom, and went back to the studio for a couple of final touches, but by this point the wine was done and so was he. In a last-minute inspiration—aided by the fact he simply couldn't be bothered to lurch back to the bedroom—he lay down on the garage floor.

Pretty quickly he got to sleep, via the intermediary of passing out.

There was a polite coughing sound, and he looked up to see someone standing over him. Not just someone, in fact, but a policeman—the young cop from yesterday.

"Hey," David said.

"Like you to come with me, sir."

"Why?"

The cop reached his hand out toward David's arm. He didn't actually touch it, but the implication was clear.

David looked around the little courtyard. Only one of the other tables was taken, a couple who were now studiously looking elsewhere. He raised his voice and directed it toward them. "You got a problem with me?"

Somehow, it turned out, it was possible for two people to look even *less* like they were there, while still remaining physically present.

David drained the last of his coffee and stood. By accident, his thigh banged against the edge of the little metal table, causing his stirring spoon to fall noisily to the flagstones. "Pah," he muttered, with vague enmity, before starting to follow the cop up the alley.

As a final touch, he turned back to the couple. "Assholes," he snarled.

The cop was waiting out on the sidewalk. David realised that rather than feeling nervous, or scared, he felt excited.

"What?" he said. "I wasn't doing nothing wrong."

The cop looked at him steadily. "Kind of a departure from photographing houses, isn't it?"

David realised the policeman wasn't dumb. He kept silent.

"So how come the drifter disguise? Which is pretty good, by the way."

"Didn't fool you."

"It's my job to keep my eyes open, keep track. It's how I know who lives in which house, too. So—what's up?"

"I'm just trying something."

"You got a problem with the people who live here?"

"No. Just... I thought it would be interesting. To see how they would react."

The cop nodded. He looked along the street. Most people were going about their business in the usual serene way. A few, mainly on the other side of the street, were watching. It was doubtless a while since they'd seen a cop talking to someone other than to cheerfully pass the time of day.

"I understand the joke, sir," he said. "Some people won't."

"Don't you think it would do them good? To be reminded?"

"I'm not talking about them, sir," he said. "And anyway... no, I don't think it would. If you've got some big thing about social equality, why not go back to the city and do something about it?"

David looked at him. Along the upper California coast, "the city" isn't a catch-all term—it specifically means San Francisco. "How do you know I'm from there?"

"Happened to run into Ron Bleist, guy who owns the cottage you're renting. Said you were a painter."

"*Happened* to run into him?"

"My point is, nobody portrays Carmel as an equal-opportunity environment. It is what it is. If you can put up with that, you're welcome here."

"And if not?"

The man shrugged.

David found he was becoming genuinely angry. "You know the really crappy thing?"

"Tell me the really crappy thing."

"Nobody here even knows the difference. You've got good eyes, presumably some experience of the real world. Everyone else I've encountered today... they can't even tell I'm not a real drifter. I'm actually kind of well known for what I do. I've got a million-dollar condo up in the city. This crap all over me is paint and dust, not real dirt. And yet nobody here can even tell."

"Maybe you're a better artist than you realise."

"Or maybe everyone here is dumber than they know."

The cop shrugged once more.

"That's it?"

"You want to string a sign round your neck, sir, declaring yourself a piece of performance art, be my guest. Otherwise, do yourself a big favour and go get cleaned up."

"Is that some kind of warning?"

"Yes, it is."


David did not go home, however. After fuming on the street for a few minutes, he stomped down to the beach. By the time he got there he was feeling hot and even more dreadful than before, so he continued down to the sea and walked straight into it. The water was very cold.

He trudged back up the beach, found some shade and sat down. When he awoke, several hours later, the hangover had abated a little. His irritation hadn't, however.

A small group of people in their early twenties were now sitting some distance away. They wore shorts and T-shirts in various shades of pale. One of the guys glanced over at David, then turned back to the group.

David pushed himself laboriously to his feet. He went over. The dried sea-salt on his clothes had made them stiff, and caused interesting tidal patterns in the paint. Another unconscious finesse.

He stood outside their circle. The same guy as before looked up at him. He was blandly good-looking, not overtly supercilious.

David croaked at him. "You got a problem with me?"

He'd noticed when talking to the cop that last night's over-indulgences had coarsened his voice. Crashing out on the beach had turned the huskiness up another big notch.

"Nothing that needs resolving right now," the boy said, mildly. He turned back to his friends, none of whom had appeared to pay David any attention at all, as if he wasn't even visible.

Turning imperiously from them, David accidentally got his feet caught on a piece of driftwood, and fell over, full-length in the sand. Nobody laughed, or jeered.

He got up and lurched away.


By now, if the truth be told, David was starting to tire of the game. He'd established that the residents and visitors of Carmel didn't much care for down-and-outs. Big deal. He could have predicted that without the rigmarole. He wandered back into the centre, deciding to milk the effect one last time before going back to the cottage. A few people stared. Others crossed the street to avoid him. Nobody shouted, nobody called the cops.

Time to go home, have a bath. Reboot. Probably not work—with a hangover like this—but get an early night instead. Tomorrow's always another day, potentially the start of a new chain. He still liked the idea of a drifter's shadow in his painting. It worked. He could be up and at it bright and early. Have it blocked out by the afternoon, put the canvas to one side and start another. Have a civilised dinner at a restaurant in the evening, get back on course.

It might even have panned out like that, too, if his route hadn't happened to take him past the grocery market, and if he hadn't found a forgotten twenty in the back pocket of his jeans.

They may not like down-and-outs in nice stores, but they'll always take their money for a big bottle of wine.

\* \* \*

She came out of the alleyway just after eight o'clock, by which time it was the other side of twilight. David had been waiting across the street by the side of a gallery that had shut some time before. Galleries in Carmel didn't have to work long hours.

He walked quickly across the street toward her. He nearly tripped on the curb—over half of the outsized bottle of wine was inside him now, and he was feeling much better for it. The barista girl from Bonnie's looked up and saw him, and her face fell.

"Why'd you call him?"

His voice came out louder than he intended.

She took a step back. "What?"

"Why'd you call the cop? I was just sitting at a table. I'd paid for my coffee. I wasn't getting in anyone's face. So why'd you call the fucking cops?"

The girl started backing toward the alleyway that led to Bonnie's, seeking safety in the work environment she'd just left. David followed.

He pressed her. "Can't you see who I am? The guy who's been coming in your place every day for a fucking week. I must have dropped fifty bucks in there. I asked you yesterday if you liked living in Carmel, remember? We had a *conversation*. Yet today, just because I look a little different, suddenly you're all over 911."

"I'm sorry," she said, still backing up the alley.

"Big deal. The point is *I'm the same guy*. Actually, that's not the point. Who even cares whether I'm the same guy? I'm *a* guy. A man. I had every right to sit there. I wasn't causing trouble. So what the *fuck*?"

"I don't understand."

"I'll tell you. There's a chain between everything you do, what you did last, what comes next. There's a chain between *people*, too, him and me—and there should be one between you and me, too. Get it? There's a duty of care. Person to person to person. If not care, just simple politeness. We're all part of the hundred percent."

She shook her head, looking miserable and scared, and kept backing up the alleyway, toward the courtyard.

David was aware this wasn't coming out as clearly as he'd hoped, and his frustration started to run away with him. "If you break the chain *nothing makes sense*. You stop picking up the brush and doing something with it, anything's better than nothing, then the paintings don't get done. And if you stop respecting me just because I look like shit, society doesn't work. We're back to being animals. Do you get what I'm talking about now, *you stupid bitch*?"

She turned and ran the last yards into the dark courtyard. David, unsure of what he was doing, or why, strode enthusiastically after her. It struck him, in a corner of his soul he'd known was there but had always refused to visit, that breaking the chain might have interesting consequences.

He'd never been a violent man. Even his ex-wife would testify to that. But that was some other David. If the chain was broken… perhaps he didn't have to remain consistent with that man's behaviour. Maybe there were other ways of being that he could try. It struck him, like a bolt from the blue, that it might actually be *interesting* to punch a snivelling woman in the face. To knock her down and then stand over her and take his time over deciding what to do next—or what things, and in what order.

He realised with a shiver that these courses of action had always been there, running side-by-side with normal life, and it was only the restraining links to his previous ways that had stopped him trying them before.

As he lurched into the courtyard after her, he saw the girl reach the other side and go banging straight into the metal gate. During the day this gate yielded access to another alley, which let out onto the next street. Right now, however, it was padlocked.

"Huh," he said, with a slow smile. "So now what?"

But she turned from the gate to face him, and he was confused to see she didn't look scared of him any more.

He realised, too late, that they were not alone in the courtyard.

Sitting at the small tables, waiting, were the young man from the beach, the woman who'd told him off for smoking the day before, and the man in the blue cap, along with several others.

They didn't look scared of David either.

\* \* \*

Two hours later the body was delivered to the cop's house. It was brought over by Bonnie—owner of the coffee store, also the lady who'd asked David not to smoke—and her husband, coincidentally an amateur watercolourist. The body's legs had already been removed and were waiting in the cold store of Max's restaurant. Bonnie would later prepare them for the long roasting procedure that would ultimately create the smoky-sweet powder that not just the restaurant and her coffee shop but every eatery in town deployed, in one way or another, according to the recipe and procedures laid down by the town's long-ago founders.

The cop received the body without enthusiasm. He'd tried to warn the guy, and he knew for a fact the village had plenty of the powder in reserve and so this didn't need to have happened. Nonetheless, he did his job.

He put the body in the trunk of his car and drove it an hour along the coast road. He took a turn off Highway 1 not far from the Big Sur River Inn, and drove a further ten miles down an old, forgotten road to the secluded cove where, once again according to protocol—this one dictated by the Watchers—he unwrapped the offering from the plastic sheeting and left it face down on the sandy beach.

An hour after he left, three figures emerged from the pounding surf. The Watchers were as always dressed in long black coats— or cloaks, no human had ever been close enough to establish the difference and survive—and tall, pointed hats. They consumed the parts of the body they had a taste for, primarily internal organs. The rest was left for the crabs.

The Watchers took care to savour the experience, as they knew its days were numbered. The Elders amongst them had started to indicate they were growing bored of the special relationship with Carmel, and that it might soon be time for the town and its inhabitants to meet their end. A date had not yet been set for the night when the Watchers would swarm en masse up from the sea and fall upon the village, but it would be soon.

Or so they thought.

Unbeknownst to them, the vast god which lives—and has always lived—in the frigid waters just off Big Sur was reaching the end of one of its own millennial cycles. Within a consciousness that moved slowly (and yet was capable of sudden and terrible decisions), was stirring the thought that it was almost time to rise up again and consume this portion of the coast—if not tonight, then the next day or the next. As usual, and by intention, the process would closely resemble an earthquake, one that would on this occasion not merely knock down a few houses, but leave the shape of the coastline permanently changed.

So much changed, in fact, that the new outline would displease the nameless being that spends most of its time in the shadows on the dark side of the moon. This dissatisfaction would eventually cause it to destroy the Earth entirely, erasing it in an instant to swirling dust, so it could start its creative work again on a fresh canvas.

There are always chains, in work and love, from birth to death.

What keeps us sane is not knowing our position along them.

# INTO THE WATER

*by* S I M O N   K U R T   U N S W O R T H

KAPENDA WATCHED THE water, and the water ate the Earth.

"Isaac, the High Street's finally going under, we need to go and catch it," said Needham from somewhere behind him. Kapenda raised his free hand in acknowledgement but didn't move. Instead, he let his eye rise, up from the new channel of brown and churning floodwater to the bank above. The house's foundations were exposed by the water so that it now teetered precariously on the edge of a gorge. *Fall*, thought Kapenda, *fall, please*. The house didn't fall but it would, soon, and he hoped to be here when it did.

"Isaac!" Needham again. The talent was already at the high street, waiting. The talent was like a child, got fractious and bored if it wasn't the centre of attention; *Don't keep the talent waiting*, was the motto. *Don't annoy the talent* was the rule. Sighing, Kapenda finally lowered the camera and turned to go.

It had rained for months, on and off. Summer had been a washout, the skies permanently thick with cloud, the sun an infrequent visitor. On the rare occasions the clouds broke and the sun struggled through, grounds steamed but didn't dry out. The water table saturated upwards, the ground remaining sodden until the first of the winter storms came and the rivers rose and the banks broke and the water was suddenly everywhere.

They were less than a mile from the town, but the journey still took several minutes. The roads were swollen with run-off, thick limbs of water flowing down the gutters and pushing up from the drains, washing across the camber and constantly tugging at the vehicle. Kapenda wasn't driving but he felt it, the way they pulled across the centre line and then back as Needham compensated. It had been like this for days now all across the south of England. Kapenda leaned against the window, peering at the rain and submerged land beyond the glass.

There were figures in the field.

Even at their reduced speed, they passed the little tableau too quickly for Kapenda to see what the figures were doing, and he had to crane back around to try and keep them in view. There were four of them, and they appeared to be crouching so that only their shoulders and heads emerged from the flooded pasture. One was holding its arms to the sky. There was something off about the shape of the figures—the arms held to the clouds were too long, the heads too bulbous. Were they moving? Still? Perhaps they were one of those odd art installations you sometimes came across, like Gormley's standing figures on Crosby beach. Kapenda had filmed a segment on them not long after they had been put in place, and watching as the tide receded to reveal a series of bronze, motionless watching figures had been quite wonderful and slightly unnerving. Had they done something similar here?

The rain thickened, and the figures were lost to its grey embrace.

The talent, a weasel of a man called Plumb whose only discernible value was a smoothly good-looking face and a reassuring yet stentorian voice, was angry with Needham and Kapenda. As Kapenda framed him in shot so that the new river flowing down Grovehill's main street and the sandbagged shops behind it could be seen over Plumb's shoulder, Plumb was moaning.

"We've missed all the dramatic stuff," he said.

"We've not," said Needham. "Just trust in Isaac, he'll make you look good.

"It's not about me looking good," said Plumb, bristling, brushing the cowlick of hair that was drooping over his forehead. "It's about the story."

"Of course it is," said Needham. "Now, have you got your script?"

They didn't get the lead item on the news, but they did get the second-string item, a cut to Plumb after the main story so that he could intone his description of Grovehill's failed flood defences. Kapenda had used the natural light to make Plumb seem larger and the water behind darker, more ominous. He was happy with the effect, especially the last tracking shot away from the talent to look up the street, lost under a caul of fast-moving flood whose surface rippled and glittered. The water looked alive, depthless and hungry, something inexorable and unknowable.

*Now that,* thought Kapenda, *is how to tell a story*, and only spotted the shape moving through the water when he was reviewing the footage a couple of hours after it had gone out. It was a dark blur just below the waves, moving against the current and it vanished after perhaps half a minute. Something tumbling through the flow, Kapenda thought, and wished it had broken the surface—it would have made a nice image to finish the film on.


Plumb had found an audience.

They were in the bar of the pub where they were staying: the tiny, cramped rooms the only place available. The flood had done the hospitality industry a world of good, Kapenda thought; every room in the area was taken with television and print reporters.

"Of course, it's all global warming's fault," Plumb said.

"Is it?" said the man he was talking to. The man's voice was deep and rich, accented in a way Kapenda always thought of as old-fashioned. It was the voice of the BBC in the 1950s, of the Pathé newsreels. He punctuated everything he said with little coughs, as though he had something caught in his throat.

"Of course," said Plumb, drawing on all the knowledge he had gained from reading one- and two-minute sound-bite pieces for local and, more latterly, national news. "The world's heating up, so it rains more. It's obvious."

"It's as simple as that," said the man, and caught Kapenda's eye over Plumb's shoulder. One of his eyes was milky and blind, Kapenda saw, and then the man, disconcertingly, winked his dead eye and smiled.

"He really is an insufferable fool, isn't he?" the man said later to Kapenda, nodding at Plumb, who was now holding court in the middle of a group of other talents. *What's the collective noun for the talent?* thought Kapenda. *A show-off? A blandness? A stupidity?* He moved a forefinger through a puddle of spilled beer on the table, swirling it out to make a circle. The man, whose name was David, dipped his own fingers in the puddle and made an intricate pattern on the wood with the liquid before wiping it away.

"He thinks he understands it," said David, and gave one of his little coughs. "But he doesn't."

"What is there to understand?" asked Needham. "It's rain. It comes down, it floods, we film it and he talks about it and tries to look dramatic and knowledgeable whilst wearing an anorak that the viewers can see and wellingtons that they can't."

"This," said David, waving a hand at the windows and the rain beyond. He was drunk; Needham was drunker. "It's not so simple as he wants to believe. There are forces at work more complex than mere global warming." He coughed again, a polite rumble.

"Pollution?" said Needham. Kapenda thought of his camera, of the eye he held to his shoulder to see the world, about how he'd frame this discussion. One at each edge of the screen, he decided, in tight close-up, David's opaque eye peering into the lens as Needham's head bobbed back and forth, up and down, like a bird. Needham was a good producer and director because he stressed over the little details, but a bad drinking companion because he got like a terrier over tiny fragments of information.

"Pollution? Possibly, but no answer about the Earth is that simple. Why is the water rising so fast? So far? Mere geography, or something more? My point is that we look to the wrong places for answers, because the real answers have faces too terrible to contemplate," said David and then stood. He was tall and solid, not fat exactly but well built, his waistcoat straining under the pressure from his ample belly.

"You're looking in the wrong place, all of you." And with that, nodding his thanks for the company, David turned and walked away. Kapenda grinned at the look of confusion on Needham's face, saw that Plumb was heading back their way and quickly rose himself.

"I need a walk," he said.

"A swim, surely?" said Needham, and he and Plumb laughed. Kapenda did not reply.

The pub was on a hill—it was why it remained mostly unaffected by the storms and the rising floodwater. The rain was coming in near-horizontal sweeps now, gusting along in cold breaths that made Kapenda shiver. Lightning crackled somewhere over the fields, followed by thunder that reminded him of David's voice and cough. The forecasters were saying that this storm would burn itself out in the next day or so, but they'd said that before and been wrong. The previous week, the rains had continued through the period they'd confidently predicted would be dry, and the groundwater rose and rose. What had he come outside for? Not air, not even to be away from Needham and Plumb, not really.

Kapenda went down towards the lights that were strung out along Grovehill's main street. Generators, housed in the nearby community hall, powered the lamps and rope barriers prevented him from getting to the water. Even at this time of night, news crews were clustered along the ropes, each filming or preparing for filming. He tried to look at the scene as though he was holding his camera—was there something here not about the floods but about the press response to it? No, that had been done.

There had to be something new, some fresh angle. As the rain pattered down around him, Kapenda thought. What was the weirdest thing he'd seen since this all started? He'd been in the tiny town of Chew Stoke a few weeks earlier, filming the remains of a vehicle that had been washed into a culvert and whose driver had died. In Grovehill, no one had died yet but there were abandoned cars strewn along the streets and surrounding tracks, hulking shapes that the water broke around and flowed over in fractured, churning flurries.

That was old. Every television station had those shots. He'd been there the year before when the police had excavated a mud-filled railway tunnel and uncovered the remains of two people who had been crushed in a landslide. What they needed was something like that here, something that showed how weak man's civilised veneer was when set against nature's uncaring ferocity. He needed something that contrasted human frailty and natural strength, something that Dalí might have painted—a boat on a roof, or a shark swimming up the main street. He needed that bloody house to collapse.

What about the figures in the field?

Actually, the fields were a good starting point. They had flooded heavily and most were under at least four or five feet of water, but due to some quirk of meteorology or geography the water on them was sitting calm. *Somewhere*, he thought, *somewhere there's an image in that smooth expanse that I can use.*


Kapenda waited until morning, and such light as came with sunrise, before investigating. He left a note for Needham, who likely wouldn't be up until mid-morning anyway, and drove back along the roads towards the field. Through the windscreen, the road ahead of him moved like a snake, constantly surging and writhing.

The dark shape was in the first field he came to, drifting slowly along, spinning. Kapenda saw it through the tangle of hedgerow and stopped, climbing out into knee-high water and lifting his camera to his shoulder. He couldn't see well, was too low, so climbed onto the vehicle's door-sill and then higher, onto its roof. Was this the field where he had seen the figures? He thought it was, although there was no sign of them now. From his raised vantage-point, he saw what the shape was, and started filming.

It was a dead cow. It was already bloating, its belly swelling from the gases trapped within, and its eye peered at him with baleful solemnity. Its tongue trailed from its open mouth, leached to a pale grey by the water. Its tail drifted after it like an eel. There was another beyond it, he saw, and more beyond that. A herd, or flock, or whatever a group of cows was called, trapped by the water and drowned.

Drowned? Well, probably, but one of the further animals looked odd. Kapenda zoomed in, focusing as he did so. The dead creature's side was a ragged mess, with strips of peeled flesh and hide along its flank exposing the muscles below. Here and there, flashes of white bone were visible. Its neck was similarly torn, the vertebrae visible through the damaged flesh. As he filmed, the creature spun more violently as a current caught it, slamming it into a tree-trunk; the collision left scraps of meat clinging to the bark. Kapenda carried on filming as the cow whirled away, watching as it caught on something under the water, jerked and then suddenly submerged, bobbing back up before vanishing again. A great bubble of air, so noxious Kapenda could smell it from his distant perch, emerged from where the cow had gone down.

It was as Kapenda climbed down from the roof that he saw the thing in the hedgerow.

It was jammed, glinting, into the tangle of branches and leaves about four feet from the ground. From the surface of the water, he amended. Leaving his camera in the jeep, he moved cautiously towards the glint, feeling ahead with his feet. The ground dropped away as he stepped off the solid surface of the road, the water rising against him. It came to his thighs and then his waist; he took his wallet and phone from his jeans and zipped them into his jacket's inner pocket; they were already in plastic bank bags, sealed against the damp. Carefully, not wanting to slip, lose his footing and be washed away like the cows, he leaned into the hedgerow and pushed his arm into it. The thing was tantalisingly out of reach. He pushed in harder, felt his feet shift along the submerged earth and then he was over, falling into the water and going under.

It was cold, clenching his head in its taut embrace and squeezing. Kapenda kicked but his feet tangled into something—branches or roots—and were held fast. Something large and dark, darker than the water around him, banged into him, began to roll over him and force him further under the water. He wanted to breathe, knew if he opened his mouth he'd take in water and drown, and clenched his jaw. The thing on him was heavy, clamped onto his shoulder and was it biting him, Jesus yes, it was biting him and pushing him down and he was trapped, was under it and couldn't shift it and then something grasped his other shoulder, hard, and he was pulled up from the water.

"No! No! Let him be!" It was David, hauling Kapenda from the water, pulling him back to the jeep. "What were you doing in the water? You could have bloody drowned!"

Kapenda collapsed to his knees, back into the water but held up by the jeep, and vomited. His breakfast came out in a soup of dirty liquid, the sight of it making him wretch even more.

"Are you okay? Do you need to go to the doctor? The hospital?" David was calmer now, more concerned than angry.

"No," said Kapenda after a moment. "I think I'm okay. What was it?"

"A dead cow," said David after a moment. "What were you doing, going into the water?"

"I saw something in the hedge," said Kapenda, and it sounded ridiculous even as he said it. He managed to rise to his feet, using the side of the jeep as a support. Water dripped from him.

"Let me see then," said David. The man looked paler in the daylight, as though he was somehow less there, his dead eye bulging from a face that was round and wan. Its milky iris peered at Kapenda. His other eye was dark, the sclera slightly yellowing. Was he a heavier drinker than he'd appeared the night before? He had patches of rough skin, Kapenda saw, dried and peeling.

There was a bike leaning against the back of the jeep and Kapenda was suddenly struck with the image of David cycling down the centre of the road, his front wheel cutting a 'V' though the water, his feet submerging and re-emerging with each revolution of the pedals, and it made him smile.

"Now, let's see this thing you were prepared to drown to get," said David, also smiling.

"Oh, I—" started Kapenda, about to say that it was still in the hedge, and then realised it wasn't. He was holding it.

It was a small figure, made from some dull metal. It had a suggestion of legs and arms and a face that was nested in tentacles, its eyes deep-set and its mouth a curved-down arc. Was it an octopus? A squid? A long chain dangled from it, fine-linked and dully golden. More figures were hooked to some of the chain's links, tiny things like toads with swollen genitalia and fish with arms and legs. David held the figure up by the chain, peering at it.

"What is it?" Kapenda asked.

David didn't answer. Instead, he spun it, watching as it caught the pallid light. Its surface was smooth, but Kapenda had the impression it was the smoothness of age and wear, that the ghosts of old marks still lay under its skin. Finally, David spoke, muttering under his breath, words that Kapenda didn't catch.

"Do you know what it is?" asked Kapenda. He was starting to shiver, the shock and the cold catching him. He wanted to go back to the hotel and dry off, warm up.

"Yes," said David. "I saw one once, as a child, and I hoped not to see one again so soon. Still, I suppose it explains a lot." He rubbed one of the patches of dry skin on his neck slowly.

"The water's coming, my friend," he said, "and there's nothing we can do to stop it. Its time is here again. Well, if you're sure you're okay to drive, I'll leave you be. Take my advice, stay out of the water."

"I will," said Kapenda, "and thank you."

"Think nothing of it," said David and coughed again, his own private punctuation. He winked his sightless eye once more and then went and mounted his bike, wheeling it around to point back to Grovehill. Moments later all Kapenda could see of him was his back, hunched over the handlebars as he went down the road. Behind him, tiny waves spread out across the water and then broke apart.

It was only when Kapenda got back into the jeep that he remembered the bite—sure enough, his jacket was torn in two semicircles, to the front and rear of his shoulder, and the skin below bruised but not broken. He got back out of the jeep to try and see the cow but it must have floated off, and the only thing to see was the flood, ever restless and ever hungry.


The house collapsed just after lunch.

They were filming at the rope barrier again, this time framing the talent against a shot down the street to show how the water wasn't retreating. "Forecasters say that, with the recent rainfall, the water levels aren't expected to recede until at least tomorrow, and if more rain comes it could conceivably be several days or more," Plumb intoned. "Great sections of the South-West are now underwater, economies ruined and livelihoods and lives destroyed. Even today, we've heard of two more deaths, a woman and child who drowned in their lounge in the village of Arnold, several miles from here. Questions are being asked of the defences that the government installed and why the Environment Agency wasn't better prepared. Here, the people merely wait, and hope."

Kapenda waited until Plumb had done his turn, letting him peer meaningfully down the flooded street, before lowering the camera. One of the other crews had found a flooded farm earlier that day and had proudly showed their footage to everyone, of the oilslick forming across the surface of the water in the barn and around it as the water worked its way into the abandoned vehicles and metal storage canisters, teasing out the oil and red diesel they contained. The rainbow patterns had been pocking and dancing in the rain, and the image had been oddly beautiful; Kapenda had been professionally impressed, and privately jealous.

"Was that good?" asked Plumb, and then stopped and listened as the air filled with a dense rumbling, grinding sound like something heavy being pushed over a stone floor.

"The building's gone," someone shouted, a runner with a phone clamped to his ear, "it's completely collapsed. The flood's surging!"

As the man spoke, a fresh wall of water appeared between the furthest buildings, higher than those that had come before it, driven by the tons of brick and wood and belongings that had suddenly crashed into the flow. The wave was a dirty red colour, curled over like a surfer's dream. Somewhere, it had picked up trees and a car, a table, a bed and other unidentifiable shapes—all of these Kapenda saw even as he was raising the camera. In the viewfinder, he caught the things in the water as they hit the buildings, saw the car crash through the window of a chemist, saw the bed hurtle into and buckle a lamp-post, saw bricks bounce and dip like salmon on their way to spawning, and then the wave was upon them.

He moved back, never stopping filming, cursing under his breath that he'd missed the actual collapse. Things churned through the water, dark shadows darting back and forward under the surface, their edges occasionally breaking through to the air only to roll back, splash their way under again.

The water level rose rapidly, submerging the makeshift barriers and eating away at the bottom of the hill. As Kapenda and Needham and the talent moved swiftly back, jostling in amongst the other film crews, cars were lifted out of the side streets and began to jolt through the water. One of the lights exploded as the water reached the electric cables, and the others shorted in a series of rapid pops that left behind ghost spots in Kapenda's eyes and an acrid smell of smoke in the air. Moments later, one of the generators made a series of groaning sounds from inside the community hall and black smoke breathed out from the windows as it, too, shorted out. The police pushed the crowd back, followed all the while by the water.

By nightfall, Grovehill was lost. The rains, which had continued to fall all day, had finally abated as the light faded but the floodwater had continued to rise, submerging most of the houses and shops up to their roofs. In the pub, the conversation was subdued, slightly awed. Most of the crews had worked on weather stories before; Kapenda himself had been at Boscastle in 2004, filming the aftermath of the flash flood, but this was worse—it showed no signs of receding.

Two cameramen had died when the building collapsed. One had been caught in the initial surge of water, swept away like so much flotsam. The other, further down the torrent, had been on the edge of the bank when something turning in the water, the branches of an uprooted tree, it was supposed, had reached out and snagged him, lifting him from his feet and carrying him off. His talent, a pretty blonde stringer for a local news programme, had been taken off in shock talking about how the water had eaten the man.

"I saw one of those in Russia," said a voice from behind him.

It was one of the other cameramen—Rice, Kapenda thought he might be called. Rice nodded at the thing Kapenda had pulled from the hedge, sitting on the table by his glass of beer.

"Russia?" asked Kapenda

"I was in Krymsk in 2010 and in Krasnodar," said Rice, "back in 2012, when the flash flood killed all those people. We found a few of those around the port in Krymsk and in the fields about Krasnodar.

We did a segment about them, but it was never shown." He picked up the figure and dangled it, much like David had done, eying it.

"It's almost identical," he said. "Strange."

"What is it?"

"We never found out, not really. I always assumed it was some kind of peasant magic, some idol to keep the floods away. If that's what it was, it didn't work though, the damn things were always where the water was at its highest. I found one hanging from a light fitting in the upper room of a school that was almost completely submerged." He put the thing back on Kapenda's table.

"What happened to your segment?"

"Got archived, I suppose," said Rice. "Pretty much what we expected. I didn't mind, not really. Russia was a nightmare, and I had bigger things to worry about than whether the piece I filmed got shown."

"Really?"

"Really. It was chaos, thousands of people made homeless, streets full of mud and water and corpses. In Krymsk, everything got washed into the Black Sea, and the harbour was blocked with debris for weeks after. The local sea-life was well fed, though."

"Jesus," said Kapenda.

"Yeah," said Rice. "You'd see them, dark shapes in the water, and then some floating body would suddenly vanish. The official estimate for Krymsk was one hundred and seventy dead, or thereabouts, but I'll be damned if it wasn't far higher though. I had a friend covered the Pakistan floods, was in Sindh and Balochistan, and he told me there were things like that there as well, hanging from the trees just above the flood-line."

"The same things?"

"Yeah," said Rice again. "And I'll tell you one other thing that's odd."

"What?"

"That old woman that died in the flood at St. Asaph the other week? That drowned in her home? There was one hanging outside her house, and one outside the house of the mother and child that drowned yesterday."

"What? How do you know?"

Rice merely smiled at Kapenda. *I have my sources*, the smile said, *and I'm keeping them secret*. "Keep it safe," he said as he turned and went back to the bar, "you never know when you might need protection against the water."

Needham was in a bad mood.

It was the next morning, and he had been trying to find someone local to interview. He wanted the talent to do some empathy work, get Plumb to listen sympathetically and nod as some teary bumpkin showed them their drenched possessions and talked about how their pictures of Granny were lost forever, but there wasn't anyone.

"They won't talk to you?" asked Kapenda.

"They've all fucking vanished!" said Needham. "There's no one in the emergency shelters, no one worth mentioning anyway, and they certainly aren't staying at any of the farms, I've checked. Most of them have been abandoned too. The police aren't sure when anyone's gone, or they're not saying if they know."

"They must be somewhere," said Kapenda.

"Must they? Well I don't know where to fucking find them," said Needham.

"Perhaps they all swam away?" said Plumb and laughed. Neither Kapenda nor Needham joined in.

"It'll be dead cows and flooded fucking bushes again, you'll see," said Needham, disconsolate. "Isaac, can't you find me something new?"

"I'll try," said Kapenda.

David was standing in the water in one of the fields a little further out from Grovehill. Kapenda saw his bike first, leaning against the hedge and half underwater, and pulled the jeep over to see what the man was doing. There was a stile in the hedge and David was beyond it, out into the field proper. Kapenda waded to the wooden gate and climbed it, perching on the top and calling, "Hello!"

"'For Behold," said David loudly, his voice rolling across the water,

"'I will bring a flood of water upon the earth to destroy all flesh in which is the breath of life under Heaven.' Hello, Isaac. They knew, you see—they understood."

"Who knew? Understood what?"

"We have always waited for the water's call, those of us with the blood, waited for the changes to come, but now? Some of us have called to it, and it has come."

"I don't understand," said Kapenda. He wished he had brought his camera—David looked both lonely and somehow potent, standing up to his chest in the water, his back to Kapenda. It was raining again, the day around them grey and murky.

"What are you doing?"

"It has been brought this far but I worry," said David, his voice lower, harder for Kapenda to hear. "How much further? How much more do we want? And what of what comes after us? The sleeping one whose symbol you found, Isaac? It wants the world, drowned and washed clean, but clean of what? Just of you? Or of everything—of us as well? We should have stayed in the deeps, but no, we have moved into the shallows and we prepare the way as though we were cleaning the feet of the sleeping one, supplicants to it. We might be terrible, Isaac, but after us? Do you have a god? Pray for its mercy, for the thing that comes after us—the thing that we open the way for—will be awful and savage beyond imagining."

"David, what are you talking about?"

"The water, Isaac. It's always about the water." David turned—in the fractured, mazy light, his face was a white shift of moonlike intensity. His eyes were swollen, turning so that they appeared to be looking to opposite sides of his head. His skin looked like old linen, rough and covered in dry and flaking patches. He seemed to have lost his hair and his neck had folded down over itself in thick, quivering ridges. "It would be best for you to leave, Isaac. You have been saved from the water once, but I suspect that once is all."

"David, please, I still don't know what you mean. Tell me what you're talking about."

"I thought we had time, that the calling that cannot be ignored would never come, but it is too late. Others have hastened it, and the water calls to us even as they call to it. I can't stand against it, Isaac. The change is come."

"David—" Kapenda began, but the older man turned and began to move off across the field, bobbing down shoulder-deep into the water with each long stride, sweeping his arms around as though swimming.

"David!" Kapenda shouted, but the man didn't turn. Just before he was lost to view, the water around him seemed suddenly full of movement, with things rising to the surface and looking back at him. Kapenda, scared, turned away and returned to the jeep.

"I've found us a boat!" said Needham when Kapenda got back. He didn't seem bothered that Kapenda hadn't found anything new to film.

"Your idea about the fields yesterday, about how smooth they are, it got me thinking," Needham continued. "Now the flow's slowing down, it's safe to go out in a boat, not in the fields but around the houses. They got film of the barns yesterday, didn't they? Well, we'll go one better, we'll get film of the houses, of Grovehill!"

Plumb was already in the boat, bobbing gently at the edge of the flood. It was a small dinghy with barely enough room for the three of them. Kapenda had to keep the camera on his shoulder as Needham steered the boat using the outboard on its back. Why had he come? Kapenda wondered.

Because, he knew, this was where he belonged, recording. Whatever David had meant, whatever this flood and the ones that had come before it were, someone had to catch them, pin them to history. Here, in this drowned and drowning world, he had to be the eyes of everyone who came after him.

Needham piloted the boat away from the centre of Grovehill, down winding lanes among houses that were underwater to their eaves. They went slowly—here and there, cars floated past them, and the tops of signs and traffic lights emerged from the flood like the stems of water plants. Kapenda filmed a few short sequences as they drifted, with Plumb making up meaningless but portentous-sounding phrases. Mostly, the imagery did the talking. At one point, they docked against a road emerging from the water that rose up to a hill upon which a cluster of houses sat, relatively safe. Kapenda focused in, hoping for footage of their occupants, but no one moved. Had they been evacuated already?

Several minutes later, they found themselves drifting over a playing field, the ghostly lines of football pitches just visible through the still, surprisingly clear water. While Plumb and Needham argued a script point, Kapenda had an idea—he fixed the water-cover to the lens of the camera and then held it over the side of the boat and into the water. The surprising clarity would hopefully allow him to obtain good images of the submerged world, eerie and silent. Leaning back and getting as comfortable as he could, Kapenda held the camera so that it filmed what was below while he listened as the talent and the director argued.

"Hey!" a voice called, perhaps twenty minutes later. It was distorted, the voice, coming from a loudhailer. Kapenda looked up. Bouncing across the surface towards them was one of the rescue boats, a policeman in its bow waving at them.

"Oh fuck," said Needham.

"What?" asked Plumb.

"I didn't actually ask permission to come out here," said Needham.

"Shit!" said Plumb. "We'll be fucking arrested!"

"We won't. Isaac, have you got enough footage?"

"Yes."

"Then we play innocent. Plumb, charm them if you can."

"You have to go back!" the policeman called. Needham raised an arm at him and as the launch pulled alongside them, the talent began to do his stuff.


By the time they sorted out the police, with many *mea culpas* from Needham and much oleaginous smiling from Plumb, it was late. The water had continued to rise, its surface now only a few feet down the hill from the pub's door. Plumb made a joke about being able to use the boat to get back to it, but it was almost true and none of them laughed.

Inside, most of the crews were quiet and there was little of the talking and boasting and arguing that Kapenda would have expected. There were less of them as well; some had already left, retreating north to the dry or hunting for other stories. In Middlesbrough and Cumbria, rivers were bursting their banks and Kapenda watched footage on the news of flooded farmland and towns losing their footing to water. In one tracking shot, he was sure he saw something behind the local talent, a tiny figure hanging in a tree, spinning lazily on a chain as the water rose to meet it.

Back in his room, Kapenda started to view the film he had taken that day. The first shots were good, nice framings of Plumb in the prow of their dinghy with Grovehill, drowned, over his shoulder. He edited the shots together and then sent them to Needham, who would work on voiceovers with Plumb.

Then he came to the underwater footage.

They were good shots, the focus correct and imagery startling. The water was clear but full of debris—paper and clothing and unidentifiable things floated past the lens as it passed over cars still parked in driveways, gardens in which plants waved, houses around which fishes swam. At one point the corpse of a cow bounced languidly along the centre of a street, lifting and falling as the gentle current carried it on. The dead animal's eyes were gone, leaving torn holes where they used to be, and one of its legs ended in a ragged stump. It remained in the centre of the shot for several minutes, keeping pace with the boat above, and then it was gone as they shifted direction. Kapenda's last view of it was its hind legs, trailing behind as it jolted slowly out of sight.

They were in a garden.

At first, he thought it was a joke. Someone had set four figures around a picnic table, seated in plastic chairs, some kind of weird garden ornamentation, and then one of the figures moved and Kapenda realised that, whatever they were, they were real.

Three were dark, the fourth paler, all squat and fat and bald. One of them held a hunk of grey meat in its hand, was taking bites from it with a mouth that was wide and lipless. Their eyes, as far as Kapenda could tell, were entirely black, bulging from the side of their heads. All four were scaly, their backs ridged. As Kapenda watched, one of the figures reached out and caught something floating past and its hand was webbed, the fingers thick and ending in savage, curved claws.

As the figures moved off the side of the screen, the palest looked up. Thick folds of skin in its neck rippled, gill-slits opening and closing. Its mouth was wide, open to reveal gums that were bleeding, raw from tiny, newly-emerging triangular teeth. It nodded, as though in greeting, and raised a webbed hand to the camera.

One of its eyes was a dead, milky white.

Kapenda turned off the camera and went to stand by the window. He took the little figure from his pocket, turning it, feeling its depth-worn smoothness as the chain moved through his fingers.

He watched as figures swam through the ever-advancing water below him, never quite breaking the surface, forming intricate patterns of ripple and wave. Rice had called the thing from the hedge an idol. Was it simple peasant magic? No, this was nothing simple, nothing innocent. The idol looked nothing like the figures in the flood, was something harsh and alien. What had David said? That it was the thing that came after?

What was coming?

The rain fell, and the water rose to eat the Earth.

# RISING, NOT DREAMING

*by* ANGELA SLATTER

"**P**LAY," THEY SAID, and I did, plucking at a harp made of bone and sinew.

"Sing," they said, and I did, weaving words with water and making my listeners weep. I drew from their depths, from souls no one suspected, the dreams that might make them slumber. I surrounded them with lullabies to send gods to sleep, to keep them *below* and render them harmless to all that breathed *above*.

Too many had been the ages of pain and death, too long had the Great Old Ones reigned. *Enough*, said my masters, *enough*. Too long had the dreams of men been troubled with the ructions of the star lords. Too often did they rise at whim from their undersea city, their R'lyeth, to walk the earth and bring darkness with them.

They wondered, my masters, how to keep the beasts beneath the waves. They thought music perhaps would lull them, that in the magic of sound there might somehow be salvation. But who to play—who *could* play—such a tune? A competition was held to judge the best musician, the most enthralling player, the finest singer-seducer. They promised immortality, my masters, that no one would forget the winner's playing—for that *one* there would *always* be an audience.

They gambled, quite correctly, upon an artist's pride and arrogance.

And I won. Gods help me, I won. I was tasked to sit upon a high mountain by the sea, to play there and let the waves of my music swell and flow, to crash against the walking monstrosities, to enchant them, to lead them like stupid children into the deep, back to their sunken city.

The spells my masters had set around me meant I would not, could not drown, that the water would be to me as the air had been. That my life would not wear out, that I would forever keep them under my thrall, my hideous listeners, eternally asleep. I did not pay attention, though, not carefully enough. Only once I'd been trapped did I replay the words in my head and realise what I'd agreed to do.

*Eternally asleep* as long as I continued to play.

I think of the wife I had, sweet and tender.

I think of her belly swelling, rich and round.

I think of how I told her it would be all right. That I would return, my masters would reward me and we would never want for anything ever again.

I thought, my pride blinding me, I need only sing them to sleep. But when the last notes of my song died away, I watched the great things stir and begin to wake. And I could not bear the thought that they would walk once more, that my wife might be endangered, that our child might be cast upon an altar for the satiation of beings that had come from dark stars.

And so I played again.

And again.

And again.

Forever again.

But lately, I am tired. I have been too long beneath the storm-tossed waves. Centuries, aeons passing while I go on in an extended state of decay, neither living nor dying. I know not if I am a thing that remembers itself a man, or a man who thinks himself a thing.

My wife long ago was bones and dust, carried along the river of time.

My masters likewise have turned to ash.

What care I for a world I no longer know?

What care I for anyone else when all I wish for is the balm of sleep? The balm I have given to these *things* for so very many years?

My fingers slow upon the strings and my song stops.

"Awake!" I say, and they do.

I watch them turn and roll, sloughing off their slumber like giants, like continents rising out of the sea with the steam and stink of Earth-birth hazing their grey-green skin. The water around us boils as if a volcano had grown.

Limbs like monumental trees shift, torsos like cliff-faces heave, visages bereft of benign intent turn themselves upward so they might find the underside of the sea's surface and know which way to go. They uncoil their bodies, stretch towards the sky and the air, think and seek to break the hold the waves have upon them and to reach once more into the dreams of men.

"Rise," I say, and they do. Released from sleep they believe it a time when they might reclaim all that had been theirs.

Their largest, their lord, their priestly god ascends first, speeds upwards fastest to break free. The strokes of his great arms cause tidal waves; the bubbles from his newly filled lungs, his once-forgotten breath, move big as buildings. Dead Cthulhu rises from his house in R'lyeth, his dreaming done and his waking mind focused upon an end, a finish, a catastrophe. Around me, his kin, his followers hum a tune of destruction, one that sounds so like my song that I feel a'sudden the keen dagger of my betrayal.

I think of what I have done. Of the promise I have broken, the covenant I have dishonoured. I think of the disappointment on my wife's face should her shade discover my treachery. And I weep though my tears mix with the sea and no one but I would know of my remorse. I feel my own sleep creep upon me; a death and a forgetting, so close, so sweet.

And I fight it.

I put my hands once more to the sinuous strings of my harp and strum a tune to draw them back, these monstrous mountains, these Great Old Ones who could bring only ruin to whatever roams above, whatever takes wing in the skies. All would fall beneath the merciless behemoth feet.

My voice catches all of them. Most of them. All but one. The others still close enough to be caught upon the sweet hook of my song, the enchanting notes of my harp, settle once more. They go back to their dead, drowned houses, open the doors of heavy stone and retire.

But the greatest, the first amongst them, him I did not snare.

Cthulhu in rising, not dreaming, escapes the bonds of slumber.

Cthulhu rose and I know not where he resides or what destruction he causes. But I remember his terrible eyes as he swam upwards, as he gave me a single contemptuous glance and knew what I had done, both to him and his, and to my own kind. He judged me a hollow water-logged thing, a thing that remembers itself a man, barely worthy of a glance.

And it is that look, that longest, shortest of looks that keeps me playing, praying that my notes will linger forever.

# THE LONG LAST NIGHT

*by* BRIAN LUMLEY

I HAD MET or bumped into the old man on what was probably the very rim of the Bgg'ha Zone. And after careful, nervous greetings (he had a gun and I didn't) and while we shared one of my cigarettes, he asked me: "Do you know why it's called that?"

He meant the Bgg'ha Zone, of course, because he had already mentioned how we should be extremely careful just being there. Shrugging by way of a partial answer, I then offered: "Because it's near the centre of it?"

"Well," he replied, "I suppose that defines it now. I mean, that's likely how most people think of it; because after a number of years a name tends to stick, no matter its actual origin. And let's face it, there's not too many of us around these days—folks who were here at the time—people like myself, who are *still* here to remember what happened."

"When the Bgg'ha Zone got its name, you mean?" I prompted him. "There's a reason it's called that? So what happened?"

Getting his thoughts together, he nodded and said, "The real reason is that shortly after that damn Twisted Tower was raised when *They* first got here, after they came down from the stars and up from the sea, or wherever, the only time anyone went anywhere near the Twisted Tower voluntarily—'to find out what it was like' I've heard it said, if you can credit someone would do such a thing!—the damn fool came out again a ragged, shrieking lunatic who couldn't do anything but scream a few mad words over and over again. 'The Bgg'ha Zone!' he would scream, laughing and skittering around and pointing at that mile-high monstrosity where it stands dead-centre of things. And: 'The Twisted Tower!' he would yelp like a dog. But he was harmless except to himself, and making those noises and a mess was *all* he did until they bound and gagged him to keep him quiet. Then his heart gave out and he died with a wet gag in his mouth and the froth of madness drying on his chin..."

"You talk too much and too loudly," I told him. "And if I really should be as afraid of this place as you make out, then what in God's name are *you* doing here?" Before he could answer I shook another Marlboro from its pack, lit it, took a drag and handed it to him. I had no reason to antagonise the old boy.

"God's name?" he turned his head and stared at me where we sat amidst the rubble, on the remains of a toppled brick wall; stared at me with his bloodshot eyes—his sunken, crying eyes that he'd rubbed until they were a rough, raw red—before accepting and sucking on that second cigarette. And: "Oh, I have my reasons for being here," he said. "Nothing to do with God, though. Not the God we used to pray to, anyway; not unless I'm here as His agent, sort of working for Him without really being aware of it. In which case you might think He would have chosen a better way to set things up."

"You're not making a lot of sense," I told him, "and you're still much too noisy. Won't they hear you? Don't they sometimes patrol outside the Bgg'ha Zone? I've heard they do."

"Patrols?" He took a deep drag, handed my smoke back to me, and went on: "You mean the hunters? And do you know what they hunt? They hunt us! We're it! *Meat!*"

He took back the cigarette, and after another drag and a sly, sidelong glance at me from eyes still bloodshot but narrowed now: "Anyway, and like I said, I have a good reason for being here. A *damn* good reason!" And he balanced a small, battered, heavy-looking old suitcase on his thighs, using his free hand to hug it to his belly.

"But as for right now—" he continued after a brief moment's pause, while the look he was directing at me became rather more pointed, "—I reckon it's your turn to state why *you* are here. I never saw you before, and I don't think you're from the SSR... So?"

"The SSR?"

"The South Side Resistance, for what *they're* worth—*huh!*" he answered. But I wasn't really listening. Having taken back my smoke again, I was watching his veined right hand moving to rest on the gun at his bony hip, as again he asked, "So?"

"I stay alive by moving around," I told him. "I don't stay too long in any one place, and I live however I can. I go where there's food, when and where I can find it, and cigarettes, and on rare occasions a little booze."

"The old grocery stores? The shattered shops?"

"Yes, of course." I nodded. "Where else? The supermarkets that were—those that aren't already completely looted out. In the lighter hours, the few short hours of partial daylight when those things sleep, if they sleep, I dig among the ruins; but stuff is getting very hard to find. Day by day, week by week, it's harder all the time, which is why I move around. I ended up here just a couple of days ago. At least I think it was days; you never can tell in this perpetual dusk. I haven't seen the sun for quite some time now, and even then it was very low on the horizon, right at the beginning of this... this—"

"—This long last night?" he helped me out. "The long last night of the human race, and certainly of Henry Chattaway!"

Then he sobbed, and only just managed to catch it before it leaked out of him, but I heard it anyway. And: "My God, how and why did *this* bloody mess happen to us?" Craning his neck he looked up to where black wisps of cloud scudded across the sky, as if searching for an answer up there—from God, perhaps?

"So—er, Henry?—in fact you *are* a believer," I said, standing up from the broken wall and dropping my smoke before it could burn my fingers. "What do you reckon, then—that we're all career sinners and paying for it?" I stepped on the glowing cigarette end, crushing it out in the red dust of powdered bricks.

Controlling his breathing, his sobbing, the old man said, "Do you mean are we being punished? I don't know—probably. Come with me and I'll show you something." And getting creakingly to his feet, he went hobbling to a more open area close by, once the corner of a street—more properly a junction of twisted blackened ruins and rubble now—where the scattered, shattered debris lay more thinly on the riven ground, and only the vaguest outlines of any actual street remained. Of course, this was hardly unusual; for all I knew the entire city, and probably every city in the world, would look pretty much the same right now.

And after tugging on the sleeve of my parka while I stood glancing here and there, only too well aware that out in the open at this once-crossroads we would be plainly visible from all points of the compass, my companion finally let go of me to point toward the north-east. So that even before my eyes followed the bearing indicated by his trembling hand and finger, I knew what I would see. And:

"Look at that!" The words were no more than a husky whisper, almost a whimper. And more urgently this time: "*Look!* Just look at it, will you! Now tell me, isn't it obvious where at least one of those names comes from?"

He was talking about the Twisted Tower—a "mile-high monstrosity" he'd called it—where it stood, leaned or seemed to stagger, perhaps a mile and a half away, or two miles at most. But matching it in ugliness was its almost obscene height... a mile high? No, but not far short; with its teetering spire stabbing up through the disc of cloud that had been lured into circling it like an aerial whirlpool or the debris of doomed planets round the sucking well of a vast black hole. It was built of the wreckage, the ravaged soul of the crushed city; of gutted high-rises; of many miles of railway carriages twined around its fat base and rising in a spiral, like the thread of a gigantic screw, to a fifth of the tower's height; of bridges and wharves torn from their anchorages; of a great round clock face recognisable even at this distance and in this gloom as that of Big Ben; of a jutting tube of concrete and glass that had once stood in the heart of the city where it had been called Centrepoint... all of these things and many more, all parts now of this Twisted Tower. But it wasn't really twisted; it was just that its design and composition were so utterly alien that they didn't conform to the mundane Euclidean geometry that a human eye or brain would automatically accept as the shapes of a genuine structure, observing them as authentic without making the viewer feel sick and dizzy.

And though I had seen it often enough before, still I took a stumbling step backwards before tearing my eyes away from it. Those crazy angles which at first seemed convex before concertinaing down to concavities… only to bulge forth again like gigantic boils on the trunk of a monster. "That mile-high monstrosity", yes—but having seen it before, if not from this angle, I had known what effect it would have on me. Which was why I concentrated my gaze on what stood in front of it, seeming to teeter or waver there as in some kind of inanimate obeisance:

It leaned there close to that colossal, warped dunce's cap, out of true at an angle of maybe twenty degrees, only a few hundred yards or so as I reckoned it in the tower's foreground; and instead of the proud dome that it had been, it now looked like half of a blackened, broken egg, or the shattered skull of some unimaginable giant, lying there in the uneven dirt of that vast, desecrated graveyard: the dome of St. Paul's Cathedral.

"Horrible, *horrible!*" the old man said and shuddered uncontrollably—then gave a start when, from somewhere not very far behind us, there came a dismal baying or hooting call; forlorn sounding, true, but in the otherwise silence of the ruins terrifying to any vulnerable man or beast. And starting again—violently this time as more hooting sounded, but closer and from a different direction—the old man said, "The Hounds! That howling is how they've learned to triangulate. We've got to get away from here!"

"But how?" I said. "The howling is from the south, while to the north-east… we're on the verge of the Bgg'ha Zone!"

"Come with me—and hurry!" he replied. "If some of these wrecked buildings were still standing we'd already be dead—or worse! The Hounds know all the angles and move through them, so we must consider ourselves lucky."

"The angles?"

"Alien geometry," he answered, limping as fast as he could back down the rubble canyon where we had met, then turning into a lesser side-street canyon. And panting, he explained: "They say that where the Hounds come from—Tindalos or somewhere—something?—there are only angles. Their universe is made of angles that let them slip through space, and they can do the same here. But London has lost most of its angles now, and with the buildings reduced to rounded and jumbled heaps of debris, the Hounds have trouble finding their way around. And whether you believe in Him or not, still you may thank God for that!"

"I'll take your word for it," I told him, sure that he told the truth. "But where are we going?"

"Where I intended to be going anyway," he replied. "But you most probably won't want to—for which I don't blame you—and anyway we're already there."

"Where?" I said, looking left, right, everywhere and seeing nothing but heaped bricks and shadowy darkness.

"Here," he answered, and ducked into the gloom of a partly caved-in iron and brick archway. And assisted by a rusted metal handrail, we made our way down tiled steps littered with rubble fallen from the ceiling, now lying under a layer of dust that thinned out a little the deeper we went.

"Where are we?" I asked after a while. "I mean, what is this place?" My questions echoed in a gloom that deepened until I could barely see.

"Used to be an old entrance to the Tube system," he told me. "This one didn't have elevators, just steps, and they must have closed it down many decades ago. But when these alien things went rioting through the city, causing earthquakes and wrecking everything, all that destruction must have cracked it open."

"You seem to know all about it," I said, as I became aware that the light was improving; either that or my eyes were growing accustomed to the dark.

The old man nodded. "I saw a dusty old plaque down here one time, not long after I found this place. A sort of memorial, it said that the last time this part of the Underground system was used was during World War II—as a shelter. It was too deep down here for the bombs to do any damage. As for now: it's still safer than most other places, at least where the Hounds are concerned, because it's too round."

"Too round?"

"It's a hole in the earth deep underground," he replied impatiently. "It's a tunnel—a tube—as round as a wormhole!"

"Ah!" I said. "I see. It doesn't have any angles!"

"Not too many, no."

"But it does have light, and it's getting brighter."

We passed under another dusty archway and were suddenly on the level: a railway platform, of course. The light was neither daylight nor electric; dim and unstable, it came and went, fluctuating.

"This filth isn't light as you know it," the old man said. "It's Shoggoth tissue, bioluminescence, probably waste elements, or shit to you! It leaks down like liquid from the wet places. Unlike the hideous things that produce it, however, those god-awful Shoggoths, it's harmless. Just look at it up there on the ceiling."

I looked, if only to satisfy his urging, at a sort of glowing mist that swirled and pulsed as it spilled along the tiled, vaulted ceiling. Gathering and dispersing, it seemed tenuous as breath on a freezing cold day. And:

"Shoggoth tissue?" I repeated the old fellow. "Alien stuff, right? But how is it you know all this? And I still don't even know why you're here. One thing I do know—I think—is that you're going the wrong way."

Having climbed down from the platform, he was striking out along the rusting tracks on a heading that my sense of direction told me lay toward—

"The north-east!" he said, as if reading my mind. "And I warned you that you wouldn't be safe coming with me. In fact if I were you I'd follow the rails going the other way, south. And sooner or later, somewhere or other, I'm sure you'd find a way out."

"But *I'm* not at all sure!" I replied, jumping down from the platform and hurrying to catch up. "Also, it's like I said: you seem to understand just about everything that goes on here, and you're obviously a survivor. As for myself, well I'd like to survive too!"

That stopped him dead in his tracks. "A survivor, you say? I was, yes—but no more. My entire family is no more! So what the hell am *I* doing trying to stay alive, eh? I'm sick to death of trying, and there's only one reason I haven't done away with myself!" By which time the catch was back in his voice, that almost-sob.

But he controlled it, then swung his small, heavy, battered old suitcase from left to right, changing hands and groaning as he stretched and flexed the strained muscles in his left arm, before swinging the suitcase back again and visibly tightening his grip on its leather handle.

"You should let me carry it," I told him, as we began walking again. "At least let me spell you. What's in it anyway? All your worldly possessions? It certainly looks heavy enough."

"Don't you worry about this suitcase!" he at once snapped, turning a narrow-eyed look on me as his right hand dipped to hover over the butt of the weapon on his hip. "And I still think you should turn around and head south while you still can, if only... if only for my stupid peace of mind's sake!" As quickly as that he had softened up again, and explained: "Because I can't help feeling guilty it's my fault you're here, and the deeper we get into the Bgg'ha Zone, the more likely it is that you won't get out again!"

"Don't you go feeling guilty about me!" I told him evenly. "I'll take my chances like I always have. But you? What about you?"

He didn't answer, just turned away and carried on walking.

"Or maybe you're a volunteer—" I hazarded a guess, though by now it was becoming more than a guess, "—like that first one who went in and came out screaming? Is that it, Henry? Are you some kind of volunteer, too?" He made no answer, remaining silent as I followed on close behind him.

And feeling frustrated in my own right, I goaded him more yet: "I mean, do you even know what you're doing, Henry, going headlong into the Bgg'ha Zone like this?"

Once again he stopped and turned to me... almost turned *on* me! "Yes," he half-growled, half-sobbed, as he pushed his wrinkled old face close to mine. "I *do* know what I'm doing. And no, I'm not some kind of volunteer. What I'm doing—everything I do—it's for me, myself. You want to know how come I know so much about what happened around here, and to the planet in general? Well, that's because I *was* here, pretty much in the middle of it; the middle of one of the centres, anyway. And you've probably never heard of them, but there was this crazy bunch, the Esoteric Order or some such. They had their own religion, if you could call it that, their own church where they got together, and their 'bibles' were these cursed, mouldy old volumes of black magic and weird, alien spells and formulas that should have been destroyed back in the dark ages. Why, I even heard it said that…"

But there he paused, cocking his head on one side and listening for something.

"What is it?" I asked him. Because all I could hear was the slow but regular *drip, drip, drip* of seeping water.

Then with a start, a sudden jerk of his head, the old man looked down at the rusting rails, where three or four inches of smelly, stagnant water glinted blackly as it slopped between the track's walls. And: "*Shhh!*" he whispered. "*Listen,* damn you!"

I did as I was told, and then I heard it: those faintest of hollow echoes; a distant grunting, muttering, and *slap-slapping* of feet in the shallow puddles back where we had come from. But the grunted—or gutturally *spoken*—sounds were hardly reassuring, and definitely not to my companion's liking.

"Damn you! *Damn you!*" the old man whispered. "Didn't I warn you to go back? You might even have made it in time before *they* came on the scene. But you can't go back there now!"

Just the tone of his hoarse voice was almost enough to make my flesh creep. "So what is it?" I queried him again. "Who or what are 'they' this time?"

"We have to get on," he replied, ignoring my question. "Have to move faster—but as quietly as we can. Their hearing isn't much to speak of, not when they're up out of their element, the water—but if they *were* to hear us…"

"They're not men?"

"Call them what you will," he told me, his voice all shuddery. "Men of a sort, I suppose—or frogs, or fish! Who can say what they are exactly? They came in from the sea, up the Thames and into the lakes and wherever there was deep water. It was as if they'd been called… no, I'm sure they *were* called, by those crazies of the Esoteric Order! But true men? Not at all, not in the least! Their fathers must have mated with women, definitely—or vice versa, maybe?—but no, they're not men…"

Which prompted me to ask: "How can you know that for sure?"

"Because I've *seen* some of them. Just the once, but it was enough. And you hear that slap-slapping? Can't you just picture the feet that slap down on the water like that? Good for swimming, but of small use for walking."

"So why are we in such a hurry?"

And once again, impatiently or yet more impatiently, he said, "Because they can call up others of their kind. A sort of telepathy maybe? Hell, I don't know!"

We moved faster, and I could almost hear him wincing each time our feet kicked up water that splashed a little too loudly. Then in a while we came across a narrow ledge to one side, where the wall had been cut back some two feet to make a maintenance walkway four feet higher than the bed of the tracks.

"Get up there," the old man told me. "It's dry and we'll be able to go faster without all the noise."

I did as he advised and reached down to help him up. He wasn't much more than a bundle of bones and couldn't be very strong, but he didn't for a second offer that small suitcase to me or release his grip on it. And with him in front we moved ahead again; until eventually, this time without my urging, he continued telling me his story from where he'd left off. His story, along with that of the alien invasion or take-over—or *walk-over*—which seemed to come a little easier to him now. So maybe he'd needed to get it off his chest.

"It was those Esoteric Order freaks. At least, that was how everyone thought of them: as folks with too few screws, and what few they had with crossed threads! But no, they weren't crazy—except maybe in what they were trying to do. And actually, that even got into the newspapers: how the Esoteric Order was trying to call up powerful creatures—god-things, they called them—from parallel dimensions and the beginning of time; beings that had come here once before, even before the evolution of true or modern man, only to be trapped and imprisoned by yet more mysterious beings and banished back to their original universes, or to forgotten, forbidden places here on Earth and under the sea…

"Well, that was a laugh, wasn't it? As daft as all those UFO stories from more than fifty years ago, and those tales of prehistoric monsters in a Scottish loch, and hairy ape men on Himalayan mountains; oh, and lots of other myths and legends of that sort. But daft? Oh, really? And if those oh-so-bloody-clever newspaper reporters, the ones who infiltrated the church and saw them at their worship and listened to their sermons—along with the other religious groups that scoffed at their 'idiotic beliefs'—if they had been right, then all well and good. But they weren't!

"And when should it happen—when *did* it happen?—but at Hallowmas: the feast of All Hallows, All Saints!

"And oh, what an awful feast that was—*Them* feasting on us, I mean—when those monstrous beings answered the call and came forth from strange dimensions, bringing their thralls, servitors and adherents with them. Up from the oceans, down from the weird skies of parallel universes, erupting from the earth and bringing all of the planet's supposedly dead volcanoes back to life, these minions of madness came; and what of humanity then, eh? What but food for their tables, fodder for their stables."

That last wasn't a question but a simple fact, and the old man was sobbing again, openly now, as he turned and grasped my arm. "My wife…" He almost choked on the word. "That poor, poor woman… she was taken at first pass! Taken, as the city reeled and the buildings crumbled, as the earth broke open and darkness ruled…!

"Ah, but according to rumour the very first to go was that blasphemous, evil old church! For the so-called 'priests' of the Esoteric Order had been fatally mistaken in calling up that which they couldn't put down again: a mighty octopus god-thing who rose in his house somewhere in the Pacific, while others of his spawn surfaced in their manses from various far-flung deeps. Not the least of these emerged in the Antarctic—along with an entire plateau! That was a *massive* upheaval, causing earthquakes and tsunamis around the world! Another rose up from the Mariana Trench, and one far closer to home from a lesser-known abyss somewhere in the mid-Atlantic. He was the one—damn him to Hell!—who built his Twisted Tower house here in the Zone. In fact the Bgg'ha Zone is named after him, for he was—he *is*—Bgg'ha!

"And there's a chant, a song, a liturgy of sorts that human worshippers—oh yes, there are such people!—sing of a night as they wander aimlessly through the rubble streets. And having heard it so often, far *too* often, dinning repeatedly in my ears while I lay as if in a coma, hardly daring to breathe until they had moved on, I learned those alien words and could even repeat them. What's more, when the SSR trapped and caught one of these madmen, these sycophants, to learn whatever they could from him, he offered them a translation. And those chanted words which I had learned, they were these:

"'*Ph'nglui gwlihu'nath, Bgg'ha Im'ykh I'ihu'nagl fhtagn.*' A single mad sentence which translates into this:

"'*From his house at Im'ykh, Bgg'ha at last is risen!*'

"And do you know, those words still ring in my ears, blocking almost everything else out? If I don't concentrate on what I'm doing, on what I'm saying, it all slips away and all I can hear is that damned chanting: *Bgg'ha at last is risen!* Ah, but since he was able to rise, maybe he can be sent back down again! And perhaps I even have... even have the means with which to do it..."

It was far more than he had ever told me before; but there he fell silent again, possibly wondering if he had said too much...

Then, as we rested for a few minutes, and as I looked down from the maintenance ledge, I saw how the dirty water glinting over the rails was much deeper here, perhaps as much as ten or twelve inches. Seeing where I was looking, my companion told me:

"Yes, there's very deep water up ahead, and likewise on the surface *over*-head."

"Ahead of us?" I repeated him, for want of something to say. "But... on the surface?"

"Mainly on the surface," he nodded. "That's where it's leaking from. We're heading for Knightsbridge, as was—which isn't far from the Serpentine—also as was, but much enlarged and far deeper now. That too was the work of Bgg'ha; he did it for some of his servitors, the kind we heard wading through that shallow water back along the tracks. There's plenty more of them in the Serpentine, which is part of a great lake now that has drowned St. James's Park and everything in between all the way to the burst banks of the Thames. We can stay down here for another mile or thereabouts, but then we may have to surface… either that or swim, and I really don't fancy that!"

"You've done this before," I said as we set off again, because it was obvious that he had, and fairly often and recently. That explained how he knew these routes so well.

He nodded and replied, "Five times, yes. But this will be the last time. For you too, your first and last."

"Or maybe not," I answered. "I mean, you never can tell how things will work out."

"You young fool!" he said, but not unkindly, even somewhat sadly. "You'll be right there in the heart of the Bgg'ha Zone, in the roots of the Twisted Tower, that loathsome creature's so-called 'house!' And I can tell you exactly how things are going to work out for you: you *won't* be coming out again!"

"But *you* did it," I answered him. "And all of five times—if you're not lying or simply crazy!"

He shook his head. "I'm not lying, and I'm not simply crazy. You're the one who's crazy! Listen, do you have any idea who I am or why I'm really here?"

I shrugged. "You're just an old man on a mad mission. That much is obvious. I may even know what your mission is, and why. It's revenge, because they took your wife, your family. But one small suitcase—even one that's full of high explosives—just isn't going to do it. Nothing short of a nuclear weapon is ever going to do it."

The look he turned on me then was sour, downcast, disappointed. And: "Have I been *that* obvious?" he said, pausing where the ledge stepped up onto an actual platform. "I suppose I must have been. But even so you're only half-right, and that makes you half-wrong."

The Shoggoth light was suddenly poorer, where the mist writhing on the tiled, vaulted expanse of the ceiling was that much thinner.

Our eyes, however, had grown accustomed to the eerie gloom and the fluctuating quality of the bioluminescence, and we were easily able to read the legend on the tunnel's opposite wall:

KNIGHTSBRIDGE

"My God!" my guide muttered then. "But I remember how this place looked in its heyday: so clean and bright with its shining tiles, its endless stairs and great elevators, its theatre and lingerie posters. But look at it now, with its evidence of earth tremors and fires; its blackened, greasy walls; its collapsed or caved-in archways and all the other damage that it's suffered. And... and... *Lord, what a mess!*"

A mess? Something of an understatement, that. The ceiling was scarred by a series of broad jagged cracks where dozens of tiles had come loose and fallen; some of the access/exit openings in the wall on our side of the tracks had buckled inwards, causing the ceiling to sag ominously where mortared debris and large blocks of concrete had crashed down; and from a source somewhere high above, a considerable waterfall was surging out of an arched exit and spilling into the central channel, drowning the tracks under a foaming torrent.

As we clambered over the rubble the old man said, "I think that I—or rather that we—are probably in trouble." And I asked myself: another understatement? How phlegmatic! And meanwhile he had continued: "Like everywhere else, this place is coming apart. It's got so much... so much worse, since the last time I passed through."

Which was when he began to ramble and sob again, only just managing to make sense:

"There's been so many earthquakes recently... if the rest of the Underground system is in the same terrible condition as this place... but then again, maybe it's not that bad... and Hyde Park Corner isn't so far away... not very far at all... and anyway, it was never my intention to surface here... there's water up there... too much water... but there's still a half-decent chance that we'll make it to Piccadilly Circus down here in the Underground... I've just *got* to make it to Piccadilly Circus... right there, under the Twisted Tower!"

Feeling I had to stop him before he broke down completely and did himself some serious harm, I grabbed his arm to slow him down where he was staggering about in the debris. And I shouted over the tumult of the water: "*Hey! Old man!* Slow down and try to stop babbling! You'll wear yourself out both physically and mentally like that!"

As we cleared the heaped rubble it seemed he heard me and knew I was right. Shaking as if in a fever, which he might well have been, he came to a halt and said: "So close, so very close... but God! I can't fail now. *Lord, don't let me fail now!*"

"You said something about not intending to surface here," I reminded him, holding him steady. "About maybe having to swim?"

At which he sat down on a block of concrete fallen from the ceiling before answering me. And as quickly as that he was more or less coherent again. "I wouldn't even try to surface here," he said, shrugging his thin shoulders. "No reason to do so. And anyway there's far too much water up there—and too many of those monsters that live in it! But we must hope that the rest of the system, between here and Piccadilly Circus, is in better condition."

"Okay," I said, grateful for the break as I sat down beside him. "Piccadilly Circus is our destination. So how do we manage it? And will it mean we have to get down in the water?"

Swaying a little as he got to his feet, he looked over the rim of the platform before answering me. "Are you worried about swimming? Well don't be. The water here isn't nearly as deep as I thought it might be... I think it must find its way into the depths of the shattered earth, maybe into a subterranean river. So even though we won't have to swim, still it appears we'll be doing a lot more wading; knee-deep at least, and maybe for quite a while. So now for the last time—even though it's already far too late—I feel I've really got to warn you: if you want to live, to stand even a remote chance, you have to turn back now. Do you understand?"

"I think so, yes," I told him. "But you know, Henry, we've been lucky so far, both of us, and maybe it's not over yet."

"I can't convince you then?"

"To go back? No." I shook my head. "I don't think I want to do that. And the truth is we all have to die sometime, whether it's at Piccadilly Circus under the Twisted Tower or back there where those—those *beings*—were splashing about in the water. I mean, what's the difference where, why, or how we do it, eh? It's got to happen eventually."

"As for me," he said, letting himself down slowly over the rim of the platform into water that rose halfway up his thighs, "it *is* a matter of where I do it, where I can be most effective. My revenge, you said, and at least you were right about that. But you: you're young, strong, apparently well-fed, which is a rare thing in itself! You probably came in from the woods, the countryside—a place where there are still birds and other wild things you could catch and eat—or so I imagine. So for you to accompany me where I'm going..." He shook his head. "It just seems a great waste to me."

There was nothing in what he'd said that I could or needed to answer; so as I let myself down into the water beside him, I simply said, "So then, are you ready to move on?" And since his only reply was to lean his bony body into the effort—for the flow of the water was against us and strong—I added, "I take it that you are! But you know, Henry, pushing against the water like this will soon drain you. So may I suggest—only a suggestion, mind you—that you let me carry the case? If you want to do the job you've set yourself, well okay, that's fine. But since I'm here why not let me help you?"

He turned to me, turned a half-thankful, half-anxious look on me, and finally reached out with his trembling arms and gave that small heavy suitcase into my care. "But don't you drop it in the water!" he told me. "In fact don't drop it at all—neither that nor bang it around—or damage it in any other way! Do you hear?"

"Of course I do, Henry," I answered. "And I think I understand. I've seen how you take care of it, and it's obvious how crucial it must be to your mission, however that turns out. Perhaps as we move along you'd care to tell me about it... but it's also fine if you don't want to. First, though, if you don't mind, could you get my cigarettes and lighter out of the top pocket of my parka?" For even though we were well above the water level, still I was hugging the case to my chest with both hands. And I explained: "The water's very cold and a drag or two may help to warm us up—our lungs, anyway. So light one up for yourself and one for me." And when he had managed that:

"Thanks, Henry," I told him out of the corner of my mouth, before dragging deeply on the scented smoke.

He smoked, too, but remained silent on the subject of the suitcase... in particular its "secret" contents, as he seemed to consider them.

As already more than hinted, I thought I might know about that anyway but would have preferred to hear it from him. Well, perhaps there was some other way I could talk him into telling me about it. So after we had waded for another ten or twelve minutes and finished our cigarettes:

"Henry, you asked me a while ago if I had any idea who you might be," I reminded him. "Well no, I don't. But it might pass some time and keep our minds active—stop them from freezing up—if you'd care to tell me."

"*Huh!*" he answered. "It's like you want to know everything about me, and I don't even know your name!"

"It's Julian," I told him. "Julian Chalmers. I was a teacher and taught the Humanities, some Politics and—of all things—Ethics, at a university in the Midlands."

"Of all... all things?" Shivering head to toe, he somehow got the question out. "How do... do you mean, 'of all things'?"

"Well, they're pretty different subjects, aren't they? Sort of jumbled and contradictory? I mean, is there any such thing as the ethics of politics? Or its 'humanity', for that matter!"

He considered it a while, then said, "Good question. And I might have known the answer once upon a time. But then I would have been talking about—God, it's c-*cold*!—about human politicians. But since the actions and mores of humanity no longer apply—"

At which he had paused, as if thinking it through. And so:

"Go on," I quickly prompted him, because I was interested. And anyway I wanted to keep him talking.

"Well, the invaders," he obliged me, "and I mean all of them—from their leaders, the huge, tentacle-faced creatures in their crazily-angled manses, to the servitors they brought with them or called up after they got settled here—all the nightmarish flying things, and those shapeless, flapping-rag horrors called Hounds, and not least those scaly half-frog, half-fish minions from their deep-sea cities—

not one of these species seems to have ever evolved politics, while the very idea of ethics might seem as alien to them as they themselves seem to us! But on the other hand, if you're talking *human* politics, human ethics—"

"I don't think I was," I said, quickly dropping the subject as another maintenance ledge came into view on the left.

We couldn't have been happier, the pair of us, to get out of the water and onto that ledge. And more than mildly surprised, we were relieved to discover that a welcoming draft of air from somewhere up ahead was strangely warm!

"Most places underground are like this," the old man tried to explain it. "When you get down to a certain depth the temperature is more or less constant. It's why the Neanderthals lived in caves. It was the same the last time I was here, which I had forgotten about, but this warm air has served to remind me that we've reached—"

## HYDE PARK CORNER

He had let the legend on the brightly tiled wall across the tracks finish the job for him, precisely and silently.

"So, what do you think?" I asked him, as we moved from the ledge onto the Underground station's platform. "How are we doing, Henry?"

"Not good enough," he answered. "We should be doing a whole lot better! My fault, I suppose, because I'm not as strong as I used to be. I'm just too frail, too weak, that's all, and I'm not afraid to admit it. It's what happens when a man gets old. But that's okay, and I can afford to push myself one last time. Because this *will be* the last time; my last effort in the long last night."

"Hey, you've done okay up to now!" I told him. "And if this warm draft keeps up it will soon dry out our trousers. That's not much, I suppose, but it may help keep our spirits up."

He glanced at me, if only for a moment conjuring up a thin, sarcastic ghost of a smile, and with an almost pitying shake of his head said: "Well okay, good, fine!—whatever you say, er, Julian?—but right now it's my turn to spell you. So if you'll just give that case back to me…"

Not for a moment wanting to upset him, I handed it over and said,

"Okay, if you're sure you can handle it—?"

"I'm sure," he replied, as we looked around the platform. And when I looked down at the tracks I could see them glinting dully under no more than twelve or fifteen inches of water. But both of the arched exits were blocked with rubble fallen from above, making my next comment completely redundant:

"It appears there's no way up, not from here."

Henry nodded. "Not even if we wanted or needed one, which we don't. Next up is Green Park, and following that—assuming we get that far—Piccadilly Circus. But Green Park is right on the edge of the water, and—"

"And that's Deep Ones territory, right?" I cut in.

He nodded, frowned and narrowed his eyes, and said, "Well yes, I do believe I've heard them called that before…"

"Of course you have," I replied. "That's what *you* called them, back there where they were splashing about in the water behind us."

Still frowning, he shook his head and slowly said, "It's a funny thing, but I don't remember that." And then with a shrug of his narrow shoulders: "Well, so what? I don't remember much of anything any more, only what needs to be done…"

And with one last look around he went on: "We have to get back down into the water. Just when we were drying out, eh? Be glad Green Park's not far from here, only one stop. But it's a hell of a junction, or used to be. It seems completely unreal, even surreal now—like some kind of weird dream—but there were three Tube lines criss-crossing Green Park in the old days. I still remember that much at least…" He gave himself a shake, and continued: "Anyway, for all that it's close to the lake, it was bone-dry the last time I was there. Let's hope nothing has changed. And after Green Park, at about the same distance again, then it's Piccadilly Circus—the end of the line, as it were. The end for us, anyway."

His comment was loaded—the last few words, definitely—but I ignored it and said, "And is that where we'll surface?"

Again Henry's nod. "It'll make your skin crawl!" he said. And matching his words, he shuddered violently; which I didn't in any way consider a consequence of his damp, clinging trousers. Then, when he'd controlled his shaking, he continued: "But yes, we'll surface there, right up Bgg'ha's jacksy, or as close as anyone would ever want to get to it!"

I waited until we were moving steadily forward again, in water that came up just inches short of our knees, and then said, "Henry, you say our skins will be made to crawl. But is there any special reason for that—or shouldn't I ask?"

"You shouldn't ask." He shook his head.

"But I'm asking anyway." Which was just natural curiosity on my part, I suppose. And whatever, I wanted the old man's take on it; because we all see things, experience things, differently.

"As you will," he said with a shrug, and went on: "Piccadilly Circus as was is lying crushed at the roots of Bgg'ha's house. That great junction, once standing so close to the heart of a city, is now in the dark basement of the Twisted Tower, that vast heap of wreckage where he or it lords it over his minions—*and over his human captives*, his 'cattle.'"

"His cattle..." I mused, because that thought or simile was still reasonably new to me. At least I had never heard it expressed that way before coming across Henry.

"As I may have told you before," the old man said, "that's all they are: food for Bgg'ha's table, fodder for his stable."

We were moving faster now, under an arched ceiling that was aglow, seemingly alive with luminous, swirling Shoggoth exhaust. And the closer we drew to Henry's goal or target, the more voluble he was becoming.

"Do you know why I'm here?" he suddenly burst out. "I think you do—or rather, *you* think you do!"

Nodding, I said: "But haven't we already decided that? It's revenge, isn't it? For your wife?"

"For my whole family!" he corrected me. And the catch, that half-sob, was back in his voice. "My poor wife, yes, of course—*but also for my girls, my daughters*! And my eldest, Janet—my God, how brave! I would never have suspected it of her, but she was braver than me. Inspiring, is how I've come to think of it: that my Janet was able to escape like that, and somehow managed to crawl back home again.

But she did, she came home to me, and then… then she died! Not yet twenty years old, and gone like that.

"She died of horror and loathing—because of what had been done to her—but never of shame, for she had fought it all the way. And it's mainly because… because of what Janet *told* me had happened to her that I've kept coming here. It's why I'm here now: for Janet, yes, but also for her younger sister, Dawn, and for their mother; and for all the other females who've been taken—*and who are still there*, maybe alive even now in that Twisted Tower!"

"Still alive?" I repeated him. "You mean, maybe they're not just fodder after all?" At which I could have bitten through my tongue as it dawned on me that it was probably very cruel of me to keep questioning him like this. But too late for that now.

Sobbing openly and making no attempt to hide it, Henry replied: "Janet was taken two months ago. They took her in broad daylight, or what we used to call daylight, on her way back home from an SSR meeting. She'd been a member since not long after her mother was taken. A boyfriend of hers from the old days saw it happen. It was those freakish flapping-rag things, those so-called Hounds. I was always telling her to stick to the shadows whenever she ventured out, but on this occasion I'd forgotten to warn her against angles. They took her on a street corner; just ninety degrees of curb that cost Janet her freedom and, as I believed at the time, her life too. But no, Janet's captors were working for that thing in the Twisted Tower, something I hadn't known until she escaped and got home just a month ago.

"That was when I found out about what goes on in that hellish place. Since when I've risked my own life five times making this trip in and out, always hoping I might see Janet's mother, or her younger sister Dawn, and that I might be able to rescue them somehow… but at the same time making certain deliveries and planning for the future… in fact planning for right now, if you really want to know. But my wife… and Dawn… that poor kid, just seventeen years old: they're somewhere in that nightmarish tower, I feel certain. But alive and suffering still, or dead and… and *eaten*! Who knows?" There he paused and made an attempt to bring himself back under control.

Feeling the need to have the old man continue, however—no

matter how painful that had to be for him—I said, "Henry, before Janet escaped... did she ever see her mother, or her younger sister Dawn, there in the Twisted Tower?"

He shook his head. "Not once. Other girls, plenty of them, but never her Ma. And where Dawn is concerned, that's completely understandable. She was taken just three days after Janet found her way home in time to... in time to die! In other words she was out of that place before Dawn was taken in." He paused for a moment or two before continuing.

"Now, I know it must sound like I've been pretty careless of my girls, but that's not so. And maybe it's best if Dawn really is dead, because of what Janet... because of what she told me was *happening* to those... those other female captives."

And as he broke down more yet, as gently as I could I asked him, "Well then, Henry, what did Janet tell you? What *was* happening in there, to the other female captives?"

Sobbing and stumbling along through the water—sobbing so loudly I thought he might sob his heart out—still he managed to reply: "Oh, that's something I see in my blackest nightmares, Julian, and I see it every night! But first let me tell you how Dawn was taken...

"I had left her at home while I went looking for a place to bury Janet. No big problem there... a hole in the ground, with plenty of bricks and rubble to fill it in. Necessary, yes, because there are packs of real hounds running wild through all the destruction. But then I'd gone rummaging for food in the ruins of a corner store I'd found: canned fruit and meats and such. But when I got back home with my haul—'home', *hah!*—a concrete cellar in a one-time museum, a wing of the old Victoria & Albert, I think it was... hard to tell in all that devastation. But anyway, when I got back Dawn was gone and the place had been completely wrecked. What few goods we'd had— sticks of furniture and such—were broken up, strewn everywhere, and the place was damp and stank of... oh, I don't know, rotting fish, weeds, and stagnant water. The evil stench of the Deep Ones, yes; and they, too, are the servants of Bgg'ha, as I believe they are of all the octopus-heads..."

And there Henry fell silent again, leaving only the echoes of his tortured voice, and the sloshing of our legs through the water. But I still couldn't let it rest; there were things he had hinted at that I would like explanations for; I wondered just how much he'd learned, how much he knew. And so:

"You said your wife was taken that first night," I reminded him, as if he needed it. "She was taken as all hell stampeded through the city and there was no defence against the turmoil, the horror. But that was a long time ago, Henry. And weren't these monsters slaughtering everyone and destroying everything in their path at that time? How could you possibly think your wife might still be alive in Bgg'ha's Twisted Tower? Especially after what Janet told you about it?"

At which the old man seemed to freeze in his tracks, jerked to a standstill, and in the next moment turned on me, snarling: "How do *you* know what Janet did or didn't tell me, eh? And how much do *you* know about that damned Twisted Tower? Tell me that, Julian Chalmers!"

Oh, I was glad in that moment that I had returned his suitcase to Henry, and that he was carrying it with both hands. He still had that gun on his hip, and if he could have reached for it without jeopardising the safety of the case and its contents I felt sure he would have done so. And who knows what he might have done then? But he couldn't and didn't, and I said:

"Henry, I didn't mean to hurt you, but those creatures in the Tower... they *eat* people, don't they? Haven't you already said as much? And it's been a very long time for your wife. Now, don't be offended, but in the light of your daughters' ages, not to mention your own obvious years, it has to be my understanding that your wife isn't a mere girl; so what good would she be, *alive*, to such as Bgg'ha and his minions? I mean, him and his monsters? Beasts in their stables? What use to them except as... well, except as—"

But that was as far as he would let me go, and I could tell by the look on his face that it wouldn't in any case be necessary to finish my question.

"*God damn you, Julian!*" he said, turning away. "It was hope—desperate, impossible hope!—that's all. And as for... as for poor

Dawn…" But he couldn't say on and so went staggering away through the sluggish, blackly glinting water, in the eerie light of the swirling Shoggoth tissue.

I gave him a few moments before catching up, then said: "I'm sorry, Henry, but you leave me confused. I know you're planning some kind of revenge—in whatever form that may take—but if you were really hoping that Dawn and your wife are still alive, might not the violence of any such revenge hurt them too, not to mention you yourself?"

Yet again he came to a halt and turned to me. "Of course it would, and will!" he said. "But far better that—a quick, clean death to them, indeed to all of us—than what they could be suffering, to what Dawn if not her mother *must be suffering*, even as we speak!" And before I could say anything more: "Now listen…

"Did you know they take young boys, too? Young men, I mean, of your age or thereabouts? And since you appear to be good at figuring things out, can you guess what *they* are used for?"

"No, not really," I replied, unwilling to disturb him further. "But in any case, maybe we should quieten it down now. I think I heard voices—some kind of sounds, anyway—from somewhere up ahead."

The old man's eyes focused as he looked all about, searching for recognisable signs on the old blackened walls. And: "Yes," he whispered, as quietly as I had suggested. "Your ears are obviously better than mine. We're only five minutes or so away from Green Park, which is one of the worst places for—"

"—Deep Ones?" I finished it for him, and he nodded. And from then on we stayed silent, creeping like mice, glad that the water level had fallen away to no more than an inch or two. And for the second time Henry entrusted his case to me…

Ahead of us, the Shoggoth light brightened up a little until it was about half as good as dim electric light used to be. Even so it suited us just fine, because Henry was right and four or five minutes later Green Park's platform loomed up out of the shadows and gloomy distance. By then, however, those barking, gutturally grunting "voices" I had heard had faded into distant echoes before ceasing almost entirely; but still there were the sounds of some sort of laborious work going on in that subterranean burrow's upper reaches. So we didn't climb up onto the platform but stayed on the tracks in the shadow of the bull-nosed wall, where we crouched down and kept the lowest possible profile as we traversed the mercifully short length of the station. And halfway across that comparatively open space, suddenly Henry paused to tug nervously on the sleeve of my parka, indicating that I should look at the platform's flagged floor.

Still keeping low but raising my head just enough to scan the length of the platform end to end, I saw what he had seen: the large, damp imprints of webbed feet where the dusty paving flags had been criss-crossed. Then, too, I detected the stench of weedy deeps and the less-than-human creatures risen up from them.

*Deep Ones!* Henry framed the words with his lips, both silently and needlessly. And: *Look!* He pointed.

From the mouths of the entry/exit archways, rubble had been cleared away and heaped aside. The stairs and one wrecked elevator, visible beyond the archways, were also clear of debris. But from one of the exits a thin stream of water was flowing forth, snaking across the platform and over the lip of the bull-noses, before finding its way down into the well and from there, presumably, into unseen channels that were deeper yet. But even in the moments we spent watching it, so the flow rapidly increased to a torrent, and at the same time a massed, triumphant shout—a hooting, snorting uproar, even at the distance—sounded from on high. But of course we already knew that the engineering going on up there wasn't the work of human beings.

And now Henry whispered, "Come on, let's get out of here!"

Minutes later and a hundred yards or more into the comparative darkness of the tunnel, finally the old man spoke up again. "We were very lucky back there, fortunate indeed!"

"Oh?" I replied. "Fortunate?"

He looked at me incredulously. "Why, the fact that they had recently gone up out of the station! And that they hadn't begun to flood the place earlier, like yesterday maybe. For if they'd done that we'd be swimming by now! Surely you know or can guess what they were doing—what they're doing even now?"

Trudging along beside him, sloshing through inches of cold, black water, I shrugged. "Well, like you said: they're flooding the place."

"Yes, but why?"

"Because… because they like the water?"

Henry offered up a derisive snort and repeated me sarcastically: "'Because they like the water'? Is that all? Man, can't you see? Don't you understand? They're terraforming—no, *aqua*-forming—the Underground system, similar to what we had planned doing to Mars before those freaks in the Esoteric Order messed everything up! They're making the Tube system suitable, comfortable, compatible— to themselves, to their loathsome way of life! Now do you see it? This maze, these endless miles of tunnels, stations and levels; these massive great rabbit-holes—*and all of them filled with water*, if not now then soon! Paradise to the Deep Ones! Subterranean temples to their master, octopus-headed Bgg'ha, with myriad submarine connections to his Twisted Tower like the strands of a gigantic sunken cobweb!"

Henry's thought or vision was fantastic and even awe-inspiring: the entire Underground system filled with water; a vast submarine labyrinth where the Deep Ones could spawn and worship their bloated black deity for as long as the Earth continued to roll in its orbit.

Then for several long minutes we remained silent, Henry and I, as we slopped along under the swirling and gradually brightening glow of Shoggoth filth.

But eventually he said, "Well then, Julian—have you figured it out yet?"

"Eh? Figured what out?"

"Why they take young men, of course."

"You mean, if not to eat them?"

"Yes," he nodded. "If not to eat them. What other use could young men be put to, eh?"

Deciding to let him tell me, I shook my head. "I've no idea, Henry." And beginning to sob again, however quietly, he said:

"It's because young men are sexually potent, Julian. Just like horses in the stud farms as once were before *They* came. That's what my girl Janet told me, but it's also why she escaped and came home worn out, dying, *and pregnant!* The baby—not much more than a foetus, I imagine or hope, poor innocent creature—he or she died with Janet. But better that than the other. And now… and now…"

I nodded and said, "I understand—I think. And now there's Dawn. Why don't you tell me about her, if you can?"

"No," he shook his head, "you *don't* understand! You haven't thought it through. But I didn't have to, because I had it from Janet, and I'll tell you anyway; or perhaps by now you can tell me? Why would a monstrous thing like Bgg'ha—and *his* monsters in that Twisted Tower of a house—why would they want children, babies, from their captives?"

We both slowly came to a halt and stood facing each other; but even knowing what he was getting at I made no reply. The old man saw that I knew and nodded an affirmative. "Oh, yes, Julian. In the long-ago era of sailing ships, men from the west would sometimes come across cannibal tribes in the South Sea Islands, and these savage people had a term for the enemies they roasted for food. They called them—or the flesh they ate off them—'long pig', because that's how we taste, apparently. Now I don't know if they ever tried 'short pig', if you follow my meaning, but what could be more tender or pure than—"

"—Yes, I do understand, Henry," I cut him short. "There's no need to torture yourself any further."

"But what horrified me most," he continued, as if he hadn't heard me at all, "wasn't the thought of those monsters at *their* repast, no, but wondering what the young men who fathered those babies—what they *themselves*, or for that matter the mothers—could be living on in the Twisted Tower! For what other source of... of *food* could there possibly be in that dreadful place? And what kind of inhuman, bestial people could bring themselves to do something as terrible as that in the first place? Surely they would rather die first... you'd think so, anyway."

"Yes, you certainly would," I replied, even though he hadn't meant it as a question.

Henry could barely stifle his soul-wrenching sobbing as he turned away from me, staggering and yet in some superhuman way seeming more determined than ever, windmilling his arms and only just managing to maintain his balance as he went splashing along the drowned, rusty tracks.

I caught up with the old man, caught his arm to steady him before he could trip and hurt himself, and said, "But there are all kinds of men, Henry. Most men couldn't do that, I think, but as for those who can, what choice do they have? They can reap what they've sown, as it were—if in this case you'll excuse such a metaphor—and eat or starve in the absence of any other choices, and that's all. But you know, some men, women too, are *very* adaptable; and in desperate times and situations the survival instinct in people such as these will quickly surface, and they'll soon become inured, accustomed to… to whatever. Yes, that kind of person can get used to almost anything."

But yet again he may not have heard a word I said. And instead of scolding me for my "logical" approach to what he had told me—however sickening and disgusting that approach must surely have seemed to him, if indeed he had heard anything of it at all—he once again began to babble about his youngest daughter, Dawn:

"You've never seen a girl so lovely, Julian. Only thirteen, or was it fourteen years old?—I don't any longer remember—when the world went to hell—growing up almost entirely underground, in that dark, damp basement we called home. What chance for poor Dawn, eh? Never had a boyfriend, never knew a man; her dark-eyed, raven-haired beauty wasted in the gloom of a cellar. And all she ever saw of the outside world on those occasions, those very rare occasions when, at her pleading, I would take her into the light of day, was the sullen sky and the shattered city… but we could never stay for long… not even crouching in the rubble … there were terrible things in the poisoned sky—Shantaks, I've heard them called, and the faceless Gaunts—and it was never very long before they would glide or slide into view, scouring the land as they searched… searched for… for what else but us! For mankind's devastated remnants! For the scattered handful of human beings who remained!

"But my Dawn… she was everything to me… as her mother before her, and her poor sister. But they were taken, all three, and what have I now—what's left for me?—except the hope of a measure… however small a measure… *of revenge!*"

It seemed to me the old man was waiting for an answer, and so I shrugged and obliged him, saying, "Well since you ask, it seems there's nothing left for you Henry, except that small measure of revenge. So you'll do what you have to, and for that matter, so will I."

"So will you?"

I nodded and said, "There's nothing much left for me either, Henry. So just like you I'll do what I have to—" And I had to bite my tongue as I almost added, '—to survive'.

The Shoggoth light ahead of us was very much brighter now, and in order to change the subject I pointed it out to my companion. "Look there, it's almost daylight up front! Or as daylight used to be, I mean."

"I see it," he answered, as his sobbing gradually subsided. "Another fifteen to twenty minutes and we'll be there. Piccadilly Circus… or ground zero, if you prefer."

"Hmm!" I said. "But I always thought that term described a point on the ground directly *beneath* the explosion—not above it."

He was obviously surprised. "Quite right, yes! But since we both know what I meant, why nit-pick?" Then, looking at me sideways and slyly: "By the way, you really have got it all figured out, haven't you?"

"Most of it." I nodded. "But I still don't know, can't see, how you've been able in the circumstances to build any kind of device powerful enough to make all of this worthwhile. I mean, you'd need a laboratory, and the know-how, and the materials."

Henry returned my nod. "Very good," he said, "very clever. But don't I remember saying that you had no idea who or what I am or was? I'm sure I do."

"Ah!" I said. "So this is what you were getting at. Except you never did get around to telling me. So then, Henry—who and what were you?"

"I am, as you know, Henry Chattaway," he replied. "But what you *don't* know is that I have an almost entire alphabet of letters after my name, that I was twice put forward as a candidate for a Nobel Prize in physics, and that…"

He paused, and I prompted him: "Yes? And that…?" For this was the one thing I had most wanted to know but hadn't dared ask him outright in case it gave me away. And:

"Well, why shouldn't I tell you?" he said, as the first signs of the man-made cavern or excavation that was the main Piccadilly Circus Underground station gradually came into view up front. "For it's too late now to do anything else but see it through: the last of my dreams come true on this long last night."

And as we climbed up from the tracks onto the platform and I returned his small heavy suitcase to him, he continued: "Julian, I was the top man—or rather, not to make too much of it, one of them—on PFDP, the Plasma Fusion Drive Project. Similar in its way to the Manhattan Project, it was very hush-hush even though no one in the scientific community gave it a snowflake's chance in hell, even as a theory. What? Abundant energy from next to nothing? You may recall that seventy years ago the same dream had given birth to the bombs that put an abrupt end to World War II. Not so much a dream as a nightmare, as it happened—at least until someone began speculating about the possible benefits: that maybe nuclear power could provide cheap energy for the entire world; which of course never really worked out. The fuel was dirty, dangerous, and had too many safety problems; the mutations and fatal diseases that followed on inevitably from the accidents and errors were hideous, while some of the infected radioactive regions remain hot even to this day.

"Well, history repeats, Julian. Plasma fusion was the next best hope for cheap energy, far better and cheaper and so much easier to produce... why, men might even go to the stars with it—if it worked! But it didn't, or rather it did, except even the smallest, most cautious of tests warned of a Pandora's Box effect. Only let it loose and it could initiate a chain reaction with anything it might touch and fuse with. That's the only and best explanation I can give to a layman, especially in what little time we have left. But enough: we stopped working on it, and the world's authorities—every single one of them, recognising the awesome power of this thing—signed up to a strictly monitored ban on any further experimentation... simply because they couldn't afford not to!"

While Henry talked, his voice gradually falling to a whisper, we had proceeded from the tunnel to the platform, then to the relatively pristine stairs and elevators. The latter, of course, had not worked since the night of the invasion; but the stairs, completely free of rubble, had taken us to the surface, which upon a time had been a landmark, a renowned open-air concourse where many streets joined in that great circus it was named for. A far different sort of circus now.

"This place," I said, letting my voice echo, "is looking rather empty. Not what one would expect, eh?"

"I know," Henry agreed in a whisper, probably wondering why I wasn't whispering too. "It's been like this each time. You would think it should be crawling, right? Which in a way it is, if not as you might expect. Not crawling with alien life, no, but with the very meaning of the word 'alien' itself!"

Crawling, yes. And making one's skin crawl, too. Even mine. It was the way it looked, its shapes and angles; its architectural features, if you could call them that; its non-Euclidean geometry.

It had four legs—or was it three? Maybe five?—all leaning inward, or was it outward? Something like the once dizzy and dizzying Eiffel Tower, but a twisted version, and what we had surfaced into was the base of one such leg that used to be Piccadilly Circus. The rest of the legs were green-misted and vague, half-obscured by distance, submarine-tinged Shoggoth light, and the intervening shapes of anomalous buttresses, columns and spiralling staircases. And adding to the confusion nothing stood still but appeared literally to crawl, each surface flowing and changing shape of its own accord.

As for the staircases: some had steps as broad as landings, others with steps like frozen ripples on a pond, but rising, of course, and a third type with no steps at all but smooth, corkscrew surfaces of some glassy substance, sometimes turning on clockwise threads and other times winding in reverse. And all of them stationary, at least until one looked at them.

We were dwarfed, Henry and I, made minuscule by the gigantic scale of everything; and screwing up his face, shielding his eyes as he peered up into reaches that receded sickeningly into skyscraper heights and vast balconied levels, Henry said, "That must be where the life is: Bgg'ha's throne room, cages to house his prisoners, dwelling areas for them that serve him. The monster himself will sit high above all that, dreaming his dreams, doing what he does, probably unaware that he's any sort of monster at all! To him it's how things are, that's all.

"But as for his underlings—the flying creatures, and Deep Ones, and Shoggoths that build and fashion for him, varnishing their works with a slime that hardens to glass hard as steel—I have to believe that a majority of them... well, perhaps not the Shoggoths, who are more like machines, however nightmarishly organic—but by far the great *majority* of them, know full well what they are about."

"I think you're right," I told him. "But you know, Henry, we're not too small to be noticed. And I can't imagine that we would be welcome here; certainly not you, suitcase and all! You need to be about your revenge, Henry, and should it work—to however small or enormous an effect—then, while you will have paid the ultimate price, at least your physicist friends may be aware of your success and will carry on your work, assuming they survive it. So why are we waiting here? And why is that awesome weapon you're carrying also waiting, if only to be put to its intended use?"

It was as if he had been asleep, or hypnotised by his alien surroundings, or maybe fully aware for the first time that this was it— the end of the long last night. For him, anyway—or so he thought. And he was right: it *was* the end of the road for him, but *not* as he thought.

"Yes," he finally answered, straightening up and no longer whispering. "The others who helped me put it all together, they will surely know. They'll see the result from the skeletal roof of the museum. When the explosion takes this leg out, the entire tower may rock a little... why, it could even topple! Bgg'ha's house, brought crashing down on the city that he has destroyed! And *that*, my friend, would be acceptable as a real and very genuine revenge! By no means an eye-for-an-eye—for who has lost more than me?—but as much as I could hope for, certainly."

"The roof of the museum?" I repeated him as he headed for a recess (an outcrop, stanchion, corner or nook?) in the seemingly restless wall. "What, the Victoria & Albert's roof, whose cellar was your home?"

"Eh?" He stared at me for long, hard moments... then shook his head. And: "No, no," he said. "Not the Victoria & Albert, but the Science Museum next door, behind that great pile of rubble that used to be the Natural History Museum."

"*Ahh!*" For at last I understood. "So that is where and how you and your team built it, eh? You used materials and apparatus rescued from the ruins of the Science Museum, and you put it all together... where?"

"In the museum's basement," he replied, as the wall seemed to enclose us in a leadenly glistening fold. "Those massive old buildings, and their cellars, were built to last. We had to work hard at it for a long time, but we turned the Science Museum's basement into our workshop. And after tonight, when they've seen the result of my work, they'll make the next bomb much bigger—big enough to melt the entire city, what's left of it..."

And that was that. Now I had all that I needed from the old man, all that I'd been ordered to extract from him. Wherefore:

*You can come for him now*, I told the Tower's creatures—or certain of them—fully aware that the nearest ones would hear me, because I knew they would have been listening out for me. But meanwhile:

We had entered or been enveloped in a fold in the irrationally angled wall, a sort of priest's hole in the flowing, alien cinder-block construction. And there in a corner—I'll call it a corner anyway, but in any case "a space"—was Henry Chattaway's device, its components contained in four more small suitcases arranged in a sort of circle with a gap where a fifth (the one we had been keeping from damage during this entire subterranean journey) would neatly fit. The cases were connected up with electrical cables, left loosely dangling in the gap where the fifth would complete the circuit; while a sixth component stood central on four short legs, looking much like the casing of a domed, cylindrical fire extinguisher. In series, obviously the cases were a kind of trigger, while the cylinder—the bomb— would have contained anything but fire retardant! And affixed to the cylinder at its domed top, standing out vividly against the metal's dull gleam, sat a bright red switch which, apart from the warning manifest in its colour, looked like nothing so much as an ordinary electrical light switch. The cylinder and its switch—a deadly however inarticulate combination, as the bomb *had recently been*—told a story all their own, but one which was now a lie!

Quickly kneeling, Henry opened his case, reached inside and carefully uncoiled a pair of cables which he connected up to the dangling cables on both sides. And now all was in order, or so he thought, and he was ready.

Screwing up his face and half-shuttering his eyes (I imagined in anticipation of a moment's pain), he reached a trembling hand over the circle of wired-up suitcases, his index finger hovering over the red switch… until, remembering something, he paused and glanced at me. And then, to my dismay because I do have something of a conscience after all, he said:

"I'm so sorry, Julian, but I did give you every opportunity to leave."

"Yes, you did," I replied, kneeling beside him and, before he could stop me, flipping open the lid of one of the suitcases. "And I'm sorry, too," I told him. "But as you can see, I knew I really didn't have to leave."

His jaw fell; his mouth opened wide; he gurgled for several long seconds, and finally said: "*Empty!*"

"All of them," I nodded. "Especially the cylinder—the bomb." But even then the truth hadn't fully sunk in, and he said:

"I don't understand. No one—nothing, not a single damned thing—ever saw me here. Not once. And this isn't a spot where anyone or thing would think to look!"

"You weren't seen here, no," I replied with a shake of my head. "But you were seen *leaving*—just the once, by Deep Ones at Green Park—the last time you made a delivery. You were correct about their telepathy, Henry. Despite the confusion, the fear in your mind, or maybe because of it, they saw something of what you had been up to and a search was made. Otherwise no one or thing might ever have come in here. But once Bgg'ha had discovered your secret he wanted to know more about you and anything else you might be doing, and how and with whom you were doing it. So you see, they do care about us—or shall we say they're at least *interested* in some of us—especially those of us who would try to kill them. And so I was sent out to look for you. Or to 'hunt' for you, if you prefer."

Hearing that and finally, fully aware of the situation, the old man snapped upright. His eyes, however bloodshot, were narrowed now; the dazed expression was gone from his face; his gun was suddenly firm in his hand, its blued-steel muzzle rammed up hard under my chin. I thought he might shoot me there and then, and I wished that I'd called out to *them* sooner.

"*God damn!*" Henry said. "But I should pay more attention to my instincts... I *knew* there was something wrong about you! But I won't kill you here; I'll do it out there in the open—or what used to be the open—so that when you're found with your face shot off they'll know there are still men in the world who aren't afraid to fight! Now get moving, you treacherous bastard! Let's get out of here."

But as we moved from the drift and slide of the continually mutating wall to the even greater visual nightmare of the Twisted Tower's leg's interior, and when I was beginning to believe I could actually feel the old fellow's finger tightening on the trigger, then I cried out:

"Henry, listen! Do you really intend to waste a bullet on me? I mean, *look what's coming, Henry...!*"

They were Shoggoths, two of them, under the direction of a solitary Deep One. They came into view apparently from nowhere, simply appearing from the suck and the thrust to glide toward us... at least the Shoggoths approached us, while the Deep One held back and kept his watery great eyes on his charges, making sure they carried out their orders—whatever those might be—to the letter. But of course I knew exactly what they had been told to do.

Suddenly gibbering, Henry released me and turned his attention on the twin pillars of blackly tossing, undulating filth, slime and alien jelly as the advancing creatures formed more huge, slithering, soulless and half-vacant eyes in addition to the many they already had, and came flowing upon him. He fired once, twice, three times... until the hammer clicked metallically, first on a dead round, and once again, but hollowly, on an empty chamber. And finally, cursing, Henry hurled the useless weapon directly into the tarry protoplasm of one of that awesome pair of nine-foot nightmares. Then, as if noticing for the first time just how close they were, he turned and made to run or stagger away from them... but too late!

Moving with scarcely believable speed, they were upon him; they towered over him to left and right, putting out ropey pseudopods to trap Henry's spindly arms. And closing with his thin, smoking, desperately vibrating body, they slowly but surely *melted* him, sucking him into themselves and burning him as fuel for the biological engines that they were...

As his agonised shrieking tapered and died, along with Henry himself, and as the smoke and gushing steam of his catabolism rose up from the feeding creatures, the loathsome fetor of Henry Chattaway's demise might have been almost as sickening as the live smell of his executioners; but *in combination*, overwhelming the already rancid air to burn like acid in my nostrils even though I had moved well away, the two taints together were far more than twice as nauseating.

And I was glad that it was finally over, for my sake if not for the old man's...

In backing away from all this I had come up against a different kind of body with a smell which I could at least tolerate; indeed I even appreciated it. The Shoggoth-herder looked at me rather curiously for a moment, his almost chinless face turned a little on one side. But then as he sniffed at me and recognised my Innsmouth heritage, my ancestry, he further acknowledged my role in these matters by turning away from me and once more taking command of the Shoggoths.

Left to my own devices I shrugged off a regretful, perhaps vaguely guilty feeling and set about climbing the stairway with the tall treads. This was hard work indeed, for I was already weary from my journey through the Underground with old man Chattaway and his suitcase full of impotent batteries.

But up there, high overhead, I knew the ovens would also be hard at work. And long or short pig, what difference did that make when I was this hungry? Hadn't men eaten fish, and in France frogs, too? But the word from others I had spoken to was that this appears to be a problem with changelings such as myself, changelings who—while waiting for their change, when at last they, too, can go down to the water—hunt humans: sooner or later they begin to sympathise, even empathise with the hunted.

However, and despite the greater effort, I soon began to climb faster. For also up there were the cages and other habitats... and at least one lovely teenage girl; a girl called Dawn, who had never known a man—or for that matter a Deep One—or not until comparatively recently, anyway. A great shame, that there were others more or less like me up there, but I expected she would still be very fresh.

And, so that I wouldn't fall victim to mistaken identity on the way up, I commenced chanting: "*Ph'nglui gwlihu'nath, Bgg'ha Im'ykh l'ihu'nagl fhtagn...!*" And surprising me even as I sang, there it was again: that oh-so-faint feeling of guilt!

But what the hell, and I shrugged it off. For after all, it was like I had told Henry: certain kinds of men can become accustomed—can get used—to almost anything.

Yes, and not only men...

# AFTERWORD

## CONTRIBUTORS' NOTES

RANDY BROECKER was born and lives in Chicago, Illinois. Inspired by the pulp magazines and EC comics he read as a child, his first published artwork appeared in Rich Hauser's seminal 1960s EC fanzine, *Spa-Fon*.

Many years later, a meeting with acclaimed publisher Donald M. Grant at the second World Fantasy Convention eventually led in 1979 to *The Black Wolf* and his first hardcover illustrations. Since then his work has appeared in books produced by PS Publishing, Robinson Publishing, Carroll & Graf, Fedogan & Bremer, Cemetery Dance, Underwood-Miller, Sarob Press, Pumpkin Books, American Fantasy, Highland Press and other imprints on both sides of the Atlantic.

He was Artist Guest of Honour at the 2002 World Horror Convention and is the author of the World Fantasy Award-nominated study *Fantasy of the 20th Century: An Illustrated History* from Collector's Press, which also formed part of a three-in-one omnibus entitled *Art of Imagination: 20th Century Visions of Science Fiction, Horror, and Fantasy*.

The artist has long been an admirer of the writings of H. P. Lovecraft and his circle. His works have taken him to picturesque Innsmouth on more than one occasion, about which he has this to say: "The people of Innsmouth have been most kind to me over the years and I've enjoyed using them as models, although—and Lovecraft knew this—the 'Innsmouth look' as he referred to it, can be a bit hard to nail down on paper. There is, quite frankly, a tendency to over-exaggerate, which I'd like to believe I've avoided with my work this time around. I only hope they are as pleased with the results as I am.

"Whether embraced by the Innsmouth folk or not," he adds, "these illustrations are dedicated to my late brother Jay—a small token for showing me the way not only to Innsmouth, but other fantastic locales as well."

Broecker was also one of the contributing artists to *Weird Shadows Over Innsmouth*, and this new edition of *Weirder Shadows Over Innsmouth* features additional illustrations that were not included in the Fedogan & Bremer hardcover.

RAMSEY CAMPBELL was born in Liverpool, where he still lives with his wife Jenny. His first book, a collection of stories entitled *The Inhabitant of the Lake and Less Welcome Tenants*, was published by August Derleth's legendary Arkham House imprint in 1964, since when his novels have included *The Doll Who Ate His Mother, The Face That Must Die, The Nameless, Incarnate, The Hungry Moon, Ancient Images, The Count of Eleven, The Long Lost, Pact of the Fathers, The Darkest Part of the Woods, The Grin of the Dark, Thieving Fear, Creatures of the Pool, The Seven Days of Cain, Ghosts Know, The Kind Folk, Bad Thoughts, Think Yourself Lucky* and the movie tie-in *Solomon Kane*.

His short fiction has been collected in such volumes as *Demons by Daylight, The Height of the Scream, Dark Companions, Scared Stiff, Waking Nightmares, Cold Print, Alone with the Horrors, Ghosts and Grisly Things, Told by the Dead,* and *Just Behind You*. He has also edited a number of anthologies, including *New Terrors, New Tales of the Cthulhu Mythos, Fine Frights: Stories That Scared Me, Uncanny Banquet, Meddling with Ghosts,* and *Gathering the Bones: Original Stories from the World's Masters of Horror* (with Dennis Etchison and Jack Dann).

PS Publishing recently published the novellas *The Pretence* and *The Last Revelation of Gla'aki*, which attempts to reconceive some of the author's early Lovecraftian ideas and develop them, along with the definitive edition of that early Arkham collection, *Inhabitant of the Lake*, which includes all the first drafts of the stories, along with new illustrations by Randy Broecker. Also available from the same publisher is a volume of all the Campbell–Derleth correspondence, edited by S. T. Joshi.

Now well into his fifth decade as one of the world's most respected authors of horror fiction, Ramsey Campbell has won multiple World Fantasy Awards, British Fantasy Awards and Bram Stoker Awards, and is a recipient of the World Horror Convention Grand Master Award, the Horror Writers Association Lifetime Achievement Award, the Howie Award of the H. P. Lovecraft Film Festival for Lifetime Achievement, and the International Horror Guild's Living Legend Award. He is also President of the Society of Fantastic Films.

"I started imitating Lovecraft more than fifty years ago," reveals Campbell. "Soon I learned to subsume his example—his careful sense of structure, his ambition to reach for awe—and mostly did without his Mythos, which in any case was largely constructed by later writers, too often to the detriment of what he was trying to achieve. He meant his inventions to suggest more than they made explicit, but the rest of us filled in so many gaps that the whole thing became as over-explained as the Victorian occultism he wanted to leave behind. Over the decades I've tried to reclaim some of his original vision, not least in my novel *The Darkest Part of the Woods*, which took *The Case of Charles Dexter Ward* as a model of how to do without his Mythos. I hope 'The Winner' also gives some sense of his vision without needing explicit references.

"I've been in pubs as unnerving as the one in this story, and perhaps they've lodged in my shadowy subconscious. The worst was in Birkenhead—a pub where as soon as you walked in you felt as if you'd announced your Jewishness at a David Irving book launch."

Campbell's early story 'The Church in the High Street' appears in *Shadows Over Innsmouth*, and the author's 'Raised by the Moon' is included in *Weird Shadows Over Innsmouth*.

ADRIAN COLE was born in 1949 in Devon, where he still lives. He is the author of twenty-five novels and numerous short stories, writing in several genres, including science fiction, fantasy, sword & sorcery and horror.

His first books were published in the 1970s—"The Dream Lords" trilogy—and he went on to write, among others, the "Omaran Saga" and the "Star Requiem" series, as well as writing two young adult novels, *Moorstones* and *The Sleep of Giants*.

More recently, he has had several books published by Wildside Press, including the "Voidal" trilogy, which collects all the original short stories from the 1970s and '80s and adds new material to complete the saga. The same imprint has also published the novel *Night of the Heroes*, an affectionate celebration of the world of pulp fiction, as well as *Young Thongor*, which Cole has edited and which includes the previously uncollected short "Thongor" stories of Lin Carter.

The author's latest SF novel is *The Shadow Academy* from EDGE Science Fiction and Fantasy Publishing, with an audio version available from Audible. His short stories have been reprinted in *The Year's Best Fantasy* and *The Year's Best Fantasy and Horror*, and he has written and performed a number of parodies of the genres he loves at various conventions in the past.

As the author explains: "'You Don't Want to Know' is the first story I wrote about Nick Nightmare, the hard-boiled private eye, most of whose adventures pit him against various villains from Mythos terrain.

"Combining the droll style of Philip Marlowe, the shoot-'em-up no-nonsense energy of Mike Hammer and the bizarre grotesquery of H. P. Lovecraft, the Nick Nightmare stories are intended to be a celebration of the old pulps and their hyper-active, madcap world."

A further tale, 'Nightmare on Mad Gull Island', was published in the fourth edition of *Cthulhu: Tales of the Cthulhu Mythos* from Spectre Press, while *Nick Nightmare Investigates* is a new collection of tales from The Alchemy Press/Airgedlámh Publications. Both publications are illustrated by Jim Pitts.

Adrian Cole's story 'The Crossing' appears in *Shadows Over Innsmouth*.

AUGUST WILLIAM DERLETH (1909–71) was a major figure in the literary and small-press publishing world. An amazingly prolific Wisconsin regional author (known for his "Sac Prairie Saga"), essayist and poet, he is best remembered today as an author, editor and publisher of weird fiction (Lovecraftian and otherwise).

He made his debut in *Weird Tales* at the age of seventeen with a story entitled 'Bat's Belfry', and most of his own macabre fiction has been collected by Arkham House—the imprint that Derleth founded in 1939 with Donald Wandrei to perpetuate the work of their friend and colleague H. P. Lovecraft—in such volumes as *Someone in the Dark, Something Near, Not Long for This World, Lonesome Places, Mr. George and Other Odd Persons* (as by "Stephen Grendon"), *Colonel Markeson and Less Pleasant People* (with Mark Schorer), *Harrigan's File, Dwellers in Darkness* and *In Lovecraft's Shadow*.

As a widely respected anthologist, he edited *Sleep No More, Who Knocks?, The Night Side, The Sleeping and the Dead, Dark of the Moon, Night's Yawning Peal: A Ghostly Company, Dark Mind Dark Heart, The Unquiet Grave, When Evil Wakes, Over the Edge, Travellers by Night, Tales of the Cthulhu Mythos* and *Dark Things*, amongst many other titles.

Derleth began corresponding with Lovecraft around the mid-1920s. "You have the real stuff," the author wrote to his young protégé in 1930, "and with the progress of time it seems to me over-whelmingly probable that you will produce literature in a major calibre."

Following Lovecraft's untimely death, Derleth developed various fragments and outlines (reputedly) discovered amongst the author's posthumous papers into Cthulhu Mythos-inspired pastiches, which can be found in such novels and collections as *The Lurker at the Threshold, The Survivor and Others, The Mask of Cthulhu, The Trail of Cthulhu* and *The Watchers Out of Time and Others*.

In 1962, he set out his own vision of the Mythos: "The deities of Lovecraft's Cthulhu Mythos consisted first of the Elder Gods, which, though beyond mundane morality, beyond 'good' and 'evil', were nevertheless proponents of order and thus represented the forces of enlightenment as against the forces of evil, represented by the Ancient Ones or the Great Old Ones, who rebelled against the Elder Gods, and were thrust—like Satan—into outer darkness."

'Innsmouth Clay' is a "posthumous pastiche" which first appeared in the 1971 anthology *Dark Things* under only Lovecraft's byline. When reprinted three years later in *The Watchers Out of Time*, it was properly identified as a collaborative effort between the two authors.

JOHN STEPHEN GLASBY (1928–2011) graduated from Nottingham University with a honours degree in Chemistry. He started his career as a research chemist for ICI in 1952 and worked for them until his retirement.

Around the same time, he began a parallel career as an extraordinarily prolific writer of novels and short stories, producing more than 300 works in all genres over the next two decades, many under such shared house pseudonyms as "Rand Le Page", "Berl Cameron", "Victor La Salle" and "John E. Muller". His most noted personal pseudonym was "A. J. Merak". He subsequently published a new collection of ghost stories, *The Substance of Shade*, the occult novel *The Dark Destroyer*, and the SF novel *Mystery of the Crater*.

More recently, Philip Harbottle compiled two collections of Glasby's supernatural fiction, *The Lonely Shadows* and *The Dark Boatman*, while the author's son, Edmund Glasby, edited *The Thing in the Mist: Selected by John S. Glasby*, collecting eleven of the author's stories from Badger Books' digest horror magazine *Supernatural Stories*.

Ramble House will publish a further collection of fiction selected from that magazine, along with a new volume of Glasby's Mythos stories, *Dwellers in Darkness and Other Tales of the Cthulhu Mythos*. Meanwhile, the author's most ambitious Lovecraftian work, *Dark Armageddon*—a trilogy of novels that unify the "Cthulhu Mythos" and bring it to a climactic conclusion—is set to appear from Centipede Press.

A long-time fan of the work of H. P. Lovecraft, in the early 1970s the author also submitted a collection of Mythos stories to August Derleth at Arkham House. Derleth suggested extensive revisions and improvements, which Glasby duly followed, but the publisher unfortunately died before the revised book could see print, and the manuscript was returned.

In his later years, Glasby returned to writing more supernatural stories in the Lovecraftian vein. 'The Quest for Y'ha-Nthlei'—a direct sequel to Lovecraft's 'The Shadow Over Innsmouth'—was written especially for *Weird Shadows Over Innsmouth*, as was 'Innsmouth Bane', which first appeared in the short-lived *H. P. Lovecraft's Magazine of Horror*, before finally being anthologised in this volume.

**B**RIAN HODGE is the award-winning author of eleven novels spanning horror, crime, and historical. He's also written over 100 short stories, novelettes and novellas, plus five full-length collections.

Recent works include *No Law Left Unbroken*, a collection of crime fiction; *The Weight of the Dead* and *Whom the Gods Would Destroy*, both stand-alone novellas; a newly revised hardcover edition of *Dark Advent*, his early post-apocalyptic epic; and his latest novel, *Leaves of Sherwood*.

He lives in Colorado, where more of everything is in the works. He also dabbles in music, sound design and photography; loves everything about organic gardening except the thieving squirrels; and trains in Krav Maga, grappling, and kickboxing, which are of no use at all against the squirrels.

As the author explains: "As many times as I've read 'The Shadow Over Innsmouth', it never occurred to me, until I read it looking for ideas, that neither H. P. Lovecraft nor anyone in the prior "Innsmouth" anthologies had accounted for the prisoners taken during the 1928 raids on the town.

"I quickly became intrigued by what must have happened to them, and how they might well constitute the original precedent for the troubling, terrorism-era US policy of endless detention without due process.

"The anomalous ocean recording in 'The Same Deep Waters as You' was a real-world event that I've wanted to play with for years. In an irresistible coincidence, the Bloop was triangulated to have originated close to where Lovecraft located the sunken city of R'lyeh. A few weeks after I finished this story, NOAA announced that the sound was similar to the sonic profile of icebergs recorded in the

Scotia Sea. They would know, although I'd love to learn more about how there would've been enough ice around Polynesia that August that its calving was heard for 3,000 miles.

"It's more fun living in a world where this remains a mystery."

CAITLÍN R. KIERNAN is the author of several novels, including *Low Red Moon*, *Daughter of Hounds*, *The Drowning Girl: A Memoir*, *The Red Tree* and *Blood Oranges*. She has recently scripted a graphic novel for Dark Horse Comics, *Alabaster*, which continues the misadventures of her character Dancy Flammarion.

Since 2000, her shorter tales of the weird, fantastic and macabre have been collected in several volumes, including *Tales of Pain and Wonder*; *From Weird and Distant Shores*, *To Charles Fort with Love*, *A is for Alien*, *The Ammonite Violin & Others* and the retrospective volume *Two Worlds and In Between: The Best of Caitlín R. Kiernan (Volume One)*. Subterranean Press has recently released *The Ape's Wife and Other Stories*, while Centipede Press is planning expanded and illustrated limited editions of her novels *The Drowning Girl: A Memoir* and *The Red Tree*.

About the sequence of stories the author has in this volume, she reveals: "'Fish Bride' has a somewhat complicated origin. In December 2005, I mentioned something in my blog about wanting to write a humorous story about a 'whorehouse in Innsmouth, circa 1924'. I'm not very good at humour, not usually, and the idea sat fallow for a long time. A couple of years later, I wrote 'Fish Bride', a very different sort of tale, not the least bit humorous, but one that grew out of that concept of a 'whorehouse in Innsmouth'. Though 'Fish Bride' isn't set in Innsmouth, the locale clearly mirrors Lovecraft's doomed seaport. It also owes a debt to R. H. Barlow's 'The Night Ocean', which was one of those stories that Lovecraft 'revised' in an attempt to scrape by and make his meagre living.

"'On the Reef' came about in the autumn of 2010," continues Kiernan, "because I was looking to write a Halloween story, and a story about masks and the role they play in mythology and religion. And because I wanted to write a story that returned to Innsmouth long after the events of Lovecraft's story. It's not like the town could have been completely erased. So, in essence it's a kind of ghost story. Only the ghost isn't the disembodied spirit of a human being, but the force that a dead town and what happened continues to exert over the present day.

"'The Transition of Elizabeth Haskings' is one of those stories that I wrote because I'm so often more interested in looking at a superficially 'horrific' situation from the point of view of the 'Other'. Probably, John Garner's *Grendel* set me on this path. In this story, I'm not interested in provoking fear from the reader, but sympathy for the protagonist, an understanding of her sense of alienation, her loneliness, and her longing for a life forever out of her reach."

Kiernan's story 'From Cabinet 34, Drawer 6', which linked Lovecraft's Deep Ones to the Creature from the Black Lagoon, appeared in *Weird Shadows Over Innsmouth*.


**H**OWARD PHILIPS LOVECRAFT (1890–1937) is one of the twentieth century's most important and influential authors of supernatural fiction.

Born in Providence, Rhode Island, he lived for much of his life there as a studious antiquarian who wrote mostly with no care for commercial reward. During his lifetime, the majority of Lovecraft's fiction, poetry and essays appeared in obscure amateur-press journals or in the pages of the struggling pulp magazine *Weird Tales*.

Following the author's untimely death, August Derleth and Donald Wandrei founded the publishing imprint of Arkham House in 1939 with the initial idea of keeping all Lovecraft's work in print. Beginning with *The Outsider and Others*, his stories were collected in such hardcover volumes as *Beyond the Wall of Sleep*, *Marginalia*, *Something About Cats and Other Pieces*, *Dreams and Fancies*, *The Dunwich Horror and Others*, *At the Mountains of Madness and Other Novels*, *Dagon and Other Macabre Tales*, *3 Tales of Horror* and *The Horror in the Museum and Other Revisions*, along with several volumes of "posthumous collaborations" with Derleth, including as *The Lurker at the Threshold*, *The Survivor and Others*, *The Mask of Cthulhu*, *The Trail of Cthulhu* and *The Watchers Out of Time and Others*.

During the decades since his death, Lovecraft himself has been acknowledged as a mainstream American writer second only to Edgar Allan Poe, while his relatively small body of work has influenced countless imitators and formed the basis of a world-wide industry of books, role-playing games, graphic novels, toys and movies based on his concepts.

BRIAN LUMLEY started his writing career by emulating the work of H. P. Lovecraft and has ended up with his own, highly enthusiastic, fan following for his world-wide best-selling series of "Necroscope'" vampire books.

Born in the coal-mining town of Horden, County Durham, on England's north-east coast, Lumley joined the British Army when he was twenty-one and served in the Corps of Royal Military Police for twenty-two years, until his retirement in December 1980.

After discovering Lovecraft's stories while stationed in Berlin in the early 1960s, he decided to try his own hand at writing horror fiction, initially based around the influential Cthulhu Mythos. He sent his early efforts to editor August Derleth, and Arkham House published two collections of the author's stories, *The Caller of the Black* and *The Horror at Oakdene and Others*, along with the short novel, *Beneath the Moors*.

The author then continued Lovecraft's themes in such novels and collections as *The Burrowers Beneath*, *The Transition of Titus Crow*, *The Clock of Dreams*, *Spawn of the Winds*, *In the Moons of Borea*, *The Compleat Crow*, *Hero of Dreams*, *Ship of Dreams*, *Mad Moon of Dreams*, *Iced on Iran and Other Dreamquests*, *The House of Cthulhu and Other Tales of the Primal Land*, *Fruiting Bodies and Other Fungi* (which includes the British Fantasy Award-winning title story), *Return of the Deep Ones and Other Mythos Tales* and *Dagon's Bell and Other Discords*.

As Lumley explains: "'The Long Last Night' in this current volume is set in the future—possibly the last, darkest and nearest future, when the stars are finally right. Firmly grounded in H. P. Lovecraft's now world-famous 'Cthulhu Mythos', this story is my third offering in Titan Books' trilogy of Lovecraftian horror: *Shadows Over Innsmouth*, *Weird*

*Shadows Over Innsmouth* and *Weirder Shadows Over Innsmouth*, though not necessarily my last connected story. For fans of HPL, especially those suffering—or with hideously developing symptoms of—the Innsmouth taint, look for 'The Changeling' in the same editor's anthology *Fearie Tales: Stories of the Grimm and Gruesome*."

Other recent works by Brian Lumley include *The Möbius Murders*, a long novella set in the Necroscope® universe, and *The Compleat Crow*, reprinting all the short adventures and longer novellas in the saga of Titus Crow, both volumes from William Schafer's Subterranean Press. And here it is worth pointing out that Titus Crow himself has had more than a handful of dealings with the monsters of the Mythos...

KIM NEWMAN is a novelist, critic and broadcaster. His fiction includes *The Night Mayor*, *Bad Dreams*, *Jago*, the *Anno Dracula* novels and stories, *The Quorum*, *The Original Dr Shade and Other Stories*, *Life's Lottery*, *Back in the USSA* (with Eugene Byrne) and *The Man from the Diogenes Club*, all under his own name, and *The Vampire Genevieve* and *Orgy of the Blood Parasites* as "Jack Yeovil".

His non-fiction books include *Ghastly Beyond Belief* (with Neil Gaiman), *Horror: 100 Best Books* and *Horror: Another 100 Best Books* (both with Stephen Jones), *Wild West Movies*, *The BFI Companion to Horror*, *Millennium Movies* and BFI Classics studies of *Cat People*, *Doctor Who* and *Quatermass and the Pit*.

He is a contributing editor to *Sight & Sound* and *Empire* magazines (supplying the latter's popular 'Video Dungeon' column), has written and broadcast widely on a range of topics, and scripted radio and television documentaries.

Newman's stories 'Week Woman' and 'Ubermensch' have been adapted into episodes of the TV series *The Hunger*, and the latter tale was also turned into an Australian short film in 2009. Following his Radio 4 play *Cry Babies*, he wrote an episode ('Phish Phood') for BBC Radio 7's series *The Man in Black*, and he was a main contributor to the 2012 stage play *The Hallowe'en Sessions*. He has also directed and written a tiny film, *Missing Girl*.

The author's most recent books include expanded reissues of his acclaimed Anno Dracula series, including the long-awaited fourth volume *Anno Dracula 1976–1991: Johnny Alucard*; the "Professor Moriarty" novel *The Hound of the d'Urbervilles*, and the stand-alone novel *An English Ghost Story* (all from Titan Books), along with a much-enlarged edition of *Nightmare Movies* (from Bloomsbury).

With Maura McHugh he scripted the comic book mini-series *Witchfinder: The Mysteries of Unland* for Dark Horse Comics. Illustrated by Tyler Crook, it is a spin-off from Mike Mignola's *Hellboy* series. Forthcoming fiction includes the novels *Kentish Glory: The Secrets of Drearcliff Grange* and *Angels of Music*.

About the setting for his 'Richard Riddle' story, Newman explains: "Lyme Regis, in the county of Dorset, is perhaps best known as the setting for John Fowles' prematurely post-modern Victorian novel *The French Lieutenant's Woman*—which makes dramatic use, as does Karel Reisz's film, of the town's distinctive stone harbour, the Cobb. Fowles was a famous, if mysterious local resident and lived quite near my fictional Orris Priory. In the 1970s, I spent many weekends around the little coast town, where my father had a yacht—a Mirror dinghy which I sometimes crewed on fishing trips in Lyme Bay, though Dad had someone more serious along when he took up boat-racing.

"Then and now, Lyme beach was known for its fine array of fossils: before anyone learned to leave paleontological finds in place, we brought home a huge chunk of rock with an embedded ammonite for use as a door-stop. Amazingly, the shingles still haven't been picked entirely clean—though taking prehistoric souvenirs is now quite properly discouraged.

"This story, which was originally written for Chris Roberson's anthology *Adventure*, draws on my own memories of pottering around Lyme. In America, the piece was taken as a tribute to boys' adventures I've not read—Tom Swift, Encyclopedia Brown, the Hardy Boys. I was actually thinking of Arthur Ransome's *Swallows and Amazons*, one of Dad's favourite books as a child (it gave him the idea of sailing in the first place), and Erich Kästner's *Emil and the Detectives* (a 1929 German young adult mystery still read in my 1970s schooldays). Other elements thrown into the mix were H. P.

Lovecraft's 'The Shadow Over Innsmouth', Edmund Gosse's brilliant 1907 memoir *Father and Son* (Philip Gosse wrote *Omphalos: An Attempt to Untie the Geological Knot*, which desperately tries to explain the existence of fossils from a fundamentalist Christian viewpoint), and the famous anecdote of the Hartlepool monkey.

"The story goes that, during the Napoleonic Wars, a ship sank off the coast of the Northern fishing town. The sole survivor was a monkey dressed in a miniature sailor's uniform. The locals, having never seen a Frenchman, took the monkey for a spy, tried the unfortunate creature and hanged it, prompting citizens of rival towns to taunt Hartlepool natives to this day with a jeer of 'Who hung the monkey?'"

Kim Newman contributed two stories—'A Quarter to Three' and 'The Big Fish' (under his "Jack Yeovil" byline)—to *Shadows Over Innsmouth* and, as the author admits, "I thought I wouldn't write yet another fish story when I finished 'Another Fish Story' for the second 'Innsmouth' anthology, but then this popped out."

REGGIE OLIVER has been a professional playwright, actor and theatre director since 1975. Besides plays, his publications include the authorised biography of Stella Gibbons, *Out of the Woodshed*, published by Bloomsbury in 1998, and several collections of stories of supernatural terror, including *Mrs Midnight*, which won the Children of the Night Award for Best Work of Supernatural Fiction in 2011.

More recently, Tartarus has reissued his first and second collections, *The Dreams of Cardinal Vittorini* and *The Complete Symphonies of Adolf Hitler*, with illustrations by the author, along with a new collection entitled *Flowers of the Sea*. His novel *The Dracula Papers I – The Scholar's Tale* is the first of a projected four, and an omnibus edition of the author's stories, entitled *Dramas from the Depths*, is published by Centipede as part of the "Masters of the Weird Tale" series.

*The Boke of the Divill* is a new novella from Dark Renaissance; it is set in the cathedral town of Morchester, which has been the setting for a number of his stories (including 'Quieta Non Movere', which appeared in *The Mammoth Book of Best New Horror Volume 23*). It is also the setting of 'The Archbishop's Well'.

"Lovecraft's weird mythology has been a source of fascination and inspiration to me for a long time," admits the author. "His sense of 'the other' is so unique and yet so resonant to the contemporary mind. (No wonder Michel Houellebecq, the brilliant *enfant terrible* of modern French intellectualism, wrote a book about him!)

"Never having been to the United States, I wanted somehow to bring Lovecraft's Innsmouth mythology (albeit with variations) to England, and so it came to the seemingly quiet West Country cathedral town of Morchester. All good weird fiction is about the collision of two worlds. In this story Lovecraft comes to the world of M. R. James (with a dash of P. G. Wodehouse thrown in).

"I like to think Lovecraft would have approved; I'm not so sure about James though."


ANGELA SLATTER is an Australian writer of dark fantasy and horror. She is the author of the Aurealis Award-winning *The Girl With No Hands and Other Tales*, the World Fantasy Award short-listed *Sourdough and Other Stories*, and the collection/mosaic novel *Midnight and Moonshine* (with Lisa L. Hannett). More recent publications include the collections *The Bitterwood Bible and Other Recountings*, *Black-Winged Angels* and (again in collaboration with Hannett) *The Female Factory*.

She has an MA and a Ph.D. in Creative Writing, and is the first Australian to win a British Fantasy Award (for her story 'The Coffin-Maker's Daughter' in *A Book of Horrors*). Her work has also appeared in Australian, British and American "Best of" anthologies, along with *Fantasy Magazine*, *Lady Churchill's Rosebud Wristlet*, *Dreaming Again*, *Steampunk II: Steampunk Reloaded*, *Fearie Tales: Stories of the Grimm and Gruesome* and *Zombie Apocalypse! Endgame*.

"My first introduction to Lovecraft was an old reprint collection of *The Shadow Over Innsmouth and Other Stories*," reveals the author. "I was about fifteen and found it (as I found many of my books then) in the book bin at the local supermarket where I worked as a checkout chick on Thursday nights and Saturday mornings.

"What stuck with me from that collection was not only the inexorable stripping away of a mystery that 'The Shadow Over Innsmouth' embodies, but also the tale of 'The Outsider'. The images and sensations from this story have stayed with me in the subsequent thirty years—the dark, dank castle, the seemingly endless staircase going up, the awful sense of having lost one's memories, the strangeness of mirrors, and, of course, the dreadful feeling of isolation and rejection that often comes with discovering a terrible truth—the broken, decaying baroque of it all. They are images and sensations that you find in much of Lovecraft's work and, when I wrote 'The Song of Sighs', I looked back to my fifteen-year-old self and mined her memories—dug into the fear and surprise that Lovecraft's stories brought, the delighted *frisson* of horror—and tried to recreate those influences while weaving them in with my own tale.

"As for 'Rising, Not Dreaming', Silvia Moreno-Garcia, the editor of *Innsmouth Free Press*, asked me for a short Cthulhu story and the result was a kind of Orpheus tale that came out of a dream. It started with the idea of the kinds of things husbands do that disappoint wives and I wanted it to be something really big, not just simply a refusal to take out the garbage or mow the lawn."

MICHAEL MARSHALL SMITH was born in Knutsford, Cheshire, and grew up in the United States, South Africa and Australia. He currently lives in Santa Cruz, California, with his wife and son.

Smith's short fiction has appeared in numerous magazines and anthologies and, under his full name, he has published the modern SF novels *Only Forward*, *Spares* and *One of Us*. He is the only person to have won the British Fantasy Award for Best Short Story four times—along with the August Derleth, International Horror Guild and Philip K. Dick awards.

Writing as "Michael Marshall" he has published a string of international best-selling novels of suspense, including the Straw Men series, *Killer Move*, *We Are Here* and *The Intruders*, the latter adapted into an eight-part mini-series for television by BBC America.

*Everything You Need* was a recent collection of short stories from Earthling Publications, and forthcoming are a tenth anniversary edition of *The Straw Men* and his next novel.

"My wife and I have been dropping into Carmel once in a while for nearly twenty years," Smith explains about the setting for his story 'The Chain'. "Our first visit was on the vacation when we got engaged—back when there were no mobile phones and you couldn't Google for restaurant or hotel advice—and we have always enjoyed the experience.

"It's a lovely little place, of course, with an interesting history and a stunning cove and tons of nice shops and galleries and a unique mishmash of cottages from modernist to Storybook. There's also a restaurant in town that serves the very best Reuben sandwich I've ever encountered (rest assured that I have not stinted in my research over the years, and so this is no idle statement).

"However, the town's always struck me as... *odd*, and I know I'm not alone. It's artificial at some very deep level, too perfect to be true, somehow both the logical extension but also the antithesis of what its arty founding fathers dreamed of. Since I came to live in Santa Cruz—only an hour's drive north—this impression has been further complicated. I've heard from more than one source that any misfit or homeless person who happens to wander into Carmel is quietly encouraged (with the assistance of a bus ticket) to go live in my town instead.

"This alleged practice, like the atmosphere of the town itself, cannot but help make you wonder what lies beneath the surface... and for how long it's been there.

"And, of course, what happens next."


SIMON KURT UNSWORTH was born in Manchester in 1972 on a night when, despite increasingly desperate research, he can find no evidence of mysterious signs or portents. He currently lives on a hill in the north of England awaiting the coming flood, where he writes essentially grumpy fiction (for which pursuit he was nominated for a 2008 World Fantasy Award for Best Short Story), whilst being tall, grouchier than he should be, and owning a wide selection of garish shirts and a rather magnificent leather waistcoat. He has a cheerfully full beard and spends most of his life in need of a haircut.

His collection, *Strange Gateways*, recently appeared from PS Publishing, following the critically acclaimed *Quiet Houses* from Dark Continents Publishing (2011) and *Lost Places* from Ash-Tree Press (2010), which was Peter Tennant from *Black Static* magazine's joint favourite collection of the year (along with Angela Slatter's *Sourdough and Other Stories*). His fiction has been published in a large number of anthologies including the World Fantasy Award-winning *Exotic Gothic 4, Terror Tales of the Cotswolds, Terror Tales of the Seaside, Where the Heart Is, At Ease with the Dead, Shades of Darkness, Exotic Gothic 3, Haunts: Reliquaries of the Dead, Hauntings, Lovecraft Unbound* and *Year's Best Fantasy 2013*. He has been represented in *The Mammoth Book of Best New Horror* six times, and he was also in *The Very Best of Best New Horror*.

The author has a further collection due—the as-yet-unnamed collection that will launch the Spectral Press Spectral Signature Editions imprint. His novel *The Devil's Detective* is due out from Doubleday in the US and Del Rey in the UK in early 2015.

You can find him on Twitter or Facebook, or in various cafés in Lancaster staring at his MacBook and muttering to himself.

"I'm not a big Lovecraft fan," admits Unsworth. "Don't get me wrong—I like the stories (some a great deal), but his stuff isn't particularly what I have in my mind when I write. The stories are sometimes stuffy, a little claustrophobic (and not in a good way) and hysterical, despite a certain elemental power that the best of them contain. They're rarely subtle, and sometimes veer dangerously close to cliché or stereotype.

"Where he comes into his own, I think, is in creating this huge world, and worlds beyond the world, in which we can play. Whether it's the audio dramatisations of the marvellous H. P. Lovecraft Historical Society or the blood-spattered glories of Stuart Gordon's *Re-animator*, there seems to be lots of space to expand on HPL's original works, and twist and flex the things he wrote about into new and (hopefully) interesting shapes. I've done it, sometimes deliberately (as in 'Into the Water'), and sometimes without really realising it until after, when I suddenly understand that I might not have actually said 'Hey, this is one of Cthulhu's children!' in the text but that's what I've intimated.

"The reason we can do this, that Lovecraft's stuff lends itself to this kind of expansion is, I think, that his horrors are emphatically external, clamouring from the Outside and trying to get in. And the Outside is huge, unbelievably massive, which means we can put whatever we want into it and it never gets full.

"For an author, that kind of freedom—a framework with unlimited playground space—is too big a thing to ignore. Besides, tentacles and things moving in the abyssal blackness below us and above us and behind us seem like such good things to write about…"

CONRAD WILLIAMS was born in 1969 and currently lives in Manchester, England, with his wife, three sons and a monster Maine Coon. He is an associate lecturer at Edge Hill University.

He is the author of seven novels (*Head Injuries, London Revenant,* the International Horror Guild Award-winning *The Unblemished,* the British Fantasy Award-winning *One, Decay Inevitable, Blonde on a Stick* and *Loss of Separation*), four novellas (*Nearly People, Game,* the British Fantasy Award-winning *The Scalding Rooms* and *Rain*) and two collections of short stories (*Use Once Then Destroy* and *Born with Teeth*). His debut anthology, *Gutshot,* was short-listed for both the British Fantasy and World Fantasy Awards.

As the author recalls: "I'd found a hag stone—a pebble with a hole bored through it by the force of water over countless years—a long time ago on a forgotten beach, but the actual story came about after a visit to Alderney last summer.

"I spent three days with my family in Fort Clonque, which has been a Landmark Trust holiday destination since 1966. It was once a naval base guarding against attack from the French and then, in 1940, it was appropriated by Nazi Germany—Hitler thought it strategically valuable—and it was re-fortified and manned in preparation for an invasion of the mainland which, of course, never came.

"The hag stone and the fort were two complementary elements that provided one of those pleasing convergences that sometimes happen for a writer from time to time. Much of what happens in the narrative is true: the outpost mentioned in the story exists, as did the poor hare, reduced to desiccated fibres on the causeway. The unfortunate incident at the beach that takes place while Adrian Stafford is trying to eat his lunch also happened (up to a point).

"It would have been a crime not to use the location in a short story, especially for an anthology such as this. The epic, rugged scenery and claustrophobic nature of the fort call to much of Lovecraft's work that I admire—an awesomeness in the wide, open skies and the unfathomable depths; the unimaginable stretches of time over which hag stones and horrors from the ocean are formed (while the old protagonist in my story appears as a mere breath in the lungs of time); and the threat of being engulfed, of beginning to understand something vast but which is nevertheless only just observable."

# ACKNOWLEDGMENTS

Special thanks to Dorothy Lumley, Randy and Sara Broecker, Bob Garcia, Philip Harbottle (Cosmos Literary Agency), Danielle Hackett (Arkham House Publishers, Inc.) and, especially, Dennis E. Weiler, Steve Saffel and Natalie Laverick, along with all the contributors.

# ABOUT THE EDITOR

**S**TEPHEN JONES was born in London, England, just across the River Thames from where his hapless namesake met a grisly fate in Hazel Heald's story 'The Horror in the Museum'. A Hugo Award nominee, he is the winner of three World Fantasy Awards, three International Horror Guild Awards, four Bram Stoker Awards, twenty-one British Fantasy Awards and a Lifetime Achievement Award from the World Horror Association. One of Britain's most acclaimed horror and dark fantasy writers and editors, he has more than 130 books to his credit, including *Shadows Over Innsmouth*, *Weird Shadows Over Innsmouth* and *Weirder Shadows Over Innsmouth*, *H. P. Lovecraft's Book of Horror* (with Dave Carson), *H. P. Lovecraft's Book of the Supernatural*, *Hallowe'en in a Suburb & Others: The Complete Poems from* Weird Tales, *Necronomicon: The Best Weird Tales of H. P. Lovecraft* and *Eldritch Tales: A Miscellany of the Macabre*, along with such author collections as *The Complete Chronicles of Conan* and *Conan's Brethren* by Robert E. Howard and *Curious Warnings: The Great Ghost Stories of M. R. James*. His many anthologies include *Fearie Tales: Stories of the Grimm and Gruesome*, *A Book of Horrors*, *The Mammoth Book of Vampires*, the Zombie Apocalypse! series, and twenty-five volumes of *The Mammoth Book of Best New Horror*. You can visit his website at: *www.stephenjoneseditor.com*

# SHADOWS OVER INNSMOUTH
## Edited by Stephen Jones

Under the unblinking eye of World Fantasy Award-winning editor
Stephen Jones, sixteen of the finest modern authors, including
Neil Gaiman, Kim Newman, Ramsey Campbell and Brian Lumley
contribute stories to the canon of Cthulhu. Also featuring the story
that started it all, by the master of horror, H. P. Lovecraft.

"A fine assembly of talented writers... A superb anthology for
Lovecraft fans." *Science Fiction Chronicle*

"Horror abounds in *Shadows Over Innsmouth*." *Publishers Weekly*

"Good, slimy fun... There are a number of genuinely frightening
pieces here." *San Francisco Chronicle*

# WEIRD SHADOWS OVER INNSMOUTH
## Edited by Stephen Jones

Respected horror anthologist Stephen Jones edits this collection of twelve stories by some of the world's most prominent Lovecraftian authors, including H. P Lovecraft himself, Ramsey Campbell, Kim Newman, Michael Marshall Smith, John Glasby, Paul McAuley, Steve Rasnic Tem, Caitlín R. Kiernan, Brian Lumley, Basil Copper, Hugh B. Cave, and Richard Lupoff.

"H. P. Lovecraft fans will revel in this fine follow-up to Jones' *Shadows Over Innsmouth*, a World Fantasy finalist." *Publishers Weekly*

"Fascinating and recommended." *All Hallows*

# BLACK WINGS OF CTHULHU
## VOLUME ONE
### Edited by S. T. Joshi

S. T. Joshi—the twenty-first century's pre-eminent expert on all things Lovecraftian—gathers twenty-one of the master's greatest modern acolytes, including Caitlín R. Kiernan, Ramsey Campbell, Michael Shea, Brian Stableford, Nicholas Royle, Darrell Schweitzer, and W. H. Pugmire, each of whom serves up a new masterpiece of cosmic terror that delves deep into the human psyche to horrify and disturb.

"[An] exceptional set of original horror tales... a breathtaking range of colorful new ideas and literary styles." *Booklist*

# BLACK WINGS OF CTHULHU
## VOLUME TWO
### Edited by S. T. Joshi

In the second volume of the critically acclaimed Black Wings series, S. T. Joshi—the world's foremost Lovecraft scholar—has assembled eighteen more brand-new and imaginative horror tales. Leading contemporary authors, including John Shirley, Caitlín R. Kiernan, Darrell Schweitzer, Nicholas Royle, and Brian Evenson, will draw from the life and work of H. P. Lovecraft to deliver a rich feast of terror.

"Every story in this collection is outstanding... This is a superb anthology not only for Lovecraft fans, but those appreciate true Gothic horror." Horror Novel Reviews